A quick note of

Thank you to Bo and Alan who found n., ...
Ben who overcame my technophobia.
Other family who were wonderfully positive when it mattered.

Also thanks to the Surfing Vet, the Minnesota Lawyer and far more expert people than myself. You know who you are.

Kate e Mark
May you breathe easy and be excitingly creative
Jago Harris

Strangling Sparrows is the second book in the series featuring investigators Joanne Li and Dane Morgan.

The first book, *A Shoe for the Unborn,* by Jago Harris is available from www.lulu.com.

Author photography on back cover by www.jamescheadle.com

Copyright © J.R. Harris 2021

The right of J.R. Harris to be identified as the Author of the Work has been asserted by him in accordance with the Copyright, Designs and Patents Act 1988.

All rights reserved. No part of this publication may be reproduced, stored in a retrieval system or transmitted in any form or by any means without prior permission of the author.

This is a work of fiction.
Names, places, events and incidents are either the products of the authors imagination or used fictitiously. Any resemblance to actual persons, living or dead or actual events is purely coincidental.

Strangling Sparrows

Chapter 1

Dane Morgan had a photographer's eye for detail but it took ten minutes of hard running on the city streets of Boston before he realised that the trainers he was wearing just didn't feel right. The Nike Air looked identical but didn't feel like the shoes he'd worn most days over the last year. On a downhill section, his toes started bunching up and something hard began digging into his instep.

He stopped, feeling ridiculous and pulled off the right shoe and realised that it wasn't his. Checking it closely, he noticed that it was half a size smaller and looked newer. But the source of his discomfort wasn't just the tight fit, he noticed the corner of a black plastic card, covered in tape that had worked its way out from its hiding place under the insole. Dane sat down on the marble steps of somebody's corporate palace and eased the card out of the shoe, scraping off the last few bits of tape with his finger nail. He got strange looks from the suited business warriors rushing up and down but he didn't care, the situation intrigued him. The simplicity and dull blackness of the card reeked of something and after a while Dane realised what it was. He smelt money, so much money that being stylishly understated was the only way to impress.

The ID or credit card was unlike anything Dane Morgan had ever seen before. On one side it had an extremely complicated series of security holograms and no numbers. There was no start or expiry date and just one name picked out in relief – Salimond. On the back there was nothing as crass as a place for a signature, it just had the Panama Gulf Bank logo and a line of what looked like Arabic characters or symbols underneath it. He thought back to when he had changed back into his track suit and running shoes after playing.

The Grosvenor Athletic and Rackets Club was a gym in the centre of the city with a history that stretched back to the 1800's. In the old days ship owners or rich merchants would celebrate a good deal or another country conquered with a game of Real Tennis followed by a Turkish Bath and massage. Now there was a steel and glass gym with a spectacular view of the city, squash courts and an open wood planked area for whatever form of Yoga or aerobic torture was currently on trend. But the Real Tennis space remained and was based on the original design used by Henry VIII in Hampton Court, which meant an enormous enclosed room with the buttresses, hazards and gallery which were such a part of this arcane game. Dane was one of the few people who enjoyed the game and he had an hour of exhausting play earlier using the old-fashioned gut and wood racket and heavy balls which hadn't changed much in centuries.

The other area which remained as it was in the 1800's was the gentlemen's changing room. This long, narrow, room was lined with battered oak lockers, each with its brass number and in the middle there was a long slatted hardwood bench with dozens of ornate brass coat-hooks on the horizontal bar above. Players tended to ignore the lockers and leave their sports gear on the benches and walk naked through to the old marble showers. Dane remembered that the area had been busy when he had come back to the lockers and full of the good-natured competitive banter and smell of muscle rub that you get after most sports. Dane only recalled one person who'd been close enough for their gear to get mixed up - a short but well muscled guy whose body looked a lot younger than the shock of white hair he could just about see through the steam and hanging towels.

Dane looked at the strange card in his hand and realised that he would have to return to the club if he was to have any chance of finding its owner and getting his own shoes back. He put it in the zipped pocket of his track top, slipped his pack on and started jogging uncomfortably in the other guy's shoes back to the club. As he got closer, he slowed because he saw that there were three big black vehicles parked outside the front doors in an area that was normally pedestrian only and blocked by barriers.

He hobbled to a halt a hundred yards away and tried to see what was going on. Dane Morgan was a professional who'd made a good living out of photography for years. He'd taken shots in beautiful places in recent times but he'd done a few years as a press photographer and gone to places where sensible people wouldn't go in an armoured Humvee. His instincts for what made a newsworthy photograph were highly tuned and he shrugged off his pack and pulled out a battered Nikon D5 – not the smallest camera around but with a great telephoto lens that he took everywhere with him.

As he looked at the vehicles, a tight group of men burst out of the club doors and violently hustled a man in sports clothes into one of the vehicles. Dane took a rapid series of shots but even at that distance, the distinctive mane of white hair on the guy being pushed into the Chrysler stood out. One of the men in suits looked up the street, saw Dane with a camera and shouted. Dane didn't hesitate, he picked up his pack and ran down an alley between two blocks and kept running until the shoes started to bite again.

He reckoned that he was a couple of miles away from the club now and that there was little chance of anyone catching him unless they checked cameras or had aerial surveillance. As he got his breath back, he wondered what instinct had made him run – whatever it was, he felt it was right. The men at the club had been smartly dressed in dark suits and all looked like they had come out of the US government agency handbook but they obviously didn't like the idea of witnesses. Dane was a photo-journalist and naturally curious, but he was in a strange country and in no position to get involved in US undercover operations or he would find his visa revoked and himself on the plane home in minutes.

He decided to call his partner Joanne Li and warn her that he might be a few hours late but that he had seen something she might find interesting, maybe even a story. Also that he'd taken a few shots and that he would email them to her. After doing that he looked down at his watch and debated what to do next. He was still far closer to the Grosvenor Club than to home, so it made sense to wait half an hour and then return to find out what he could without making it too obvious. CCTV might be tracking him but there was little he could do other than pull a cap over his eyes and strip down to his T-Shirt to make his appearance a little different.

Joanne Li was the most committed environmental campaigner he'd ever met. Jo had uncovered a bio-medical disaster a couple of years ago and was kidnapped and nearly killed so she couldn't expose the global group who'd caused it. She'd been imprisoned for months before he'd rescued her and was still getting over the trauma. Jo was fragile but still obsessed with uncovering the damage the multi-national corporations were doing to the planet.

The work she had done exposing the SCC spill in New Zealand had made her international news and done her credibility as a campaigning journalist no harm at all. But government agencies were definitely wary of her as she'd also exposed state corruption in a number of foreign administrations and embarrassed US state department officials.

They had been in her home town of Boston for nearly a year now and his work as a freelance photographer had been put on hold apart from two trips where he photographed Peruvian mountain ranges and de-forestation in the Amazon basin for European clients. Dane had impeccable credentials when it came to landscape photography and his work had been published in media as influential as the New York Times, Sunday Times and National Geographic.

His earlier work as a war photographer had not won him awards but had given him a reputation amongst his fellow photographers as someone who got great shots in places even a drone wouldn't go. But since he'd met Jo, everything had changed, he was now as committed to her environmental work as she was and had photographed devastated forests, polluted rivers and dead animals to great affect and knew that they made a great team.

Jo, as a US citizen, had less problems working locally and had got a few leading articles in the environmental columns immediately after her release. She didn't trust companies or politicians and thought that regulations needed to be backed up by effective checking and policing that was totally independent. She said that it would need to be strong enough to prevent spills like the SCC disaster happening or being covered up again. Her solutions included thermal monitoring by satellite and the use of smart drones in more remote areas, all ideas which were possible but likely to be ignored by politicians and CEO's.

Dane knew that Joanne was frustrated because her stories mainly appeared in the specialist media and not in the international press and websites. She thought that pollution was of global importance but she knew that it needed a sensational story to get editors interested. Her current crusade was air pollution and the part it played in the huge rise in asthma and allergies amongst kids - old news as far as places like California was concerned – but just as dangerous in other cities where the populations were less informed.

Despite being sceptical about Jo's environmental paranoia when he had first met her, Dane was now 100% behind her and enjoyed giving her stories visual impact with his photography. She was on a mission now but Dane worried that she was still too fragile to be working this hard.

Dane's love for Joanne Li had almost become a burden. For a man who had gone through life for over 30 years without needing anyone, it was a shock to care so much. He had to stop himself from checking on her safety hourly and still had nightmares about her kidnapping most nights. But she was better informed, better motivated and more beautiful than any woman he'd ever met, and she obviously loved him too, so the burden was worth carrying.

Dane realised that he'd been daydreaming for too long and it was around 45 minutes since he'd sent the shots to Jo. He didn't quite know why he felt so intrigued but the fact that the guys in black suits had been so worried by his camera showed that they had something to hide. He quietly made his way back to the club avoiding main routes and stopped at a corner where he could see the front doors of the Grosvenor. The black SUV's had gone so he walked up to the big old doors and pushed through.

"Mr Morgan – are you back with us already?" asked the aged retainer who looked like something out of P. G. Wodehouse but was actually a world class Real Tennis coach.
"Yes, Gerald, I left something in the locker room – was there some trouble earlier? I tried to come through but the lane was full of official vehicles. What was going on?"
Gerald looked pointedly at someone sitting in the shadows and Dane could see a bulky man in a suit who looked like he had been made from the same mould as the team earlier.
"No, Mr Morgan, nothing to worry about.... now what did you say about the locker room? Nothing has been handed in.."

Dane Morgan said that he'd go and check and Gerald buzzed him through the outer door. As he walked down the corridor, he tried to remember what locker and hook he had been using earlier. The system was quite archaic and members were given a big brass locker key when they signed in and threw it in a large Mahogany box near the exit when they left. As it turned out, Dane didn't have to worry because he could see a pair of Nikes on the bench at the far end of the room when he entered. There were fewer people and much less conversation than earlier but there was a large, bearded guy who looked like an ageing gorilla sitting just a few feet away from the shoes.
"Hello, you limey bastard" said the gorilla amiably.
"I've told you hundreds of times, I'm half English and half Irish" Dane said with a smile.
"Hello half limey, half mick, bastard, then ..."

The gorilla was actually an extremely civilised lecturer in economics called James Spencer and of Irish ancestry anyway. Dane and he had met at a reception held by Jo's father who was also a lecturer

and they found that they shared a similarly unusual and sometimes insulting, sense of humour.
"I left my shoes here earlier" Dane said, pointing towards the trainers a few feet away.
"Are all your shoes matching Nikes?" The Professor said observing Dane's feet.
"No, not normally James." Dane said with a smile and went on to explain what had happened on his early morning run back to the club. Professor Spencer looked intrigued and they speculated who had been arrested or abducted.
"What did the guy look like?"

Dane described the short, brown skinned guy with the shock of white hair and the Professor furrowed his brow in concentration. "It could be that guy from Panama – he's some kind of green technology guru or something – can't quite remember his name – but I think that he's a scientist."

Dane thanked him and picked up the shoes from the bench, checking the inside and yes, they were his size. He put them on with relief and put the others back in his pack until he decided what to do with them. He said his goodbyes and walked out of the locker room and back to the foyer.

"Mr Morgan" a voice stopped him before he could exit and he turned round. It was the guy in the suit he'd seen earlier, trying to look friendly and not muscular without quite succeeding.
"Yeh?"
"Do you mind if I see your papers?"
"Only if you show me yours first," Dane responded.
The man very slowly reached into his inside pocket and made sure that Dane saw the shoulder-holster as he pulled a black wallet out. Flicking it open, Dane could see "Bradley Kowolski, Agent, US Environmental Agency."
"I'm a foreign citizen but I didn't carry my passport with me to the gym because I didn't think that this was a police state. But if you give me your address, I'll be happy to bring it in tomorrow," Dane looked at the guy questioningly.
"The agency will be in touch with you, if we need to, Mr Morgan – we can always find foreign nationals." The guy turned and went back to his seat, trying to look sinister and succeeding.
Dane nodded at Gerald, put on his pack and left the building. During the 30 minute run back to the house he went over what little he knew about the mysterious white-haired guy. Maybe a scientist, maybe into the environment, maybe from Panama, probably about

45, possibly of foreign extraction, certainly in trouble with US Environmental Agency. This was an agency that Dane knew nothing about and not one you would imagine sent armed bruisers to abduct scientists. He couldn't wait to get to Jo's parents' place and tell her what had happened.

Joanne had been intrigued by Dane's call as he had sounded more excited than he had for months. She knew that he was frustrated by not being able to take on much photographic work and was staying in the USA because of her. So anything that got him interested was good as far as she was concerned. She loved the tall, rangy white guy because he didn't quite fit into any national stereotype and yet seemed comfortable anywhere in the world. He was Anglo/Irish, had been a soldier, a photo-journalist and was a great landscape photographer.

They had first met in Thailand where they had eventually become lovers and shared more passion than she had ever thought possible. They also started to work together on environmental stories and his shots of polluted fish farms and ravaged forests were stunning. Then she had been kidnapped and held for months thousands of miles away in New Zealand and he hadn't rested until he had found her. So their relationship had been forged in fire and showed little sign off cooling down.

Jo also had a mixed heritage as her parents had come from Indonesia and Singapore a few decades ago with a burning ambition to succeed in academia and banking in the US. They had succeeded in their professional lives but not been great parents along the way. After the kidnap, Jo had returned to Boston and her parents, realising how close they had been to losing their daughter, had become over-protective. Luckily, they both got on well with Dane Morgan and they could see just how much the couple loved each other. But there were pressures, Dane really needed to be in Europe to restart his career and Jo, who had been such an inveterate world traveller, was nervous about travel since the kidnapping.

Dane got close to the beautiful old house in the Bay area that the Li family had owned for years and looked down the street at the five and six storey homes which had such individual style. Theirs was a double fronted, middle-terrace gem with curved bays and exquisite brickwork. He ran up the steps and opened the door, hoping that she was in. An inner door opened and she was there. He thought that she was even more extraordinary now. His photographer's eye took in the slim, swimmer's figure and long legs. The olive skin and black hair and those amazing eyes with the Asian lift. Even after all this time, seeing her made him catch his breath and he couldn't believe that she loved him too. But the look in her eyes proved it.

They embraced and walked through to the kitchen holding hands and sat down at the old scrubbed pine table. After a few minutes the Professor walked in with a huge mug of his favourite Costa Rican coffee and sat down opposite. Dane mentioned that he'd seen the Professor's colleague at the club and described what had happened with the white haired man and government agents. Jo and her father looked intrigued – neither had heard much about the US Environmental Agency or knew anyone from Panama. Professor Li wandered away with a thoughtful look on his face and Jo moved her chair closer to Dane and whispered. "You know I think you were right, I have a good feeling about this, I don't know why, but I think that we have something here... let's do a bit of digging."

They both went to their computers and started their research. Dane checked out the US agency whose heavies arrested the guy. The nearest he found to the description he remembered from the card was the US Environmental Protection Agency – an institution with the aim of cleaning up the air and water of the US with an annual budget of around 9 billion dollars. It seemed to have powers – indeed it had fined oil companies and chemical plants millions of dollars to make them clean up their processes – but it didn't look as though it would employ armed agents to abduct businessmen. Dane couldn't be certain what had been on the agent's ID card, but it definitely had "environmental agency" somewhere on it. He found the press contact on the EPA website and emailed them. Using his UK Press Association number, Dane stated that he was working on a story for a European magazine and requested information about the arrest of a scientist at the Grosvenor Athletic Club in Boston that day.

If anyone at the other end checked him out, they would find just enough on his website to back up his credentials but most of the press work was a couple of years old. Dane didn't really expect a quick answer but with freedom of information being a supposed priority, he thought it might illicit some kind of reaction. He had an automated response within seconds but knew that anything more complete would take time and the whole thing might turn out to be a waste of time.

Joanne concentrated on researching green technology and

Panamanian scientists and found little that was useful. Neither of them had been to Panama and apart from the canal, she knew nothing about it. She had always imagined that it would be a tropical marshy isthmus with nothing much else but the canal cutting through the jungle. What she found online was Panama City, which looked more like a Middle-Eastern or Asian city with high-rise monstrosities showing just how rich the country was. She wondered where all the money was coming from and found press coverage about dubious shell companies and tax avoidance by politicians and uber-rich that she vaguely remembered.

The Professor came into the room and waited for his daughter to finish on the keyboard. "I meant to tell you the other day, we're finally doing something to clean up the city."
"What's that?"
"Boston is now the first city in the US to invest in the Greenwatch air monitoring system."
Joanne smiled up at her father – she knew that he wasn't exactly a green campaigner himself but that he had really tried to understand her beliefs since the kidnapping.
"Ok, what is Greenwatch?"
"According to the papers it's the best air monitoring system in the world. Developed in the UK but using science developed right here in Shelford University. The Mayor is supporting it and the US government is using Boston as the first test and will introduce it nationally if it goes well.
"Yeh, yeh. Can you see this government investing billions in something that does good?" Joanne asked her father with a wry smile.
"You're just too cynical sometimes" her father said with a sigh. "The monitors are going to be on most blocks in the city and will have a digital readout of harmful particulates that everyone can see – that can't be bad, surely Jo?"
"Maybe... what's the timing on this?"
"The first monitors will be on the streets soon."
"Just before the national elections – what a surprise" Jo said, turning back to her computer.

Professor Li left the room wondering what on earth had turned Joanne into such a suspicious woman. It wasn't just the cover up of the chemical spill she'd exposed in New Zealand which involved government ministers and international business leaders. It wasn't the kidnap she'd suffered during the investigation. Both would have been good cause, but she had suspected big business for years before either of these had happened and had dedicated herself to exposing corporate malpractice from the minute she started as an investigative journalist. He thought that Dane Morgan might have had a moderating effect on her – he was a much more laid back sort of guy – but if anything he had encouraged her. Also his photography was hugely effective at supporting her stories. His shots of devastated rain forests and polluted waterways even convinced the Professor that something had to be done.

Having done as much research on his computer as possible for the moment, Dane went back to basics and phoned the guy on the desk at the gym.
"Gerald, this is Dane Morgan – I spoke to you earlier about my lost shoes."
"Yes Mr Morgan, I remember."
"Gerald, is that government heavy still there?"
"No, Mr Morgan, he left a couple of hours ago – not the most pleasant person we've had in the club."
"Gerald, what was the guy's name who was arrested?" There was a noticeable hesitation and Dane realised that he'd probably been sworn to secrecy by the government agents so sought to reassure him.
"Please don't worry, I've emailed the agency as well – I'm just trying to return his property."
"OK, Mr Morgan, I think that you will find that his name is Carlos Fantoni and I think that he is based in Panama. He was a great tennis player, by the way, worth watching."
"Many thanks for the help Gerald, I'll see you next week."

Dane and Jo had compared notes later about what they'd both found out in their research but got side tracked for a few hours when they heard that SCC, the company they'd exposed a year or so back as having caused birth problems, had been taken over by the Chinese. The original drug produced by the group was meant to vastly improve fertility rates amongst thousands of people who were desperate for children and the inventor had tried to insist on the price being low. The treatment had been incredibly successful since but the price had been extortionate. This was unlikely to be different with the Chinese in control.

Dane worried that any mention of SCC might have upset Jo but was reassured when she said they needed to sit down right away and discuss the Carlos Fantoni arrest. He was walking back to the kitchen with a mug in his hand when his mobile rang, looking down he saw a strange international number on the screen. He was curious and pressed receive.

"Hello son." Said an Irish voice he hadn't heard for years and Dane felt the old anger welling up in his gut. He looked for a moment at the phone and then threw it against the wall with such force that it splintered into fragments.

Eugene Morgan fathered Dane 34 years ago but he was hardly an ideal parent. Bent banker, sometime dubious entrepreneur, he had charmed himself into the trust of some of the best families in Europe and the US and cheated them so well that they had barely recognised it. He could also be a violent, hard man who would intimidate rich men into paying him thousands in order to keep their families and their businesses safe.

Dane had been sent away to school and didn't see what was going on but unlike other kids, he seemed to go back to a different home every holiday. Most of the time he was collected by his mother in their beaten-up Range Rover but once or twice his father arrived in something exotic like a McLaren or a Bugatti which impressed the other kids. Once he even sent a chauffeur in a vintage Bentley limousine to drive Dane to the Georgian mansion his father seemed to have acquired for a few months. Then Eugene Morgan disappeared and the Morgan family's lifestyle radically changed for the worse.

Dane's mother had money from a family trust fund and she had thought that it would keep them going until Eugene reappeared. He'd disappeared before but only for a couple of weeks, so she waited a month for him to make contact then reported his absence to the UK police and contacted her solicitor about the trust fund. She was shocked to find that it had virtually nothing in it and that Eugene had bled it dry over a number of years using forged signatures. That had been twenty years ago and it had broken Dane's mother into pieces.

Her problems had been made worse by the uncertainty as to whether he was alive or dead and the difficulty of getting his estate resolved. She had always suspected that Eugene was involved with some dubious people but never really knew how he made money. The way the police had reacted to her enquiries made her think that he wasn't exactly unknown to them. But that first year had been incredibly tough financially and emotionally.

Two years later a lawyer from somewhere in Central America got in touch with Dane's mother and told her that Eugene was still alive and had instructed him to give them $100,000 dollars. This was significantly less than her trust fund but it helped keep the financial wolf from the door for the next few years. More importantly for Rosalind Morgan, she now knew that her husband was alive and she prayed every day that he might return to them.

Eugene Morgan only returned once. Dane had been 15 years old and asleep in his room when he became aware of someone else in the darkness. He hadn't seen his father for years and didn't recognise the large figure sitting in the corner.
"Hello Dane." Said a soft Irish voice. "I'm your father."
Dane didn't know what to say, sat up in bed and moved to put the bedside light on. Before he could, a large brown hand stopped him and whispered. "Leave the light off son, I'm in a bit of trouble and it's better that we continue this conversation in the dark, just in case anyone sees us."

Over the next five minutes Eugene Morgan bared his soul and appeared desperate to apologise for his absence. He explained that he had done a deal with some very bad people and had been in fear of his life ever since – hiding out in Panama and South America. But things were now looking a little bit better and he would pay the gang back if he could do one more deal. He asked Dane not to tell his mother about his visit because he didn't want to get her hopes up until he could come back forever. Finally, Eugene took his gold watch off and handed it to Dane and said that he wanted him to have it, before saying his goodbyes and creeping out of the room.

Dane had been confused and didn't want to be disloyal to his mother but the explanation had sounded so plausible in his father's cultured Irish voice that he had decided to say nothing about the visit. Then he heard his mother crying the next morning and found out that all her jewellery had been stolen. He had never seen her so angry and knew that despite all the fine-sounding bullshit, Eugene had been behind the theft. Dane told her about the visit and handed over the watch – a Rolex Cosmograph Daytona in gold which was obviously worth a few thousand dollars – but his mother told him to keep it because it was likely to be the only genuine thing he'd ever get from his father.

Dane hadn't heard anything from his father since, so the call a few minutes ago had been an unpleasant shock. The bastard must have got his number from his work website – it was always important in his line of work to be contactable and he was damned if he was going to change it just to avoid his father. He walked to the corner and tried to find all the bits of his phone and tried to put it together again. Shit, what chaos was that con-man about to cause now?

Jo came back into the kitchen and Dane tried to explain why the phone was in a dozen pieces which inevitably led to her asking about the father that Dane had never mentioned before. He gave her a brief version of what he knew about Eugene – serial conman on a huge scale, Irish, known to have been in South America, hadn't been in touch for years, probably after money – that was about it. Jo looked curious but knew by the expression on Dane's face that further questions would be pointless. So she looked round the kitchen for the last bit of phone and helped him stick it together. He was short of work at present, so the last thing he needed was to be out of contact.

Jo's delicate hands found the pieces that mattered and meticulously put them together. Amazingly the screen still lit up and his all-important contact list still functioned. For some reason, she quietly looked at the recent calls record and took a note of Dane's father's number whilst he was out of the room. She didn't know why, but some instinct told her to keep a record of it.

But Jo and Dane had a more important mystery than a call from Eugene Morgan to solve. Why had an important climate scientist been abducted by armed men and where was he now?

Chapter 2

The Boston city mayor was a two-faced, self-serving bastard, which made him perfect for the job when he was first elected. He'd made his money ten years ago by inheriting a fleet of delivery vans that were low on safety and high on profit. The drivers didn't stay long as he avoided union rates and paid peanuts, fining them a fortune for every minute late and every other transgression he could invent. After trading for a few years, he sold out for a few million dollars to a sucker who believed the figures quoted by Bonelli and discovered the truth a year later when the business went bust and the sucker felt the need to quietly hang himself.

Having succeeded in business Bonelli thought that his formula for success could be transferred to politics where the real power was. It worked and after a campaign of lies against his Democrat rival he'd been elected and enjoyed the first few months of power in his huge office. Then he realised that being mayor was more than just TV appearances and big dinners. Now he was having to deal with issues like gender and transgender politics and environmental do-gooders which was waste of time as far as he was concerned.

He had entered politics because he liked control but after a few months he realised that all the real power was in Washington. Lots of the legal responsibility for executing policy, however, was still at his door and he kept his lawyers busy. One confidential report he'd received early on in his first year had really worried him. This showed that despite all the moves to different engine types over recent years, the real level of air pollution in cities like his was extremely high. Not that he really gave a shit about anything other than the risk of him losing the next election but appearances matter.

The mayor loosened his belt and eased the discomfort on his capacious gut. It seemed that no sooner had he ordered a new set of silk shirts from his tailor, then his diet of Italian pasta and rich deserts, had rendered them obsolete. He looked out from his air conditioned office on the 30th floor and could see the haze across the city. He remembered the figures from the original study on air pollution which was made in Europe - 9,000 premature deaths every year in London and 600,000 in Europe as a whole. The deaths abroad didn't bother him but the fact that he might be seen as legally responsible for deaths in his own city certainly did. Most of the press weren't a problem, but that campaigning bitch Joanne Li had been scaremongering on social media over recent months about kids dying in Boston of air pollution. Washington had heard about it and been hassling him about the danger of such stories in pre-election years.

One additional thing had really started to capture the imagination of some people – mainly the do-gooders and lily-livered campaigners who made his life difficult by demonstrating outside his office. The birds in the city centre started dying and some days he couldn't count how many finches and sparrows were on the floor.

He knew that simple images often have the power to shock more than endless facts and quietly had some of the birds analysed. He'd employed a retired pathologist he knew from Rotary Club and asked him to let him know confidentially what had killed the birds, which were mainly small, common birds like Sparrows and the occasional Robin. He didn't have access to his full laboratory any more but thought that they had been poisoned in some way. Looking at the black linings to their lungs he thought that they had choked to death by breathing in some sort of pollutant. Bonelli could see the images in his imagination of dead birds littering the ground under dead trees and knew that he had to do something before Joanne Li or one of her friends got this on TV.

Bonelli arranged for a private contractor to work in the city centre of Boston every night and clear the bird corpses from the trees and parks where they roosted. The team were sworn to secrecy and paid enough money to make it worthwhile. They were also given a lucrative year's contract and told that it would be renewed as long as they kept the streets clear of dead birds and dumped the bodies well away from Boston. The scheme worked well for months because the larger birds still survived in the city and there were enough small birds in the suburbs for no-one to notice. But Bonelli was worried that someone eventually was going to discover his pollution problem and expose his undercover work to hide it.

Then a scientist called Fantoni had made a presentation about the Greenwatch system and the mayor had listened with real self-interest. What he heard was something that could turn him into an environmental saviour and be his path out of this fucking city and to central government in Washington. The fact that this system was already working in London and had been developed in partnership with Shelford made it perfect.

Fantoni had shown film of a Greenwatch unit on a country road where the figures flashed green and then switched to a typical US city street where it flashed red. Underneath the dangerous particulates found scrolled across the screen, along with the damage done which included lowered fertility, increased menopause problems, decreased intelligence, birth defects, premature deaths and a terrifying list of other problems. When the mayor heard that there was also a substantial bonus payable to him if he signed up for a test, Bonelli had said yes and the first units were installed some weeks later.

After the Greenwatch units had been in place for a few months, they were already helping his approval ratings. The President's office had seen the political value of the Greenwatch system too. The Republican President had a turbulent first term beset by scandals and cock-ups of their own making so they had serious re-election challenges. Climate Change and pollution had been the cause of global unrest and organisations like Extinction Rebellion had started getting serious media exposure across the world a few years ago. Public interest waned during other disasters like Corona but the President had seen the figures and knew that air quality in cities was a disaster waiting to happen. So Greenwatch was a very visible way of showing that the President cared about such things and having a test in Boston was perfect because the mayor was a staunch Republican and hugely ambitious.

Bonelli suddenly had total co-operation from Washington and all kinds of funding had suddenly been made available. The Department of the Environment had got involved at the beginning and appeared to have almost unlimited money to throw at the problem of city air pollution. The fact that the President was using Greenwatch as a mainstay of his advertising and social media campaign might have had something to do with it.

The mayor looked at the big screen at the end of his office and saw the commercial that had been showing at every break on stations across the country. The high-tech looking box with the digital read out was on a pole on a state highway then it switched to another box in a city centre situation and the digital figures changed. He knew the script by heart but he turned up the sound to hear the President address the nation.

"Only one President and only one party has really started to clean up your cities. The Greenwatch system is already showing how we're reducing air pollution in Boston and I am promising to put it in every major city in the US. Vote for Me and Breathe Easy."

The advertising campaign had started months ago with an extremely frightening sequence of what appeared to be documentary footage showing children and old people gasping for breath in polluted city streets clogged with traffic. Then the scene switched to hospitals with distressed people hooked up to ventilators and the bottom of the screen showed the startling figures of those in US cities who were dying prematurely from air pollution. The President had then come on screen with his most worried and presidential expression and stated that air quality was killing US citizens and that if it was the last thing he did in office he was going to change things. Over recent months the public health approach had changed to the more direct political message appearing on TV now. But there was no doubt that the President had chosen a great issue to base his campaign on as the poll results showed. The Democrat campaign based on health care and unemployment looked weak in response.

The Mayor intended to follow the same approach with his own local campaign. After all, the Greenwatch system may have been tested in London first, but it had been developed in partnership with Boston scientists from Shelford University, so it had strong local provenance.

The guy Carlos Fantoni had been very convincing in the initial presentations and genuinely emotional when he'd talked about the death of his parents in Lima. One of the key elements in Fantoni's presentation had been the test they'd done in London which had taken place recently in the city shopping centre. The London Mayor realised that air quality had been dreadful and that one way to justify his stringent controls on diesel motors and punitive taxes on traffic was to show the people 'pollution' in a very public way. Greenwatch units were fitted along Oxford Street, Regent Street and in Trafalgar Square and whenever the air got dangerous the displays turned red and flashed. Fantoni told him that within weeks of the Greenwatch system being installed in London, opposition to increased congestion charges and bans declined by 85%. Equally importantly, the real polluters in each area were starting to be identified and shamed into remedial action.

Mayor Bonelli in Boston was nothing if not an opportunist, and had insisted on Greenwatch being installed across his city centre for a test even larger than that in London. Washington was happy to help finance it and there was a race to see who could make most political capital out of it.

The President's election was months ahead of Bonelli's so he had the national TV and social media campaigns running now. But the mayor had local advantage and made sure that he was photographed in hospitals looking sympathetic at the bedside of patients with respiratory problems. Bonelli also made sure that he was seen at the commissioning of every new unit and his "Friends of Greenwatch" social media campaign got brilliant local traction.

Even the dead birds became the Mayor's allies and he was seen in tears with a dead Robin in his hand on TV saying that bad air had killed this poor defenceless bird but Mayor Bonelli was going to undo the damage created by man and bring back birdsong to the city. It made brilliant local TV and the demonstrators disappeared from outside his office. Campaigners like Joanne Li, also appeared to have stopped haranguing him on social media.

Everything had been going so well. The London test was rolling out to more areas having been considered a great success and the Boston test was proving so popular with voters that Mayor Bonelli had a popularity rating greater then when he'd first been voted in. Then he had a message from Carlos Fantoni, the scientist behind Greenwatch and the mayor's political world started to implode.

Chapter 3

Joanne Li knew that her father worried about her cynical attitude to government or company environmental policies. He and his wife had come to the US many years ago believing in the American dream and they had made it work – he as an academic and she as a banker.

Jo had been born in the US and during her work as a journalist learned that many respected institutions preferred profit or popularity to real corporate responsibility.

She had spent months in a stinking hut because a global group preferred to keep her kidnapped rather than let her reveal the disaster they had caused. Even government ministers had conspired with them to prevent the scandal getting out and falsified evidence to have her extradited from New Zealand. She and Dane had been forced to sign 'gagging orders' to avoid imprisonment. Dane as a foreign national had to tread especially carefully – a quality which didn't come naturally. So they both thought their cynicism about large corporates and those in power was fully justified.

Joanne and Dane had talked it through and looked again at the shots and knew instinctively that there was something suspicious about the arrest of the white haired guy from the Grosvenor club. They needed to do their research carefully and avoid stirring up a hornets nest until they had to.
Dane had been researching Carlos Fantoni, the name mentioned by the doorman and Salimond, the name on the black card Dane had found in his shoe.

When he put the Fantoni name in the search engines it showed a couple of years' worth of press and online mentions in the UK and US. According to the London Times, Fantoni – Dr Fantoni as he was titled – was a highly committed environmental scientist who had worked with research bodies like Shelford University to produce a revolutionary device called Greenwatch which measured particulates in the air at a fraction of the cost of previous devices. Shelford was where Jo's father lectured, so Dane was a little surprised Professor Li hadn't mentioned him.

According to the press Fantoni was claiming that there were over 7 million premature deaths worldwide every year caused by bad air. Bringing it close to home the article said that even in 'civilised' Europe, 600,000 people were dying prematurely and in cities like London, around 9,000 people were killed every year. In terms of the causes Fantoni quoted road transport as being one of the major causes, creating around 90% of the carbon monoxide and 62% of the other dangerous particulates measured.

The sources quoted looked reliable, like the World Health Organisation and the World Atlas of Atmospheric Pollution but Dane couldn't believe the figures. His first view was that the figures must be wrong but drilling down he realised that 7 million deaths was probably a conservative estimate. So why was this not on the front pages every day - it was either wilful ignorance or the biggest cover-up of all time.

Researching the Salimond name on the card, he found less information. The company was registered in Panama and described as an environmental science company established in 2010. It had a turnover the previous year of $2.5 billion dollars and a five star credit rating. Professor Coombes was listed as CEO and there were no other directors shown. The website was impressive with shots of virgin forest and tropical flowers showing the groups commitment to a cleaner world and shots of a pristine research lab. Greenwatch was shown working in a London city street and there was a brief description of what it did. At the back of one of the London shots with Big Ben and a group of politicians was a white-haired man that Dane recognised. Dane went through to the kitchen and updated Jo with all that he'd found out. She was less surprised by the pollution figures that he'd seen, having been concerned with air quality for some time, but agreed that the lack of media attention was odd.

Over the years there had been many reports covering everything from air quality damage done to embryos, bad effects on intelligence in school children through to dementia and premature death. All important stories, which got relatively small coverage in the media. It was difficult not to see this as some kind of conspiracy of silence and the two of them knew that they had to expose this scandal in every way they could.

Greenwatch was the only positive action they'd seen in years to counter bad air quality. They had seen that it was working in London and was starting to be used in the US, which had to be good news. Yet the man behind it, Carlos Fantoni, the man who was going to solve pollution here in Boston, had been abducted by the US

Environmental Agency. It didn't make any sense at all.

Dane phoned the agency again and repeated his questions about the guy he'd seen arrested at the Grosvenor but mentioned the name Fantoni for the first time. There was more hesitation this time and Morgan was put through to a senior woman who took his name and address with great care and consulted her computer. She then repeated the same denial that any arrest had been made or knowledge of anyone called Fantoni.

Joanne and Dane often went to bed in the afternoons for what they called a 'siesta.' At the beginning Professor Li and his wife considered this habit a little too European for their tastes but they were normally out furthering their careers in academia and banking to be there to notice. The one time Mrs Li came back in mid afternoon she heard noises from upstairs which brought a distinct flush to her cheeks and she quietly let herself out, feeling rather moist in a place that she'd rather forget during a long working day.

The truth was that Jo and Dane needed to make love daily in a way that was almost like an addiction. The memory of her kidnap and the long enforced separation had made them needy for each other. When they had first met a few years ago in Thailand, Dane had been incredibly patient for such a passionate man and it was Jo who made the first moves. She still remembered the waves of orgasm her body had felt when she had mounted Dane and thought of that beachside shack in Krabi often when she was feeling depressed or frightened. Now love was something they both initiated but the intensity of it hadn't changed.

Dane had rescued her from that hell over a year ago and they had been in Boston ever since, but he still marvelled at the beauty of this woman he had so nearly lost. He loved her long lithe body and her green eyes with the Asian lift. She was still the most exotically lovely woman he had ever seen in years of travelling the world. They had a few games which they both loved to play when then were alone in the house. One was to choose a small part of the other's body and use any trick to get them aroused by touching it, stroking it or in some way stimulating it. Today it was Joanne's turn to choose.

She led him upstairs to their room and told him to strip. His body still turned her on – well over 6 feet tall and slim but with muscles in all the right places and startling blue eyes that normally had a sardonic look in them. Right now, his expression had a look of ripe expectation and she could see from his shorts that she had already started to win the contest. She ripped them off and pushed him face down on the bed so that his beautiful butt was angled towards her.

At that moment a few miles away inside the ivy-clad buildings of the college building Professor Li and Professor James Spencer were discussing particulate pollution in major western cities with David Watson a business manager within the facility with particular responsibility for fund raising and donations. The two Professors headed the economics and chemistry faculties and were unlikely but close friends who shared a concern about the commercial influence that had permeated the college in recent years and which was, in their opinion spoiling the academic purity of the institution.

"David, the College has been quoted as a partner in the development of the Greenwatch system, yet I can't find any of our colleagues in biomedicine or environmental studies who were involved in the research," Professor Li looked questioningly over to the young man across the table.
"Yes Professor, they were rather naughty about that – they were supposed to keep our name out of it."
"Naughty, thundered Spencer – have you any idea how important our good name is?"
David Watson went a dark purple and spluttered "The head of corporate affairs looked at all the London test data and it looked excellent – Greenwatch are going to fund a chair in environmental studies – millions of dollars...."

Professor Li waved a placatory hand in the direction of James Spencer who looked as though he was going to explode and said "David, this Greenwatch system is being used by the President and our mayor as a major part of their political campaigns and they say it will solve our air quality problems. If that's true then I'm sure that we will all back it wholeheartedly, but I'm not sure that we have done all the due diligence or I as head of department, would have been involved."
Watson looked uncomfortable "Professor, the Chancellor has also sanctioned our involvement with Greenwatch and he looked at all the data personally."

The two Professors looked at each other and realised that there was little point in carrying on the interrogation of David Watson. The Chancellor had arrived with a great fanfare a couple of years ago stating that he was going to end the 'ivory tower' and isolationist attitude that had driven wedges between the ivy league institutions and business or government." He had certainly improved the colleges funding by linking with a number of international corporations. The college had also started throwing honorary doctorates around the Republican Party like they were confetti. The press thought that the Chancellor was wonderful and he went out of his way to show that the admiration was mutual.

Professor Li asked Watson for a copy of the Greenwatch test data to be on his desk in the next 24 hours and Watson left the room with barely concealed relief. As he walked down the corridor, he got out his mobile and dialled his boss. "Sir, Professor Li and Professor Spencer have demanded to see the Greenwatch data by tomorrow – what should I do?" There was an expletive from his boss and Watson was told under no circumstances to comply and that the Dean's office would be dealing with this from now on. As soon as he returned to his desk Watson opened his laptop and booked two weeks leave starting immediately. In the circumstances he was sure that this would be accepted and picked up his backpack and left.

The two academics had parted vowing to continue a quiet investigation of Greenwatch. Professor Li had mentioned his daughter's interest in the system and they both thought that she should be encouraged to find out what she could about the system and the people behind it.

The Chancellor looked at one of the three screens on his desk and again reviewed the Greenwatch data. He was concerned that those troublesome old Professors were interfering again in his day to day business. The problem of air pollution was one of the great unrecognised problems of the modern age and he wanted his university to be at the centre of the solution and to have a constant source of income when the system rolled out globally. The Chancellor knew that he had broken a few rules when it came to establishing the partnership between the two organisations but Dr Fantoni had assured him that this would be kept confidential until after the Boston test results were analysed. This promise was broken catastrophically when the President and mayor started selling the College and Greenwatch connection strongly as part of their environmental clean-up campaign. The reality of the situation was that Coombes had invented the technology and he had left Shelford under a cloud, so the connection was tenuous to say the least.

One of the other TV screens was constantly on CNN with the sound switched off. Out of the corner of his eye he saw the familiar Greenwatch box showing its digital read-out and the text underneath scrolled... "President backs Greenwatch for state roll-out." The Chancellor smashed his fist down on to the desk, God, he wished that he'd never met Salimond or ever heard of the US Environmental Agency. This had the potential to be a problem of Shakespearian proportions and he could easily be the villain of the piece.

At around the same time in Professor Li's house in old town Boston, Dane had rolled exhaustedly off an equally exhausted Joanne Li. Jo had won the sex game again and what she had achieved with some cream and a few little fingers had been extraordinary. It was all Dane could do to avoid going off at half-cock and he would have had to admit defeat in the first couple of minutes had she not stopped and allowed him time to cool down. After a while he had started working on her and kept her waiting – stopping just as he felt her skin changing – and then building up her climax gently. Finally, she could stand no more and dragged him into her, demanding that he move hard and fast. My God, she thought, they were getting good at this. It was his turn to choose the erogenous game tomorrow and she couldn't wait.

After a while they showered in the enormous wet room at the back of the house and got dressed. Even in ancient Levis and a faded blue sweatshirt from Thailand which had some chameleon-like creature on it, she looked fabulous. He had a more European style and very seldom wore jeans no matter how hard she tried to change him. But his linen trousers, old highly polished brogues and dark blue cotton shirt from somewhere in London looked pretty good to her. He always looked different from everyone else she saw on the streets and had an unconscious sense of style which she loved.

They were both hungry and grazed on a few snacks in the fridge before making hot drinks and sitting in the study to watch the local news. Dane hated US news but forced himself to watch the endless political comment and pseudo facts that were always a part of pre-election time in the states. If you believed the pollsters then the incumbent Republicans were in for a hammering though there had been some swing back to the party after recent rallies had endorsed the new "clean up our cities" policy and promised to roll out the installation of air monitoring systems nationwide. Then the newscaster switched to a more urgent tone of voice.

"We have some breaking news.... there was a suspected terrorist incident a few hours ago ..." The screen switched to a dramatically staged scene with flashing police lights and people in FBI crime

scene overalls. "According to police, a foreign national was intercepted whilst trying to plant a device in a government office.. We have few details but apparently there was only one fatality and that was the perpetrator. The anti-terrorist unit have just tweeted that a major explosion has been averted."
"Shit, did you see that?" Dane asked.
"What?" Jo asked.
"I think that was Kowolski.... you know that Environmental Agency guy who threatened me at the Grosvenor club a couple of days ago.." They switched channels and frantically tried to find more news, eventually they found a local station using the same footage and Dane freeze-framed the image.
"Look at that... it's him."
"Dane – I didn't see him, but if you say so..."

Dane went out of the room and returned a few seconds later with his camera. Scrolling through the shots on the back of the Nikon he found the one he'd taken outside the Grosvenor Club and Aenlarged it. Jo peered at it closely and saw the guy being bundled into the big black wagon surrounded by agents in suits one of whom was Kowolski. It was amazing, she thought, Dane made every shot – even snapshots - look brilliant.
"Yes, it could be him, but I can't be sure."
"Don't forget, I saw him in the gym reception and he was as close as you are now." Dane responded.
"Well, if it is him, why are the US Environmental Agency and their agents getting involved in anti-terrorism?"
"That my love, is a question we need to ask them. And does it mean they think that our friend Fantoni is a terrorist?"

Chapter 4

Carlos Antonio Fantoni was born in Lima, Peru in 1968, the only son of a government official and a seamstress. His first memory was of rain hammering on the balcony of the small apartment his family lived in and his parents shouting. That was the only rain he ever saw in the years he lived in Lima – despite being a city of 7 million it almost never rains and all water has to come from the Andes many miles away. Another memory was looking across and seeing Turkey Vultures ripping a carcass to pieces on a flat roof across the street. Every time he walked to school, he looked up and was scared that the vultures would swoop down and carry him away.

If it hadn't been for two skills, Carlos might have become a minor official like his father, making a living by petty corruption or a criminal in one of Lima's many gangs. The first skill was languages, Carlos was speaking local Spanish proficiently by the age of 3 years old with a vocabulary that was greater than kids 10 years older. He devoured US TV programmes and loved the old film stars like Cary Grant or Jimmie Stewart and became fairly good at English – speaking it in the refined American accent much favoured by that era. He could understand and speak it himself before he was 8 years old. His skill with languages stayed with him all his life and by the end he spoke many of the European languages and had become reasonably good at Cantonese.

His second skill was tennis. Carlos attended a Catholic charity school until the age of 12 where he was seen as the star pupil and as far as the Franciscan friar who ran the school was concerned, he was destined for the church and finally the Vatican. One of his beliefs was that a healthy body with young boys was nearly as important as a healthy mind. So the courtyard behind the old Spanish monastery where the school was situated had an old tennis court and there was a primitive gymnasium in one of the outbuildings.

About the time that Carlos was old enough to be interested in sport, there was a TV feature on Jaime Yzaga and other leading Peruvian tennis players and their attempts to break into big-time tennis in the America's Cup. Something clicked with Fantoni and he found a couple of old Dunlop Maxply rackets and some balls in the back of the school and started to practise. Within a week he was beating boys five years older, within a month, he was beating one of the teachers who was an experienced player.

Physically, Carlos Fantoni had a mix of the qualities of his Inca forebears – slim build, golden skin and a slight slant of the eyes. He was to grow into a man with immense stamina and obvious intelligence. But without a little bit of luck when he was 12 years old, he might still have had to make his living on the hard, hot streets of Lima.

The teachers had arranged for one of the wealthy patrons of the charity that supported the school to come and talk to the students on one of the many saints' days celebrated. The big man delivered a standard speech telling students to work hard, fear God and always be a useful member of the Peruvian society. The patron himself did none of these things – being a member of one of the elite families who'd always prospered out of influence and corruption, but he loved to play the benefactor.

After the speech, the patron was given a tour of the school and Carlos Fantoni was chosen to take him round. When they got to the courtyard, the patron told the boy of his interest in tennis and how he had two grass courts at his home in the hills behind Lima. Carlos was visibly impressed – grass courts - he never knew that such things existed in Peru. Summoning up his courage, the boy said that he would play at Wimbledon one day. Astonished, the man called the friar over and asked him a few questions about the boy in English. He was even more surprised when Carlos repeated the promise in perfect English.

Over the next few months Jose Luiz Malagariga, the school patron, took a personal interest in Carlos and even asked him up to play on his grass courts in the hills. Here many of the young, rich sporting types in the capital liked to show off their prowess. Malagariga challenged many of the most arrogant to play against the boy and placed a few substantial side-bets amongst his friends. He never lost except against a semi-professional who took three sets to do it and was amazed by the kid's raw talent.

Carlos was astute enough to play the dumb kid routine and not crow too loud about his academic achievements or his victories. He was also aware that Malagariga's interest in him was not always sporting and learned to run as fast away from him as he had to avoid the lascivious attentions of Father Lopez at school. His benefactor didn't seem to be upset and in the end just decided to help him. This meant getting him proper coaching and after a gentle request from

Fantoni, finding him a tutor to bring him up to speed with his academic learning. His tutor was astonished by the boy's ability to learn languages and his proficiency in mathematics and science.

Fantoni's parents were initially worried about their son's involvement with one of the families who were notorious for screwing the poor of Lima. But gradually they realised that Carlos was starting to blossom under the patrons care and would have opportunities that few other kids had. He still returned home every night and was as helpful round the house and respectful to his parents as he had always been. But they sensed a subtle change in the boy as he became used to the better things in life and grew in knowledge.

By the age of 15, Carlos Fantoni was known as the best junior tennis player in the country and able to give many of the senior players a serious fright. Academically, he was years ahead of the best in his school but he knew that in both areas Peru was not going to be the country where he could fully reach his potential. His benefactor knew that too and one day after a particularly entertaining game against a player from the states, he called Carlos into his office. Carlos had never been allowed into this inner sanctum before and sat uneasily on the big leather chair and looked across at the big, swarthy, man who'd helped him so much. "Have I done something wrong uncle?"

Malagariga smiled at the honorary title that Carlos had started to use a few months previously and smiled reassuringly. "No, Carlos, the exact opposite, you have become almost like a son to me and I want to discuss your future. We are running out of people you haven't beaten and you need better coaching than I can find round here."

Carlos's look of relief was so palpable that Malagariga smiled again and continued, "I have some contacts in a West Coast College in the US – in fact you've just played one of their better players. They will offer you a sports scholarship from the end of this year, which means that every aspect of your game will be helped and academically you will have chances to achieve the highest levels possible. I know that you will make us proud Carlos?"

Every thought imaginable had flooded through his mind – joy, terror, fear, what his parents would say – but he fixed a smile on his face and said. "Uncle, you are so generous, but we cannot afford such a trip – my family...." Malagariga interrupted him. "Carlos, my boy, I will speak to your parents and tell them that I will pay for your further education and make sure that you are looked after in California."

The US was the first new country he'd ever visited and Fantoni remembered flying over the city of Los Angeles for what seemed like an hour with the lights twinkling down below. When he came into land for the first time he felt as though he was going to embarrass himself by throwing up, but he breathed deeply and the spasm passed.

He was only in LA for a couple of days but saw the Hollywood sign and went on the film tour to see where many of those movies he'd watched on TV had been made. He was astonished by the city but couldn't believe the traffic and the smelly smog that permeated everywhere.

From the moment he arrived, he stood out as looking different. He was smaller, brown skinned but obviously not Mexican, which was good because the country was going through one of its anti-immigrant phases and Mexico was seen as the enemy. His face betrayed his Inca heritage and looked rather exotic, so most American's he met were friendly, especially when he talked to them in accent-less English.

Over the next few years at the college Carlos Fantoni developed his skills exponentially and became a tennis player who was always asked to play for his country despite being only in his late teens. His academic achievements were also astonishing and his professors were convinced that he had the makings of a Nobel scientist or leading academic. Despite their concern about taking on Fantoni originally because of the donation his patron had made to the sports facility, the college authorities now viewed him as one of their rising stars and they used him in their prospectus as an example of how they developed skills in their students of humbler backgrounds.

Fantoni still enjoyed playing tennis competitively but in recent months he had resisted entering the pre professional circuit his coaches had planned for him. His benefactor was disappointed too and tried to pressure him but found that the adult Fantoni had developed a stubborn streak. After sending Carlos some airline tickets and requesting that he play in the annual charity tennis tournament he now hosted in Lima, Malagariga retired to his study and tried to work out why Fantoni had lost his tennis ambitions.

On the day of the tournament Malagariga realised that the cause wasn't lack of skill, Fantoni's serve was now absolutely deadly and despite his slight stature he seemed to be able to deliver 90 mph aces almost at will. And the rest of his game was immensely sophisticated – so much so that he struggled to allow the opposition who were the best of local talent any points. On court Fantoni looked in total control and good enough to achieve that youthful ambition of playing in a Wimbledon final. So what was the problem that was stopping him?

In the office after the game Carlos and Malagariga were alone for the first time. Carlos had been still wearing his tennis kit with a Lacoste track top on loosely over his shoulders and his benefactor could see how troubled he was. The boy had always had the gift of silence and sat waiting for Malagariga to speak first. Malagariga himself felt strangely nervous and realised how much he had grown to love Carlos and almost think of him as a son.
"Carlos, my boy, you played well..."
"Thank you Uncle."
"You must know that your coaches' think you could be the best player that Peru has ever produced... more than that, they think that you can be world class." Malagariga looked intently at the boy's expression but as always, he could read nothing from those Inca eyes. "Don't you want to play Wimbledon in a couple of years?"

Carlos looked uncomfortable but answered softly. "No Uncle, I am sorry and I am really grateful for everything you have done... but tennis is not my future."
Malagariga eased his bulk forward until his face was as close to his protégé's as possible and asked in an ominously controlled voice. "So what do you want to do with the rest of your life, Carlos?"
"I want to save the world from total destruction, Uncle."

Chapter 5

If a particularly ambitious US mayor had been in Malagariga's office on that day five years ago he would have eviscerated that naïve shit Fantoni before he'd had chance to cause the problems that now threatened to kill off his campaign and severely damage the presidential re-election. Bonelli thought the pressure coming from just about every direction was going to kill him and he loosened his tie and tried to breathe deeply. But the anti-stress mechanisms his specialist had taught him just didn't seem to work.

Fantoni had been so plausible. His first presentation of Greenwatch rang with total sincerity because he was genuinely committed to cleaning up the air and stopping the waste of life caused by air pollution. He said that bad air quality had killed his parents in Lima and that he had given up a promising career in professional tennis and devoted himself to his environmental studies because it was of global importance.

The team had checked him out and Fantoni was academically highly qualified – a double first in Environmental Studies and Chemical Engineering from a major West Coast University and a visiting professorship at the World Institute of Climate Change in Lima. The company he represented was a little harder to research but Salimond appeared to be a well funded company in Panama City with strong connections to a major bank. Fantoni had said that it was financed by a number of benefactors who shared his environmental views but preferred to be anonymous. This had concerned the researchers initially but when Fantoni had said that the US President's office was already in conversation with them about Greenwatch, then the team were reassured that due diligence would be carried out on the organisation further up the chain in Washington.

Carlos Fantoni's attitude to life had changed fundamentally when he had made one of his rare visits to his parents before the annual tennis game at his patron's place. He felt guilty that he had not been in contact enough but the demands of the tennis coaches had been exhausting and his academic studies were challenging to say the least. But he knew that was not the real reason, as he walked down the hot dusty streets of Lima and looked up at the familiar high rise apartments, each with its group of black vultures, he knew that he had become used to better things. As usual, the lift was out of order so he had to walk up the five floors to his parents' home, he almost rang the bell and cursed himself for being so nervous, then turned the greasy door handle and went into the small apartment he had been born in. The money he'd sent over the years had bought them a washing machine and a larger TV but the place was still small and damp.

He had phoned the previous day and his father sounded oddly subdued. As he entered the hall and shouted out a greeting, Carlos was aware of a strange smell and someone coughing as they tried to answer. As he walked into the main room, he saw a sight that reminded him of those religious paintings that had covered the walls of his Catholic school in Lima.

His mother was dressed in a long white hospital gown and she was reclining on some kind of day bed with her head and shoulders propped up by four or five pillows. Her face had a pallid beauty that reminded him of the Saints or Mother Mary shown in his school chapel. The smell of cheap disinfectant and urine was almost unbearable and Carlos had to force himself to move closer and kiss his mother on her forehead. Instinctively, he knew that she was close to death and cursed himself for not having contacted his parents for months, knowing that they would never have contacted him for help as they wouldn't have wanted to bother their wonderful son.

Carlos had tried to throw money at the problem and a series of doctors came to the apartment over the next few days, but nothing really helped. His mother refused to go to hospital and tried to hide the blood she was coughing up constantly. One specialist said that his mother's lungs had been damaged by pollution and that it was endemic in Lima but that no-one talked about it. Quietly in the corridor outside the apartment, the doctor added to Fantoni's grief by telling him that his father's lungs were also badly damaged and that in his opinion, it was only looking after his wife that was keeping him going.

At that point Carlos had vowed to himself that he would dedicate himself to finding a solution to the problem of environmental pollution. The death of both parents over the next few months from the same cause doubled his resolve.

Over the following months Fantoni graduated with honours faster than any other student and greatly reduced his coaching which didn't please his patron. At the beginning Mallagariga tried to change his mind by cutting off his funding and Fantoni had to work in bars and stack shelves in order to eat. But eventually his benefactor relented because he could see that his strategy would not work with someone like Fantoni.

Malagariga also sensed a business opportunity. He could see that the environment was something that the family business might just make some clean money out of for a change. A couple of weeks after Carlos had made his decision, Malagariga had been in Panama City to deposit some money when he heard about Salimond from a banking friend. According to him they were extremely well funded and dedicated to developing technology that improved the environment. They sounded ideal for Carlos Fantoni to approach, so he arranged an initial meeting.

Most people have heard about the Panama Canal but only a few know about Panama City. The Malagariga family had used a number of banks in Panama City for hiding and laundering money since WW2 when they had first started to make illegal money out of arms dealing. Panama is a legal offshore financial centre but has always had a dark side and been a place where everyone from Nazi criminals through to terrorists stashed money they didn't want anyone else to know about.

For most of its history the area was paranoid about avoiding publicity. After the fall of old communism, money had flown in from Russia and China because it was seen as a good haven for bad money. Then a WikiLeaks social media storm exposed just how many politicians, dictators and industrialists were hiding money in Panama banks which brought unwanted publicity to the city and things looked difficult. But within a year the media stopped talking about it and dirty money started flooding in again.

Amongst the organisations in the city Panama Gulf Bank was amongst the most secretive and discrete and had been used by royal families, dictators and emperors for a century. Nobody had ever known who was behind the bank and it had a 100% record of keeping clients affairs secret. For the last few decades Panama Gulf had surprised the markets by funding a number of initiatives which had a genuine global benefit. These included a much improved de-desalination system and improvements in intensive agriculture productivity. These were known about by bank clients and were an excellent salve for their consciences. For the bank their reasons were rather more pragmatic but it looked good as a corporate social responsibility exercise. The initiatives also had the capacity to make profit, which was a cultural necessity.

Salimond was an organisation which had almost unlimited funding through Panama Gulf Bank and which was seemingly dedicated to the ending of air pollution. Only a few people worldwide had access to this funding through the bank and had the unique black card to identify them. Only three organisations knew where the money came from – a European car manufacturer, a Japanese Industrial Group and a small consortium of oil producers. None of the groups showed Salimond or any funding from it on their annual reports and were totally secretive about its aims. But the fact that some of these organisations had been accused of falsifying emissions data and others were strong supporters of the oil lobby, might have given an informed observer some doubts about their motivation.

Greenwatch was developed by Salimond and it was genuinely good technology. Carlos Fantoni went through six weeks of due diligence on the invention in a lab in Panama City with two scientists showing the way that offending particulates could be identified and measured in the air. As part of the demonstration they had all got in 4x4's and driven six hours up into the Andes and one of the scientists got a green box out of the wagon and put it on a rocky outcrop above them. He flipped a switch and the digital read-out on the screen started. After a few seconds the figures for nitrogen dioxides shone out and shortly afterwards the figure for carbon monoxide was revealed.

The team then loaded the unit back in the car and went back to downtown Panama and placed the green box at a major intersection. Within seconds the Greenwatch unit was flashing red as it registered the dangerous levels of harmful particulates that commuters were breathing.

Carlos was a well qualified scientist and had been convinced by the demonstration and joined the company. For the first time he could see an antidote to all the ignorance about air quality and something that could end all the unnecessary deaths. He couldn't wait to get started.

First, he had to go through some induction days with people at Salimond who were more like interrogators than HR people. The training was extremely thorough and he became familiar with all aspects of the company and signed document after document to prove that he was fully informed.
He was told that he would have a permanent office within the lab in

Panama City and an apartment close by. But, the director who came in at the end of the session stated that he would be spending most of the time travelling round the world selling Greenwatch technology, not at home in Panama. That suited his ambitions perfectly.

The last session of the induction was at 3.00 o'clock in the morning when a tall well-dressed woman came in and handed him a small leather wallet. Inside were six different credit cards in his name and one black card he had never seen before.
"This is a most important card," the woman said in an accent which might have been German. "With it you can withdraw millions of dollars at any of our banks, worldwide, without question."
"Why on earth would I need that much money." Carlos asked.
"It is an imperfect world," she said with a sad smile. "In some places you may have to offer a cash incentive in order to get Greenwatch used."
Carlos felt his anger growing. "I'm not going to bribe people – pollution is killing millions, it's something anyone would want to solve..."
The woman shrugged, shook his hand, left the room and that was the last time he saw her.

The following day he was picked up and taken to an office in the old colonial part of Panama City and found that he had a desk and various assistants already installed. It felt rather surreal in those first days when he sat in his big office with glass walls looking over a team of people he was responsible for.

One of the first reports Fantoni was given showed data on air pollution in cities worldwide and a top analyst had looked at the areas most likely to be open to Greenwatch. The figures in some parts of China and Asia were horrific but governments were unlikely to have the political will to invest millions in a solution. Europe was seen as being a far more likely market. According to published data, air pollution was costing Europe around $2 trillion a year – roughly equivalent to a tenth of the continent's GDP. This according to the World Health Organisation was causing around 600,000 premature deaths every year across Europe. The analyst stated that although this was a good potential market, the European Union was extremely bureaucratic and it would be easier to start with a single city as a demonstration first.

London was not in the EU but had recognised the problem of pollution years ago and introduced a 'congestion charge' on drivers in the centre and zero emission zones. But it was estimated that there were still around 9,000 premature deaths because of bad air in the city every year. According to the World Atlas of Atmospheric Pollution, road transport accounted for 88% of carbon monoxide, 62% of particulate matter and 53% of nitrogen dioxides in London. Though there had been some improvements in air quality since, the team agreed that this city of nine million was an ideal candidate for the first Greenwatch test.

Salimond or the bank seemed to know people at the top everywhere and Carlos had a meeting set with the deputy mayor in London within a couple of months. Salimond had also negotiated a deal with top US University Shelford, to sponsor a chair in Environmental Studies which Fantoni realised would add tremendous credibility to his presentations.

The researchers had been right, London was desperate for a solution to the air quality problem as traffic taxation had not done enough to stop the rise in air pollution and it was only a matter of time before it became the subject of serious litigation. Various governments had banned diesel and petrol cars from 2040 and electric or hybrid cars had grown strongly at the beginning of the 2020's but then tailed off as subsidies reduced and petrol became cheaper. Cities like London knew that air quality needed action and needed it now.

The trip across the Atlantic had been the first long-haul flight Carlos had taken since he'd flown into the States. When the Boeing came in over the Thames and he could see those landmarks like London Bridge and Parliament, he really felt that his mission to make the world a better place had started. He'd cleared security in an hour and been met by a driver who whisked him away in an electric Range Rover and dropped him at the Savoy – handing him a small leather folder as he left and warning him to be in the foyer by 8.00 a.m. the following morning.

Carlos had felt like a superstar or someone in the old Cary Grant movies he'd watched as a kid in Lima. The suite was huge and the bathroom was bigger than his parents' living room but he gradually found his way round and realised that he was ravenously hungry. He showered and changed into one of the six new suits that Salimond had tailored for him and went down to find the restaurant. Over the next few months Carlos Fantoni would become used to the best hotels and restaurants but on this first occasion he just stood in the entrance of the River Room with his mouth open.

Seeing the confusion of the well-dressed young man, Emilio the head waiter had glided over and politely asked in English if he wanted a table. Carlos nodded and Emilio asked one of the waiters to take him to Table 8. Carlos turned to him and asked in perfect Italian whether that was really the best table available. Taken aback but amused, Emilio changed the table immediately to one with a view. Fantoni couldn't remember afterwards what he'd had, but it was wonderful and at Emilios' suggestion he finished with an espresso and small Cognac.

Carlos digested the information about London in the folder before the same driver arrived and they left the hotel. He knew that the meeting with the mayor's office was at 11.00 a.m. but first the car went to a branch of the Panama Gulf Bank in South Kensington and the driver instructed him to use the black card to withdraw 200k in dollars.

A senior manager met him inside the vast foyer of the bank and escorted him up to the 15th floor, where he was taken to a small windowless office equipped with a strange piece of equipment and a computer. Carlos had been guided to the retinal scanner and paused there whilst each eye was recorded, then his face was photographed from both sides and put into the banks facial recognition system. He was told that he was now on the system and that he could draw up to $10 million a month at black card machines inside Panama Gulf Banks worldwide. In an emergency, he was told that he could even use their standard outside ATM's to draw up to $200,000 expenses.

On this first occasion he was guided back down to the main bank floor and told to use his black card at one of the normal cash machines. He put the black card in the slot and the screen changed, welcoming him and requesting information about the transaction. He filled in $200,000 and the system authorised payment requesting that he stayed by the machine. Within a few minutes a manager came out from an office with a black attaché case and handed it to him. Carlos then left the bank and went back to the car, which was parked outside with the driver holding open the door. As he entered the beautiful cream leather interior, Carlos again felt like he was in some kind of movie but was interrupted by his driver in broad East London demanding the case, which he handed over as if it were red hot. $200,000 was more money than his parents could have ever dreamt of and he was being asked to give it away as a bribe. He knew that his home city ran on corruption but he never thought that London would be the same.

The bribe was handed over with extreme secrecy to someone influential in the mayor's office and Carlos didn't see the transaction or have time to object. The presentation to eight people including the Deputy mayor had gone extremely well and all of them had walked down to Westminster Bridge where Carlos repeated the roadside test they'd done in Panama. The Greenwatch box had flashed red on two of the danger particulates and when the team returned to the office, another Greenwatch box was live streamed on their computers from the Chilton Hills, showing far safer levels of particulates.

Fantoni made it clear that Greenwatch was a highly sophisticated monitor, not a cure in itself. But because it was highly visible it was ideal for those who wanted to get an electorate in favour of the dramatic measures really needed to curb air pollution in cities like London. The faces round the table were guarded but it was obvious from the positive questions at the end that the team were impressed.

He had got on well with his driver and Carlos started to consider him almost a friend in a strange land. Fantoni had ranted about never wanting to be involved in corruption ever again and the driver had swerved to the side of the road and wrenched open the rear door. As he climbed in Carlos saw the gun under his jacket and wondered exactly what was coming.
"Mr Fantoni" the man said in an angry undertone. "If you think that everyone wants to save the world, you're a fucking idiot. There are people out there prepared to spend millions to keep the oil wells pumping.. they don't care who dies." Horns from cars stuck behind the Range Rover got his attention and the guy buttoned up his jacket and got back in the driver's seat and drove back to the hotel. Wondering what had happened to the deferential and rather smooth English driver, Carlos slumped back in his seat.

After dinner in the Savoy and a few minutes practising his Italian with head waiter Emilio, Carlos decided to go out for a walk. He went out through the revolving doors, past the top-hatted doormen and walked out to the street. It was dark in the shadows and he didn't see the tall figure wearing evening dress follow him. The man looked like a throwback to the Edwardian age and was wearing a black frock coat over his silk waistcoat and black tie. A silver topped walking stick completed the outfit and he tapped it on the pavement every other step in the approved manner as he followed his quarry down the Strand and right down a small side street.

"Mr Fantoni" said a deep voice from just behind Carlos which gave him a shock and he turned, realising how dark the side street was.
"What do you want..?" Carlos asked in a voice that was little more than a squeak. He was young and an athlete so he shouldn't have felt threatened by the old man in the strange outfit but there was something really sinister about him. Carlos gathered his courage and repeated the question in a slightly stronger voice. He didn't even see the stick as the man swung it into his balls. As he slumped to his knees, he found that the assassin had gracefully pulled a long thin sword from the stick and passed the point across his throat with incredible speed. Carlos felt a sick, cold pain in his groin and knew that he was only alive because the guy wanted it that way so he stayed still.

"Mr Fantoni, my principles have asked me to pass on a message, which is to stop what you are doing with Greenwatch. If you don't then we will meet again and I will have a chance to practise my surgical skills." The assassin put the blade back into the stick with a mechanical click, turned and walked unhurriedly away into the shadows.

When he looked in the mirror later, he could see a razor cut that passed from shoulder to shoulder on his Saville Row suit and that his throat showed a line of blood from side to side which was steadily seeping on to his shirt front and tie. The whole thing was over so quickly, it was difficult to believe it had happened. If it hadn't been for the ruined shirt and jacket, he might have put it down to a nightmare.

Everything had moved quickly in the days after that and London agreed to a two year test on a fixed number of major roads in the city centre. Having sold the initial concept in, Carlos had little further direct involvement with London Council and was involved planning with Salimond head office about targets elsewhere. He'd binned the shirt and pushed the suit to the back of the wardrobe, so thought less and less about the threats.

He was told to wait a week or so to check that the initial units were installed successfully, so he spent plenty of time in the Savoy cocktail bar whilst he was there. Later, he was to wonder whether it was accidental or he was manipulated into talking to the attractive woman who'd been sitting a few feet away. The woman had been complaining loudly to the barman about the congestion charges and low emission areas in the city. Carlos had drunk a couple of dry martini cocktails and was emboldened to butt in and tell her just how many premature deaths were caused by bad air quality in London. She looked shocked and asked how he knew.

Diane Fallow was a junior reporter on the Financial Times who had been trying to get one of the few traditional journalist jobs left in the hard press for four years before she finally got in. She'd got a Masters in Journalism & Politics in her early 20's and worked for some influential online publishers but her real love was the Press. Hard copy newspapers had been dying for centuries and many great journalists had been thrown on the scrap heap, but Diane loved the medium and had taken a pay cut to work for one of the best – the FT.

Most of her colleagues thought of Diane as one of the blokes, an impression she encouraged. She was tall, well built and had her auburn hair cropped short and acted the hard-nosed hack around the office. But underneath all the attitude she was actually quite attractive, she could also turn on the charms when it was useful and it was definitely useful in the case of Carlos Fantoni. Her feminine side was certainly attracted by the slim, brown-skinned guy with the strange Inca eyes she met in the bar at the Savoy. She'd known the barman and he'd tipped her off about Mr Fantoni and how he'd been having high level talks with the mayor, so she'd deliberately made contact one night in the bar. But what he'd told her made the effort worthwhile as she had genuinely been shocked at the death rate and professionally interested in the likely adoption of the Greenwatch system in London.

Carlos had liked the woman in the bar and gave her his new business card. He knew that she was a journalist but was naïve – very naïve about the way the Press worked. A couple of days later the FT ran a small front page story about the city of London investing in a new air pollution monitoring system called Greenwatch.

The mayor's office had been incandescent about the premature announcement but presumed that it had come from the notoriously leaky council press office. Fantoni had learnt a lesson that day and phoned Diane Fallow, complaining about the leak and asking her to warn him about any other stories before they happened. She apologised and agreed to meet him in a few days knowing in her heart that she wanted more from Carlos than just a good story. She called him and they met over dinner and ended up in his suite which was exactly what she'd hoped for and the start of a passionate relationship which would be repeated whenever he was in London and she wasn't working.

Fantoni used London as his base for a several weeks and appeared on TV a few times supporting the start of the test in the city. The story of how his parents had died from air pollution in Lima had obvious emotional appeal and his sincerity shone through about his mission to clean up city air. So he appeared alongside the London Mayor on a number of occasions and did huge amounts to sell the idea of Greenwatch. He also travelled to the US and back once using the early London data to pre-sell Greenwatch in Boston and the US. The response had been gratifyingly good.

After his encounter with the assassin Carlos tried not to leave the Savoy at night on his own. He was worried that if he told the hotel manager or his driver about the tall, elegantly dressed man with the swordstick, they would ridicule him. But Ralph his driver knew something was wrong and tried to protect his back whenever they were together, but he normally went off duty about 6.00 p.m. No matter how often he asked Fantoni what was wrong, he just shook his head and said it was nothing.

After a while, the threat of the attack receded and Carlos was sleeping well. Diane Fallow wasn't with him for once, which was disappointing, but considerably more restful as her pale, full breasted body and auburn hair really turned him on. The comfort of the suite at the Savoy was wonderful and the bed was like a haven after all the travelling. He was dreaming wonderful dreams when an alarm blasted out and high intensity, blinding lights started flashing in his room. He shocked himself awake and tried to see what time it was, groggily pulling on his dressing gown and groping towards where he thought the door was.

Few people look at the emergency instructions on hotel doors and Carlos was no exception, so he pulled open the door into the corridor and had no idea which way to turn. He looked round for any sign of an emergency exit and what he found was pandemonium. Smoke was billowing out of air vents, the siren was even more intense but he could see a green exit sign at the end of the corridor and tried to battle his way through. He fell once and nearly choked on the acrid fumes but forced himself to the end and pushed open the fire door.

Once through, things were a little easier. He pulled the door hard shut behind him and was relieved to find that the air was clearer and the sound muffled. Carlos ran down four flights of stairs to a door on the ground floor where he pushed on the escape bar and burst out into the cold, fresh air, gasping.

"Mr Fantoni, I told you we would meet again." The tall figure in the frock coat stepped out of the darkness and unsheathed the swordstick.

Chapter 6

At the beginning of the project when Fantoni was in London, the real board of Salimond met in a suite on the 54th floor of the Burg Al Arab, Dubai. The inventor Dr Coombes and Carlos Fantoni were not invited. There were only three people present – a middle-aged German who was a major shareholder in a car manufacturer found guilty of giving false emissions data about its products. An older Iranian representing a small cartel of oil producers which were family owned. Finally, a young woman who was heir-apparent to one of the largest privately owned Japanese industrial conglomerates. All of these had a major interest in the continued use of petrochemicals and so their involvement in Greenwatch would have astonished anyone who knew them.

Wolf Bayer had looked out at the futuristic world on the Dubai coastline below and realised that very little of it would have existed if it hadn't been for oil. Whenever he had any doubt about what Salimond was doing – which wasn't often – he thought of this view. He looked up and realised that the others were waiting for him to talk. He had confirmed that London was ready to go ahead and that six Greenwatch units would be in place by the end of the month. In fact, they were installed far earlier because the mayor's office wanted to deflect criticism from environmentalists. The Salimond inner board had agreed that the bribe paid to city officials had been a useful investment since it had been captured on film for future use.

Sheikh Bin Hadad had raised a point at the end of the meeting which concerned the board greatly. He had heard rumours that another oil producer was so concerned about Greenwatch that they had put out a contract on Carlos Fantoni in London. There was total agreement from the board members that there was no way they could reveal the true purpose of Salimond to the oil people, no matter how similar their interests. It was also vital that Carlos Fantoni was protected until he had finished his job.

Ms Tanaka of the Japanese Group said that she could mobilise a number of resources the company had in London and that they could be operational within a couple of hours. She had made a call at 12.45 p.m. London time and confirmed that undercover protection would be in place before the following night. There was general discussion about how Fantoni could be protected on a long term basis when he left the UK.

The minutes show that there was a lengthy report from each board member on the state of each company's problems, many of which related to air pollution or decline in oil usage. Wolf Bayer stated that although the German group had been found falsifying pollution data some years previously they had delayed any final culpability by promising compensation and creating a fog of legal misinformation. The Technical Director had been sacrificed at the time and was now living in disgrace in South America with an obscenely large pay-off. The new CEO appeared to be a great supporter of hybrid and electric power but 90% of their cars were still using traditional fuels and generated all of their profit.

Bin Hadad represented a number of smaller oil producing areas where ruling families had spent trillions to keep the general populations happy enough to not need democracy or any political change that affected the obscene amount of wealth that went to a relatively small number of family members. In the old days, the family would not have cared at all if outside opinion was critical of them but now all businesses were global and bad public image could affect share price and the value of their portfolio.

The Arab spring had been short lived but had frightened family members, who knew that if they wanted to keep the value of their assets high for generations to come, then they had to be clever. The move to make oil the major culprit with air pollution was a major threat to income and the sheikhs had been desperate to delay any bans on petrol or diesel for as long as possible. Bin Hadad reported that the family saw the Salimond idea as a way of achieving these objectives and was prepared to increase their investment in the company at any time if required.

Ms Tanaka also promised that the considerable resources of her company would be available to the project if necessary but that total secrecy was essential. To the outside world, Harakiko Group would have appeared to be less vulnerable to pressure from the anti-oil lobby as they made everything from musical instruments to scientific equipment and pharmaceuticals. But the vast wealth of the dynasty that owned it had been put into major shareholdings within US automotive groups many years ago. They were also involved directly in one of the oldest Japanese truck and car manufacturers who would have been found guilty of the falsification of emission figures had it not used its political power to keep them suppressed.

Harakiko had thought that the investment required to make those vehicles eco-friendly was prohibitive and that in any case they preferred to invest in driverless technology. But for the next few years they were committed to petrol and diesel and Salimond was offering a creative way to reduce their risk. This also meant that they might continue to sell their most polluting vehicles to third world countries and nobody would be any the wiser.

The board members all had an obvious interest in maintaining the status quo as far as petrol consumption was concerned. So observers would have been amazed if they had found out about their financing of Salimond and backing of Greenwatch, a device dedicated to making the public aware of the high levels of air pollution on their streets.

When Wolf Bayer had been approached by dissident scientist Dr Coombes a couple of years previously, his first reaction was fear. The man had left Ivy League college Shelford after an argument about IP rights and was trying to sell what Bayer could see was a brilliant answer to air monitoring for German cities. Coombes was approaching the venture capital company, of which Bayer was head, for finance to fund the European launch. Bayer had been impressed with the technology and his first thought had been to kill the idea and possibly even Dr Coombes before he had chance to sell it to anyone else and ruin the automotive business. Then he had a brilliant thought.

Just like the person who owns a newspaper often controls what news is passed on and in what form, to a gullible public, a person who owned a measuring device could influence what it measured and how accurate it was. But first you had to build trust, otherwise the information would be regarded as unreliable as many emissions' figures had turned out to be in the past. Bayer could see a way of delaying, deflecting and possibly killing off most of the criticism his group had been suffering for the last few years. He told Coombes he would totally finance the project and over the next few weeks tied him up with contracts, promises and a salary that was ten times what he'd earned at Shelford.

Bayer's next meeting had been with a long haired youth who he'd been told was an expert hacker. After a few days sitting in the youth's cellar surrounded by more computers than he'd ever seen, he was convinced he had an extra package that could be offered to selected clients. This would cost them considerably more than the system itself. The Greenwatch monitor had superb accuracy in measuring all the particulates considered damaging to health. If the extra package was bought then those figures could be reduced by up to 50% and the monitors could be manipulated remotely from a laptop or smart device.

The political and corporate benefits of this to certain sectors were obvious. Solving air pollution for real would require so much investment and such a change to consumer behaviour that most leaders found it easier to leave the problem to the next administration. Greenwatch with the extra package would allow some to demonstrate lower levels of particulates than reality or false levels of improvement. He knew that would be incredibly attractive to some and still have the benefit to Salimond of delaying the demise of traditional fuels.

This was too big for even Bayer's group to finance. His family had used Panama Gulf Bank to store illicit assets back in WW2 and he'd used them himself so had contacts there and knew that their security was 100%. He asked them to approach a number of companies with his concept which was detailed enough for those targeted to recognise the basic principles without knowing how it would be achieved. Obviously, Bayer was anonymous at this stage, but after an intense series of meetings the bank had three groups, including his own, who would invest as long as their involvement was totally secret and the funding invisible. Each group designated one person to attend board meetings but obviously Salimond needed some sort of infrastructure.

To this end Bayer and the bank had set up an office for Salimond in the old Spanish quarter of Panama City two years previously and had recruited genuine scientists and research staff. All of the board members had invested considerable funds to start the project. At the time of the Dubai board meeting Salimond had a staff of 30 including Dr Coombes, who was enjoying the benefits of his new wealth rather too much. Carlos Fantoni, however, had been there six months and was proving an excellent choice as head of the Greenwatch team as he had already proved in London. Keeping Fantoni in ignorance of the extra package that the unscrupulous might buy was essential. Bayer himself, handled that selling.

London was chosen for the first installation of Greenwatch because it had an ambitious city mayor with a reasonable amount of autonomy. It was also a capital city with a worldwide reputation whose opinions would be respected globally. Data from this test would be seen as reliable by other potential buyers as it had a severe pollution problem. Wolf Bayer's staff had also found some members of the environmental committee who were willing to receive a substantial amount of money to recommend Greenwatch.

The London test was already going well at the time of the board meeting but everyone knew that the biggest target was the US. Here again the analysts had done a good job and chosen Boston as an ideal city to start with and Fantoni had already begun some initial conversations. Boston was ideal for Greenwatch because it had an air quality problem which was already being exposed by campaigners. Similar to London it had an ambitious mayor with substantial local power. The city was big enough to be influential in national politics and had a strong academic institution with which the board had already negotiated an advantageous financial deal. The connection between Greenwatch, Dr Coombes and the University may have been a little tenuous, but the Chancellor was prepared to overlook that as Shelford needed the money. Also, he was keen to do anything possible to enhance his reputation as a green innovator.

The minutes of the Dubai board meeting were seized by the Federal authorities over 5 years after the London test and investigators started to piece together what had been behind the Greenwatch scandal. It was obvious that many of the people employed by Salimond – including Carlos Fantoni - had genuinely thought they were there to help improve air quality and stop thousands of premature deaths worldwide. Those early board minutes had confirmed how vital the inner circle thought Fantoni was to future success. It was noted that he had objected to the bribery involved in London and had been extremely annoyed. It was agreed that he be protected from any further involvement in the corrupt side of negotiations. His innocence and sincerity were extremely important to the success of the exercise. At all cost, he must be allowed to remain ignorant of the capacity of Greenwatch to falsify readings when required.

The threat to Fantoni in London had been seen as immediate. The Japanese representative had confirmed at the end of the meeting that four special forces bodyguards had been assigned to secretly guard Fantoni at the Savoy and whilst he was travelling in the city. They had been briefed to use extreme measures if necessary to protect him from harm.

Chapter 7

Carlos Fantoni was paralysed with fear. After the adrenalin of the escape through the smoke and fire alarm he suspected that it had been a trick to get him out of the hotel. The tall man dressed in the Edwardian frock coat should have been grotesque but was just terrifying as he remembered. His warning last time, to dissect Fantoni if he continued with Greenwatch, had been frightening but he hadn't truly believed it. Why would anyone want to hurt him, when all he wanted to do was save people?

Fantoni forced himself to concentrate. He pulled the big white dressing gown around him and tried to move his legs. He looked around for a way to escape and heard the fire door click automatically behind him and realised that retreat wasn't possible. There was only one way out of the long, dark, alley and though he could see the lights and hear the noise of the Strand a few yards away, he didn't think that he could get past the blade of his assassin.
"Why are you trying to kill me?" Fantoni croaked.
The figure stepped back and sighed in a bored and slightly exasperated manner. "Because I'm being paid an inordinate amount of money to do it and I rather enjoy the creative aspect of my work."

Fantoni was more composed now. He was damned if he was going to give up his life that easily, he'd been an athlete and been brought up in the slums of Lima. An urge to rush the assassin came over him and he was aware of every sound and light as his senses went into overload. He gathered himself up with adrenalin pumping but the man seemed to know what he intended and took two steps back, drawing out the long, thin blade and looking balanced in the way that an Olympic fencer does.

Confusingly, Fantoni felt a tug on the back of his dressing gown and before he had time to think, someone pulled him with great strength back down the alley and through the fire door. Fantoni had nearly pissed himself with fright but realised that he was back in the hotel with a door between him and the assassin. He turned, wondering what threat he was having to face now and found himself facing a guy with oriental eyes, dressed head to foot in black, carrying some sort of automatic weapon, who bowed.

"You are safe, Mr Fantoni, please let me take you to your room, my name is Henry and I am employed by Panama Gulf Bank." Fantoni trudged back up the flights of stairs with every limb shaking with spent adrenalin and went through the door at the top. This time there was no smoke, no alarms and it was obvious that someone had the resources to manipulate the Savoy systems in order to trick him into escaping as there was no real fire. His saviour seemed to have obtained a room key and opened his door, checked carefully round the suite before shaking his hand and saying that he would be close by all night and not to worry. Fantoni checked every room and opened every wardrobe. Amazingly, he had then slept well and only woken when his driver had rung to say the car was downstairs.

Carlos Fantoni told the driver that any appointments had to be delayed until he talked to someone on the Salimond board. He mentioned the supposed fire, the attempts on his life and rescue the previous night and the eyes in the rear view mirror looked suitably concerned. After a few minutes conversation on his mobile, the driver suggested that Carlos went back into the hotel for breakfast and he would call when he had something arranged. He agreed and walked back into the foyer and through into the magnificent dining room.

Breakfast was not normally his meal. However he ordered an Omelette Arnold Bennett which the head waiter said had been invented for customers in need of a restorative and he certainly felt as though he qualified, plus a pot of strong coffee which really started his brain operating. Despite all the doubts and distractions, Fantoni remembered that breakfast as one of the best he'd ever eaten and had felt suitably restored when the mobile rang.

The driver had arranged a meeting at the Panama Gulf Bank branch that he had visited previously to withdraw cash. Fantoni found himself in a large windowless room at the top of the building facing a man called Wolf Bayer who claimed to be one of the main backers of Salimond and Greenwatch. The tall, grey haired man apologised that he had not met Fantoni before but said that his involvement in Greenwatch had to be kept totally secret. He explained that his family owned one of the largest automotive groups in the world and his involvement in Greenwatch would be seen as against the interests of the company, who still produced traditional petrol- driven vehicles by the thousand. Bayer added that as a token of his trust in Fantoni he had broken his own security rules to deal with this problem.

Fantoni told him about the attempts on his life and what the assassin had said about continuing with Greenwatch. Bayer asked him detailed questions about the attempt and said that they had heard about the threat so late that they couldn't warn him. He was profuse in his apologies and gave Fantoni the opportunity to resign from the project immediately but added that it would be considerably easier to protect him if he stayed.

Carlos asked who was behind the threats and the German spent considerable time outlining possible threats before admitting they didn't know who it was, but someone in the oil or automotive sector was most likely. The guy with the swordstick was a very expensive assassin based in the UK who worked for anyone with the money and he apparently had a 100% record of success.

With a lack of prudence that he would regret later, Fantoni had said that he would stay and take Greenwatch to the next stage. He still believed totally in the Greenwatch project and was convinced that accurate and honest monitoring could save thousands of lives in cities everywhere.

That night Carlos had questioned his own logic and wondered whether he was being naïve. Ever since his early days on the tennis circuit he had an instinctive distrust of the big business tycoons who'd tried to sponsor him. These fat, rich men and women thought that by paying a young sportsperson they were becoming skilled athletes themselves.

His introduction to Salimond and Greenwatch had been it was a small dedicated team, committed to improving things for real, working people like his parents. Now the projects big backers were becoming more obvious and he was starting to feel that they weren't as idealistic as they had claimed. But the technology worked and he was uniquely qualified to make it a success, so after a few hours thought, he decided to dedicate himself to it, whatever the threat.

There was one event from those early days that Bayer had organised that gave Fantoni great pleasure. The Range Rover picked him up and his driver looked excited but refused to tell him what was going on. They drove out of the centre and took what seemed hours navigating the big car through the suburbs until he saw a sign which gave him a clue. Wimbledon, the place that as a young tennis player had seemed as far away as the moon and yet had fired his ambition to play better than anyone else, was a few miles away. He hoped that he might get a glimpse of the most famous club in the world. But Bayer had arranged much more than that.

The Chairman of the All England Lawn Tennis and Croquet Club had been told that Carlos Fantoni was once an international standard junior tennis player and arranged for him to play a few games on centre court against a club pro. Fantoni was overwhelmed and wondered what he was going to wear on the most famous tennis court in the world. His two minders opened the tailgate of the Range Rover and got out a Farrah & Brown sports bag. Inside was a pair of Nike shoes in his size, Classic Fred Perry shirts and shorts and a pair of Wilson Professional racquets.

The next couple of hours had gone by in a dream. From changing in the old-fashioned players' room, through to five games on centre court, where he had forced a couple of games off the pro, everything had been amazing. He realised that he had definitely not lost his mojo when it came to the top class game. The pro was an Argentinian and they had chatted about the difficulties faced by young, poor players trying to turn professional. Carlos explained that he loved the game but had given up the US professional circuit after his parents in Lima had died and he vowed to do something about pollution. The pro had been polite but secretly thought he was crazy.

The tour round afterwards had been extraordinary and Carlos spent a good deal of time looking at the trophies and photographs of early winners like Fred Perry, Rod Laver, Bjorn Borg as well as those he'd seen as a kid like Murray, the Williams sisters and Federer.

Afterwards the Chairman and a number of younger members entertained him to lunch in a panelled room that dated back to the late 1800's. They had a glass of Nyetimber English sparkling wine to start with then sat down at the long walnut table. Down the centre was a large salmon which had come down from the Tay the previous day and a four-rib of English Longhorn beef, both served cold and surrounded by a variety of salads. After a lengthy description of the Gewürztraminer, Burgundy and Claret available from the club cellar, Carlos gave up hope of trying to remember it all and helped himself to a few slices of salmon and pointed to one of the bottles nearby in a frosted bucket. The white wine was also English and the guy said it was from an ancient Roman vineyard in Kent. It was absolutely delicious.

Only one thing spoiled the end of the lunch, he was looking out of the window of the members' dining room at one of the courts below. There, standing in the shadows in a corner of the court was a figure in a black frock coat carrying a silver-topped stick. The man had touched the rim of his hat in greeting and slowly walked off court.

Carlos had left his mobile in the car and didn't want to contact any of the club officials. So, to the amazement of his hosts, he ran down the stairs and back to the car where he found his driver and minder having a quiet smoke behind the Range Rover. He explained that his assassin was around and knew he was there. Henry ran off in the direction of Court 3 with his phone clamped to his ear and the driver escorted him back to the members' dining room.

Over the next few days there had been many things to do on Greenwatch and Fantoni had grown tired of the signing ceremonies, photo-calls and had no time to worry about threats. When he asked his minders, they had just said that the threat had been neutralised – whatever that meant – and not to worry. He didn't believe them really but he knew that he was due to fly out of the UK soon and hoped to be out of harm's way in Panama, so he hadn't worried too much.

There was a call on his mobile before he left the UK from Diane Fallow, the journalist he'd met in the cocktail bar of the Savoy who'd prematurely published the news about the Greenwatch test in London. He'd been extremely wary but listened when she said that she wanted to apologise by buying him a bottle of champagne. Carlos had found the woman extremely attractive so despite his misgivings he agreed. He didn't feel safe despite everyone saying that the assassin had been neutralised, so didn't want to go far. In the end, they arranged to meet at Simpsons on the Strand which was just a few yards away from the hotel. Despite the proximity, Henry got a black taxi for him and promised to be just behind, guarding his back. The cabbie thought he was mad but accepted gladly when he saw the £20 tip he was being offered for a 1 minute journey.

Carlos hadn't known much about the 100 year history of Simpsons of the Strand but learned that it had only been refurbished a few years ago because parts of the structure had started to disintegrate. There were fears at the time that the unique atmosphere of the place would be destroyed but looking around at the panelled hall and old oak desk it was hard to see anything that looked too modern. The bar upstairs had black walls covered in cartoons of old judges, actors or politicians and looked as though it hadn't been touched for centuries. He sat on one of the long sofas and waited. Her colleagues would barely have recognised Diane Fallow who wore jeans and jackets most of the year. She had dressed to impress in a long Ballencia dress that she'd bought from a charity shop in Knightsbridge which had the head waiter drooling when he helped her out of her coat. It showed off her tall, voluptuous figure and cropped auburn hair to perfection and certainly got Fantoni's approval.

When the staff had taken their drinks order and left, she touched him on the arm and been hugely apologetic about the premature release of the London Greenwatch test. Though Fantoni had been very much on his guard, he found himself warming to this tall, strangely attractive woman with every glass. By the time they went downstairs to the restaurant, they were laughing together like lovers.

The restaurant was large, dark and dominated by a number of giant silver salvers with domed covers that Diane said were the trademark of Simpsons. The waiter had taken them to a large oak table at the far end of the room and presented them with a menu, called a Bill of Fayre that looked like it was made from parchment or something old. They left the wine to the Sommelier who after he had heard their order, brought them each a glass of French white Burgundy which had a slightly hard edge they knew would go well with the potted shrimp and salmon they ordered as starters.
Before they chose from the meat trolleys Carlos had bared his soul to Diane about the damage that bad air quality had done to his parents and his almost evangelical need to improve the lot of poor city dwellers everywhere.

She had a journalist's cynicism but warmed to his obvious sincerity and with this warmth came an increasing desire for this immaculately dressed and exotic looking man opposite. By the time the carver had given her a slice of rare Scottish beef and Carlos had chosen Welsh lamb from the trolley, their legs had touched 'accidentally' under the table and stayed there. After a glass or two each of Hospice de Beaune brought by an amused sommelier, they both knew where they were going when the meal finished.

Carlos hadn't even thought about threats to his life, he'd just grabbed her hand and rushed out of Simpsons and round the corner into the Savoy. A few minutes later they were in his suite and Fantoni realised that it had been months since he'd made love to anyone. They both hesitated – embarrassed for a moment – then she shrugged out of her gown and stood in front of him. The lovemaking for the first time had been urgent and intense but the second and third times had been a delicious journey for them both. They loved each other's bodies – she was full breasted and full hipped with a body that would have made a 1950's Italian film director sign her up. He was exotic with light olive skin, good muscle definition and that strange Inca face which made him stand out in a crowd. She even loved the thick white hair as it lay on the pillow next to her auburn crop.

They were creatures from different worlds who would spend weeks apart but become friends and lovers who rejoiced in each other's company. She had an instinctive distrust of the Greenwatch project from the beginning and tried to warn him but in his innocence, he chose not to listen. The public in London loved Greenwatch. After a few months, the system had an 85% approval rating where it was operating and growing levels of acceptance elsewhere. On days when the Greenwatch monitors flashed red it was front page news and politicians were forced to identify culprits and take action.

Encouragingly for Fantoni, there were strong indications from the politicians in the media that Greenwatch would be rolled out further in London and to large cities in the UK which meant a huge contract for Salimond and Greenwatch. The Prime Minister was well aware of Greenwatch and saw it as a serious threat in many ways. The costs of actually rectifying the air quality problems in the main cities would be astronomical and require increased taxation at a level his party could not ever accept. Wolf Bayer attended a top secret meeting in Downing Street a few months after the start of the test. Bayer understood the PM's problems and offered him a confidential update to the system which might make it more acceptable. Both parties understood the risk and realised that any exposure of the deal would almost inevitably end in disgrace or prosecution.

Even before the London test had been rolled out to other parts of the city, Fantoni and his team had done a major sell-in for Greenwatch with the Federal authorities in Washington and to the mayor of Boston. Salimond analysts had done their job well, revealing that the Republicans nationally were in decline and needed something to give their political campaign a difference. Boston had been seen as a perfect test because the Shelford university connection would play well with local electorates. They had also tried to enhance connections with the college by granting them ten million dollars for an environmental research programme starting the next year.

Mayor Bonelli had signed up for the test immediately. He knew that Washington was keen on Greenwatch because he'd heard from the President and so he railroaded the proposal through and had Greenwatch units on the streets of Boston within a couple of weeks of the first data coming out of London. The Greenwatch units had been there for a year now and had been a great public success. The Presidential campaign 'Vote for Me and Breathe Easy' was getting brilliant exposure for them both and Carlos Fantoni was delighted with the progress he was making with Greenwatch in the UK and Boston. He was a regular flier now between London and the US but every trip seemed to be successful and he was already way above target in terms of units installed. More importantly, people were seeing on the Greenwatch units just how bad their air was and taking action.

The FT journalist Diane Fallow met Carlos on most trips and she knew that he loved her. She thought that she loved him too but now she had to make a call that would ruin his day. She had finished her investigation into London Council Members and found lies and corruption involved in the Greenwatch deal. More importantly she had information that questioned the accuracy of the test data. There was a serious scandal brewing, so even though it was three in the morning in Boston, she had to call Carlos right away and tell him to stop Greenwatch.

Chapter 8

Diane Fallow was a junior reporter, but she was a good investigator with a tenacious grip on anything that might turn into a lead story. She had to admit, however, that she'd been lucky on the subject of Greenwatch. She'd been given the brief a year ago by her editor at the Financial Times to investigate local government corruption in London. Not that he thought there was much there, but it was a way of getting Diane out of the office and off his back. She was a constant irritant to him with her demands to be given serious stories to work on and not just trivia. He respected her ambition but didn't really have the time to show it.

Her first move was to talk to a woman she knew from Yoga who worked for Greater London Council. The two met for a coffee in a trendy little place with just a glimpse of the Thames and Fallow told her she was doing a story on gender issues in the workplace. From her Diane got an idea where some of the young workers went to relax after work and planned to visit them on pay day at the end of the month. Her real mission was obviously to look for corruption but she didn't want to alarm her friend or give her the opportunity to warn the council what she was doing.

After many drinks in bars frequented by the local government staff, she'd been tipped off about a guy who was acting way above the standard of living that his salary could afford. After a holiday in Panama and a new car, this guy had pissed off most of his associates and one of them was delighted to give Fallow his name on the understanding that she wouldn't reveal her sources. So, for the last few weeks she had been investigating Rick Duckley, a middle ranking officer on the Environmental and Air Quality Committee. Within a few days it became obvious that Duckley had far more cash than anyone would expect and enjoyed spending it. She'd got hold of a copy of his recent bank statements and he didn't look like a rich man on paper but he spent cash like a billionaire.

She'd followed him one Thursday night from his depressing flat, south of the river, into a number of bars frequented by the bankers and traders in the big offices nearby. He didn't seem to have any close friends but often joined groups where he flashed his money around buying rounds as if it would buy him popularity. Some groups tried to refuse his generosity but he insisted claiming loudly that he'd made a killing on the markets. It was obvious from the looks behind his back that few people believed him but they took his drinks anyway.

Fallow had worried that as a good looking female she might have stood out in the places Duckley went but she needn't have worried. These days there were more females on the trading floors and in financial services and they liked to party just like the men. So she always attached herself to the edge of such groups and kept close enough to see what Duckley was doing. That night she estimated that he had spent close to six hundred pounds in cash – not bad for a government clerk. As visual proof of his excesses, she had quietly filmed him sharing a magnum of vintage champagne with his new found friends. The film quality wasn't great on her phone but it was good enough for her editor to recognise Duckley and see the celebration.

When she went in the FT offices the next day, she was full of hope that the film would give her editor the confidence to finance a bigger investigation but when he walked into the glass walled office, she could tell that he was in a foul mood and also had his head in his hands. She knocked on the door quietly.
"Fuck off, I'm busy," he said without looking up.
"Boss, I'm sorry," she said, determined not to be intimidated
"Diane, when I gave you the last decent trainee journalist job in the UK, I thought that you would develop some common fucking sense – go away."
Diane put the iPhone in front of him and started playing the last nights film. Despite himself, the guy couldn't resist looking at the picture.
"What's this, your birthday party? We must be paying you too much."
"This is a guy who works in local government in a crap job, he earns less than I do – which is a pittance by the way, and yet he spent around six hundred quid on drinks last night."
"Who is he? "
"His name is Rick Duckley and he's on the air quality and pollution sub committee at London Council."
"Has he been involved in this Greenwatch device that the mayor is always spouting off about?"
"Not sure."
"Well fuck off and find out," which was the nearest the editor came to authorising what she went on to do.

Fallow had gone back to the desk she shared with a couple of more senior staff and planned her next moves. She'd researched Greenwatch and come across a shot of Carlos Fantoni who looked rather exotic but someone she'd definitely like to meet on a dark night. It had taken a few days before she'd been able to engineer a meeting with Fantoni and even today he didn't know that their first encounter had not been accidental. On that first date he had been so sincere and enthusiastic about cleaning up London that she'd warmed to him. The fact that they eventually ended up in bed had not been planned but she hadn't regretted a minute. In fact, she repeated the experience whenever he was in London.

Over the next month she'd seen plenty about Greenwatch on local TV as local politicians were making a big deal about it. Years ago, The Times newspaper had analysed air quality and found dangerous levels of pollution around 6,500 schools, educating 2.6 million children. It was likely that things in London had got even worse since then. Friends of the Earth, World Health Organisation and scientists had been warning that the young, elderly and sick were badly affected by bad air quality for years. What was equally concerning for local government was the trend towards litigation against authorities who caused bad health in their areas. And it was obvious that this affected not just London but most big cities worldwide.

Diane could see that the London politicians loved it because they were doing something good for a change. She'd been out on the streets and had seen the Greenwatch units flashing red because the air was bad and had also seen the leaders scurrying away to find the bad buses, dirty trucks or smoking factories who were behind it to ban them. She may have been sceptical about Greenwatch at the beginning but she was starting to understand Carlos Fantoni's belief that this device could save thousands of premature deaths in the UK alone. The only problem was Rick Duckley - if that shit was involved in Greenwatch then she was worried.

Diane's editor had complained loudly about her expenses after nearly a month of expensive drinks in the bars Duckley visited with not enough progress. She pointed out that she was doing this in her own time and her editor had snorted and said that if she wanted to keep her job, she had one more week to get a real story. She had been frustrated by Duckley's absence for part of this period and realised when he'd come back with a tan that he'd been somewhere sunny. She decided on a high risk strategy that might force the guy to open up to her and planned to visit his favourite bar on Friday night.
"Duckley, we know that you're on the take," said Fallow, flashing her FT Press card.

"Whaa...." said Duckley, dropping his cocktail on the floor and turning crimson. They were in the darkest corner of 'The London Broker.' Duckley had thought his luck had been in when this attractive woman had asked him to buy her a drink and they had moved away from the Friday crowd at the bar. Now he couldn't stop spluttering and he looked as though he was going to run. "Duckley, you've got one hope of keeping off the front page."
"You've got it wrong... it's not me.." he whined, moving towards the door.
"Duckley, I'm phoning the police now if you run you, bastard." Fallow shouted, grabbing him by the jacket. People were looking over and she pulled him back. "It's not you we're after," she said quietly in his ear and he turned back with a little more hope in his face.

She confronted him with the evidence and claimed that there was no way a man on his salary could have spent the thousands of pounds without getting it illegally. She also forestalled any excuses about winning lottery tickets or betting success by telling him that she had inside information from a reliable source that he had taken bribes. This was not strictly true but Fallow had a very convincing manner about her and Duckley looked as guilty as sin.

Over the next 30 minutes Duckley told her everything after the assurance that "a journalist always protects her sources" and other bullshit that Fallow told him. He claimed that his boss on the environmental and air quality committee had taken two hundred thousand dollars and he'd got a lousy fifty grand just to approve a contract.

Duckley had tried to excuse it by complaining about the miserable salaries paid to government officials and spiralling cost of living in London. Fallow tutted encouragingly and said that she quite understood but pushed hard for information on what the bribe was for. Duckley looked like a hunted animal who was going to run until Diane grabbed his arm and reminded him that the only way he could avoid exposure was to tell all. He stopped abruptly and turned to Fallow, whispering that the bribes were to approve Greenwatch. Duckley then pulled away and ran out of the bar, generating astonished stares and derisive shouts from those he'd been drinking with.

Diane Fallow couldn't understand why something that she'd discussed with Carlos Fantoni, something that he genuinely thought would save thousands of lives, would require such a bribe to get it installed. She hid her surprise and left the bar, needing time to collect her thoughts and as Duckley was a slimy bastard, she needed to check his story out. She was short on proof and sensed that he hadn't told her everything.

The editor moved her off the story for a few days and on to a company director scandal which was occupying a lot of column inches in the tabloids and which needed some FT level accuracy. She enjoyed the challenge but the Greenwatch investigation was still the most important thing on her agenda and she knew that it needed more substance before she took the story to the editor.

A few days later she ambushed Duckley as he was leaving his office and told him that her editor didn't believe his story about Greenwatch and they were going to run a straightforward corruption story about him. She said that no-one could understand why such beneficial technology would need a big bribe for it to be accepted. Duckley was really terrified as he'd obviously thought that his previous confession had been enough to grant him anonymity and tried to explain why Greenwatch had required such a bribe in order to get it through.

Greenwatch technology was excellent and the boss of the committee had checked it out very carefully during the test on various streets in London. But he'd also noted on one street that the readings had been ridiculously low and had seen that Dr Coombes, the inventor of Greenwatch was working on his computer in the specially equipped SUV they had with them. They questioned him about the odd figures and he explained that he had been manipulating the figures on his laptop. When confronted the inventor stated that some countries and areas that were likely to buy Greenwatch would find it very useful to be able to alter the readouts remotely. It took a while for the implications of this to sink in but his was absolute dynamite and Fallow started to see why so much of a bribe was necessary.

The falsification of emissions was big news years ago when VAG, the huge German car group lied about fuel economy and pollution. They were not alone and just about every form of petrol driven transport was guilty of quoting inaccurate figures. This had been a huge scandal but multi-national lawyers and the global PR machine managed to obfuscate the facts for decades. Thinking about it Fallow couldn't understand how such companies hadn't been bankrupted and were still selling cars and trucks by the thousand.

Greenwatch was something the public thought they could trust. It was brilliant technology and it was on the streets where real people could see it. Its independence and honesty were the big selling point so if people thought that its results could be manipulated by the politicians or companies they distrusted so much, then the billions invested in it could be wasted.

Duckley had said that this wasn't just a matter for London Council – he'd heard rumours that Downing Street had been made aware of what Dr Coombes had been doing with the Greenwatch accuracy and wanted it kept quiet. Diane knew that she was ahead of anyone else and that this was the biggest expose she had ever dealt with. She would draft the story over the next few hours and take it into the editor in the morning. First, she had to call Boston and ruin her lover's life.

Carlos Fantoni had been asleep for hours when the call came. He'd been exhausted after another round of visits to US cities selling Greenwatch and now he was back in Boston, the city which already had some units on test for several months. He'd been interviewed on TV, radio and press and thought that it would have been a lot easier if every politician including the local mayor, hadn't always wanted to be in front of the media with him. He was back in the same downtown hotel that he'd stayed in before. It wasn't the Savoy but it was perfectly acceptable and had a beautiful view over the city. The noise from his phone and computer was insistent and the screen showed that it was Diane Fallow and the thought gave him an almost instant stirring in his groin. But the call was a real passion killer and he switched on all the lights and tried to concentrate on what she was saying.

It took him half an hour to calm himself enough to think straight. He knew about the bribes in London of course, but was too ashamed to admit it to Diane Fallow. But the main thing that terrified him was the fact that the data on the Greenwatch screens might be capable of being altered.
Suddenly everything he'd believed in – Salimond, Greenwatch - started to crumble and he realised that he had to try and stop the tests in Boston quickly. He picked up his mobile and phoned the Mayor of Boston's personal number.
"Sir, this is Carlos Fantoni of Greenwatch, you need to stop the roll out of the units now. There are real doubts about the accuracy of the data and I think that they could be hacked into. Please let Washington know what I've said, it is essential that Greenwatch is stopped."

There was a shocked gasp from Mayor Bonelli when he'd heard the message that Fantoni had left early in the morning and he tried to get him back on his mobile with no success. He then called a few numbers in Washington and caused absolute panic amongst the Presidential team involved in his campaign. They all knew where Fantoni was staying in Boston and agreed that he had to be silenced before he could de-rail millions of dollars of political campaign.

Carlos had paced around his hotel room for an hour wondering whether to confront anyone at Salimond with the disastrous news he'd heard from London. He had a number for Wolf Bayer but when he tried it was unobtainable. He rang his office in Panama and it rang for five minutes with no-one answering. He realised that he didn't really have any other means of talking to the real powers behind Greenwatch, Salimond or Panama Gulf Bank especially at this time in the morning.

After a few more minutes, Carlos realised that he needed to get out of the hotel and clear his head. After an hour's exercise he would be far better equipped to deal with the cataclysm that he was about to create. He didn't take much apart from the Panama Gulf Bank black card which was worth so much he didn't like leaving it. He didn't trust safes or lockers, he always hid it in his trainers when he went out for a run or exercise. It felt safer for some reason.

At the Grosvenor Athletic Club, he tried to go through the archaic signing in process which always seemed so tedious. But the reception wasn't manned so he couldn't get a locker key or sign the register. In the end he just pushed the door open and walked through to the changing rooms. There were a surprisingly large number of people already exercising and some who were changing into their city clothes ready for a day of corporate raiding or digital madness. This was a city where making money started early and most would be at their desks by 7.00 a.m.

He pushed passed a couple of members and dumped his bag on the bench. The old part of the gym was like a museum but he loved the Real Tennis Court which was the origin of the sport he'd been so good at as a youth. He could see from the board that one of the courts was already booked but that the other was free. Carlos changed out of his track suit and into tennis gear leaving everything on the benches without really thinking about the black card hidden under the insole of the Nikes. He had an almost superstitious love of his old Dunlop Green Flash shoes and always changed into them for tennis. He moved to the base line on court and practised hitting lots of practice balls round the hazards and walls hoping to come up with a plan to save the Greenwatch project but not quite succeeding.

He'd been there for an hour when he heard a lot of noise from somewhere in the building and the shouting was getting closer. He stopped and wondered whether there was some kind of emergency as this place was normally relatively quiet apart from the sound of rackets hitting balls and players chatting on the adjoining court.

The side entry to the court was suddenly full of suited men. Two burst through with guns drawn and told him to stay still. He dropped his racket and tried to question the nearest guy, who told him to shut up and flipped a wallet with a gold badge open. Carlos couldn't really see what it said before he was dragged bodily off court and through to the locker room. One man picked up his sports bag and they made for the exit. Gerald tried to complain but he was pulled past him and out through the front doors and into a large black vehicle. The last thing Carlos remembered was struggling with one of his captors, a sharp pain in his arm and everything going black.

Chapter 9

Dane Morgan had seen the white haired young guy being hustled into the government vehicle over a week ago at the Grosvenor Athletic Club and shown the shots he'd taken to his partner, Joanne Li. As a campaigning journalist, she was always after a big story and as an experienced photographer, Dane knew the way to take shots with news appeal. Looking back at the three or four shots he'd taken on the Nikon and enlarging them on the laptop, they were sure that at least one guy was armed with a Glock or some other non environmentally friendly weapon. This was strange when they were supposedly from the US Environmental Agency.

Dane and Jo had worked together on some tough assignments. They discovered an environmental disaster a year back that a global group and national government wanted to cover up so badly that Jo was kidnapped and nearly killed. They had a strong instinct for such things and the abduction of the man who was almost certainly Carlos Fantoni felt like – as Dane said in his English vernacular - somebody trying to cover their arse.

They'd done a bit of research, Fantoni was the man behind Greenwatch, a system on test in Boston that should be a genuine lifesaver. Joanne had been campaigning against poor air quality in the US for months and even her cynical attitude to political motivation hadn't been able to criticise this new technology. Why the man behind it should 'be disappeared' so violently defied explanation. Their investigation had also shown that the US Environmental Agency was genuine and there to stop pollution round factories and mines. But it would be hard to imagine that they would abduct people or be involved in anti-terrorist work like their agent Kowolski. Despite many calls and emails, despite threats of freedom of information and Jo flashing her press credentials, the agency denied any knowledge of the arrest of Fantoni.

So they decided that the only way they might get to the truth would be to investigate Fantoni's background further. The website had showed that Greenwatch technology had been developed by Salimond Group which had connections with the Panama Gulf Bank. When Dane had learnt this he'd become extremely excited and pulled out the card he'd found hidden in Carlos Fantoni's shoes. The card was still a mystery, it had more security holograms than he'd ever seen on a normal credit card and had Salimond and Panama Gulf Bank names on it. It was likely to be important as Fantoni had obviously tried to hide it before he was taken.

Jo's father was helpful about the publicised links between Greenwatch technology and Shelford University, where he was a professor. US politicians nationally had made a big deal out of the fact that Greenwatch technology had been developed locally but Professor Li said that certain academics were questioning these links and there was a serious scandal brewing. Presidents like Trump had encouraged financial links between universities and business but many thought that this had gone too far. Greenwatch had sponsored research and environmental studies worth millions and Professor Li was concerned that they might have been exploited.

Jo's reputation as a fearless environmental campaigner had been enhanced a year or so back. She'd investigated a chemical spill in New Zealand which had been covered up by some very powerful people. Joanne had been held in isolation for months to prevent her from exposing the tragedy and would have been killed if Dane and local police not found her. They'd both had to sign Non Disclosure Agreements to get out but Jo had used blogs and the dark net to expose the disaster. The result had been a couple of high level resignations and a clean lake. The frustration for Jo was that she still had not been able to get the story in the mainstream media.

Dane and Jo had become a highly effective team over the last couple of years as well as lovers. His dramatic shots of polluted fish farms in Thailand and dead lakes in China had given Jo's stories power in the past and helped get them published in some of the most influential magazines and websites. Now he was frustrated by having signed an NDA and being here on a temporary visa which meant not being able to work as freely as normal. As an Anglo/Irish he could normally get into most countries and as a war photographer he'd got into some pretty dangerous ones, but the US had only allowed him in to join Jo on the understanding that he didn't break their rules. With their present investigation into Fantoni and the US Environment Agency, he knew that he was at great risk of being quietly extradited.

So they thought that getting out of the US might be a good idea for a few days. They'd seen the Greenwatch presentation that Fantoni had made to US politicians and knew that Salimond had its HQ in Panama and that the Greenwatch R&D facility was in the same city. Fantoni had an office there and the Panama Gulf Bank was a major funder of the organisation, so they decided to fly to Panama City as soon as possible.

Before they booked flights, Jo decided to have a go at confronting Mayor Bonelli again about local air pollution and to see what he thought about the Greenwatch arrest. Bonelli was in mid-term and had been suffering badly in the polls until he'd seen Greenwatch and promised to clean up the city. Now he was riding high in the approval ratings and looking a much stronger bet for his re-election in two years' time.

Bonelli's new friend, the President, was up for re-election far more immediately and thought Greenwatch was a brilliant idea for his own campaign and had already spent billions promoting it. 'Vote for Me and Breathe Easy' was his campaign line and it was working. Bonelli was happy that the President had stolen his idea – millions of extra dollars had flowed into Boston to help the test and he was getting plenty of reflected glory. Jo suspected that Bonelli's ambitions were for a trip to Washington anyway and not just as mayor.

Joanne called Mayor Bonelli's office and decided that a full frontal attack might just yield some interesting results. Dane stopped working on his computer to listen, he loved it when Jo got the bit between her teeth and really ran with something. They both knew that there was something really wrong and that the politicians were trying to cover it up. After being unable to get Bonelli directly Jo told his press secretary that she knew that the man behind Greenwatch had been arrested and that she was going to get the story out in the next few hours unless she heard from the mayor. She also used her 'Corporate Li's' blog to put out the same message.

At that moment Mayor Bonelli was standing in his office looking across the haze of the city and wondering whether he was going to die. He could feel the blood rushing as his heart hammered in his chest and his shirt and trousers felt as though they were strangling him. He pulled off his tie and broke a button trying to open the top of his shirt. He could hear someone banging on the door but ignored them. He tried to breathe deeply, he must control himself or he genuinely thought he'd be dead.

Everything had been going well for Bonelli until the call a couple of days ago from Fantoni had questioned the Greenwatch test accuracy. Fantoni had begged him to stop the test in Boston until he checked out the claims by the London Times reporter that Greenwatch readouts could be falsified. Bonelli had been stunned and agreed, promising to get back to Fantoni after he'd made a few calls. He knew how important Greenwatch was to the President's campaign and his own rise in popularity. Ironically the electors even loved it when the units flashed red to show danger because he was able to rush to the area, get maximum media attention, and ban traffic for a day. Greenwatch seemed to be trusted and even that pain in the ass Joanne Li had shut up for a few days.

Bonelli thought back to those years in his haulage business. In those days oil and diesel was public enemy number one and everyone would have predicted that by now they would have been banned. Covid 19 seemed to stop everyone in their tracks and reduced subsidies for green engines and much lower petrol prices seemed to keep the traditional gas guzzlers on the road a lot longer. Bonelli had a 5 litre Cadillac and couldn't see himself going electric any time soon.

"Contain-ability." That was what the President's special aide said they needed when Bonelli had told him about the Fantoni threat. It took a while for him to realise that meant preventing the man from exposing any problems at all costs. They had known where he was staying so arranged an anti- terrorist squad with false credentials to snatch him before he had time to talk to anyone else. They were at the back entrance to his hotel within 30 minutes but were delayed because he had left. It took a further frustrating 50 minutes before they could get him from the Grosvenor Club and that was a little more public than they'd planned. But hopefully they'd put the fear of God into the club secretary who was one of the few members there at that time.

Bonelli had breathed a sigh of relief because Fantoni was now too far away to cause trouble. Their plan was to carry on with the test in Boston – without anyone from Salimond if necessary. Bonelli was sure that with their Shelford connections they could take the whole project to the next stage without too many problems.

Washington told Bonelli about their other worries. With the help of GCHQ in England, the US team had heard about the call Diane Fallows made to Fantoni telling him about the bribes and falsification of results involved in the test. They knew she was a journalist who would almost certainly want to publish the story soon.

The London authorities were extremely worried about exposure too as the Greenwatch initial test had been popular with the voters and was being rolled out to streets in the rest of the city. Parliament had also passed budgets for Greenwatch to be installed in the largest cities in the UK and MP's were seeing that for the first time since Brexit, the popularity/trust ratings of politicians had reached double figures. Scandal now would be disastrous and the Prime Minister's office said, confidentially to their US counterparts, that they would take extreme action to stop Fallow from publishing.

Mayor Bonelli had thought that with Fantoni out of the way and SIS dealing with the London journalist, his chances of surviving might have increased a little. But today he had local problems with the fucking Li family and unless stopped, they could de-rail Greenwatch themselves. First there was Professor Li complaining that the technology hadn't been developed at Shelford, which had been a major selling point for Washington to back the project. Then that interfering bitch Joanne Li was the latest problem. She'd been complaining about Boston air quality for months and Greenwatch had shut her up. Now she called to say that she'd seen the arrest of the Greenwatch scientist and was going to tell all. Bonelli clutched his chest and slid to the floor.

Joanne and Dane stayed around for a few hours but got no response from the mayor, so it looked as though the bluff about publishing the arrest story hadn't paid off. Even Jo started to doubt herself, after all what did they really know? A man had been taken by the US Environmental Agency and he might be connected to Greenwatch. All the mayor's secretary had said, was that he was ill and unable to talk right now. Surely if their suspicions about Fantoni had been true then the mayor would have dragged himself to the phone, even if he was half dead?

In the mayor's office they were not convinced that Bonelli would survive the day. His press officer had burst in despite instructions from the secretary not to disturb the Mayor in any circumstances, but the call from Joanne Li had been too important to ignore. He had only managed to blurt out a little of what Li had had threatened to do before Mayor Bonelli went purple and collapsed. They called 911 and a team were there within 4 minutes. Bonelli was given CPR at the scene by the paramedics and rushed over town to Boston General. Now he was on life support with a number of extremely concerned doctors checking his vital signs and a local TV crew on stand-by waiting for anything dramatic to happen.

The evening news carried the story as second lead. Stock footage of racing ambulances and heart monitor machines gave it drama and an interview with the deputy mayor gave an impression of sincere sadness that Bonelli would not be able to carry on his great work. It was obvious that Mayor Bonelli had suffered a pretty massive heart attack and that his survival was by no means certain. The discussion then moved on to the national political scene and the success that the Presidential campaign was having with the Greenwatch "Breathe easy" idea. There was even a heart-felt interview from the oval office where the President thanked Bonelli for all his tireless work and wished him a speedy recovery.

Dane Morgan and Joanne Li saw the evening news and realised that their plan to confront Mayor Bonelli about the arrest of Fantoni was now impossible. The US Environmental Agency lead was also dead and nothing – including the threat of freedom of information lawyers – would get them to admit that they had ever heard of Fantoni. This re-enforced the need to travel to Panama and investigate the head office of Salimond, the company behind Greenwatch. They checked online and found a direct Delta flight which would get them into Panama City in a couple of days and booked it, one way.

The booking was also noted by Bradley Kowolski in Washington who'd last been seen carrying a US Environmental Agency badge and a shoulder holster in Boston. He remembered Dane Morgan extremely well and was fully informed about the campaigner, Joanne Li. Having them off US soil and into an area where the authorities were less vigilant about human rights might be extremely useful. He guessed that they would be checking up on Salimond as they couldn't possibly know that Fantoni had been taken there too. Someone at the top of Black Ops had made that decision because they had worked out that having everyone involved in the Greenwatch fiasco, Coombes, Fantoni etc, might be an advantage if a fatal accident was seen as being necessary. It was also a good place because the US had control of an old prison which had been used for prisoners who didn't really exist – or wouldn't for very much longer.

Chapter 10

Joanne Li had travelled to many parts of the world as a freelance reporter but spent most time in Thailand, Malaysia and China. Despite the relative closeness, she'd never been to Central America or to Panama, their next destination.

She'd started in journalism five years ago but had to work for nothing as an environmental campaigner for ages. Luckily, she'd had a small inheritance to help finance her mission and had been able to travel extensively in the Far East. There she uncovered examples of corporate greed and political ignorance which had resulted in huge damage to the natural world. Despite her first-class degrees, getting stories published by mainstream media had been difficult at the beginning when she had no reputation. Then she discovered the SCC chemical spill in New Zealand and was kidnapped to prevent her publishing. The story of her rescue had been big news in the US and Europe and some of the serious press started to take notice of her for the first time.

Frustratingly, Joanne had been prevented by non-disclosure agreements from telling the full story about the disaster and there had been a massive cover-up in New Zealand, Thailand and the US. But she'd carefully used an anonymous blog to tell the truth and those in power had not got away with it. Dane had signed the same NDA's and was not a US citizen so he could be thrown out in minutes if he offended any local laws. Though NDA's had been discredited in many circumstances, they knew that the federal lawyers would use them mercilessly if necessary and they didn't have the sort of money it would require to defend themselves in court.

Air pollution had been Joanne Li's main cause since she'd returned to Boston. She'd first seen the figures years ago and not believed them. A study by the World Health Organisation quoted that 600,000 premature deaths in Europe were caused by air pollution every year. In the US an authoritative report calculated that no less than 133 million US citizens lived with dangerous levels of air pollution with profound effects on their health. The figures were staggering and the situation was even worse in the third world. But there had been no national outcry anywhere, which amazed her and she suspected that there was some kind of cover up or wilful ignorance about the sick state of our cities.

Jo remembered that there had been a few landmark legal cases in the 2020's where individuals sued city authorities because they or their children had been damaged by bad air. But nothing dramatic seemed to happen and litigants were either bought off or discouraged by high-price lawyers. Some cities taxed traffic, some restricted hours of travel but no-one really seemed to have the motivation to change things dramatically. London was a recent exception and she had read with hope about the street monitoring test a couple of months ago. Now she knew that this was Greenwatch, the system that Boston had signed up for which had been promoted by Carlos Fantoni, the man arrested at the Grosvenor Club.

She was on her way to Panama to find out more about this man and the company he worked for. She hadn't been out of the US since the kidnapping and needed a change of scene. She also hadn't been to Central America before and was excited to see the canal and the city. The Delta Airlines Boeing was in the air for nearly 6 hours before they could see the dozens of tiny ships below stacked up waiting to enter the Panama Canal. Dane had flown in 15 years previously just as they were opening a massive second entrance for the latest mega tankers. He'd been astonished at how many ships were there in the bay and learned that the canal had a one-way system going from Atlantic to Pacific coasts in the morning and reversing the flow in the afternoon.

When you consider that the alternative was to sail the full length of South America, it is not surprising that the French engineers thought, in the 19th Century, that the vast cost in lives and money was worth the investment. In the end they went bankrupt and the US took over the construction in the early 1900's and finished it because they could see the vast military and commercial potential.

As a landscape photographer Dane hadn't found much to interest him about the Canal Zone on his last trip – especially after the Andes and Costa Rican jungles which he'd travelled through on the way. Now his mission was different and he had a fraction of the equipment he normally carried, but felt the weight of the Nikon in his backpack and was confident that he could handle most things. Up to a couple of years ago, Dane had insisted on using a film camera for his landscapes, which most people thought archaic but he thought it gave more beautiful results. In the end getting film processed became almost impossible and he was forced to go digital, but on a job like this it was considerably more convenient. Since he'd started working with Jo it had been important to be able to quickly shoot a spill or dead forest and email it to a magazine or website. Looking down as they came into land it was difficult to know what his camera might be needed for this time but he knew that it would be ready.

Joanne had been reading about Panama on the flight over and knew more about the areas history. The more she read the more she wondered why anyone respectable would use Panama as a base. As the plane circled, she too saw the dozens of ships, each with its pall of smoke waiting outside the canal entrance. And the tankers were enormous and full of the oil that was killing the world. What chance did two people have to change things? She sighed and held on to Dane's arm as the aircraft banked sharply and came into land crossing over three islands that she remembered were used for storing gold in Spanish times.

Last off the plane was a strange figure who looked like he'd come out of an early colonial photograph. Instead of the frock coat he normally wore in England, he had a three piece cream linen suit, a wing collared shirt and an ancient Panama hat. He was carrying the same silver-topped stick that he carried in London and one that might have bothered the security scanners had he not been whisked through on a diplomatic passport.

No one else on the flight would have recognised him but Carlos Fantoni would have shuddered if he had seen him. Alexander Brown was the name he was known by and he had a unique reputation amongst assassins as the man who had never ever failed to carry out a mission. Brown had an impeccable English pedigree and served as a surgeon in Iran and Afghanistan for the army, until he realised that he was more interested in taking lives than saving them and that it could be an extremely profitable occupation.

Brown had been employed by a consortium of oil producing families months ago to eliminate Carlos Fantoni before he made Greenwatch successful anywhere else. One of life's great ironies was that had they known the true reason behind Greenwatch and the motivation of Salimond then they would probably have asked for his protection. But the paranoia of big business during this point of history knew no bounds as they saw their sources of riches threatened on every front.

The attempt at the Savoy in London had been frustrated by some special protection squad that Brown had never seen before but he hadn't given up. His reputation for never failing was at stake and that was extremely important as far as future jobs were concerned. But he had to find Fantoni first, he knew he had left the London hotel a couple of days later, but did not know his destination. As always, the Greenwatch website was helpful and the news section showed Fantoni was due to address a climate change group in Boston in a few days. Brown booked his trip immediately and got on a Virgin flight from Heathrow to Boston leaving at 08.10 the following morning.

Mid flight, Brown checked his laptop and realised that his plans needed to change. He had worked off the books for the NSA a year back and someone there had emailed him to say that Fantoni had been smuggled out of the country to Panama where they had him in a high-security prison. Brown was extremely concerned as to how the agency knew he was after Fantoni and whether to trust the information. Thinking it through, however, he couldn't see why this could be misinformation and decided that he needed to get to Panama. He emailed his employers and relaxed in the Premium seat knowing that he had four more hours before they touched down. He reclined his seat and slept the sleep of the unjust.

When Brown awoke, he saw from his messages that his clients had booked him on a Delta Airlines flight to Panama the following morning and a quiet apartment in the old town had been arranged for him close to the sea. He was still slightly confused about the NSA involvement but he had worked for them before and suspected that this was a black op where everyone would disavow everyone if things went wrong. Brown had his own agenda, Fantoni was becoming tedious and had already caused an inordinate amount of inconvenience. To use a quaint English phrase, Brown intended to have his guts for garters.

Jo and Dane had booked a cheap hotel through Trip Advisor which appeared to be not too far from the banking district so they could check out Salimond and Panama Gulf Bank which were the names on the black card Fantoni had left hidden. They had saved money by finding an unlicensed taxi just outside the airport and the 1950's Cadillac looked great but hadn't had air-con for 20 years, so they roasted. When they were dropped off at the end of the road, the heat in the centre of the old town was like a furnace even to those used to warm climates and Dane felt his shirt sticking to his back and his scalp starting to prickle. Remembering where he was, he vowed to get himself a straw hat as soon as possible before his head fried.

The Hotel Tantalo was an oasis of cool and they dumped their bags and went up to the roof bar for a well deserved drink. Joanne ordered a Pisco Sour and Dane a Corona beer and they looked

across the many rooftops to the Palacio and the sea. They were close enough to see the Pelicans patrolling the sea, diving suicidally into the water and scooping fish into their enormous bucket-like beaks. Further out to sea they could see a couple of islands and dozens of tankers, cruise ships and other vessels that were always there waiting for the canal. The scene should have been idyllic but Joanne shivered.
"You know, I really don't like the feel of this place, it has a terrible history. Did you know that the Spanish killed millions of Incas and other civilisations just to get their gold back to Spain through here?"
"Yes, but that was hundreds of years ago." Dane replied quietly.
"Do you know how many virtual slaves and forced labourers died during the building of the canal?
"No"
"The French didn't keep great records, but they reckon it was 250,000 and that was recent history," Jo said bitterly.

Dane put his arm round her. He knew that Joanne was a sensitive woman in many ways and that she was right, if any city was built on blood, it was probably this one. A few feet away a lone guy in a business suit heard the conversation on his ear-piece and nodded to himself.

Panama City has been the home of opportunists, pirates and brigands for centuries. The Spanish had a port through which most of the gold plundered from South America passed on the way back to Spain. They thought that it was well defended with massive guns pointing out to sea but in 1671 British privateer Henry Morgan marched overland and attacked it from the rear. The haul was so immense that Morgan eventually became respectable and was made Governor of Barbados. The Spanish learned their lesson and built a more defendable port on the peninsular where the old town now stood and continued to export gold and silver for another century.

In the 20th Century, Panama City was a dangerous frontier town which eventually found a new niche as a tax haven for money launderers and bent bankers. According to some investigations everyone from mafia bosses to Russian oligarchs had billions stashed as did a few supposedly respectable corporations. But such stories died down as they always do and Panama City carried on as usual, not in the old town, but in the towering city which had grown like a parasite alongside it.

Jo was feeling guilty. The only secret she had ever kept from Dane

was the fact she'd kept a note of Dane's father's mobile number. She knew that he was a conman and had swindled the family out of thousands but Eugene Morgan had tried to reach out to Dane and she thought that he deserved a chance. Dane's reaction when he'd heard his father's voice had been violent and it had taken an hour for her to piece the broken phone together and save its contact list. Her plan was to try and arrange a reconciliation – after all any father of Dane couldn't be that bad, could he? The other thing she remembered from Dane's story was that Eugene knew Central America and she thought that he might be able to help in this crazy search for Fantoni and Salimond. After a restless sleep she dithered for hours and then crept out of the room and dialled the number.
"Hello" said a sleepy Irish voice.
"God.... I'm sorry, I didn't think what time it was – it's 6.00 a.m. here."
"Who is that? and don't worry about the time, it's fuckin early here too.. How did you get my number?" Joanne was tempted to hang up but screwed up her courage.
"Listen, I'm sorry, but I'm a friend of Danes..."
"You know Dane?" Eugene interrupted in a desperate voice.
"Yes, but he doesn't know I'm calling you.. in fact..."
"Listen. Please listen. I know that Dane has every reason not to talk to me, but I just want to warn him... it's incredibly important... where are you now?"
"Panama City"
"Oh Jeezus that's the last place I'd want him to be... listen... get him to meet me inside the Cathedral Metropolitana in the old town at 11.00 this morning. Tell him this is not a con, you are in great danger..."
"Ok, I'll try.." Joanne said and wondered just what can of worms she'd opened this time.

Dane was still asleep and she left him a note and walked down the narrow white stairs and pulled open the big front door with a noise that could have woken the dead. It was still early and the insects were loud in the trees and the roads were deserted apart from someone a block away who was emptying a week's bottles into a refuse truck. It was hot and humid already and she could feel the sweat building under her shirt as she walked towards a large cream building with flags which seemed to be close to the bay.

This didn't feel like a South American town, it felt like some of the French or Spanish places she'd visited on her school trip to Europe. It had narrow streets for coolness, a really grand town hall and a Cathedral that was five times the size of any other building. The place she was walking past now was obviously the Presidential

Palace and had the flags to prove it. Only the large palm trees that lined the bay gave it a more tropical look. As did the Pelicans who were back out fishing with their bucket beaks and the amazingly brightly coloured parrots who were arguing in the trees. She rehearsed all the different ways she was going to break the news to Dane and none of them seemed to work. Why she had taken a note of Eugene's number before Dane wiped it, she still didn't know but she'd learned to trust her instincts.

She walked past the palace and turned right down a street where some of the shops were opening shutters, then right again back to the Tantalo Hotel. There on a balcony she saw a familiar tall figure wearing an unfamiliar straw hat and could see the joy on his face as he waved down at her. She ran up the stairs and into the room to find that Dane wasn't wearing the new hat, he wasn't wearing anything at all and he was obviously pleased to see her. She felt a thrill of excitement and a moistness where it mattered and pushed him back into the chair.

They didn't even kiss, she straddled him and pulled him inside with a gasp. She moved up and down slowly like she wanted this to last for hours. He pulled off her T-Shirt and stroked her breasts gently watching first one nipple go hard and then the other. God, he thought this is such a turn-on but I must hold out until she comes. She started to rise and fall quicker and they both knew that holding on wasn't an option, Dane grabbed her by both hips and pulled her hard down on to him, grinding hard and listening to her gasp with pleasure.

It took ten minutes before she remembered just what had been bothering her. She showered and dressed in an electric blue silk robe from Thailand she knew made her look good and told him to sit down. Her serious, worried face confused him and he pulled over a cane chair from the balcony and tried to listen and not touch.
"Back in Boston, I did something that might upset you or make you angry."
"What?" He asked, testing his brain with the horrible possibilities of things unspeakable that she might have done..
"Listen, you know that I wouldn't do anything to hurt you..." she said leaning over and stroking his cheek, "but I spoke to your father..."
Dane didn't know whether to feel relief that it wasn't an affair with one of her many admirers or anger that she'd spoken to that bastard Eugene but in the end just sighed deeply and nodded for her to continue.
"I called him early this morning and found out that he's here in

Panama. What's more important he says that we are in danger and he needs to see you this morning."

"I wouldn't trust him to tell the truth even if his own life depended on it, the guy is a bastard." Dane shouted down at her. Jo felt a tear rolling down her cheek and brushed it away impatiently as Dane stormed out of the room slamming the door behind him.

Dane did what he often did when he needed to think, he went for a run. The streets were still pretty empty and he ran at top speed down to the edge of the sea knowing that he needed to get rid of a lot of steam before he could bear to go back to the room. He passed the palace at top speed frightening the birds that were roosting in the eves and had to turn right after a few minutes and passed a theatre on one side and some kind of beach club on his left. He realised that he was not going to be able to sustain this pace, so he slowed down when he reached a tall monument and tried to get his breath back. God he was getting unfit. He looked down at the Nikes on his feet and remembered that he hadn't run anywhere since Boston on that day when he had seen Fantoni taken from the Grosvenor Club and found the strange black card.

He stretched his legs on the plinth of the monument and saw the inscription which said it was the Placia Francia and was to honour the French who had died building the Panama Canal. If Jo was right then they were just a small proportion of the thousands of others who died digging it out and were never recorded.

He looked around and realised that he was on a peninsular with a spectacular view of Panama Bay on one side and the Pacific on the other. He sat down on the steps and breathed the sea air deeply looking out at the many fishing birds close in and the ships of all kinds queuing for the canal. Some of them were so big they looked like land mass on the horizon and he presumed that they would be waiting for the newer Panamax Plus entrance further away. Until you came to a place like this, it was difficult to remember just how much cargo still moves around the world by sea. Looking at the smoke coming out of the many funnels Dane also remembered that it wasn't just cars in cities that destroyed the air and many fleets had done nothing to improve their emission levels. God, he thought, I'm starting to think just like Jo.

Dane looked at his watch and realised that he'd been away half an hour and he'd left Jo in the room. His anger had subsided and he couldn't believe that Joanne was capable of bad stuff. No-one could understand what a plausible bastard his father was and what damage he'd done. He jogged gently back across town through streets that were now heaving with people, past the Cathedral until he saw the flags of the Presidential Palace and knew that he was near the Tantalo Hotel. As he got close, he saw Jo on their balcony.

He went up the stairs and didn't resist when Jo put her arms around him. Her beautiful oriental face was still streaked with tears and he sat down and listened to her explanation about the call to Eugene. He knew that she trusted her instincts and didn't interrupt when she said that Eugene had sounded genuinely terrified for their safety and that she believed him. But when she said that he had to meet Eugene in the Cathedral at 11.00 a.m. he flatly refused because he couldn't trust himself not to kill the man. Then Jo said she'd go instead but he knew that he couldn't pollute her with his father's company, so he reluctantly agreed to go and looking at his watch realised he only had an hour.

Dane had passed a number of churches on his run back so had to check for the Metropolitan Cathedral on his tourist map. He realised that it was the twin towered white building he'd gone past and that it was just a few minutes away, so he relaxed, showered and changed into a Sea Island cotton polo shirt and chinos. At ten minutes to the hour Dane walked slowly down the narrow stairs and out into the heat of the day and sighed knowing that there was no way out of this, he'd promised Joanne that he'd be calm and listen to Eugene. He crossed over an intersection full of shouting people and noisy vehicles and walked along the side of the cathedral and round to the front. There he could see an ancient weathered stone facade flanked by two white towers and wide stone steps leading up to massive dark double doors. He climbed them unwillingly and turned the worn handle on a smaller door obviously used by thousands of worshipers and stepped inside.

Inside it was cold, dark, eerily silent and Dane could smell the incense of centuries. He walked carefully further into the body of the cathedral and looked round holding onto the back of a pew for stability. He hated churches like this and the way that even in poor places they were full of gold and riches sweated out of the poor. He still couldn't see anything and walked further down the aisle to where a shaft of light was streaming through a window in the North. There he saw something in the front pew near the confessional, a large, hunched figure in dark clothes who had his back to the church and who was strangely still.

Chapter 11

Carlos Fantoni was gagging with thirst, his arm ached but he was surprised that he was still alive. His captors may have been wearing suits and ties but they were violent men. You could tell by their eyes that they were killers and their guns were obvious every time they moved him. He had regained consciousness in some sort of plane, strapped down tight on a stretcher and vomited on the floor. His guards had cursed and tried to clean him up with an old towel.

After landing he'd been hustled through a deserted part of a large airport and straight into a closed vehicle. He didn't think that he was in the US because he had seen jungle out of the windows and heard birdsong that reminded him of home in Peru. He really had no idea where he had been taken, but had the feeling it was a long way from anyone he knew or cared for. He was free to sit up now and realised that he was still wearing the tennis gear he'd been playing in, now with the sweet smell of vomit. In a moment of panic, he looked round for the Nikes in which he'd hidden the million dollar card and realised they weren't there. So the card he had hidden had gone, but now he probably had more immediate things to worry about – like survival.

The room he was in looked like a cell that hadn't been used for years. There was no sound of warders doing their rounds or other prisoners, Fantoni felt completely alone. There was one barred window high on the wall which allowed insects to come through at night but he couldn't hear anything, not even aircraft or vehicles, no matter how hard he tried.

The men had told him nothing except someone would be coming soon and that he would have to answer their questions. Fantoni demanded that he see somebody senior and mentioned the names of officials in the Washington administration he'd met during the Greenwatch presentations.
They had not seemed impressed. Then he demanded a mobile phone so he could call his office and lawyer at which the larger of the guys laughed unpleasantly, walked over and casually kicked him in the guts. He'd doubled up in pain and retreated to his bunk.

Fantoni was an intelligent guy and knew that he had probably caused all this trouble himself. Ever since the call from Diane Fallow he'd been in turmoil. She'd told him about the bribes paid to London officials – which he knew about and justified in his own mind because of the number of lives Greenwatch would save. But the falsification of emission readouts she'd found was horrific and something he'd never believed possible. From that moment he knew he had to stop the whole thing before all public trust was lost.

The VW/Audi emissions scandals twenty years ago caused many people to distrust all automotive figures on fuel economy or emissions. Greenwatch was supposed to be the antidote to all this and his call to Mayor Bonelli in Boston had been his first attempt to get the tests stopped before they could do any more damage. It was obvious now that someone in the US administration didn't want Greenwatch stopped.

He had lots of time to work out what he would do if he was free and was certain that he could save the project. The Greenwatch technology was excellent but it needed to be trusted. Once you put it in the hands of politicians or big business, then you put the whole thing at risk. So it needed a totally independent watchdog everywhere in order to work. But when you think about the millions of lives you could save, then surely it was possible.

His guards left him alone for many hours and Fantoni spent much of it on his bunk thinking about Diane Fallow and remembering the nights they had shared. He had never been in love before and ached for her in a way that was almost like physical pain. He worried about her, she had risked her career to tell him about this scandal and he knew that some powerful people would be working against them both. He reckoned that it was about 10 days since she'd called him and knew that she would be worried about the lack of contact.

At about the time Fantoni was curled up in pain in his cell there was an extraordinary meeting of the Salimond board members responsible for the Greenwatch project. Wolf Bayer apologised for calling them together again so quickly but said there had been dramatic things happening and action had been necessary. He played a recording of Fallow's telephone call to Carlos the week previously and waited for the uproar amongst the board members to die down. He then played the recordings of Fantoni's message to Mayor Bonelli demanding the stop of the test and his panicked call to Washington.

"Those recordings were sent to me from GCHQ, the global monitoring centre in the UK. They were also sent to various officials in Washington. The first call was from a Diane Fallow who is a Financial Times journalist and Carlos Fantoni's lover. Publication of her story would, as you could imagine, be disastrous to the Greenwatch project." Bayer paused dramatically.

"I should tell you also that Fantoni was taken in Boston a couple of hours after those calls and I don't know who took him. But before I get to that, I must tell you I realised that the most urgent thing to deal with was the London journalist and her proof. She might have published a couple of days ago but I had help from the UK government who also didn't want Greenwatch stopped." Wolf Bayer could not resist a little smile as he held up a copy of the Daily Mail front cover from a previous day, **"Journalist killed by drug crazy councillor."**

Bayer explained the story being told, was that the journalist Diane Fallow was visiting corrupt official Rick Duckley at his apartment, and her editor knew that she was going to confront him about his lavish lifestyle. Duckley had apparently killed himself shortly after battering Fallow to death. Police found a massive amount of heroin in his body and a considerable amount of other drugs on the premises. Duckley's high living was thus being put down to drug dealing and not to corruption that might have reflected badly on Greenwatch.

There was considerable relief round the board room table at the creative way someone had eliminated the problem in London. There was agreement that the plan to expand throughout the UK need not be halted for very long. Apart from the expansion in London, Bayer said that there were eight more large cities in the UK who were already signed up for Greenwatch and the potential turnover in this country alone was billions. Europe would be next and Bayer projected a graph on the wall showing the next five years turnover which astonished them all. Bayer paused dramatically and held up his hand for silence.

"We mustn't forget something. We all run global industrial groups who've been eviscerated by governments all round the world for years. We've employed millions of their people, been vital to their economies but they've taxed us nearly to death. Now they are trying to turn us into Public Enemy Number One again because we've used fossil fuels. We backed Greenwatch because it is the most efficient system of measuring air pollution we found." Here Bayer paused for emphasis. "But it can be controlled to show much lower readings if necessary. This is something that the more enlightened governments and cities are already willing to pay considerably more for. Personally, I look on it as fair compensation for all the lost profits we've suffered in recent years." There were nods of approval round the table. "But the absence of Fantoni does present some problems as he has been our chief salesman since the beginning."

Wolf Bayer had an incoming call and excused himself for a few minutes and said that he would need to call back someone in Washington to find out more about Fantoni whilst the board had lunch. When he returned his expression was perplexed.

"The Americans have taken Fantoni because they don't want Greenwatch screwed up at this stage of the election campaign. We agree with them there." Bayer said ironically. "But what their plans are for him, they won't tell me. I did share with them, the information that the original leak in London had been eliminated and the official seemed quite relieved."
"The other news is rather irritating. Mayor Bonelli, who you will remember signed up for the test in Boston, has had a heart attack." There were curses in various languages round the table and then Bayer continued. "So mayoral support has stopped for the moment... but I gather that the Greenwatch test will continue as the President is certainly keen to continue backing it."

The board discussed whether it might be worth trying to find Fantoni and assess whether there was any chance of persuading him to back Greenwatch again. They knew how much he'd actually been told by the London journalist and it was that Greenwatch had the capacity to falsify readings. The London test readings were actually accurate most of the time because there was a vested interest in them being bad. There was no obvious candidate to replace Fantoni as Dr Coombes was turning into an alcoholic so the board decided it was worth trying to find Fantoni wherever the Americans had put him to see whether he might be reassured enough about the technology to carry on. Wolf Bayer thought that the chances of persuading Fantoni to rejoin the team again were low and that threats might be a more productive method. Either way, it would be good to know exactly where he was and then Salimond could control things more directly.

Fantoni had not marked the days on the walls of his cell and had only a rough idea how long he'd been there. He had endured dozens of the ready meals they forced him to eat and in the steel mirror his beard was pretty established, so he estimated that he'd been there about ten days. Still no-one had been to question him.

At least they had taken away the stained tennis gear he'd arrived in and given him fresh clothes. The orange overalls were relatively clean but looked as though they'd been kept in a cupboard for a few years and smelt musty. The orange colour made him think of terrorist prisoners he had seen on TV recently. But on reflection he thought not as this place looked as though it hadn't been occupied for years. On his weekly trip to the showers, he passed unoccupied cells and heard no other prisoners. This didn't feel like a normal prison.

He was tortured by doubt as to how anyone could be cynical enough to ruin Greenwatch. The technology was brilliant and it could save thousands of lives so why would anyone try to affect its accuracy. He thought that he had checked it out carefully and desperately wanted to speak to the scientists in his lab to see whether Greenwatch was capable of being manipulated as Diane Fallow had stated. Most of all he needed to speak to Diane, she had a down to earth attitude that helped him see things more clearly. As more time went on, the more he worried that he might have been premature in phoning Bonelli and demanding that Greenwatch was stopped. Perhaps he should have thought things through, spoken to Wolf Bayer and waited.

Sitting in an old office fifty yards away from the cell was a very angry man. Bradley Kowolski was part of a squad that didn't exist on any set of official documents. He'd occasionally be eliminating problem people like suspected terrorists as part of a NSA special enforcement squad. He wasn't trained to babysit Peruvian midgets for weeks just because he'd been on duty in Boston setting up a hit and was available. It should have been a simple hotel snatch with no witnesses but as always, the intelligence was wrong and they'd had to get him out of that fancy gym with far too many people watching for comfort. Kowolski had been instructed to get Fantoni to a special facility in Panama and to stick with him. Since then, there had been a deafening silence from anyone until this morning. Now finally he'd heard that someone senior from the President's office would be visiting tomorrow to question Fantoni directly. Maybe Kowolski would get the chance to finally get out of this bug infested hellhole and stop being a fucking nanny.

The Presidential aide had actually already reached Panama and had some basic research on the way about Salimond and Panama Gulf Bank. A Washington team had done the same when the President had thought about backing Greenwatch but they really hadn't done due diligence because with his CIA resources, he'd found pretty quickly that Salimond had rather dubious backers and Panama Gulf Bank was full of dirty money. The fact that Greenwatch had been developed at Shelford was also a half truth which was being contested rather vigorously at present. Carlos Fantoni however checked out pretty well both academically and morally but might have to be sacrificed if he got in the way of the President's plans. That would be clear tomorrow when he interviewed him.

Another problem the President was aware of was the campaigning journalist Joanne Li was in Panama too. Her and her partner Dane Morgan had been asking embarrassing questions about Greenwatch and Fantoni ever since the arrest and had a CIA surveillance team checking their every move. The aide had heard recordings of their conversations and knew that they planned to check out Salimond head office and try and find out about Carlos Fantoni. The aide had authority to arrange accidents for them if they started to interfere too much. The Washington team were paranoid about Joanne Li as her blogs and tweets seemed to frighten politicians witless these days.

Fantoni didn't actually sleep much that night. The big American had come in with his supper in a foul mood and when he tried to question him about the visit tomorrow, he'd hit him so hard in the chest that he thought he wouldn't be able to breathe. It took him minutes of gasping on the floor before he could breathe in. After a few hours of fitful sleep, he woke up when it was virtually dark with a feeling of dread and knew there was something in the room. He quietly sat up from his bunk and tried to see. There on the wall, just visible by the moonlight from the high window was a spider that looked huge and was very tentatively moving down towards him. He'd seen big spiders in Peru but this didn't scuttle away when he banged his shoe on the wall like they had, it kept coming. Fantoni shouted furiously for help and the cell flooded with light. After a few seconds Kowalski burst in, gun drawn and looked round. Seeing the spider, he reversed the gun and hammered it to a pulp with the butt.

At first light Fantoni heard the dawn chorus of birds and what sounded like apes in the distance and tried to work out again where he was. The temperature in the cell varied from sweltering in daylight to freezing at night and humidity was a real problem. He was convinced that he was in a jungle somewhere and with the US connection wondered if it was Guantanamo Bay or somewhere like it. He tried to get himself clean in the tiny metal basin and clear up the rubbish that had accumulated after a few dozen ready meals and pile it in the corner. After last night's visitor, he didn't want anything that might attract local insect life to be close to his bunk. The orange overalls he was given when he'd first been imprisoned were changed weekly and were relatively clean. So Fantoni was as prepared as he could be for the visitor he'd been told to expect.

It was a couple of hours before the Presidential aide found his way to the prison. For security reasons he had to drive himself in a locally hired Toyota Land Cruiser and the directions were sketchy. Once he found the Canal Zone, he was told to look for a shipyard called Martinez and go through to the back of the deserted yard and open the big steel gates. Keeping the water to his left he was told to travel for 5 miles on the single track road. It looked as though the track had only been used a few times and the ruts and holes required his total concentration as did the jungle which was pushing in from both sides. Despite the air con the journey was hot, sticky and dangerous and once he had to stop whilst a troop of monkeys crossed the track, the leader giving him a challenging glance whilst they passed. The aide was far more used to the political jungles of Washington than this steamy hell and all he wanted to do was get the questioning over and get back to his own natural habitat.

The building had been US property for 80 years. It was a high security prison which was state of the art in the last century and had the watchtowers, searchlights and high walls of a miniature Alcatraz. Its most famous residents had been some old style mafia dons who had spent their last days there well away from any family connections. The jungle had invaded the prison from almost every direction since and creepers like serpents had pushed through the crumbling concrete. The aide saw that there had been some attempt to clear the main gates of vegetation and blasted his horn when he was alongside the gatehouse.

Fantoni heard the car and knew his interrogator had arrived. He had recovered his courage after the events of the night and was determined not to be intimidated by this situation. He had dragged his way out of the slums of Lima and survived the tennis circuit without weakening. Over the years he had met gangsters, bent politicians and con men and what had kept him going was belief that he could improve the world by making sure Greenwatch was used everywhere. His parents had died because of pollution and he was a scientist who could make sure that sort of tragedy never happened again.

It took the aide around twenty minutes to realise that if released, Fantoni would never keep quiet about the problems associated with Greenwatch. He had tried intimidation, bribery and gentle persuasion but Fantoni was still adamant about going public.

This was a crucial time in the Presidential re-election campaign and though he was backing away from Greenwatch a little, the general view of 'Vote for Me and Breathe Easy' was so strong, it should not be changed. It was tempting to just leave Fantoni here to rot but he knew that the journalists were also in the area trying to find him so the pressure was on to find a permanent solution.

Difficult situations sometimes create strange alliances. The aide was informed that there had been a call from Wolf Bayer of Salimond to someone senior in Washington. The nub of the matter was the board of Salimond were aware that Fantoni had been taken by the US and was in Panama. After a long and extremely guarded conversation it became clear that he thought Salimond and the President had a shared interest in keeping any problems associated with Greenwatch quiet. Having confirmed to everyone that Fantoni would definitely not cooperate with any cover up, the aide was told that a permanent solution needed to be found.

Fantoni's days were numbered from the minute he stopped talking to the aide – nobody now wanted him to spoil their plans. There had already been too many breaches of security very visibly involving US forces and Fantoni. During every Presidential election campaign there were journalists like Joanne Li circling like vultures trying to find scandal. The President and the US needed to be totally blameless when it came to Carlos Fantoni and anything that might happen to him. A possible solution was suggested by a member of the black ops team. There was somebody who might do the job who was totally deniable. His name was Alexander Brown and according to the files he was a high-function psychopath.

Chapter 12

Dane Morgan didn't want to be there, the smell of incense made him gag. Panama Cathedral was dark and so full of doom that bright sunlight through the dirty stained glass window couldn't dispel it. The large figure slumped in the front pew could have been alive or dead and could have been anybody. He hadn't seen Eugene for 20 years and after the way he had conned his mother, he had hoped never to see him again. Morgan slid awkwardly down the row behind to be closer and looked over to the person who was still motionless. Just when the suspense was getting unbearable the head turned and a large hand beckoned him.
"Hello son, come over here," the soft Irish brogue was as familiar as Guinness and just as bitter. "I know you don't want to talk, but please listen for five minutes because you and Ms Li are in danger."

Dane sat down in the pew a few feet behind where he didn't have to be next to the man who'd created such misery in his mother's life. He could see the thick white hair and big face from the photographs his mother still insisted on keeping in her bedroom. The face was tanned and deeply lined but the eyes were as blue as ever as Eugene turned and looked awkwardly back at Dane.
"You're looking good Dane."
"Get on with it – I don't want to be here at all." Dane said with the anger barely contained in his voice.
"I heard a couple of weeks back that you were checking up on Carlos Fantoni and Greenwatch in Boston and tried to warn you by phone."
Dane was astonished at his father's knowledge but kept his voice level. "Yeh, well, your call wasn't exactly welcome."
"Well, I had to tell you, the people involved are more dangerous than you could possibly imagine. Panama Gulf Bank are involved and I've worked with them before. They would kill anyone who got in their way and your names were mentioned but you were in Boston. Why the fuck did you come to their home ground?"
Dane hesitated. "We are looking into Salimond, the company behind Greenwatch... and trying to find a chap called Fantoni..."
"Fantoni's here – the Yanks have got him in some godforsaken prison down river." Eugene whispered. "But his days are numbered, ever since he turned whistleblower... don't go near him."
"Why the fuck should I listen to you? "Dane asked with contempt in his voice.
"Listen son, I've done many things I regret – especially when I was married to your mother – but I never meant to hurt her, but these guys... well they deal in trillions and power is everything to them.

Don't get in their way."

"Yeh, well I've been in plenty of dangerous places before, I don't get put off that easily and Joanne feels the same, especially when it comes to big company corruption."

"Eugene laughed sarcastically." I read all about her and the SCC disaster and she did a real good job on that story but those people were civilised compared to this lot. Here you're dealing with the bank that holds most of the bad money in the world from Nazi gold through to mafia reserves. Now you've also got the dirty tricks side of the NSA involved too. Both won't let anything get in the way of Greenwatch."

"Why on earth are they all so worried, what's the problem?" Dane asked, rising to his feet.

"I don't know," Eugene answered, "but it will be about power."

Dane shuffled to the end of the pew and started to walk out of the cathedral, he could hear Eugene calling him back but pushed open the heavy front door and stepped out into the sunshine, which was blindingly white after the gloom. He gradually focussed and wondered whether anything Eugene had said could be trusted, but he had seemed genuinely scared for them.

He walked slowly back to the hotel re-running everything his father had told him and worrying about what to tell Jo. She had suffered greatly during the SCC kidnap and he had hoped to protect her from the kind of stress involved in investigations like this. But this looked as though it could be even more dangerous than the last time they worked together and the sooner he discussed it with her the better. Dane pulled out his mobile half way there and rang her. After a few rings it clicked to answer phone and Dane was surprised that she wasn't eagerly waiting for him to report on the meeting. He was even more worried when he went up to the room and found her gone.

He looked round for messages, checked his phone again and found nothing. He ran down to reception and looked in the hotel bar but it was empty. Dane started to get a really bad feeling in his gut and dialled her number again but it went through to message. He knew the worst thing to do when someone is missing is to move around so he forced himself to sit on a pavement seat outside the hotel and wait.

After 20 minutes, Dane's phone rang and he could see it was Jo's number. He answered with huge relief but heard an unfamiliar and slightly accented male voice.

"Mr Morgan, we've brought Ms Li in for questioning."

"Who are you and where is she?" Dane demanded, remembering just how far away from home they were. "Please be careful with her, she has been very ill," he ended rather lamely.
"She didn't show any sign of illness when she was resisting arrest." The officer stated ironically.
"I repeat, who are you?"
"We are the Policia – Officer Fernandez is my name."
"Where are you? Ms Li is a well known journalist in the US and you will find that she is extremely well connected. I will come for her right away."
Officer Fernandez didn't sound particularly impressed but gave Dane the address of the Central Police Building in Panama City.

The taxi took him to an ugly concrete building in the modern part of Panama City. They passed amazing high-rise architectural masterpieces that looked like twisted spirals and glass fantasy towers that were the equal of Dubai or Singapore. Many were banks or hotels and Dane realised just how much money was flowing through this city. One was the Panama Gulf Bank Building which looked more like an alien space ship than a structure for business.

Eventually Dane paid off the cab and passed through the security barriers and into the police building, which had all the charm of a fortified multi-story car park. There were men with automatic weapons everywhere and Dane threaded his way round the guards and found a reception desk occupied by two swarthy women who studiously ignored him for what seemed like five minutes. Eventually he shouted "Officer Fernandez" in his best British accent and actually got some attention.
"Colonel Fernandez, you mean" said one of the women stiffly.
"Yes, probably." Dane responded hoping he hadn't upgraded the problem. "Whoever it is has arrested my partner Joanne Li, who is a US citizen."
The woman consulted her computer and nodded affirmatively. "I will contact him right away." She spoke softly on the phone in a language Dane couldn't understand and confirmed that someone would be down shortly.

Dane walked to the end of a line of seats in the filthy waiting area and looked around. It looked like the detritus of the world was sharing the room with him. There was a man in Arab dress covered in blood with a wife in tears, an evil looking couple of Hispanic men with scars and tattoos. There were a couple of obvious hookers in obscenely scanty dresses. Finally, there was a man in a good suit who looked as though he had been seriously mugged. He really couldn't understand why anyone would think that Joanne Li should be in a place like this.

After 15 minutes, a tall black woman in a beautifully cut suit stepped out of the lift and looked with distain at the waiting area. After a while Dane realised that she was calling his name and he stood up. She introduced herself as the Colonel's PA and Dane realised that she was as tall as he was and he felt like a badly dressed peasant alongside her. She pressed 5 on the lift control panel and they travelled in silence until the doors opened. The corridor could not have been more different to the ground floor, there was good carpet on the floor, glass walled offices and the sound of hushed efficiency as they walked to a corner office. The woman knocked and she held open the door for him to enter. The first thing he heard was the beautiful sound of Jo laughing.

Dane walked into one of the largest offices he'd ever seen and spotted Jo sitting opposite a guy who looked like an Italian film star, something like a cross between George Clooney and Roberto Rasile. The guy smiled pleasantly at Dane and waved him over to a large black leather chair that was the twin of the one that Jo was sitting in.
"Are you alright Jo?" was the only thing to say in the circumstances.
"Yes, fine Dane, but Colonel Fernandez has been apologising for the way his men took me from the hotel – they thought I was a sort of terrorist or something."
Fernandez nodded apologetically and said that he had received an email from the local US security people stating that Joanne Li was in Panama and was a 'Person of Interest.' Normally that was a euphemism for a dangerous person and as there was a major international banker's conference happening in the city this week, they decided to detain Ms Li before she had chance to cause any problems. They now realised that she was a respectable journalist and the daughter of Professor Li who Fernandez had met at Shelford when he was doing his degree.

Dane just wanted to get Jo out of there and bring her up to date with the conversation he'd had with his father, so he asked whether they could leave and Fernandez said that he would arrange for a car to take them back to the hotel. It looked churlish to refuse so they said yes and talked about trivia for five minutes until the tall black PA knocked on the door and took them down to the back entrance to where there was a Mercedes 500 SEL with blank plates waiting for them.
Before they left the woman gave Jo a card with Colonel Fernandez's

direct number in case she had any more trouble. Jo thanked her and they stepped into the air conditioned leather of the Mercedes.

On the back seat Jo started to ask about his visit to the cathedral and Dane shook his head and touched his finger to his lips. He suddenly realised that their mobiles had also probably been tracked since the states and resolved to buy burners tomorrow. Jo got his drift and said it had been very scary when the police had come because they were armed and in full riot gear. They had picked her up and bundled her into a police wagon and taken her mobile and iPad before she had time to object. Dane commiserated with her and made all the right noises because he was sure that their conversations in the car would be listened to.

Rather than going straight to their room, Dane suggested a coffee in a square not far away and they walked hand in hand in silence. Locals were just finishing lunch in the noisy square with large trees providing shade over the dozen or so tables. It was hot and humid and the smell of cigarette smoke filled the air but Dane found a place just near the main building and they sat. After ordering a Coke and an iced tea from a waiter who obviously wanted to finish his shift and go, Dane leaned close and looked into those lovely green eyes and tried to tell her about the conversation with Eugene. It may have been the close encounter with danger or the close proximity of one of the loveliest women he'd ever met, but it was difficult to stop feeling incredibly randy. She was looking close into his eyes, sensed his mood and quietly stroked his thigh under the table.

It took about an hour back in the room before he could actually talk seriously about his father's warnings. Lovemaking at that level drove everything else out of their minds and the outside world and its problems seemed a long way away. But he forced himself to summarise the key points which were that Salimond was behind Greenwatch and part of Panama Gulf Bank. This was a bank where dirty money from all round the world was kept and they killed anyone who got in their way. Fantoni had been abducted by the US for reasons unknown and was being kept in a prison somewhere in the Canal Zone. The other major point was that Salimond or Panama Gulf Bank knew about their enquiries and felt threatened in some way so Eugene said that they should stop and get out of town as fast as they could.

After a few minutes discussion, Jo and Dane agreed that there was no way they were going to give up now. They both sensed that this was a big story, they just had to find what worried a major crime bank and the US so much that they were prepared to imprison somebody illegally and be willing to kill to keep it from coming out. They had a few lines of enquiry: the black bank or ID card that Dane found at the beginning, Salimond headquarters and Carlos Fantoni, wherever he was imprisoned.

Social media had been extremely useful in the past to get difficult stories of corruption and scandal out relatively anonymously. There was a blog titled 'Corporate Li's' that had been used by Jo and others and they decided to use it with one of the shots taken of Carlos's arrest. **"Carlos Fantoni was behind Greenwatch and there are rumours that he's been illegally imprisoned. The US Environmental Agency deny that they've met him. Is this a case of Corporate Li's?"**
The blog had been dormant recently but had been really active during the SCC scandal so it took a few days for interest to build and Jo planned to keep the momentum up so that it might get attention from mainstream and environmental influencers. **"The President said that Greenwatch would help us all breathe easy but the scientist involved has disappeared. Is this a case of Corporate Li's?"** Jo included a shot of one of the Greenwatch units on the streets of Boston. The search engines did their job and Jo could see the hit rate growing exponentially over the first few hours. They decided to leave things for now and carry on with their research in Panama. She also distributed both stories on the Dark Web knowing that even some quite respectable journalists referred to it.

The Presidential aide had a long conversation with the President and confirmed that Fantoni was never going to cooperate with them as far as Greenwatch was concerned. The President tended to talk in coded language as if he expected every call to be recorded and played back but it was obvious that he was worried. He stated that Fantoni was a problem both he and the British Prime Minister were talking about later that day and everyone hoped that the aide could find a permanent solution well before the election.

The aide had an address for the assassin Alexander Brown and nothing else, so he called up Kowolski who was still on Fantoni guard duty and they agreed to meet in a couple of hours to visit him in the old part of Panama. Brown had a fearsome reputation as a highly motivated psychopath and according to the information someone had passed on, he had already been employed by another oil cartel to take Fantoni out. The plan was to offer him more money and give him Fantoni's location so that he could succeed with his mission. This was seen as having two major benefits: getting rid of the troublesome Fantoni but also being able to blame the consortium of oil producers who originally employed him if things went wrong.

The two Americans met in a quiet square at 6.00 p.m. and checked their guns. Kowolski led the way and they came to small white three storey house with a balcony facing the sea. There was no sign of life so they climbed the outside staircase which seemed to be only access to the upper floors. The aide was definitely feeling spooked by the reputation of this man and kept close to the back of Kowolski as they climbed. At the top there was a door and the NSA guy hammered on it with his gun butt and stepped to one side in case anyone shot through the door. There was no answer and Kowolski tried the handle and cautiously stepped in shouting Brown's name and that they were from the NSA.

It only took a few minutes to check out the small apartment and find it empty. They debated what to do and in the end, left a note on the desk with the aide's business card which had an impressive presidential seal on it. Alexander Brown didn't generally like Americans, after several tours as an army surgeon in Afghanistan and Iran, he'd found the officers loud, over confident and amateur. The enlisted men he'd found lacking in anything resembling culture and so poorly educated that they didn't have any idea of where in the world they were.

From his hiding space above the ceiling, he observed his two visitors who'd tripped at least two silent alarms on the way in and given him plenty of time to hide. They were not great examples of manhood but he was intrigued by the mention of Fantoni and knew that the US was not afraid to spend money.

Brown had to admit he was grateful to the Americans for another thing. It was an obnoxious Master Sergeant at Camp Bastion who first got him into the killing game. After sewing him up, the guy was so rude that the surgeon decided to wait until he had been discharged from hospital and have his revenge. The darkness there was intense and he knew that the guy got pissed with his fellow sergeants in a tent on the outside of camp, every night. The surgeon had bought an antique cavalry sword left over from some 19th century conflict in a flea market months ago. He'd polished it and honed its edges until they were like razors. He'd waited and confronted the guy who'd drawn his sidearm but looked amusingly surprised as the sabre took off the hand holding it. He then sliced the guy from throat to gut, cutting through his uniform like paper. Brown revelled in the fact that he could name every organ as it spilled onto the ground. He knew then that the thrill of taking life was far greater than that of saving it and his career as an assassin started from that moment.

Assassination is a competitive marketplace. Alexander Brown realised that there were already expert snipers by the dozen, those for whom explosives were a work of art and even those for whom untraceable accidental death was a speciality. He needed a difference, a USP as they say in marketing and it was a chance viewing of a Victorian Murder Mystery book which gave him that edge. He decided to capitalise on his ancient lineage and always dress in antique clothing such as frock coats and wing collars like his ancestors. Also, to use his skills as an Olympic standard fencer in a slightly different way by always killing his prey with either sabre or foil. Over the years he realised that for practical reasons, a sword stick was much easier to carry and almost as enjoyable to kill with.

The English Gentleman killer image went down well with the Far East, Middle East and US clients and the fact that he had never failed made him extremely sought after. Over the last 10 years he had made millions of dollars, but as they say in the business, you are only as good as your last kill and with Fantoni he had failed so far. A call to the number on the card made it even more profitable to assassinate Carlos Fantoni and they had helpfully told him where he was imprisoned and that his guards would be removed in 2 days. Alexander Brown resolved to use the next 48 hours to plan his mission and visualise the successful disembowelment of his quarry.

Chapter 13

The last few weeks of the Presidential re-election campaign had gone extremely well. He had only a short time to survive before the Tuesday in November which was the traditional date for votes to be cast. But the wrong move now and he could still lose ground.

The President used Air Force One to quickly get to Bonelli's bedside in Boston to show support for the fellow Republican who'd introduced Greenwatch to him and given his own campaign such a great advantage. It would make great TV to show the new caring President.

Greenwatch may have given him a few concerns recently but he had been assured that Fantoni was no longer an issue and he could carry on using Greenwatch as a major campaign advantage.
Boston had been a brilliant opportunity. Not only had he achieved brilliant TV coverage of him looking tearful at the mayor's bedside with the Life Support Machine bleeping dramatically in the background. The President had also taken a leaf out of Bonelli's book and visited Greenwatch units already on test in the centre of the city and shown shock when the readouts flashed red and indicated unhealthy levels of pollution.

He then reminded the audience that he had promised to clean up US cities and that his slogan was 'Vote for Me and Breathe Easy.' This bit of free advertising itself was worth millions of dollars and was seen on Facebook, YouTube and Twitter as well as mainstream TV and radio.

Before he left, he took the Presidential cavalcade of two armoured limousines and three SUV protection vehicles to the mayor's office for yet another photo-opp and to give a stirring speech to the mayoral staff to keep them motivated on Greenwatch. If anyone thought about the pollution caused by five high powered vehicles and Air Force One passing over their city, they kept it to themselves. But the President was becoming hyper sensitive about such matters and made a note to talk to Tesla and Cadillac about a new electric Presidential fleet when he was re-elected.

He needed to be a little careful however, as a member of one of the richest oil and gas families had been a major contributor to the campaign fund that got him elected last time. The job of balancing obligations to his fundraisers with the needs of the country was an almost impossible one and he was grateful sometimes that a

President can have no more than two terms in office. But he had to win this next one first.

Back in the oval office a few hours later he pondered just how many times this room had been featured on film. He'd seen it blown up by terrorists who kidnapped the incumbent, seen it occupied by devious, cunning men and women in House of Cards, he'd even seen it invaded by Lex Luthor and friends who were there to defeat Superman and the world with their Kryptonite. There were very few real heroes seen on film in the room – perhaps Kennedy before the gloss faded or Obama when he stood for idealism and a new equality. But the last few years had been difficult for the oval office and although Trump had his own unique qualities, very few looked back on his term now with affection.

In his own opinion the present President had brought more dignity and more statesmanlike qualities to the job but in the end, something always arose that tested his principles and forced him to be pragmatic. In his second year Special Forces had captured a Muslim extremist, reputed to have been behind many bombings, in a part of Africa where the US had no real excuse to be there. His first instinct was to bring him back and give him a show trial but his advisors pointed out that in legal terms we had no chance of winning because of where we captured him and the fact that witnesses to his atrocities would be impossible to find. In the end he devolved the decision to his closest aide and the terrorist just disappeared from his list of problems.

The same aide had become invaluable since, he had experience in the military before he entered politics and still had links with some of the more shadowy organisations tasked with keeping the US safe. The unusual thing about him is that he seemed to have no political ambitions himself but obviously enjoyed being a power behind the throne. The aide was in Panama City at present and had already found out more about Greenwatch in a few hours than the officials he'd tasked with checking out the system a few months back. According to the aide, the companies behind Greenwatch had extremely dubious provenance and it was suspected that there was some kind of criminal intent behind it. Having talked to Carlos Fantoni, the guy who'd sold the whole Greenwatch idea to the President's office in the first place, the problem was apparently that the read outs could be falsified. The aide was convinced that Fantoni was an unwilling dupe in this process as after he was interviewed and set free, he was determined to go public immediately. For the President in Washington and the Prime

Minister in London, the timing of such an expose would be disastrous.

The President was enjoying a brief moment alone and sipping a wonderful cup of four teas blended for him in London by Liptons. He was drinking it out of an ancient Spode tea set that had been a gift from Queen Victoria & Albert to the White House in 1890 and pondering on the nature of duty. Albert was a polymath who had done more than anyone else to bring Science, Culture and Art of the highest quality to Great Britain which is why there are so many museums and concert halls still carrying his name. He was also outward looking and had a huge sense of duty to the country who'd given him such power. This sense of responsibility had permeated through to all of his children and had meant the British Royal Family had survived when many others had failed.

The President's sense of duty to his country was also well developed but he knew that he only had a few more weeks to win the second term of office and he needed to achieve more of his objectives. The UK was nowhere near as important as it had been in the last century but the Special Relationship still had some power – especially when both countries had the same agenda. The President looked at his world clock and realised that it was early morning over there and put a secure call through the Prime Minister's hotline.
"Mr President, how can I help you this morning?" Answered the cultured, deep voice of the man who'd single-handedly got the UK back on track after the fiasco that was Brexit.
"Greenwatch is a name that I suspect we both know?" The President asked wondering just how much the PM had been told by his staff.
"Yes, and what have you heard?" The PM enquired wondering the same thing.
"Your Financial Times was going to publish a story that discredited Greenwatch technology."
"Not anymore," the PM interjected. "Unfortunately, the journalist involved was killed in a drug related incident and the story found to be inaccurate."
"How regrettable." The President responded with barely concealed relief in his voice.
"Speaking personally, I can tell you that the Greenwatch test in London was a triumph. After all the false data we've suffered from the automotive and oil industries in past years, this was something the people could trust. For the first time, I was seeing the political will across both sides of Parliament to get all polluting vehicles off

the road."

"Did your scientists double check the results after this problem first arose?"

"Yes, the technology is everything it was claimed to be and the results of the London test were mainly accurate." The PM paused, "but, and this is a big but, our team found that it could be hacked into and manipulated if someone really needed to alter them."

"Needed?" The President asked pointedly.

"Someone on the London team was told confidentially that the system readings could be manipulated at extra cost. This was apparently designed for the Chinese or Indian markets which according to Salimond were much less particular about accuracy."

"But that would destroy Greenwatch as a credible expenditure for us," the President said.

"But it's such a strong part of your re-election campaign, surely you can't change now?"

"Really doubtful... really can't see how, so I'm going to have to make it work." The President said.

The PM hesitated wondering just how honest to be. "Fantoni is the immediate problem and if he goes public then we are both in trouble – but I suspect you know where he is don't you?"

"That's possible," was the guarded reply.

"I also gather that the people behind Greenwatch, who are not as respectable as they seemed, also don't want Carlos Fantoni to reappear." The PM stated hoping that he wouldn't be asked to name his sources.

"That's very interesting." The President concluded, firing a message off to his aide as he talked.

The two men ended the conversation with the promise to talk again. In these days of recorded conversations, freedom of information acts and leaks at very high levels, it was almost impossible to say anything too directly these days, but they both knew that Greenwatch was vital to their futures. For Fantoni, however, the future looked extremely bleak.

Chapter 14

Joanne and Dane went down to the old town for a meal. It was a noisy, hot square surrounded on three sides by public buildings that could not have been more different to the new city they'd seen earlier. Most looked around 200 years old and had been built to impress, with fluted pillars and ornate ironwork balconies. They looked like the finance houses or government offices Dane had seen in the old parts of Dublin and London but instead of dark granite, they were marble and blindingly white stone.

The noise from the mopeds and trucks on the narrow streets was intense, so they crossed over to the far side of the square where there was a couple of cafes under wide leaved trees that looked like acacia. A stooped, old waiter came out of the building and gestured them to a table deep in shade at the back and they followed. Jo wrinkled her nose up at the acrid smoke from an adjoining table and Dane pointed to a table away from the smokers. The waiter looked insulted, like only old waiters can when customers disagree with them, but followed them over.

They hadn't eaten for hours and looked at the simple menu with genuine interest. First Jo asked for an iced tea and Dane a Balboa beer, and the waiter hobbled back to the bar muttering under his breath. Dane and Jo giggled to themselves and concentrated on the food choice. The drinks when they came were excellent, the iced tea wasn't canned or sweet it was home made and gloriously cold and sharp in a thick glass jar. The beer was dark and bitter and Dane drained it in one appreciative gulp.

When the waiter returned, he looked at them with genuine pleasure at their enjoyment. He suggested a plate of Yuca Frita as a snack which they had a few minutes later with another two drinks. Dane tried his rudimentary Spanish on the waiter and asked a couple of questions about their choice but didn't really understand the answers. They had a rule never to order anything like Pizza or Burger anywhere other than the countries that invented them, so ended up choosing something called Ceviche for Jo and Sancocho for Dane. They saw another table with a bucket of frosted white wine and pointed to that. The waiter was now their friend and nodded happily all the way back to the kitchen.

Whilst they were waiting for food, Jo fired up the iPad and saw that the blogs about Carlos Fantoni she'd done earlier had achieved a reasonable number of hits. She knew there was a risk that she'd stirred up a hornets' nest by mentioning the President - in fact she was banking on it. With only a few months until the elections they both knew they had to find out answers soon. After lunch they were going to find the Salimond "centre of excellence" mentioned in the original Greenwatch sales material. Then they were going to take the mysterious black card to the Panama Gulf Bank and see what happened. First they had to get a mobile.

Dane saw a local VIP car hire company advertising in the hotel magazine and did the normal bullshit about him being a famous photographer needing a great car for a photoshoot at special rates. He could hear the sales manager slowing down enough to access Dane's website whilst they talked and knew that the landscape work for Discovery Channel, New York Times or Sunday Times, would do the trick. Within a few minutes, they'd agreed a price for a 4x4 to be collected in the morning and Dane agreed to photograph the company boss and his personal car.

The lunch was wonderful. Jo's Ceviche turned out to be raw fish marinated in a sharp lime juice served with tortilla chips that was so good she refused Dane a taste. The Sancocho was a good honest meat stew served in a large earthenware bowl with chunks of flat bread. They never found out what the wine was, but it was dry and flinty and perfect with Jo's dish. Dane reverted to the Balboa beer with his stew and sighed with contentment.

They realised they hadn't talked about anything important for 10 minutes and felt rather guilty as they both leant back in their chairs and ordered expresso coffee. They thought that the Salimond office was just a short distance outside the old part of Panama and was worth a visit later when they looked more business-like. The coffee did its job and they paid the bill with a tip that made their waiter even more friendly and walked back to their hotel.

An hour later, Jo was dressed in the blue silk trouser suit she had not worn since her business meetings in Thailand, with flat Converse pumps and a black leather courier bag. Not the most coordinated outfit she had but she still looked stunning. Dane changed into a cream linen jacket from Hacket of London and dark blue canvas chinos. As always, he carried one of his faithful Nikon cameras, this time a D850 with a 16.6x zoom in his backpack.

The Salimond office was 15 minutes' walk away in a quiet street just on the edge of the new business district. The building was a modern 6-storey construction with dark smoked glass mirroring the outside world. Eventually they found an entrance door with wording on a metal plate *'Salimond Group – green solutions, worldwide.'* Jo pressed the buzzer and when a voice answered, Jo said it was Joanne Li and that she had an appointment with Dr Fantoni. Admiring her cunning, Dane stood back and eventually the voice from the box squawked in a very panicked way that Dr Fantoni was not available. Jo then applied maximum pressure and said that she was the environmental correspondent of the New York Times and they had travelled all the way from the US to have an interview, which in view of the US President's interest at present, she was sure they wouldn't want to refuse.

There was a long pause and then the door buzzed and they went up to a reception on the first floor. This was a large open room with brilliant graphics of smog covered cities alongside Green Planet type aerial shots of pristine rain forests and leaping whales. One side had glass windows looking over what appeared to be research labs with a number of white-coated scientists hard at work. Salimond looked genuine as did the elderly professor who strode across the room to greet them.

"Hello, my name is Professor Coombes, we didn't know you were coming. Dr Fantoni is missing at the moment – which is rather worrying – but I'm sure that I can help as Greenwatch was my invention." Dane for something to do, started taking photographs of the Professor in the same way the paparazzi shoot reluctant celebrities. The Prof didn't know whether to be scared or flattered but ushered them into a meeting room behind reception. Despite the air conditioning it was hard not to notice the smell of strong drink on him as he sat down and his bleary eyes.
"Ms Li, where are you from?"
"Boston."
"Ah, are you related to a Professor Li, by any chance?"
"Err.. Yes."
"Shit... pardon me... but he joined Shelford after I left and now he's causing problems and questioning Greenwatch and my involvement there. I really think you'd better leave," the Professor stood up and tried to walk out. Jo grabbed his arm.
"Listen, we think that Dr Fantoni has been abducted and that Salimond is a front for something extremely dangerous. You will be on all the news websites tonight unless you give us some true answers - just what is going on here?"

The Professor hesitated, slumped down in a chair and appeared to be sobbing. Dane and Jo waited patiently for him to recover his

composure and when he recovered, he looked up meaningfully at a small box in the corner of the room and escorted them out of the office and out to the lift.
"Fantoni is a good man you know..." The scientist shouted as the lift doors started to close.
"That's why we need to find him.." Jo said putting her arm through the closing doors.
"And Greenwatch does work, you know." They heard him shout as the lift descended.

Dane and Jo compared opinions after the encounter and agreed that the meeting hadn't really got them much further in their search for Carlos Fantoni. All they knew was what Eugene had said, that he was in a prison somewhere in the Canal Zone and Dane didn't believe anything his bastard of a father said. They walked across town to a tourist office and got a large scale map of the canal area. Nothing was shown on the map that resembled a prison but one of the older guides behind the counter said he thought he remembered his father talking about some gangster who might have been imprisoned in the Canal Zone many years ago, but he couldn't be sure.

The day was coming to an end but it was still hot and sticky. They walked back to the street where the Salimond building was to find some shade and maybe see the scientist or anyone else from the company they might question. Eventually Professor Coombes came out and looked shocked to see them, it was getting dark and the man looked hunted. Joanne went up to him leaving Dane leaning against the wall opposite. She reckoned that she looked less threatening than a 6ft 2inch man as he already looked terrified.
"What do you want?"
"The truth about Greenwatch." She said quietly.
"No it's too dangerous.."
"I told you, we'll publish anyway – we've got shots of you, the office, everything." Jo said.
"Come with me." The Professor took her arm and led her to the end of the street where there was a small park where mothers and children were playing in the cool of the evening. Dane followed well behind and watched as Jo and the Professor sat down on a small bench behind the swings and appeared to be deep in conversation. As happens in the tropics, the sun was going down quickly and the insects started to hum in the trees. The two were talking for a long time and Dane saw the mothers, one by one, shout to their kids and leave the park.

Finally, the figure of the Professor stood up and walked quickly out using a gate at the far side of the playground. Dane crossed and sat next to Jo on the bench and asked what he'd said. Joanne seemed to be really excited and it took her a while before she could calm down enough to tell him.

"We were right... there is a real problem with the Greenwatch system, it measures pollution alright but the guy said the real reason Salimond are backing it so hard is because it can be altered in certain circumstances to show false readings. The guy said Salimond is backed by a major oil family, an automotive group and a Japanese industrial conglomerate – all of whom have a vested interest in keeping the petrol pumps pumping. He believes that the US government is now also involved in some way. He's really scared, he's been paid millions for the technology but his passport has been taken and he feels that he is a prisoner here."

"Wow" was all Dane could say.

"The important thing – the really important thing – is that he's agreed to come to our hotel tonight so we can film him for our next blog – he's going to tell all."

"What time?" Said Dane looking at his watch.

"Ten o'clock."

The unidirectional microphone carried by the CIA local had picked up everything and been transmitted to an office a few miles away. After a hurried discussion it was decided to pass on a message to a recently acquired asset situated across the old town in an apartment at the edge of Panama Bay. Alexander Black looked at the special mobile supplied by his new US employers, scanned the message and happily sighed. This was going to be an extremely profitable and rather amusing few days.

The Professor had been terrified when he'd been confronted by Joanne Li but part of him now felt the need to confess. After all, Greenwatch was his life's work and it was meant to save thousands of lives, but he'd been persuaded to hand it all over to Salimond. Persuaded was too gentle a word – he'd been told that if he didn't comply, his family back in the US would suffer and so would he. He'd got lots of money in his bank account, but that was the Panama Gulf Bank and he didn't trust them one bit. Now he had a chance to make things right and make a clean breast of things.

The Professor had been in his Panama apartment for a couple of years with only a monthly trip home to keep in touch with his wife and kids. They were happy, his academic career had not been particularly well paid and his wife had expensive taste in clothes and cars. Now she was able to run a brand new Mercedes Sports and they had moved to a really expensive part of Boston.

In some ways he loved Panama City, the place was so vibrant and his apartment was a three bedroomed luxury design that looked as though it should have been in a James Bond movie.
Professor Coombes looked at the Rolex on his wrist and realised that he only had half an hour to cross town to the Hotel Tantalo where he'd agreed to meet Joanne Li. He knocked back another "Makers Mark", checked his shirt, knotted his tie and buttoned his jacket one more time in the mirror. He wanted to look good in the film, which as an intelligent man, he knew might be his last. He was sure that when his bosses saw the film, he'd be fired but he'd never meant to sell out to Salimond, he'd genuinely wanted to help the world with his invention. Now was the time to make amends.

Coombes went down to the ground floor and greeted the concierge, who nodded and pressed the exit button behind his desk. It was dark down the narrow street and Coombes suddenly felt a shiver of almost primeval fear which he knew was ridiculous. He'd walked out at night dozens of times and never worried and though it was a rough city, there was little crime in this area. He gathered himself and walked to the light at the end and turned down Avenue Central where he passed some of his favourite cafes and bars until he reached the Cathedral and the turning for Hotel Tantalo. The Cathedral loomed dark above him and he was aware of a strange figure standing very still on the steps. The figure looked like something out of an Edwardian melodrama in a long black coat and silk top hat.
"Professor Coombes, how wonderful to meet you." The figure said in the most cultured English.
"Wha.."
Alexander Brown stepped forward and with almost balletic grace drew the sword out of its container. Coombes shivered with fear and felt his bowels loosen at the sight of the tall black figure who looked like something out of his childish nightmares. His eyes saw the gleaming silver blade which was as thin as a needle and his hearing heard the metallic scrape of the sword as it left its container. He knew that no one could help him and part of him knew that he deserved to die.

The assassin took a few steps forward and drew the blade down and across the Professor's body with surgical precision. This was a traditional "drawing and quartering" that Brown had been dying to try ever since he'd seen it in a medieval book of punishment. The results were gratifying and the assassin was able to send a photograph to his client of the target sitting down holding most of his guts in his lap, obviously quite dead.

Now, unless the Americans found him another surprise client, there was just one person left in Panama to eliminate. Alexander Brown had something even more special planned for him.

Chapter 15

Carlos Fantoni was getting desperate. He couldn't work out exactly how long he'd been imprisoned but it felt a long time and nothing had changed. He'd built his hopes up when he knew the man from Washington was coming to interrogate him because it was something different. Now a couple had tried to persuade him not to expose the problems with Greenwatch and he'd been tempted. They had been persuasive, saying that they promised to sort out the problems. All he had to do was tell everyone how good the system was and not expose the potential dangers and he would be out of this prison and back saving the world in a couple of hours.

He answered the same way he'd done with the first guy. "I'm not being any part of a con-trick or fraud, the public have had enough of those over the years and the only way to save Greenwatch is to expose its dangers so the public can guard against unscrupulous people misusing it." Fantoni was under no illusions about the danger this put him in, with a Presidential election months away and Greenwatch the mainstay of his campaign. He bet the politicians in London were equally committed to the system and didn't want any embarrassing questions now they were getting public opinion on their side.

Even that thug Kowolski seemed to have lost interest in him. The violence he'd shown in the early days had subsided and talk was restricted to a monosyllabic grunt when he brought his food in. He knew Kowolski's name because of the name tag he'd worn when he was abducted but the other guy was a complete mystery and said even less than Kowolski. But one evening when they were closing up the other guy said "48 hours and we're outa here, thank God" to Kowolski as the door shut. So maybe something was about to change.

Fantoni reckoned that his chances of getting out were slim. They were in a jungle, miles away from the US and no one apart from his girlfriend Diane Fallow would really care where he was. As she was the journalist who found out about the Greenwatch con, Carlos knew that she wouldn't give up easily. Hopefully by now the story had run in the Financial Times and she was trying to find where he was. But she was the other side of the Atlantic and wouldn't find it easy if the US authorities were hiding him in somewhere like Guantanamo. He hadn't tried to escape other than trying the door a few times because the only opening was the small window high on the wall which no human being could get through. The big spider that had entered at the beginning of his imprisonment had been scary but other than small insects, nothing had come through since. The experience had made him wary, however, and remembering stories about some deadly Australian spiders that specialised in lavatories made him doubly careful on the loo in the corner too.

The only time he got out of his cell was three times a week when his guards gave him soap and a towel and marched him down the corridor to a shower that looked as though it had been designed for 20 people or more. So he was relatively clean but his beard had grown tremendously and the face that looked at him in the mirror looked like some Inca prophet and not the athlete he'd been before. There were no windows, or doors en-route and he was watched by the two armed guards, so there was no way he could see of escaping. And judging by what the guard had said things were coming to a head soon.

Five thousand miles away in a city that looked like Panama on steroids, the board of Salimond had a progress meeting high in the Burj Al Arab. Present were the inner circle which was Sheikh Bin Hadad from the consortium of oil families, Ms Tanaka from the Japanese industrial conglomerate and Wolf Bayer, from the German automotive group. Bayer as usual chaired the meeting and asked for patience as a security guy swept the room for bugs and declared it safe to start.
The hotel was old-fashioned by modern standards and its 70 floors were dwarfed by more recent architecture in Dubai. But the Bin Hadad family had provided some of the original money for the construction and the board got extra special treatment. The only downside was security and though the Salimond board changed meeting rooms every time, the building was not as impervious to outside observation as many others. Micro-drones and improved satellite technology had made confidential meetings a nightmare. Every meeting held by Salimond needed to be totally secure as its objectives were not shared by even some directors of the companies represented. Wolf Bayer, for example, was only one of two members of the family who owned the car group, who was aware of Greenwatch and their involvement.
"We have met today because Ms Tanaka wishes to make an announcement."
The tall Japanese woman was an exception in the group. She wasn't a member of an influential family, she wasn't part of a powerful dynasty. But she'd forced herself to the top of this traditional Japanese group through sheer intelligence and ruthlessness. Along the way she'd worked in New York, London and

was rumoured to be the heir apparent to an old fashioned Japanese business warlord who would normally have passed things on to his son.

"I have been told by my principals, that they want to withdraw their support to Salimond." There was a stunned silence round the room and Wolf Bayer stood up.

"Ms Tanaka, you can tell Hattori Kenshin and the rest of the family that there is no way out of Salimond. I know that he now has a division producing electric vehicles and isn't as committed to oil as he once was, but there is no way that he can get the millions back or reduce the commitment you made."

"My principals are not concerned about the money – the few billion invested is less than their worldwide R&D budget. But their reputation matters and when Salimond starts hiring cheap assassins to get rid of obstacles... well."

"May I remind your principals, that 200,000 people supposedly die each year because of air pollution, so a journalist or two in London and Fantoni in Panama hardly registers on the conscience front? Also.." Here Bayer warmed to his task. "When it comes to assassins, your entire dynasty is based on Shogun warriors – and what were they if not assassins?"

Ms Tanaka waited for quiet and added a final point. "Also my company is concerned about Joanne Li."

"Who?" Bayer asked in total surprise.

"A year or so back an environmental campaigner called Joanne Li started a social media campaign which nearly brought down an international chemical group called SCC and caused the resignation of senior politicians. She is not to be underestimated."

"What's that to do with us?" Asked Sheikh Bin Hadad.

"Over the last few weeks, she's been blogging about Greenwatch and the Fantoni disappearance and even the US President is worried about her."

"Indeed, and that explains why the US agencies were also so keen to have Fantoni disappear," Bayer added thoughtfully.

"Finally," Tanaka waited for everyone to stop talking. "I have it from reliable sources that Joanne Li and her partner are in Panama now."

There was a pause whilst they all assimilated this new information. As always Wolf Bayer was the first to collect his thoughts.

"We will obviously look into that right away. But first, I want to make a general point... My group employs hundreds of thousands of people and its very existence was threatened by those do-gooding fools who wanted to ban oil. I know that your companies were also threatened by the same pressures and we thought that all of you had the courage to do something about it.

As you know, my belief was that cities have always been polluted and that the environmentalists had overstated the problem. When I first saw Greenwatch I saw a real threat to our existence but then I realised that given a certain amount of adaptation the technology could buy us time and protect our profits. Petrol and Diesel engines in my vehicles are more efficient than they've ever been and I think that we could be selling them for years to come with a little help from Greenwatch.

You also have very tangible benefits from this project if you don't lose commitment. We are members of the Salimond club for life, if involvement in this project became public knowledge then everybody's company could suffer catastrophic reputation damage or worse."

Ms Tanaka looked annoyed but nodded in acknowledgement and promised to pass the message on to Hattori Kenshin. She knew nothing more about Joanne Li herself and thought that the information had only been received by Kenshin's office a few hours ago. Cutting to the essence of the problem, she agreed with the board that the most urgent thing was the elimination of Carlos Fantoni and then Joanne Li would have very little to investigate.

Wolf Bayer was a lot more worried than he dared show to the board. Things had moved out of his control for the moment and the unholy alliance he had made with the CIA/NSA or whatever set of initials the thugs from Washington were using, could be dangerous. Both parties wanted Greenwatch and no adverse publicity at present and were prepared to kill to ensure it. Professor Coombes the inventor had been seen as a threat by someone and been eliminated. The journalist in London who had been the source of the original expose had also ceased to exist. Bayer was going to keep this secret from the board for the moment and hope to get control of the situation. In the meantime, everyone agreed that the major threat to success was sitting in prison somewhere in Panama.

Carlos Fantoni would not have been surprised that he was the object of so much interest. The visitors from Washington had obviously been very senior and very worried by his plans to expose things. Before he'd been taken in Boston, he'd seen some of the Presidential campaign and knew that it relied on Greenwatch. He knew that he threatened to derail that campaign and suspected that the politicians in the UK would also have been upset by the Financial Times story. God he hoped Diane Fallow missed him and was trying to find him.

He thought he heard the guards leave during the night and suspected that something was going to change because the second guard had brought in a lot more water and food than normal. As he left the guy looked back and quietly said. "I'm sorry, you don't deserve this" and "good luck – you'll need it," before he slammed the door and left. Now it was first light and the prison was quieter than he'd ever known.

Dane Morgan was awake early and took his coffee out to the balcony where he could watch the street waking up. They had waited for the scientist for hours last night but he hadn't turned up to film his story and they presumed that Coombes had lost his courage. They found out differently when they switched on the TV in the hotel room. The news coverage didn't spare anybody's feelings and though it was in Spanish it was obvious that Coombes had been disembowelled by someone before he reached the hotel. This was just too convenient to be a coincidence and Dane suspected that the conversation Jo had with him was overheard or the scientist had told someone. Either way, this proved that they were investigating someone who would kill rather than let the truth about Greenwatch or Fantoni out.

They hadn't really understood why everyone was so scared until the conversation with Coombes.
Having heard from the Professor yesterday that the valuable bonus with the system was that its results could be falsified by unscrupulous governments they were starting to see why. They still had no proof of any of these facts and the only person left who could prove it was Carlos Fantoni and they still didn't know where he was.

Joanne did another blog with a graphic image from the TV news on the Corporate Li's site stating that the inventor of Greenwatch had been murdered, Carlos Fantoni had been abducted and was the US involved? Along with the previous blogs they hoped that someone out there was listening and would pass on the messages to as many people as possible. The previous blogs had done well in terms of hits so she thought that the murder story would get even more traction. Jo shut her iPad and they discussed the plans for the day, frustrated that they still knew so little about Fantoni's location.

Dane reminded her that he had arranged a 4x4 vehicle and was due at the dealer at 9.00 a.m. Then they were going to try the mystery black card that had started all this at the Panama Gulf Bank to see what happened. It was obviously important in some way because Fantoni had tried so hard to conceal it before he was abducted in Boston.

VIP Motors (Panama) was a few miles away by taxi and when they arrived the boss was already outside with a classic Ferrari Dino that dated back to the 1970's which was obviously his pride and joy. For a cheap rate on his hire Dane had offered to take shots of him and his favourite car and after looking at his website, the guy's vanity had got the better of him. Dane's shots had been published in influential newspapers like the London Times and Washington Post and in some major online publications. Given that many of the recent shots were of landscapes or disasters, some of them might not have impressed him. But older ones were brilliant studies of faces and people including a series of F1 Drivers with their private cars that he knew would impress anyone in the motor business. They did.

Jose Forte Malagariga, was a small dark man of mixed Spanish/Argentinian ancestry who thought there were only two cars ever made that were as beautiful as his first mistress. One was the 1965 Jaguar V12 E-Type convertible, the other was the 1974 Ferrari Dino 246. The Ferrari had cost him half a million dollars but the mistress was in danger of costing him a lot more. Luckily Malagariga could afford it as he was one of the first to introduce hybrid and electric 4x4's into Central America. Despite his real love of V8's and V12 engines he had become a real fan of electric cars and raced a Jaguar I-Pace in the national championships.

Dane was a fan of original Land Rover 4x4's and had a 1958 split screen version in bits at an old friend's farm in Leicestershire, England. Some day he hoped to have the time and money to restore it. To him the sophistication of modern cars ruined the drivers experience by making them feel invulnerable with automatic braking, lane departure warnings and buzzers that sounded if any danger was likely anywhere. He found that Malagariga held similar opinions and they had a good-natured argument about the relative merits off road of Land Rover Defenders and Toyota Land Cruisers.

Dane took some great shots of the boss and his Ferrari then of him in front of a huge Bugatti All Road much favoured by local crime bosses. He showed the boss many of the shots on his laptop and promised to email them over to him in the next 24 hours. Malagariga asked where he was going in his hire car and Dane said that he needed off-road capability and reasonable load carrying capacity and something really tough, but he wasn't quite sure. Malagariga led them round the back of his showroom and through some double doors to a workshop with around 6 vehicles being worked on by

mechanics in immaculate white overalls. They looked more like a pit crew than normal mechanics. The guy led them out through the back and into the backyard and pointed to the only vehicle in the place that didn't have a high gloss shine.
"This is my original Jaguar I-Pace, I don't race it any more, it's 5 years old but it's fully maintained and has a few special features that I think you'll like. It might just convince you that an electric Jaguar is better than any old Land Rover diesel-engine antique. Look after it."

The car looked as though it had been through a sandstorm. The paint was a faded red, the wheels were utilitarian black with knobbly all terrain tyres and the vehicle looked 4 inches higher than most Jaguar 4x4's he'd seen. Dane opened the door and the inside was stripped of any luxury, just Recaro racing seats in the front and a simple bench in the back. Despite his inbuilt prejudice against modern, he had to admit to being impressed.
"Listen this has slightly less range than the standard I-Pace but you're unlikely to run out of electricity round here in the two days you've got it. But let me know if you do." Jose said.
"I'll look after it." Dane promised.

Joanne didn't share Dane's odd taste when it came to cars and cameras but didn't say anything. She knew that he was an excellent driver and willingly got in the passenger side as Dane pushed the starter button. It was still odd to see all the dials on the dashboard light up and no noise from the engine. Dane waved to the guys and gently pulled out of the workshop and into the bright sunshine.
"We need to speak to your father." Jo delivered this bombshell whilst Dane was trying to pull into a multi lane highway that crossed the city. Dane grunted but concentrated on negotiating his way through in rush hour traffic.
"We still don't know where Fantoni is and he's the only one who might know," she added.
Dane looked angry and considered it for a few seconds. "I still don't trust that bastard but if you want to contact him, then I won't stop you." Jo still had his mobile number and called it. Much to Dane's annoyance the Jaguar system picked it up on Bluetooth or something and Eugene's voice was blasted out on 8 speakers.
"It's Joanne Li, Mr Morgan."
"Yes Ms Li, how can I help?"
"Do you know exactly where Carlos Fantoni is?"
Eugene's voice became extremely guarded and he asked where she was calling from. When she said Panama City, he became almost hysterical and said that he would meet them at the same place as before at mid-day. He then ended the call and Jo couldn't

get him back no matter how many times she called.

Dane said nothing but punched in an address on the satnav and followed its directions to a small industrial estate on the outskirts of the city. The building had Drone Zone in big letters and Jo groaned in anticipation of a techfest conversation from the guy behind the counter and her partner. Dane was a great landscape photographer and before that he'd taken shots in war zones that most people have never heard of and he had to get in really close. Once he'd dug in for two days in a snake and ant infested desert just to get a photograph of a drug lord making an exchange. In all that time he'd never used a drone and the prospect of using one to find Fantoni was really exciting him but he needed advice.

After talking things through with the guy, Dane hired a DJ Mavic drone because it was the cheapest and already had a camera installed. They went out into the yard and Dane practised for 20 minutes controlling its flight path and got reasonably proficient. The camera quality wasn't up to his normal standards but it didn't need to be, they would use it to overfly the area and use Jo's iPad to see what the camera was seeing real time.

They left the area with the drone in the boot and headed towards the centre of the city and the banking area. What they planned next was one of the most risky parts of the investigation, to try the black card – either at an ATM or counter and see what happened. The city looked beautiful in the morning sun with reflections off the mirrored high rises and statement buildings like the magnificent barley-sugar tower. The Panama Gulf Bank headquarters was amongst the most impressive being a pure gold arrow shape pointing up into the clouds.

They drove quietly past a few times and tried to see where everything was. After a few passes they spotted some ATM's at the end of the building and parked on the pavement outside. Feeling slightly ridiculous Dane put his sunglasses and Panama hat on as protection against CCTV and got out of the Jaguar. He walked round the car and towards the machine, looking back he could see Jo peering out of the passenger window and she was as white as a sheet. The sun was shining on the screen and he really had to concentrate on where the slot was. With a slightly trembling hand Dane pulled the card out and slid it into the slot. For what seemed like hours the machine did nothing and then a message appeared on screen.
Good morning Mr Fantoni, what currency do you require?

Alongside the side of the screen were a great number of icons representing the main currencies and Dane pressed US Dollars.
Do you require banker's draft, cheque, transfer or cash?
Dane opted for cash.
Please fill in the amount of US dollars you require.
Without thinking too much about it, Dane filled in $100,000.

The machine paused for 30 seconds, which felt like an hour. Then it started pushing out $100 bills at the rate of about 1 per second. Dane was aghast, but he managed to put the first 10 or more hundred dollar notes in one pocket, then as more arrived he stuffed more down his shirt, then down his trousers and notes were starting to spill on the floor as he ran out of places to put the money. Joanne saw what was happening and couldn't stop laughing but finally ran to the back of the car and pulled out a shopping bag and rushed over stuffing what notes she could into it. Luckily this was a city where there were few pedestrians, otherwise they would have created quite a scene. With Jo and Dane helping they managed to get lots of the money off the floor but a thousand notes obviously take up a surprisingly large amount of space. And the bills just kept coming.

Jo couldn't believe that they were getting away with this, surely someone would notice soon? She looked up and down the street waiting for the sound of security men running or police sirens, but nothing happened. Then the machine stopped, leaving one note half way out of the ATM slot, which Dane for some crazy reason battled to get out until Jo punched him on the shoulder. Then they were aware of a siren from inside the bank that cut through the traffic noise and they realised it was time to leave.

They ran back to the car and threw the money in the back feeling like bank robbers in a cheap getaway movie. Dane couldn't believe what they'd just done, they'd just robbed Carlos Fantoni, or Salimond, or Greenwatch or the bank. It really shouldn't be that easy, but they were not criminals and he really didn't know what to do with the money now. Perhaps they'd ask Fantoni if they ever found him? But if they were caught in this part of the world, the authorities would have every justification to put them in jail and throw away the key.

Instinct made Dane look in the mirror, and he realised that there was a large SUV that had come round the corner at great speed with lights blazing. He didn't think, he floored the accelerator and the Jaguar leapt forward faster than anything he'd ever driven before. A standard Jaguar I-Pace was advertised when launched in 2019 as being faster to accelerate than many supercars. Indeed, it was faster that its own F-Type Sports coupe. In the years following, it had become even more of a benchmark for those wanting to design a vehicle with reasonable off road capacity and extraordinary road speed. Malagariga had modified the suspension and wheels to make the handling extraordinary at the expense of some comfort. He'd also squeezed about an extra 15% of acceleration, which made the performance staggering.

Dane realised that he couldn't see the Mercedes in the mirror anymore and they were already at 80 mph heading towards a busy junction. He braked and yanked the wheel right and the car went round like on rails but unfortunately, straight into a one-way system the wrong way. He saw a huge Mac truck radiator and swerved round it, hearing the angry blast of the horn and the hiss of air brakes as he did. It all felt so strange - like a driving game with the sound off – the Jag was doing great speeds but there was only squealing from the tyres, virtually no noise at all from the engine. He weaved round other traffic until he reached another turning and managed to get the car heading the same way as everyone else.

During the chase the bag with the $100 notes had flown across the car covering everything with dollars. Joanne recovered enough to start stuffing them back into the bag and Dane started trying to empty his pockets whilst slowly driving across town. He had no real idea where he was until he switched the screen on and realised that he was close to the city limits. They pulled to the side of the road in a deserted petrol station and drew breath.

Inside the Panama Gulf Bank, there was very little concern because only one person knew what the special account was. The black card was only used by 4 people – the directors of Salimond and Carlos Fantoni – and none of them wanted their transactions to be recorded in any way. It had been argued that many of them might be for payments to corrupt officials or other illegal payments and that neither side wanted any evidence that could be used against them. All black card holders had unlimited credit so the amount withdrawn would never be a problem but ironically the machine only had 150K of US dollars and the ATM issued an alert when it was starting to run out. A cashier noticed the danger and the fact that the card being used was one he'd never seen before and checked with his boss.

The director knew that the black card was special and that one person had recently been taken off the list of authorised users – Carlos Fantoni. But he had forgotten to reprogramme the ATM and now he was in deep shit. He picked up his phone to security and told them to detain anybody operating the furthest cash machine now because there was a robbery in progress. The team were out of the building in just a few minutes and saw a vehicle parked illegally outside the bank which they tried to catch but lost when it went the wrong way round the one-way system.

After 30 minutes of suspense the security team called the director and said the criminals had been driving some kind of highly tuned getaway car and their old Mercedes couldn't keep up. Having thought it through the bank director was quietly grateful they were not caught because that would have revealed his own error and with an outfit like Salimond, he was not sure they would be very understanding. He just decided to do nothing.

Joanne suddenly realised that they had been sitting in the car for ten minutes and no one had found them. They still had their bag of money but they still needed to find its owner, Carlos Fantoni, and Eugene was the only way she could think of to do it. She looked down at the bright green Swatch that Dane had bought for her when they'd met because it matched her eyes. It was 11.30 a.m. and they only had 30 minutes to get back to the cathedral for the meeting.

Dane pressed the starter button and the Jaguar glided away from the curb and turned back to town. This time they both went to the cathedral and it was quite busy. Two elderly ladies in black were lighting candles at the front, a small group of French tourists were being given a tour of the artworks by a local guide. There were around a dozen people scattered around the pews, either praying or just resting out of the hot sun. At first there was no trace of Eugene, Dane went over to the pews by the confessional where they'd met before but there was no sign. So that they didn't stand out too much they both sat down in a pew near the front and waited.

For such a big man, Eugene Morgan moved very quietly and the first awareness they had was when he gently tapped Dane on the shoulder from behind. Dane tried to hide his shock but the fact that he'd jumped up made it a little difficult, he was too tall a man not to stick out. Jo gently pulled him back down into his seat and worried whether Dane might throttle his father. Dane was a gentle man normally but what his father had done to the family brought out the dark side in him. Eugene claimed to be a reformed character but it was obvious that he still moved in some highly dubious circles,

which is why he was in Panama City.
"We need to find out exactly where Carlos Fantoni is and we're not going anywhere until we find him." Jo said with real determination in her voice.
'Keep your voice down... what makes you think, I can help?" Eugene said softly.
"You mentioned him last time and I think you know where he is," she continued.
"Listen, I might know something.. but you guys are already getting noticed by some very dangerous people – I just wish that you go home." Eugene's accent became more Irish the more excited he got.
"Listen.." Dane couldn't quite bring himself to use the word Dad.. "Listen, you say you care, but I don't believe it, but if you do, then just tell us where Fantoni is."
Eugene paused dramatically until he had their total attention. "Fantoni, will be dead in a few hours, they've sent some psycho Englishman to take him out."
"If I believe you and why should I, then we need to find him now."
"No"
"We'll go anyway.. anywhere until we get noticed."
Do you have a four wheel drive?" Eugene asked with an exasperated tone.
Dane nodded.
"Then I'll come with you."
Dane shook his head.
"It's the only way you'll fucking find him." Eugene said more loudly and at least three worshipers muttered words of outrage and looked over. Eugene waved in apology and started to leave the pew, stopping to stoop and cross himself in front of the altar. Marvelling at the power of an Irish education, Dane pulled on Jo's arm and they were forced to stand up and follow.

An hour later the three of them were parked at the back of deserted boatyard at the side of the canal and Dane got the drone out of the Jaguar and started the machine up. Eugene knew that Fantoni's jail was through the gates at the end but didn't know how far down the canal it was. It could be a few yards or many miles because the maps showed nothing and access might have to be by river, he didn't know.

Dane got the four rotor drone buzzing quietly above and they could see themselves on the iPad standing amongst the debris of the yard below. Altering the controls, he moved the machine away from overhead and could see the canal and other boatyards next door to where they were. The resolution was better than he'd expected and gaining altitude, he saw the bright blue and red jumble of boxes that he knew was the Biomuseo building. Closer there were some ships and a canal pilot boat exiting the old canal entrance. Further away he could see enormous grey and blue shapes that must have been mega tankers coming through the much larger Panamax entrance. He remembered that every ship, from the smallest yacht to the new largest tankers had to pay a large toll and carry a pilot. It was no wonder that the canal had a stacking system as sophisticated as the largest airports because the income generated was absolutely staggering.

Dane had to be careful not to be too obvious; drones had been used for terrorist attacks and a naval vessel would have no compunction in shooting it down. Even some larger cargo vessels would have some form of laser defence system to keep drones at bay. So he kept away from the ships and concentrated on the inland side of the canal edge where the jungle was dense and looked for any kind of building. After a while Dane became more adept with the drone and Jo directed him with the iPad on her lap next to him. The drone had left the busy part of the entrance area and was flying parallel to the lake with no buildings visible and endless green jungle. Dane moved the flight path slightly to the right to look for any track which might have been used. He experimented with different heights until he found the best and both of them concentrated intently on the screen. Jo cried out and there it was, a narrow track cut straight through the jungle that had to be man-made.

Eugene had lost interest a while ago and was wandering around the far end of the yard with his mobile clamped to his ear and a worried expression on his face. Interestingly Dane noticed that he had moved over to the gates and was playing with the entrance system. Then Jo grabbed his attention because they had lost the track underneath. It took a few minutes to find it again and then it required total concentration because the jungle was getting dense and they kept on losing the path.

The drone had a range of around 15 miles but it was difficult to estimate how far they'd gone, but it must be around 5 miles. Gaining altitude Dane realised that there was something ahead that could be a clearing in the jungle and maybe some kind of structure poking through the trees and called Jo over. They closed in and realised that the tower was just like the prison towers they used to see in all those Alcatraz movies and it was on the end of a large building partly hidden by undergrowth. Going down they could see an open gate which Dane thought was odd in a prison and another tower. Moving round they could see a block of faded white buildings which could have been the jail itself and the rest of the perimeter wall. There was no sign of life, no vehicles, no people, but some fresh vehicle tracks leading into the jungle, showed that someone had been there recently.

Dane had the drone doing a lazy circuit round the building whilst he and Jo tried to plan their next move. If anything, Eugene was looking more concerned and his pacing up and down at the far side of the car park was getting more frenetic and he kept on wiping his brow nervously. But Dane and Jo had to concentrate on their own situation.

"Do you think it's the right place?" Jo asked the obvious question.
"There's no sign of people and the gates are open so I don't know."
"Let's get really close to the building and see if we can see anything."

Dane nodded and he made the drone get down to roof height where he scanned the top windows and found nothing. Then he moved to a tower hoping to see whether the searchlights were functional and as he went close a figure popped up and pointed some kind of weapon. There was a flash of light and they both instinctively threw themselves back in the seats. The drone controls ceased to work, the picture on the iPad ceased to exist and though Jo tried to reboot it, they both knew it was the end.

Their stunned silence was shattered by Eugene hammering on their car door. Dane buzzed the window down and saw that Eugene's normally florid face was as white as a sheet.
"I've just spoken to someone on the inside I know in Panama City. They've already dismissed the guards and sent an assassin to take out Carlos Fantoni."

Chapter 16

Alexander Brown's career in the British Army was mainly in front line surgical units in Afghanistan and Iran. He had basic training on land vehicles and could drive trucks and even a tank if necessary but he didn't feel at home in boats. The rib with the twin outboards looked the business, it was mat black, powerful and looked as though it could handle seas a lot more demanding than the Canal Zone he was having to travel on but there had been no time to practice. The call from someone from the NSA or CIA that someone was overflying the prison with a drone meant that he had to move his plans forward by 24 hours which was irritating.

The other thing that made it difficult was the instruction to travel at dusk when canal traffic was light and police activity was low. He'd been told to meet someone at a particular grid reference late afternoon on the lake a mile west of the eastern entrances to the canal. The assassin could navigate perfectly well and knew that he could find the rendezvous but was less confident about handling the boat. But 50% of his fee was already in his bank account and Brown had been paid a generous bonus for taking out that idiot Professor Coombes. Considering that Brown would have come to Panama for free anyway, just to keep his 100% success record intact, he decided that he must consider any present difficulties of minor consequence. God Bless America!

The assassin had prepared well. He packed his frock-coat neatly in a backpack and cleaned and sharpened his blade. He then put his wing-collared shirt, tie waistcoat and trousers on and checked himself in the mirror, after all, in his business image was important and he had a superstitious belief that he could only make truly stylish kills whilst wearing the outfit. The only concession he'd made for the trip was a light waterproof camouflage jacket that he wore over the top.

The old Honda with local plates was at the end of the street as promised and he found the keys underneath the seat. It was starting to get cooler, thank God and he'd followed the route he'd been given for half an hour until there were no houses on either side of the road. The old warehouse he'd been told to look for had "Forwarding Agents and Exporters" in faded letters on the gable end. Brown had parked by its gates as instructed and a small guy in a Triumph baseball cap had come out of an office and beckoned for him to follow.

The inside of the warehouse was full of all kinds of goods from crates of Japanese whisky, to white goods, wide screen TV's and even a few large Harley-Davidson motorcycles shrink-wrapped in plastic. Brown had little doubt that few of them had come through official channels. He'd followed the guy past them all until they reached the far side and he'd pushed open a small door. In what remained of the day, he could see a small wharf with petrol pumps and a couple of boats which is how he now found himself in the black inflatable listening to the guy talking in broken English about the controls just as the light started to fade. The guy passed on a grid reference of the prison where Fantoni was being held and gave him a portable sat nav. The man said that the guards had now left and the distance by water was about 5 miles.

Brown stepped into the rib and felt extremely uneasy as it rocked from side to side. He clambered forward and sat in the high racing type seat and pressed the starter button. The twin Honda outboards roared into life and the guy pointed to the throttles by his right side and pushed them gently forward as he tried to move the boat out of the quay and into open water. The rib came to a juddering halt and Brown realised that he hadn't cast off at the rear. The guy in the baseball hat ran back, untied and threw the lines into the stern and watched him with barely concealed distain as he tried to manoeuvre the vessel out.

The assassin didn't like losing face at anything and knew that only one thing was going to improve his foul temper. As much as he wanted to go back to the wharf and wipe the smile off the face of the boat man with his blade, he would keep all his righteous anger ready for his next client Mr Fantoni.

Dane and Jo knew that they had to find Carlos Fantoni quickly and pushed open the gates pointed out by Eugene. Though they had seen the track and the prison from the drone they only had a rough idea how far away it was and they were losing daylight fast. The way looked easy to find at first but the jungle started to close in on both sides pretty quickly. The Jaguars lights were good but the surface of the track was treacherous and judging by the paint on one tree, another vehicle had slid into a trunk fairly recently after misjudging a rock fall a mile or so in. But Dane was an experienced four-wheel drive user and kept the pace to around 30 mph.
"What's this?" Asked Eugene, picking up the heavy carrier bag from the floor. "Jeezus," he exclaimed as the hundred dollar notes spilled out.
"Not bloody yours." Said Dane, nearly sliding into a ditch as he

realised what his father had found." Put it back."

"Alright son, don't panic, I have seen money before you know. Not normally as much as this, though."

"Put it fucking back, or I'll throw you out!" Dane jammed on the brakes and turned to glare at his father.

"Listen, both of you, shut up, or you'll get us killed – Eugene pass that bag over here." Jo shouted in exasperation.

Eugene reluctantly picked up the loose notes and put them in the bag before passing it to the front where Jo tried to hide it under the seat without really succeeding. Eugene looked longingly over to where she was stowing the money and Jo knew that given half a chance, he would be very tempted to do a runner.

The car was at a standstill and Dane buzzed the window down. He still couldn't get his head round the fact the I-Pace was electric and totally silent. They could hear all kinds of jungle noises: the cicadas were starting their rough rattle and in the distance they could hear howler monkeys calling to each other. A moth or insect the size of a man's hand tried to fly in and the heat from the outside started to become oppressive so Dane closed the window and took a deep breath and looked over at Jo with an understanding look in his eye.
"Ok, let's get on."

The tyres slipped for a while and it looked as though they might get bogged down but Dane had learned how to drive on old Land Rovers and knew how to rock the vehicle back and forward until it came free. The power of the Jaguar was astounding and wasted on a track like this but it had high ground clearance and clever four wheel drive which is all you needed as long as you kept an eye on the track surface for logs or rocks. After half an hour of slow driving the trees were so close on both sides that the big green leaves were brushing the vehicle and Dane had to avoid more substantial branches in case they smashed the windscreen.

Visibility was now low. It felt like darkness had fallen as the forest canopy met above so you couldn't see the sky overhead. Mist was seeping out of the trees reducing visibility even further as the halogen headlights tended to reflect back in his eyes. Dane stopped for a while as a large ape or monkey looked at him curiously from a tree ahead and crossed in a languorous overhand swing that seemed to be absolutely effortless. He took a sip of water from the metal bottle that had been given free by the hotel Tantalo to reduce plastics and rubbed his eyes to clear them.

"Have you thought what you'll do if you find Fantoni, son?" asked a voice from the back.

Dane realised that he'd not really thought that far ahead and so Joanne answered first. "We need to get him back to the states so he can expose this Greenwatch scandal."

"And how are you going to do that when the CIA and just about everyone else wants him out of the way or dead?" Eugene asked. The truth of what Eugene was saying started to sink in. They looked at each other in slight panic and realised they had rushed into this whole exercise with no plan as to what might happen if they succeeded.

"Dane, put this number into your contact list." They both got out their mobiles and put in the long number that Eugene read out to them. "There's no way you'll ever get him out using airports or by road, the CIA or NSA have technology that you wouldn't believe. That number is for a man I know who has been known to do a little people smuggling. It'll cost you, but it's the only way you'll get anyone out."

Whilst they were digesting that logic, Dane pressed the starter button and all the screens lit up like some kind of entertainment console. He gently pressed the accelerator and the Jaguar glided forward, silent apart from the noise of the big knobbly tyres on the stones of the track. He looked at the sat nav screen and realised that he had travelled 3.6 miles. He looked at the battery indicator and realised that he only had 60% charge left but had no real idea what that meant in terms of range. The guy in the garage had thought that there was little chance of them running out of power during the short time he'd wanted the car but no-one had expected that to include an hour on rough terrain and a high speed car chase in Panama City.

They travelled in silence for the next ten minutes and only had to stop once to move a branch that had fallen across the track. Dane got out and the humidity and heat hit him like a blow, but he managed to move the obstacle to one side noticing that there was more insect life under the leaves than he'd ever seen in one place before. He shuddered and got back into the car, clearing the bugs off the screen with the wipers and was astounded that anyone could live in a place so infested with things that bite like this place.

The screen was showing 5.6 miles travel distance and Jo thought that she could see some sort of building ahead. Unbelievably Eugene was on his telephone and was talking urgently in low tones hunched up on the back seat. As the SUV coasted to a halt, they could see one of the towers that they'd seen from the drone and as it had been shot down, they needed to be careful. Eugene had been told that the guards had left a few hours ago by boat and they hadn't met anyone on the track but nothing was certain. They also knew that an assassin was on his way to kill Fantoni, so the situation was doubly risky.

They all got quietly out of the car and Eugene came round and handed Dane a small hand gun.
"That's a spare, but it's fully loaded, so be careful. I'm going to the river to meet someone so don't wait for me if I'm not back because I'll return by the river. It will be a lot more comfortable than your fuckin driving Dane – see you son."

Dane felt uneasy with the gun but had been in war zones enough to know how to use it. He still didn't have any trust for his father and got Jo to check that the money bag was there before he locked the car and saw Eugene walking down a path that led away from the prison towards the water.

The assassin had taken around 10 minutes to get the hang of the boat and got quite confident with the throttles and steering. The problem was that full throttle was incredibly noisy and the rib bows went so far in the air that he couldn't see ahead. He'd settled on about half throttle which was frustratingly slow but even with reasonable eyesight he'd found it difficult otherwise to avoid the sunken logs and weed that threatened to tangle his propellers or capsize him. In the end he moved about 10 yards away from the bank and the going had become a lot easier.

After about an hour of travelling his sat nav glowed green in the dark and he realised that he had about a mile to go and better prepare himself for action. He took off the camouflage outer jacket and pulled out the frock-coat from his back pack. It was slightly difficult to put it on in a slowly moving boat but once he'd managed, he felt so much better.

This was his uniform, his working clothes that he'd worn during fifteen kills and which, with the sword stick, had earned him thousands of dollars. When he thought back to the early days, it was embarrassing he was so lacking in creativity, but this kill was going to be his pièce de résistance, his masterpiece. He was so absorbed by his own thoughts that he woke with a jolt when the sat nav bleeped. Looking to the right he could see an old landing stage and turned towards it, throttling right back and looking for somewhere to tie up.

With a certain amount of bumping in the semi darkness Brown managed to get the rib parallel with the platform and to tie the rope round a kind of hook, which held, but the rest of the boat began to swing out and away. He experimented with the power, direction and steering until he finally got the front of the rib tied off too. Then he switched off the engines, put his stick carefully on the landing stage and stepped out of the boat and on to the old quay, which was reassuringly solid apart from bits where rot had made it dangerous.

Alexander Brown vowed to himself that he would avoid future contracts with a marine content and restrict his work to dry land where he could work more confidently. He shone his torch down the path he knew led to the prison and started to walk carefully heading south. He disliked the jungle and brushed carefully through the big wet leaves that tried to block his way and which could hide spiders, snakes and all kinds of killers. The path was easy to follow and had obviously been cleared recently but the undergrowth was already starting to take back control.

Brown thought with regret that this place was so remote that very few people were ever likely to see his handiwork. But at least the way was clear and his progress down the path was good until a large figure carrying what appeared to be a large Steyre 9mm handgun stepped into the torchlight.
"I'm from the CIA, Mr Brown and I'd like you to stop exactly where you are." The Irish accent was not exactly typical of the Central Intelligence Agency but the gun was convincing.

Joanne was concerned about Eugene's departure but knew they couldn't delay with the assassin due at any moment. Dane was glad to be rid of him because he still didn't trust him an inch and with a hundred grand in a carrier bag close by, that was true in spades. The fact that Eugene knew so much showed that he was still close to the dark forces involved in all this and Dane thought that the minute things got tough he would revert to type and betray them. Jo wasn't as hard about him but knew there was no time to waste and that Eugene could probably look after himself.

They walked past an old concrete gate house which looked like it hadn't been occupied for decades, indeed the whole prison appeared like something out of the last century. In the torch light, they could see part of the walls had crumbled with a giant vine or creeper growing through the cracks.

There were numerous tyre tracks round the yard, but no vehicles there now thank God. They almost tripped over the drone they'd hired and wondered just how they were going to explain the neat round hole through its centre. Dane put it to one side to collect later and they moved silently to a door in the main building that was possibly the main entrance. It had obviously been used recently because there was no dust or vegetation over it. They tried the big metal handle which turned with a creak and they found themselves in a hall which was surrounded on two sides by glass fronted offices that looked as though they were abandoned years ago.

Visibility with just the Maglite torch was getting difficult but they couldn't delay. Jo looked around for any kind of illumination and tried an old light switch on the wall. This fell off with a clatter of loose plaster which scared the daylights out of them both. In the fading beam of the torch they moved further into the building and almost fell over a portable generator and battery pack. Dane looked at this carefully and soon had it running, which made a certain amount of a noise but illuminated a line of bulbs strung down the corridor.

They both felt incredibly vulnerable because any remaining guards would be alerted and anyone searching for Fantoni would also know they were there. But at least they knew that their suspicions had been correct and someone had been here in the last few days. As they followed the bulbs down the corridor, they passed an office full of rubbish that had obviously been used for cooking and living because there were empty water bottles and food cartons everywhere. They looked into a shower which still had water dripping on to the tiled floor and kept moving until they could see the last bulb at the end.

There was one metal door with a spy window in it. The door was shut but it had a large metal key still in the lock. The spy window was clean and Dane looked through. Inside he could see a man with white hair and a black beard on a bed, looking up at him with terror in his eyes.

The assassin was sitting down with his hands on his head as the old Irish fart had told him. The guy was overweight, middle aged and if he really was from the CIA then the agency was having a serious recruitment problem. But the gun was steady and he knew that it had around 9 bullets in the magazine so it deserved respect. One of the problems with the assassin's modus operandi was the fact that he always killed by blade and never carried a gun. It just wouldn't be the gentlemanly thing to do.

But the Irish guy kept talking nervously about the people he knew in Panama who were probably the people who had employed him. He mentioned the CIA, the NSA and at least half a dozen people whose names he'd never heard of, who were probably the cream of the criminal fraternity. In the end, Brown seriously worried that the guy was trying to bore him into submission and then his mobile rang.

It only needed one moment of distraction from the Irishman. Whilst he looked for his phone, Brown picked up his stick, withdrew the blade and pushed it deep into the man's chest without even having to stand up. His victim didn't even seem to have noticed what trouble he was in until a spurt of deep red blood sprayed out of his front and he seemed to lose the ability to move. He made an impressive gurgling noise in his throat and fell forward.

The assassin was disgusted with himself. The killing had no elegance, no finesse and gave him no pleasure at all. He threw the gun into the undergrowth, pulled the body out of the way and set off down the path. After a few minutes pushing his way through the undergrowth he found the path down to the prison and picked up speed. His employers had said that it would take only a few minutes to find the prison but he was hampered by the darkness. He hesitated briefly because he thought he could hear voices below, which was concerning as he'd been told that the guards would be long gone by now. The other strange thing was that he thought he could see lights down through the trees.

He loosened the blade in its container and carefully pushed downhill through the last few leaves on the path where he could see the side a large concrete building which was obviously the prison. He had a thrill of anticipation as he imagined what he was going to do to Mr Fantoni but as he moved round the wall a large SUV burst out of the courtyard with lights blazing and blasted up a track into the trees. Within seconds the vehicle had been swallowed by the jungle and Brown knew instinctively that his quarry had gone and felt a deep pang of disappointment.

Chapter 17

Jo had tried Eugene a few times on his mobile before they left the prison and got no response. Dane was not concerned after a lifetime of hating his father, it was going to take a lot more than a few hours of good behaviour to change his attitude and Eugene had said he was going back by river anyway. They had Carlos Fantoni, which was the main thing and they had to get him out of the jungle and away from the prison as fast as possible.

The big xenon headlights cut through the night well and the mists had cleared, so they just had branches and flying insects to worry about. Dane had done plenty of travelling but he'd never encountered a place with so many large spiders, flying insects the size of birds and other assorted wildlife. Thank goodness they were in a vehicle.

Fantoni had been scared to death when they'd arrived. He was an intelligent guy and he'd been expecting someone would be coming to eliminate him. The fact that Jo was there reassured him a little as he couldn't imagine a tall, slim, beautiful woman would be in the assassination business. When she mentioned the work she'd done as an environmental journalist and that she was the daughter of Professor Li, Fantoni started to believe their story.

Fantoni was anxious to start calling a few people, especially his girlfriend in London but Dane said they needed to be incredibly cautious and get to a place of safety first. At this stage it was best to assume that everyone was a threat including the US government and Salimond. On that basis, it was probably unsafe to take Carlos back to their hotel and an unkempt man with a wild black beard in a Guantanamo style orange overall would be hard to hide. Jo remembered that there was a slightly downmarket motel not far from the industrial estate they had hired the drone from, and reckoned it was worth a look.

It took an hour to get back to the boatyard where they accessed the track and it was totally dark when they opened the gates and looked round. They were incredibly careful as there could have been an army hiding in the shadows of the building but they pushed on and out of the area picking up speed as they hit the main road. Dane looked in the mirror and there was no tell-tale sign of headlights or vehicles following them.

Captain Morgan's Retreat was the name on the front of the building and it looked like the sort of place that rented rooms by the hour rather than the day. It was late but Dane went in and was told there was only one room left and it was the bridal suite. Dane asked the going rate per night and was given an outrageous figure. Dane told him to fuck off in his best Anglo-Irish and started to walk out. In the end the guy agreed to rent out two adjoining rooms for three nights at a reasonable rate for cash and Dane walked away with two sets of keys.

The rooms were at the far end of the single story building and there were parking spaces directly outside. He parked the Jaguar and smuggled Carlos in whilst he was shielded by the car door and got him settled in the bedroom. All their gear was at the hotel, so they just put Dane's backpack and camera in the other room and left the bag of money in the car. They hadn't eaten for hours but there were the garish lights of an all night truck stop further along the main road and Dane pulled in alongside the Kenwoods, Fords and other big rigs parked alongside a long low cafe. Dane couldn't believe how busy it was but managed to order some pizzas and coffees to take out despite the language difficulties.

Sitting on the bed with Jo and Carlos Fantoni seemed strange when they hardly knew him but he ripped into the Margarita pizza like someone who hadn't been fed for weeks. The pizzas were surprisingly good and the coffee would have kept Rip Van Winkle awake for hours. After a few minutes they all felt considerably better but Fantoni looked exhausted.
"We have a small confession to make." Dane needed to clear his conscience.
"What's that."
"This whole thing started because our shoes got mixed up at the Grosvenor and I found this." Dane held up the black card.
Fantoni looked surprised. "I wondered what had happened to that."
Dane coughed. "Jo and I tried it at the Panama bank and ended up with this." Dane pushed the carrier bag of money over.
Fantoni started laughing, almost hysterically and didn't stop. He tried to talk and couldn't get the words out through laughter. "How much is there?" he eventually got out.
"About a hundred thousand dollars." Jo said.
"Well, you could have asked for a million, but you wouldn't have been able to carry it." Fantoni said with a further chuckle.

Fantoni went on to explain what the black card was, how he'd been asked to use it for bribes in London and how he'd hated everything about it. He tried to explain why he'd got involved in Greenwatch but they could see that he was running out of energy. Dane stopped him and said he should lock himself in, **put a do not disturb sign on the outside of the door and get some sleep.** They would be back in daylight with some basic supplies and a plan.

After seeing him put the sign outside the door, the two decided to go back to the Hotel Tantalo where all their gear was and try to act as normal. They parked the Jaguar a block away and walked to the hotel where they had a key to the night entrance and went up to their room. It felt as though they'd been away for weeks but it was only 24 hours and yet so much had happened. They had become a little paranoid about being overheard and were very guarded in their conversation but decided to get some sleep whilst they could and get up early.

The alarm went off four hours later and it was light outside. They needed to get Fantoni some clothes and toiletries so he didn't stand out from the crowd. In the end they found a hypermarket on the edge of the city and Jo got T-Shirts, underwear, sports socks and a black Adidas track suit but wondered about shoes. With a flash of genius, Dane remembered that he was a similar shoe size to himself, and got him a pair of trainers that were in the sale. Shaving kit, toothbrush and other basics they got from the other side of the store. Dane noticed that Jo was paying with hundred dollar notes.
"Where did that come from?"
"Where do you think?" Jo answered with a wink.

They were in a hurry to get back to Fantoni and worried he might have absconded during the night. The sign was still on the door and he eventually answered after checking them out from behind the curtain. He asked again to phone his girlfriend and Dane said that he needed his permission to use some of the cash they'd got with the card because it would be traceable if they used credit cards.
"Use it – use it all, I don't want it, but please get me a phone." Fantoni pleaded.
Jo gave him the clothes and the toiletries and they suggested he got changed and cleaned up whilst they ran a few more errands and got phones.

Dane took the bag of money and first went to the drone hire place where the guy wasn't impressed by the drone's condition but managed to live with it when Dane handed him a few hundred dollar bills. Dane told the assistant that he'd been trying to catch out a guy who'd been screwing his wife and the drone had got too close to the action. The guy had nodded sympathetically and pocketed the cash.

He was still in the Jaguar and despite being covered in fresh mud from the jungle, it was in far better shape than he'd expected. But it was too visible to continue with for much longer and Dane emailed Malagariga the owner saying that it was a great vehicle but he'd drop it into the showroom later when he'd arranged a replacement. Being the wheeler-dealer that he was, the boss said he had a few high mileage used vehicles out back he would hire out for cash but could Dane take another shot of him with a special Bentley Continental he had just acquired.

Dane got a few smart phones for cash that he thought were untraceable and went over to the motel where he passed them to Jo and they exchanged numbers. He asked her to keep them secret from Fantoni and said that he was going to take the Jag back, explaining about the deal. Before he left, he put a thousand dollars in his pocket and gave the bag with the rest of the money to Jo.

Whilst the light was good Dane took a photograph of Jose Malagariga in front of a beautiful
1958 Bentley S1 Continental with bodywork by HJ Mulliner. This was such a huge departure from the guy's obsession with Jaguar and Ferrari that Dane couldn't resist asking about it. Malagariga winked and said mysteriously that not everyone knew the value of old cars.

Malagariga looked proudly at the shots Dane had emailed and asked him how long he needed a car for. Dane guessed a week but said that he was broke and couldn't afford anything exotic as he was waiting for another job to come in. The boss nodded understandingly and Dane ended up with a Toyota Hi-Lux diesel with crew cab and about 100K miles on the clock. This vehicle couldn't be better, there were dozens of them around, it had local plates and had generated absolutely no paperwork at all.

Dane fired up the Toyota which was reassuringly noisy and clattered out of the lot waving to Malagariga as he went. He went back to the Hotel Tantalo and loaded their clothes and gear into their cases, which he carried out and round to where he'd parked the Toyota. He then went back to the hotel and paid cash, thanking the manager most warmly for his hospitality and tipping him royally. As the guy had seen Jo arrested by armed police, he probably thought that they were some kind of criminals and warned them that a couple of

Americans had been asking after them earlier and he hadn't liked the look of them. Dane thanked him and said that if they came back to tell them they were travelling on to Brazil.

The Captain Morgan Retreat didn't look any better in daylight but Carlos Fantoni did. He'd shaved off the beard and binned the orange overalls and showered. The track suit and shoes fitted well and it was only the distinctive mane of white hair that made him stand out. The big TV screen on the wall was on a 24 hour news channel and Fantoni was distracted by coverage of the US President at a convention. The sub titles summed things up in English.

'The President was in confident form yesterday at the Republican convention. With only a few months to go and now ten points ahead in most polls, he can afford to be.'

Fantoni looked incredibly angry.
"We've got to stop him, he can't be trusted with Greenwatch. Please give me a phone."
"Who would you phone?" Jo asked gently.
"I don't know.... someone in the US press.... I don't know." Fantoni answered lamely.
"No-one is going to believe you but I've got a better idea." Jo said softly.

Over the next half an hour Jo explained about her Corporate Li's blog and how she'd used it anonymously to get difficult stories over in the past. Carlos Fantoni hadn't really got involved in social media other than a brief time when he was at university to keep up with girlfriends. He was fascinated by the way that Jo had used it to provoke the US establishment and saw the blogs she'd sent after his arrest and about the Presidential 'Breathe Easy' campaign which depended on Greenwatch. Jo suggested that Carlos do a video explaining what had happened to him, how he'd escaped and what the problems with Greenwatch were. Over the next hour they worked on a rough script and edited it down to a brief but dramatic statement that should really shake things up.

Dane listened patiently to them working on the video but had to interrupt. "Listen you guys, I'm sure that the video will really work but we need to work out what we do afterwards."
"What do you mean?" Jo asked. "We don't have to worry about the NDA's we signed years ago because this is a different subject."
"Maybe you're right but I'll still get thrown out of the US, that's not what I mean."
"Ok what then?" Jo asked.
"I'm talking about Mr Fantoni. The US or Salimond or somebody has

already tried to kill him and after that video he will be an even bigger threat – we can't just take him out through an airport, can we?"

Carlos and Jo looked thoughtful and tried to think of any options which didn't involve official borders and failed. Sadly, neither Dane or Jo had any contacts who might provide false passports and Eugene, who probably would know such people, still wasn't answering his mobile.
"I still want to do the video now, whatever the risk." Carlos interjected. "But who's going to see it?"
"We can't guarantee any of the nationals will pick it up, but we'll do our best." Said Jo, clearing the table and asking Dane to set up the camera.

Dane drew the curtains and checked the background had nothing that gave any hint of where they were including a couple of prints of pirate ships that someone thought gave the Captain Morgan's Retreat a real nautical feel. Carlos Fantoni sat down behind the table and started his speech.
"My name is Carlos Fantoni and I have been illegally imprisoned in Panama by the United States. Until recently I was in charge of Greenwatch which as you know is meant to identify air pollution in your cities. Sadly, I found out that some people were using Greenwatch to falsify the results and tried to report this to the authorities. Before I could do this, I was kidnapped by the US Environmental Agency and smuggled out of the country. Luckily I have been rescued by environmental campaigners and am trying to get back."

Carlos continued for another few minutes and then finished up with a plea for the US President and UK Prime Minister to stop using Greenwatch until someone with total honesty could take over from Salimond. He also warned everyone about Wolf Bayer, the Chief Executive of Salimond who he thought was totally unscrupulous and prepared to kill thousands of people rather than lose profit.
Dane whistled in admiration at the way Fantoni had exposed all the guilty parties and got the message across. Jo would intercut with past footage of Greenwatch on the streets and Dane's shots of the arrest in Boston to get the final video finished and posted in a couple of hours.

A few minutes later, Carlos Fantoni asked for a telephone. Remembering that he'd been desperate to make a call and concerned about security, Dane asked who he wanted to call.
"A woman called Diane Fallow who's a journalist in London - she

was the one who told me about the Greenwatch scandal in the first place."

"Do you remember her number?"

"Yes, she and I were... lovers."

Carlos picked up the phone and dialled the number and got an unobtainable tone.

"Did you include the international code?" Jo asked helpfully.

"Of course, I was always calling her from abroad."

"Who does she work for, perhaps she's at work" Dane added, looking at his watch.

"The Financial Times in London."

"I've done some work for them in the past, I'll get the number for you." Dane looked down his contact list and dialled a number, putting it on speaker and handing it to Carlos. There was an audible series of clicks as the call went through.

"Financial Times, how can I help?" A very English female voice answered.

"Diane Fallow in features." Carlos asked.

There was a noticeable hesitation and a voice answered.

"Newsroom, can I help?"

"Diane Fallow, please."

"Who's that speaking?"

"It's Carlos Fantoni – I'm a friend of Diane but I've been away abroad for quite some time."

"Just a minute, I'll transfer you to the editor."

"Mr Fantoni, I remember Diane mentioning your name. I'm really, really, sorry... Diane was murdered a few weeks ago."

Chapter 18

People smuggling is a growth business. Everywhere in the world there are people who feel deprived or threatened wanting to reach places they feel are privileged and safe. And most of the places don't want them unless they're rich or geniuses. Thousands of people want to get into Europe and thousands want to get into the US and some employ smugglers. There are plenty of people wanting to get into North America but not many want to leave from Panama.

The guy who had been on Eugene Morgan's contact list specialised in getting people into the US by giving them a completely new identity and was incredibly expensive. Dane beat him down to $20,000, $10k now and $10k when he reached the US. When the smuggler asked where he wanted to go in specific terms, Dane answered Boston because at least there Jo had family connections. The guy said that might take a little time to organise but he'd ring over the next few days.

As everyone knows, the Panama Canal connects two oceans, the Pacific and the Caribbean and saves thousands of miles of sea travel. Thousands of boats of all kinds of sizes pass through and everyone has to carry an official Panama pilot and go through the relatively small locks that take the vessels from ocean level to canal level in around 30 minutes.

Juan Arias had a good family background in Panama and great connections but had never made enough money in politics or the military to pay for his preferred lifestyle. Then a few years ago he managed to get a friend on the run from the gangs out of Panama and into Canada and made a lot of cash. Arias was a modest man and his two bedroomed apartment, in the centre of town, was seen as extremely unfashionable by many of his friends as was his 12 year old Toyota. But his property in the US and his 50ft Sunseeker Predator in Spain was considerably more impressive and locals there thought of him as some kind of dotcom millionaire.

Arias was 30 years old, tall and had such a permanent tan that he looked Spanish but was born and bred local. He had a small office in Panama and generally dressed in a modest suit and most people just thought of him as a businessman. When asked what he did he sometimes answered that he organised tours, which was at least partly true.

One of Juan Arias' uncles was a licensed Panama Pilot and he occasionally helped him when boats of interest were passing through, so his face was known by the tight group of people who operated there. With any boat, going through the system, the regular captains were used to seeing four or five guys in the yellow hi-viz jackets who moved from point to point working the ropes and clipboards like a corps of ballet dancers in Swan Lake. What they all did was a mystery but as long as they got through quickly that was all that mattered.

The small Holland-Sweden Line clipper had 500 guests and 600 crew and was aimed at those wealthy people who'd been disgusted by the mega cruise liners with thousands of guests where you never got to meet anybody like yourself. The ship was based on an early tea clipper design with four masts and a long narrow hull which fitted through the old canal entrance easily. The sails were only used when the wind was right and the big diesel engines did the work most of the time but the sails were majestic when hoisted and made everyone feel like genuine seafarers.

The clipper specialised in going to destinations that the big liners didn't and this trip included exclusive destinations in South America, though the Panama Canal and on to Cuba, Bahamas, the deep south of the US and then Boston. Its guests thought that they were far more eco-friendly than those without sails and revelled in the fact they were not going to the standard large cruise destinations like Venice or Dubrovnik, which had been ruined by mass tourism.

The boat had an overnight stop in Boston where guests disembarked and given cultural tours of the old city and New England plus an exclusive dinner cooked by a French Creole chef. For obvious reasons Juan Arias thought this ship was perfect to transport his next client and had already discussed terms on the phone with the Filipino steward he'd dealt with on a previous trip and warned him there would be an extra member of the crew who would join the ship when the pilot boarded at one of the locks.

Dane and Jo had been trying to console Carlos Fantoni for days after he'd heard about the murder of his girlfriend Diane Fallow. When he talked to her editor it just got worse. The story that she had been killed by the man she accused of Greenwatch corruption and that drugs were the source of his money, just dragged him down as did the tabloid media coverage of the murder he found online.

Then after a while he started to doubt the truth of the story in the UK press as too many things didn't add up and he knew a bribe had been paid to Duckley because he'd been involved in the process. He also knew that the US guy who'd interviewed him in prison had been desperate for him not to mention that Greenwatch could be manipulated. Finally, there was the fact that the inventor of Greenwatch had told Joanne the results could be falsified but had been killed before he could be recorded. Disturbingly, everyone who tried to blow the whistle on Greenwatch was dead and by now those wanting to keep its secrets would know that he hadn't been killed. To say he was in grave danger if he stayed would be the understatement of the century.

In the end, Dane had phoned the guy Eugene said could get people out of the country and negotiated the fee but that was a couple of days ago. Eugene himself had gone completely out of contact and Dane suspected he'd done what he did every time things became difficult, which was to disappear. The smuggler answered the phone in Spanish but changed to English when Eugene's name was mentioned. The phone was on speaker and it took ten minutes to explain their needs and for the guy to respond with his requirements which included photographs, details of nationality and all the other information a false passport needed.

The three of them looked at each other in the motel room and checked through the list. After a few minutes deliberation with the phone on mute, they worked out how to supply everything needed. Then the guy mentioned the cost and Dane had the good sense to barter because it was an outrageous figure. Eventually they agreed on a figure that would knock a large hole in the dollars they had left from the Panama Bank black card, but it didn't seem to matter to Carlos as it was extremely dirty money and would be good for it to be used for a good cause.

The wait was tedious and the sitting around in the tacky motel room was unpleasant, especially for Carlos who had barely been out. More importantly the chance of someone finding them increased every day and Carlos knew that if he didn't get back to the US soon, then his chance of stopping the Presidential re-election campaign and exploitation of Greenwatch was zero.

The video-blog he'd done had achieved plenty of hits but hadn't stopped the momentum of the re-election campaign one bit. Carlos needed to be there, live in the US, being interviewed on TV - then he might achieve something. And Carlos knew that he owed it to

Diane Fallow, who'd given her life to exposing truth, to make it happen.

Carlos had nearly blown it all a couple of hours ago. He was bored, stir crazy and Dane and Jo were out. He grabbed a few dollars and quietly opened the door of the room for the first time in daylight and stepped out. It was about 10.00 o'clock and the autumn sun was hot and blinding as he looked up the busy road. He could see the sun reflecting off the long low buildings across the road and decided to run gently along the carriageway until he found somewhere he could have a juice or a coffee. He stretched his legs a little and realised how unfit he'd become since his tennis days. But he could still run and as he ran further and further up the side of the road, he started to loosen up and feel just a little more human.

The trucks were a pain, absolutely huge interstate wagons and trailers that nearly blew him off his feet as they passed at maximum cruising speed. The hard shoulder was unpleasant too with glass bottles, cans and the occasional roadkill to avoid. So, at the next intersection Carlos turned left on the plain and within minutes was re-entering the jungle on a road that was turning into a track. Ahead was a burnt-out car with a couple of trees growing through it and behind that a shanty with a guy sitting on a rocking chair in the shade with what appeared to be a shotgun or rifle across his knees.

Carlos slowed gently and tried to look casual as he tied his laces and stretched his knees. He couldn't help noticing, that parked on the far side of the shed was a new Lexus 4x4 that didn't look as though it belonged to the shack.

It took a few minutes to run back to the main road and Carlos was hypersensitive to any sound, especially the sound of a big engine starting behind him or a shotgun being loaded. Luckily all he heard was the raucous caw of parrots from the trees and the drone of the insects. As he got back to the main highway it was all drowned out by the constant roar of the trucks and Carlos realised that he'd been away from the hotel for an hour and taken too big a risk. He kept his head down on the way back and increased speed so that by the time he got back his heart was hammering and he was covered in sweat. Dane and Jo were not back so he had chance to shower and change before he heard the noise of the Toyota pick-up returning.

The people smuggler had been in touch with them and a suitable boat was due through the canal tomorrow, so Carlos had to get enough supplies together for a week and only had a backpack to keep them in. The passport was delivered and Carlos Fantoni was now Juan Lopez, a Spaniard who was normally resident in Madrid. His Spanish was perfect, so the nationality stated was no problem, but Fantoni would have preferred to know more about his homeland, which he'd only visited once. His command of languages was impressive and the smugglers could have chosen one of a dozen other nationalities and Carlos could have managed. But his native Peruvian was too unusual, there were too few people travelling on the cruises of his nationality and he would stand out too much.

His appearance was more difficult to deal with. He looked like an Inca from some old painting and his shock of white hair made him even more conspicuous. So Jo got some hair clippers from the store and ceremoniously got to work on Fantoni's head in front of the bedroom mirror. She piled the hair into a plastic bag for dumping later and they looked at the new man in the mirror. Jo was no hairdresser and she'd eventually had to clip, layer by layer until it was effectively what was called a 'number 2' in Europe or a crop everywhere else.

Dane thought that Carlos looked pretty good. More like an athlete than a thug, more like a guru than a businessman, but at least he wouldn't have any problems with his hair whilst he was on his sea trip. Carlos was apparently going to be hidden somewhere in the clipper and not be visible but they thought that he still needed to look as though he was crew in case he was seen by accident. Temperatures at this time of year were still warm but there was always the chance of a tropical storm so he needed some extra clothing. In the end Carlos insisted on accompanying Dane when they went to the outdoor store and bought his own gear. In the end the dark jeans, heavy duty boots, white T-Shirts, insulated gilet and black Berghaus waterproof jacket fitted in well with most groups and the knitted woollen hat was worn by outdoor workers everywhere. The heavier clothing would be worn on the transfer leaving the backpack for underwear, toiletries, water bottle, survival rations and his remaining money. Dane travelled pretty light himself and approved, just suggesting that he put in a mobile phone and cheap radio too.

When they returned to the hotel, the three discussed what they needed to do before Carlos departed. They decided not to do any more videos but Jo did a few more written blogs, mentioning Greenwatch, Carlos Fantoni and the President which she knew would keep Washington on edge. Everything seemed to be going to plan but then Carlos heard a big engine outside the motel and peeped out through the shutters. What he saw was a big Lexus 4x4 cruising down the length of the motel car park with two guys peering into the windows as they passed. He was sure that it was the same as the one he'd seen outside the shanty and knew he had to tell Dane and Jo about the run. They noticed his alarm and listened when he admitted he'd gone for a jog and also looked out of the room for the Lexus, but it had roared off.

Juan Arias dressed early in the morning in the outfit he wore whenever he worked down at the canal. Most of his gear was dark working clothes but the most important elements were the hi-viz waistcoat with Panama Canal Authority stamped on the back and the lanyard with his photograph and licence number on an official badge. The clipper was making an early transit and his uncle had warned him that he needed to be down at the locks by 6.00 a.m. with his guest.

Arias may have been a smuggler but he had very few connections with the criminal gangs in Panama City. But no one could have been ignorant of the vast manhunt that was going on for Fantoni. Vast rewards were being offered by one of the largest gangs and also by a US agency that Arias suspected must be NSA, CIA or one of the other shadowy organisations that operated illegally in this part of the world. Arias wasn't tempted as both parties had a habit of terminating anyone who was stupid enough to take their money. Another reason was tennis. Arias was a keen amateur player and he'd seen Fantoni play years ago in the Central American Cup and recognised his genius. The thought that a player of his skill would be killed by the mob or the spooks was horrible and Arias was determined to get him out of the country safely.

Arias had googled Fantoni once he'd recognised the photograph and seen that he'd been behind Greenwatch, a device dedicated to cleaning up cities, which was a mission that Arias strongly believed in. Panama City was almost unbearable to walk in and he knew that his parents wore masks against the pollution even for short walks.

It was barely light when Arias met his client in the carpark of the transport cafe just up the road from the motel. It was a good place to meet as vehicles were coming and going all the time at this time of the day, and they didn't stand out.

He didn't recognise the Peruvian at first as his hair had been cropped and his hair with the premature white streak had always been memorable even when he was a kid. But peering into the back of the Toyota he started to recognise his Indian looks and nodded to the other two occupants in the vehicle. The tall European guy gave him the required amount of money in a bag and Arias passed over a hi-viz waistcoat and badge to Fantoni that were identical to those worn by himself. Fantoni had a whispered conversation with the other two and got out of the Toyota. He quickly crossed the few yards that separated it from Arias' Hyundai and pulled himself into its front seat.

Juan Arias looked over at the man in his passenger seat and noticed that he was quietly crying and wondered what terrors he'd been subjected to over the last few weeks. He said nothing to him for ten minutes, just concentrating on the drive down to the Canal Zone. As he got closer, he couldn't resist mentioning the game he'd seen Fantoni play and the man's face lit up with the memory. As they got closer, he concentrated on instructions for the transfer and gave Fantoni a list of do's and don'ts for the voyage that was almost as complete as those given out to official passengers.

In the end the plan worked well. The clipper was unusual with its four masts and associated rigging and longer than many, so it seemed natural for more members of the canal staff to be involved. The first officer on the vessel had been told that an apprentice would be coming on board as well as the pilot and they had good natured banter about the quality of young trainees that was universal. Fantoni looked the part and had been told to go aft checking ropes as he went and he would be met by a steward by the canvas roof that covered the crew rest area.

Before his eyes adjusted to the darkness, from under the awning a brown arm pulled him sideways and he found himself being led down some stairs, through a few doors and down a narrow corridor. He never really saw the steward clearly but found himself pushed into a cabin with a porthole, an en-suite bathroom and a fridge. The guy said "stay in room" in heavily accented English and threw a key at him and backed out quickly.

Fantoni could hear the water rushing all around him as the lock made the adjustment in levels necessary for the vessel to exit into the Caribbean. It was obvious that he was right at the bottom of the boat and all he could see was the walls of the lock itself moving. Whilst he was waiting, he was relieved to find that the loo worked and that the fridge was stocked with water and snacks. This was far more comfortable than he'd feared and he stretched out on the bed with a sigh.

Bradley Kowolski was an angry man. Just when he thought he was on the plane home to Boston, he heard from the assassin that Fantoni had been rescued before he could be eliminated. The shit had hit the fan in a big way in Washington and been doubled in power when the bastard did a video blog accusing the US of kidnap, murder and fraud. Kowolski had been stuck in Panama ever since trying to find Fantoni and bribed half the criminals in the area to help him. The assassin was equally angry and said by text that he still considered the contract live and would kill Fantoni wherever he was at no extra cost. But until a few minutes ago, no one had the slightest idea where he was. Then someone sent him a grainy photograph, obviously taken from a great distance, of a man wearing a hi-viz jacket and a hat who might just be Fantoni.

Chapter 19

The President had done eight rallies in the last 12 months and funding was at record levels for his re-election campaign. 'Vote for Me and Breathe Easy' was his strap line and Greenwatch was the difference, the USP that had motivated his volunteers, his staff and most importantly, the electorate. If it hadn't been for the mayor of Boston, he might never had come across this technology and it was a great sadness that Mayor Bonelli was still on life support in Boston. But you had to hand it to the guy, he knew how to choose a campaign platform. Pollution in cities was big news and Greenwatch allowed you to present an answer rather than to be blamed for the levels of bad air.

The President did not consider himself to be a bad man but commitment to Greenwatch had already made him sanction some bad things. In London and in Panama people had died and he suspected that his staff were involved. His aide returned from Panama City and had been locked in his office since, only telling him want he really needed to know and giving him deniability as far as the rest were concerned.

But one bit of bad news got through. The President had been in the Oval Office catching up when someone junior from the Press Office came in with a tablet and showed him a short bit of film. The young man was David Rainbird, a highly ambitious intern of Native American ancestry who knew that he had to push himself constantly to try and break through the barriers put there by the traditionally minded political staffers, who all went to the same schools and knew each other. The established order was not WASP any more but it didn't include someone who'd spent his first years on the reservation. Rainbird knew that anything of interest was supposed to be shown to the President's Aide before it went through to the Oval Office, but he wasn't in the office at the moment and the video was something that needed to be seen. So Rainbird told the battle-axe in the outer office that he had something urgent to show the President and much to his amazement he was buzzed though.

Rainbird was in total awe but tried not to show it. He looked directly at the President and told him there was some film on an influential blog that he thought he needed to see urgently. The Leader waved him round and the intern set up his laptop so that he could see the screen.
The young man on the video looked Indian and had a shock of thick white hair but was speaking in educated English. Knowing that no-

one would interrupt him with something trivial at this time of day and fearing some kind of terrorist demand, the President concentrated carefully on what was being said. When the guy claimed to be Carlos Fantoni he gasped and felt himself going cold with apprehension as the statement continued. At the end he tried to collect himself but it was obvious that the President was extremely concerned about its content.
"Has my special aide seen this?"
"No sir, he's not in yet."
"Well make sure he sees it now.... what's your name son?"
"Rainbird sir."

The President recognised an ambitious intern, when he saw one – he'd been one himself, so he complemented Rainbird lavishly and asked him to leave the laptop with him and keep everything totally confidential for the moment. As the young man backed respectfully out of the office, nearly tripping over the coffee table, the President called his aide on his mobile and brought him up to date. The aide was incandescent with rage that the intern had not informed him but calmed down eventually when the President outlined his plan of action.

In a basement somewhere in Langley is an office known to very few people and almost as confidential as the nuclear countdown codes. The basement is bomb-proof, impermeable to electronic interference and staffed by a hundred people who have a higher security clearance than the President. One of its objectives is similar to GCHQ in the UK, which is to monitor all forms of communication. But it has another brief which would send liberal-minded wimps running to the hills if they ever found out about its secret. The department had the capacity to close down sections of the internet completely and in extreme circumstances to change content. This misinformation brief had only been used in extreme circumstances to interfere with terrorist communications but it had saved thousands of lives.

The staff of this department had always called themselves the Newshawks and the legend or approved story they told their girlfriends or families was that they were censors, trawling the internet for unacceptable content and trying to stop it. Politically any President would have found it suicidal to admit that they had the same capacity to silence the internet that China and North Korea had. Indeed, the legal advice received 20 years ago was that it would be immediate grounds for impeachment, so they kept it to themselves. In fact, not every President had been told about the department, those of a more left wing attitude were kept in blissful ignorance and funding was hidden in an impenetrable mix of CIA/NSA and Homeland Security budgets that no one could fathom.

The current Republican President knew of the department but had never used its skills before. His special aide was fully aware of the Newshawks and when they both looked at the Corporate Li's blog over the last few months, they realised that they had to stop it.

The President had been aware of some adverse comments on social media but nothing as potentially damaging as this video. He had also been under the impression that the aide had solved the Carlos Fantoni problem, though he had no wish to be aware of the details. Now it seemed all the threats to his campaign were just as live as they had been a few weeks ago. In truth the aide hadn't informed the President of the escape of Fantoni because he'd hoped to have solved it permanently by now. He couldn't believe that with all the resources the US had in Panama, no-one had managed to find him and eliminate him.

The aide apologised and reassured the President that the Corporate Li's blog would suffer technical problems from now on and be seen by no-one. He also said that Fantoni had been spotted and that he would cease to be a threat to anyone. The President looked unconvinced but reminded his special aide that the final rally was next week and then it was the elections in the second week of November. Greenwatch was the most important part of his campaign and used properly, it could save thousands of lives. The aide nodded, thinking rather libellously that if the leader had the chance to win *or* save lives then he knew that this politician, like most of the rest, would choose victory. But his job was to get on and clear the obstacles, so he'd better get on with it.

The aide pulled Rainbird into his office after his meeting in the Oval Office and put the fear of God in him. The guy stammered out an apology which looked about as sincere as a politician's promise and asked what he could do to help. He was told to trawl the internet for anything similar that mentioned Greenwatch, the President or Fantoni and only report to the aide. He went back to his workspace and got started. The aide had to arrange a meeting with the head of the Newshawks urgently and called him on his direct number as he walked out of the Presidential suite.
"Bill, I've just been with the President and we have an online threat that might need your particular skills."

Bill Troutman looked like a storybook version of a geek or eccentric professor. He wore hand-knitted cardigans that were fraying in many places, over 1960's rock tour T-Shirts. Corduroy trousers in green or brown were his normal attire below the waist and Converse baseball boots completed the outfit. Despite his eccentric look everyone deferred to his knowledge of hacking, propaganda, deception and other internet based fun. Troutman had headed up the Newshawks during the reigns of three US Presidents, though not all of them had known he was there. The present incumbent did know about the department and seemed to be a great improvement on the last one but Troutman took his responsibility very seriously and wouldn't use his skills unless the US was threatened. So he was guarded in his response.
"I can see you later this afternoon, if it's urgent."

It was 4.00 p.m. and the sky over Langley was dark with storm clouds as the aide pulled into the car park. Rain that was almost sleet slanted down as the aide ran the hundred yards to the anonymous looking office. He pressed the entry buzzer and looked up at the camera that appeared normal but actually incorporated some extremely sophisticated face recognition software. The aide was on the system so after he asked for Troutman, the door quickly opened and he was in a featureless waiting area with two grey chairs and a coffee table. He sat down and watched the rain bouncing off the tarmac and went over his approach to the Newshawks in his head. Troutman had a reputation of being a bit difficult and the aide knew that asking him to help the President's election campaign would not work. Only a threat to the nation would motivate the Newshawks.
"How are things in Washington." The deep voice from a few yards away shocked the aide out of his reverie and he stood up to greet him. Troutman didn't disappoint visually, he was wearing a Bonzo Dog T-Shirt that looked new and an orange cable-knit waistcoat over the top. The aide was subjected to a vigorous hand shake and ushered through a side door and into a windowless meeting room that still had used coffee cups littering the top. Another guy came in and requested that he hand over his phone, tablet and other devices which he did reluctantly.
"Don't worry, they will all be put in an electronic dead zone for the next half an hour, but you'll get them back soon." Troutman said soothingly.

The aide felt naked without them but presumed that it was necessary. Everyone knew about the tracking of phones and despite the highest level of security possible on staff devices, it was obvious that a facility like this had to take extra precautions.

"You may have seen that the President wants to put air quality monitors in US cities?"

Troutman nodded "It's a big part of his election campaign, isn't it?"

"Yes, but it could genuinely save thousands of lives – it's not just politics." The aide said with a shade more defensiveness than he'd intended.

Troutman gave a grunt which could have meant anything "How can we help?"

"We've been having problems with a person called Joanne Li and a blog titled 'Corporate Li's.'"

"Is this something Chinese?" Troutman said with barely concealed enthusiasm.

"Not quite – but there might be some Chinese connections – we don't know really. But they are telling all kinds of lies about Greenwatch and Carlos Fantoni which could stop the introduction of these monitoring units. There are enough people from the oil and car makers against this already and the President thinks that if they see these blogs then they could cause big problems."

As he was talking Troutman had been working on his keyboard and got the Corporate Li's blog on a big screen at the end of the room. The video of Carlos Fantoni blasted out at high volume and they watched it through.

"The name Carlos Fantoni seems to be running through all these recent blogs – who is he and did we kidnap him?" Troutman asked.

The aide hesitated, "Fantoni was the main man selling Greenwatch to us and he did a good job, but we think that someone may have bribed or intimidated him – as I said there are people from the oil companies who would spend billions to stop Greenwatch. Now he's trying to say that it's no good, which is ridiculous. All we want him to do is stop him spreading false news at such a sensitive time."

"And this is from the President." Troutman asked.

"Well, it's from everyone who wants the air in our cities to improve. It's already being used in London you know and it's made a real difference." The aide said knowing that Troutman was quite proud of his English ancestors.

"Is it, well its simple enough to stop, if you want?"

"Yes Please."

Troutman spoke on the phone to someone in his department and looked over to the aide. "Done,"
he added. The aide thanked him and stood up. Within two minutes he had collected his electronics and was back in the car. The weather had turned into a beautiful autumn day that matched his

mood completely. He texted the President and started up his Buick and returned.

Back in Washington David Rainbird was extremely confused. He'd been asked to trawl the net for anything about Greenwatch, Fantoni and related subjects and he'd saved quite a number of mentions from the UK and US. But when he referred back to the local mentions, they had completely disappeared. He went back through exactly the same processes and used the same search parameters but it was like any mention had never existed. The blog Corporate Li's had been a good source of comments but there was now nothing at all. It was all very confusing.

When the aide returned to the White House, Rainbird intercepted him and gave him a file of the material he'd found about Greenwatch which was almost completely European. He also said that much to his surprise he couldn't find anything from the US, even the film he'd shown the President earlier. The aide told him not to worry but to look for any other mentions of Greenwatch over future days and prepare an analysis by the end of the month. He was told under no circumstances to talk to anyone else or his internship would be terminated immediately and he wouldn't ever get a job in Washington again. Rainbird believed him and slunk back to his workspace, vowing to himself to never play political games again.

The President googled 'Corporate Li's' when the aide reported back and was relieved to find that the blog had disappeared. In the guarded language that senior politicians use when trying to put over unpleasant instructions in a non-attributable way, the President said he hoped that he would never have to deal with Carlos Fantoni again and that he had disappeared forever. The aide nodded and agreed.

Bradley Kowolski's temper hadn't improved much. It had taken hours for the CIA photographic specialists to enhance the grainy shot he'd been sent and he still wasn't sure it was Fantoni. The photograph had been sent by one of the gang member spotters he'd employed who'd at least said that it was taken at the entrance to the Panama Canal and looked like someone stowing away on a large clipper. Kowolski looked again at the enhanced shot, which showed a slim guy wearing a hi-viz jacket with Panama Pilot markings and a hat which made it impossible to see whether he had white hair or not. Despite the way that it's shown on the movies, he didn't have instant access to satellite images to double check things because they were operating in other more active theatres but he did have a time slot on the shot which would make it possible to check ship movements. Also, the big sailing ship was unusual which would make it easier to identify and he expected to have an email within the hour telling him what the name of the vessel was and where its next port of call was.

Alexander Brown found there was only one way he reduced stress and that was by taking it out physically on someone else. The body count in Panama City was low – only the idiot Coombes and that Irish idiot had given him any opportunity to show his surgical skills which was many days ago. The fact his original target had escaped before he could reach the prison was frustrating and the news that he'd failed to complete his contract twice was appalling and would tarnish his reputation immensely. Brown was known as the assassin who never failed and the only way to recover his 100% record would be to chase Fantoni to the ends of the earth, if necessary, and kill him with great cruelty. In the meantime, he just had a few hours to indulge himself before the flight he'd booked to the US departed and he had a particular target in mind.

Windjammer was the name of the ship that was going through the canal locks at precisely the time shown on the photograph sent to Kowolski. It was a replica of an old tea-clipper which carried a lot more crew than passengers because whenever the conditions were right, they hoisted the sails. This required a lot of man power but the results made it stand out in every harbour in the world and meant that despite the high costs they were booked up years ahead. The large crew meant that customer service was extraordinary, with a ratio of 5 to 1 even those who'd been on the most expensive but traditional cruises were impressed. The crew worked for four months solid and then had a month off and were well paid by average standards.

The Filipino steward bribed by Arias had been on duty for a month whilst the Windjammer had visited Peru, Equador and Columbia and then crossed the continent through the Panama Canal. The plan was to visit Cuba, the Bahamas and then to sail up the east coast of the US making various stops until they reached Boston for a special celebration. This was a long voyage and would take another three weeks before the ship reached its destination. His unofficial guest had been in a cabin for three days now and was no trouble at all and the steward had been careful not to be seen even when he dropped the occasional meal outside the door.

Fantoni had enjoyed the first few days. After the pressure of the last few weeks where he constantly faced death and the tension leading up to him becoming a stowaway, he slept for hours. The cabin was very comfortable, it had been planned as a first class suite originally but the owners realised it was too close to the engines and noisy. It was only used now when the ship had overbooked or when off-duty officers wanted free passage. The steward knew that no-one would need it for the next few weeks as the crew were too busy to visit a cabin, they knew was always empty.

Kowolski now knew the ship and every port of call and decided that it must be the vessel on which Fantoni had stowed away. He had this confirmed when he sweated a minor smuggler called Arias who a contact had betrayed for a few dollars. He used the old electric drill trick which worked so well in the old days and he only had to damage one knee before the guy gave him everything he needed to know. At least the smuggler survived which is more than Fantoni would do when they caught up with him. Kowolski passed on the information to the assassin and knew that the English psycho would find some way of finding him. If not then some of his own associates would deal with him when he reached the US. The main benefit was that Fantoni had been silent as had Joanne Li since he boarded which had taken some of the pressure off, but Washington needed them both to remain silent – preferably permanently.

Alexander Brown was now more relaxed, the assassin had waited in the darkness of the cathedral for the Bishop to enter as he knew he would before the late service. Brown was in his favourite black frock-coat and felt properly dressed for work in a church. He wasn't very fond of the religious community and had suffered badly from an expensive Catholic education in England. He heard the front door creak and saw the clergyman walk down the church aisle looking at the tall figure leaning casually on his stick with curiosity. Brown stepped towards him and muttering a few words he remembered from the Latin mass, he drew the razor-sharp blade in a perfect cross across the man's torso and saw him collapse directly in line with the altar. It was simple, elegant and made the assassin happy. So did the recent information he'd received about the location of Fantoni.

But after three more days Fantoni was starting to get cabin fever. He'd been stuck in prison cells, motel rooms and confined for weeks now and needed some air. He had also used his phone to go online and now realised that this was a long voyage and by the time he got to Boston the election would be over and it would be too late to confront the President during his "Breathe Easy" campaign. So he had to get back to the US quickly and the next stop was the Bahamas. But Boston was the only place where he had contacts and the help of Dane and Joanne so he still needed to get there – but quicker. Also, as the first city in the US where Greenwatch was on test, it was the right place to expose the way unscrupulous people could manipulate its results.

He waited until mid-night and put on a clean T-Shirt, jeans and pushed open the door of his cabin. There was a swell running and the ship was rolling gently as the Windjammer pushed through the waves at top speed. The sails were down and the powerful diesels were pushing ahead whilst most guests were asleep so they could make landfall in Nassau sometime over the next 24 hours.
Fantoni walked cautiously down a narrow corridor past three or four cabins and to a double door with porthole style windows. He looked through them carefully and could see a set of wide steps with brass handrails leading up to the next level. He pushed through and hesitated but realised that if he was to have any chance of getting off, then he needed to know the layout.

"Good Evening sir, is everything alright? "A female voice asked from a low desk behind him. He nearly ran but remembered his identity and answered in perfect Spanish, reverting to accented English with a smile and saying that he just wanted a little air. The girl smiled back and he went up the stairs to the next level. Eventually he found himself on the open deck and sucked in the air gratefully. The girl hadn't been suspicious - jeans and T-shirts are worn by rich and poor alike and his hair had grown and was now a respectable crew cut.

On deck you could see just how impressive this clipper was. The masts towered up above him and the mass of spars and rigging creaked even though the sails were furled. Over the next few hours Fantoni surveyed the vessel from bow to stern and got its geography clear in his head. He had seen at previous ports that the Windjammer either tied up alongside a harbour wall or moored off-shore and a tender took passengers to the shore. He wasn't sure what they did at Nassau but he intended to be ready to try to disembark with the guests.

Fantoni had been back in his cabin for most of the following day when he heard the announcements and could see the land through his porthole. Windjammer was not going to moor in Nassau harbour with the masses it was scheduled to join the super yachts and mega-yachts across the islands at New Providence. The crew all assembled on deck to raise the sails as the captain wanted to make an entrance and Fantoni could hear the ropes and pulleys working as he packed everything in his back pack and got himself ready. The sun was going down and he made his way on deck and joined the other guests as they watched the clipper enter the harbour. He looked around at the five or six enormous private yachts already moored - it was hard to imagine that any one person could afford a ship that size. Most of them were motor vessels and he could see that even billionaires could be impressed by clippers judging by the way they were looking over at Windjammer as it came round under full sail.

Talking to one of the deck hands, he found out that they were able to tie up at one of the quays because they were only due to stay in the Bahamas long enough for guests to have dinner in the 6 star hotel a few yards away and do a little shopping. He joined a stylish group of French passengers ready to go down the gangplank, and chatted in excellent French, hoping that he could hide amongst the dozen of them whilst they loudly complained about the food onboard and their hopes for dinner. It worked and they laughed and joked as they headed to the security gate that was the way out to the marina buildings and designer shops. They pushed through, waving at the ship's officer who was giving out leaflets. Fantoni would have followed if he hadn't seen a tall figure in an antique cream linen suit and a silver topped stick looking at the passengers ahead of him and felt a shiver of recognition.

Chapter 20

Dane Morgan and Joanne Li were back in Boston. They had left the remainder of the illicit cash with Fantoni and booked return air fares using their own credit cards. When they thought what they'd done to annoy the establishment over the last week, they were certain they'd get intercepted before they got on their flight. But they got through security at Panama faster than normal and had a trouble free arrival in the US. It was all a little unreal.

They'd not tried to contact Carlos Fantoni as they were paranoid about traceability but worked out from the Windjammer's website that it was probably in the Bahamas by now. Looking at the rest of the itinerary they realised that it would take far too long by ship for him to get to Boston if they were planning to disrupt the President's campaign. What made it worse was the fact that someone had taken all Jo's social media down and the Corporate Li's blog looked as though it had never happened. All the blogs about the kidnapping of Fantoni, the death of Coombes and the manipulation of the results of Greenwatch didn't exist anymore.

They were now back in the kitchen of the old house in Boston that Professor Li and his wife had lived in for years. Dane and Jo had spent months together there and loved it, they had made love in Jo's bedroom dozens of times and had renewed their habit of having a siesta every afternoon. This had awoken their passions in more ways than one but they still kept on wondering what state Carlos Fantoni was in.

They had an exhausting and totally satisfying session of lovemaking in the shower that afternoon and totally forgot about him. Jo's lithe body covered in fragrant soap bubbles was an immense turn on for Dane and the difference in their heights was no problem at all. She found herself way off the ground with her back sliding on the Italian tiles, impaled upon Dane, who's penis seemed to have grown another two inches since the last time. They had an incredibly intense orgasm almost simultaneously and collapsed on the floor with amazement on their faces, that two bodies could do that so beautifully.

At that moment Carlos was 100ft in the air. He had no idea whether the assassin had seen him in the queue of passengers trying to exit the marina but panicked and ran back to the ship shouting to the

French crowd that he'd forgotten his phone. He ran back up the gangplank startling the officers relaxing at the top and used the same excuse, pushing past and deciding that going back to his cabin would be dangerous. The last thing he wanted was to be cornered by the psycho with the sword stick who'd tried to kill him in London.

On deck he was hidden amongst the rigging and masts but needed to see the shore. In order not to be seen, he looked up and saw the masts with huge ropes coming down from each side and cross pieces half way up to hold the sails. For a moment he considered climbing up the lines but realised that even a monkey would have trouble on those tarred ropes. He moved further towards the bows and saw a crow's nest at the top of the main mast with a rope net all the way to the platform.

Fantoni found the side away from the quay and saw where the net started. He looked round the deck and saw it was deserted and carefully climbed out on the narrow edge of the ship holding on to the base of the rope ladder. It was a network of holds which was wide at the base but got narrower and narrower as it got close to the top. The first bit was quite easy as long as you had at least one foot and one arm on the rope at all times, but as Carlos climbed up further the rope started to sway alarmingly. He really had to summon his courage, remembering that sailors did this in storms and gales but he was in harbour. When he looked up it still seemed a huge climb and realised the mast was swaying in the wind but he reached up and grabbed another handhold and forced his left foot to move up as high as it could. He knew that looking down would be fatal so concentrated on the last few yards of climb which was getting narrower and narrower.

At the top of the netting, he could see the underneath of the platform which had an opening barely wide enough for anyone. For a second, he thought he might fall, the wind was howling and the ladder was now so narrow that it took just one hand. He gritted his teeth and reached up using his left leg to rise and pushed his head through the hatch. With a gasp, he pulled his hand and arm through and levered himself into the crow's nest on his elbows. Up here the wind noise was deafening and Fantoni lay full length holding on to some stout ropes until the shaking in his body stopped.

He couldn't believe how much the climbing had taken out of him. He was young, supposedly an athlete but it took five minutes for Fantoni to recover sufficiently to stand and look down from the crow's nest. The view from the top was extraordinary and yet he was completely invisible. It was just as well because he couldn't believe how close he'd been to walking straight into the guy who'd threatened him in London. Fantoni would have recognised him anywhere, it wasn't just the antique clothing or even the stick, it was the pale drawn face and dead eyes he seen from close quarters outside the Savoy. He looked like a man who'd lost his soul and Fantoni couldn't believe that he'd tracked him here. Hopefully the group of French people in front had shielded him and he could stay out of sight until the Windjammer departed.

Fantoni was in the crow's nest for hours and he had to put on all the clothes in his back pack to try and keep warm. He checked how much cash he had left and worked out he had about $70K in $100 notes left which would be necessary as he had no credit cards and a false passport that hadn't yet been tested.

But the hours alone had convinced him of one thing. All his trials so far were because he wanted pollution ended. It had killed his parents and it was killing thousands around the world at the moment. Rich industrialists like Wolf Bayer and Salimond had lied about the facts for centuries and got away with it. Greenwatch could be an answer but it had to be run by the right people and at the moment that wasn't the US President, it wasn't the UK Prime Minister and it certainly wasn't Salimond. Even if it killed him, Fantoni was determined to get the real facts about Greenwatch in front of the public.

He realised how dark it was below and yet Fantoni could hear the distant sound of voices and the crew sliding down the gangplank. He put his pack back on and wondered how he was going to do the reverse journey down from the crow's nest. He waited for half an hour and the noises of returning passengers reached its peak. Judging by the shouts in many languages and merry laughter the evening special dinner at the hotel had been a success. One of the French guests he had talked to earlier had said that the man behind the dinner ran a three star Michelin restaurant in Spain so it would be good. The fact that he was French also meant that the meal was likely to be light years better than the food on board which she thought was "merde."

Dinner was something Fantoni dreamed of. There was no way he could pretend to be a guest in the dining room. Things are more checked there than anywhere else as management live in terror that someone might escape without paying their drinks bill. The steward brought the occasional meal from the dining room at the beginning and there was plenty of fruit and snacks in the fridge but not enough to stop him being hungry most of the time. He had no way to contact his man and didn't know what he looked like but knew that he had to get more food. It was difficult to work out how he was going to do it without risking discovery.

First, he had to get down from the top of the mast and try to be sure that the assassin wasn't on board too. The first bit was the most terrifying as he had to lower his body down through the hatch and feel with his feet for a piece of net he could rely on. It took a considerable amount of courage to let go of the wooden platform and hold on to the narrow square of rope with his hand. His mind found it difficult to reverse the climbing process but eventually he reached down with his hand and held on to a piece of net about two feet down on his right. He pulled his left hand down level and then the downward movement became more instinctive and before he had time to think he realised that the net was wide and he must be getting close to the bottom. He heard voices on deck not far away and froze on the ladder.

Jo and Dane were lazing on their bed after their exertions when Dane suddenly sat up. "Listen the blog may have been taken down but we haven't lost everything."
"What are you talking about?" Jo enquired, with just a trace of hope in her voice.
"Everything I took – the original shots from the Grosvenor Club right through to the interview with Carlos, is still on my camera" Dane jumped out of bed and ran to the wardrobe pulling out his Nikon and bringing it back to the bed. He turned on the camera, tried scrolling through the shots but his expression got more and more despondent. "Shit, the bastards have found some way of wiping all my shots off."
"I thought that was too easy, they probably did it when they were checking our hand luggage coming back from Panama." Jo said.
 "Yeh, I suppose so..... But hang on, everything was on my laptop too…." Dane leapt up again and left the room, returning a few minutes later with his Apple Mac. After a few minutes checking he realised that the bastards had been too clever and also deleted everything on his laptop.

They were both really depressed as they realised they had nothing left at all. People would have seen the Corporate Li blogs over the last few weeks but memories fade and no one could look back at them now. If they still had the shots and the interviews then Jo could have done a new social media message and tried to build interest. She was a journalist with a growing reputation but any editor she approached would demand that she showed them the original material. Now it didn't exist and the man at the centre of the scandal - Carlos Fantoni - was not available. Suddenly Jo sat up so swiftly that Dane jumped with shock.

"Hang on Dane, didn't you tell me years ago that iCloud charges were getting ridiculous."

"Yeh, so what?"

"Well didn't you say that it backed up your files automatically?"

"Yes." Dane said with an understanding smile.

They needed to think this through and not jump in too quickly but there was just a hope that the techies who'd blanked his camera and laptop had not thought about Cloud back up. With more hope than they'd had in hours they held this in their minds but were worried that even trying to access the Cloud might alert somebody. Dane said he would talk to one of his friends in IT when it was a civilised time in the UK and check the best way to do it.

Quite a few things had changed since they'd got back to Boston. Professor Li and his wife had been scared witless that they had got themselves involved in something dangerous like they had with the SCC scandal in New Zealand. They had uncovered an environmental disaster but they ended up in trouble with two governments and in great physical danger. Jo had taken months to get over those problems but her parents could see she was a changed person. She was happy, enthusiastic and determined to help solve the air quality problem.

They all sat down at the kitchen table when they returned from Panama and Dane updated them on most of the things that had happened but left out the dangerous bits of the journey. The Li's were astonished at the treatment of Carlos Fantoni and disgusted that US officials had probably abducted him and maybe tried to kill him. Everyone agreed that the best thing was to get Fantoni back as soon as possible and get him on the news.

Professor Li added an interesting update on the university situation. Greenwatch had been sold to the US authorities as being technology developed in conjunction with Harvard. This had turned out to be misinformation as Coombes, the inventor, had been at the institution but developed the technology after he'd left. He had also been asked to leave because of some sort of financial irregularity that the Professor had not been able to discover. What made this all the more complicated was that Salimond had sponsored at great cost a chair in Environmental Studies which the Dean was now extremely defensive about. At this point it looked as though Jo was going to explode and her father held up his hand to stop her having a rant about the way that big companies exploited academics and added that there was now an internal investigation on the whole subject. He added that he and several other academics were determined to expose any corruption in the organisation and David Watson, the business manager, had already resigned.

Jo seemed slightly mollified but added that if anyone thought of asking Coombes to appear at the inquiry then they better think again because he'd been murdered in Panama only a few days ago. Also, if anyone wanted to investigate Salimond then they'd better speak to the boss Wolf Bayer and ask where his money came from.

Carlos Fantoni kept as still as he could but the gunwale was slippy and his arms were getting tired from hanging on to the rope. Luckily it was dark but the voices got closer and sounded like two people sitting on the deck chairs on the deck close by. They were young Americans and discussing just how boring the holiday had been with their respective parents. Interesting as it might have been anthropologically, Carlos really hoped this early exercise about 'on board romance' would end soon in a shared bunk or rushed kiss. Listening to the teenage voices, he realised that neither could be the assassin but he still had to be extremely careful as he could be anywhere.
The kids were still there five minutes later and his hands were turning numb so he had to act. He pulled himself up and swung his legs over the edge of the ship and on to the wooden ledge that ran down the length of the bows.

"The rigging is OK sir. "He shouted to a non-existent officer aloft and nodded to the shocked youngsters snogging in the chairs. He walked slowly down the ship looking behind every mast and peering into the shadows. When he got to one of the gangway doors, he peered through the porthole and seeing nothing, went through and down to the next deck. There was more noise and Fantoni realised that this was the level where the dining room was situated and remembered just how hungry he was. He looked down at his T-Shirt and realised that it was filthy and there was no way he could pass for a passenger so went a few decks down until he found his cabin.

Carlos had intended to have left the ship by now and had left the door open. He pushed the cabin door open and saw that the steward had left him some food and water on the bed. It was more fruit and some kind of rice dish but Carlos wolfed the food down like it was the best meal he'd ever tasted.

Realising that he better take no more risks he locked the door from the inside and went through into the bathroom to see what sort of state he was in. In the mirror he saw a badly shaven ruffian with a badly stained shirt who would never pass as a passenger. So he stripped off his clothes and had a thorough shower, hair wash and tried to get the t-shirt clean by rinsing it in the shower. His jacket was OK because it had been in his pack and his trainers were fine but his jeans were a mess. Somehow, he had got tar or creosote from the rigging all over the front of the denims and it would be impossible to wash it off. If he intended to get off at the next port of call then he needed to look far better dressed than he was now.

As he lay back on the bed, he heard the shouts of the crew and realised they were casting off from Barbados and would be travelling overnight to the USA. He checked the door again but thought that once underway he was less likely to encounter the sinister English assassin he'd seen onshore but he wasn't sure. Carlos tried to work out how he'd known about him stopping in Barbados. Thinking it through however, someone must have talked, whether it was the smuggler or someone else he didn't know but they were obviously going to stop at nothing.

He looked at the ship's itinerary and saw that the ship was due to stop in Charlestown, South Carolina in a couple of days and the guests were to be taken on a tour of this historic town. When he googled the area, he found that there was a marina with berths for super yachts so Windjammer might be moored on the quay rather than out in the bay, but he couldn't be sure. Importantly he could see that the area had an airport which had regular flights to Boston and hoped that his passport would be good enough for the flight.

By now he could tell that Windjammer had cast off and was underway. It was late so Fantoni reckoned most passengers would be in their cabins but he planned to wait another hour before he left the cabin to look for any source of food and clothing. Food was the easier of the options as he'd seen the dining room and the doors of the galley kitchen were visible at the far end. Clothing was extremely difficult and stealing from someone else's cabin seemed far too risky. But looking in his own wardrobe he saw something that gave him an idea.

After what seemed like hours, Carlos opened his door and peered out. There was still a chance that his attacker was on board and knew where he was so he crept out listening carefully at every junction. The ship was obviously out of shelter now and was rolling slightly and the noise of the wash made it difficult to hear clearly. He went up a gangway to the dining room level noticing that all lights were out in the room apart from the kitchen. He was shocked to hear voices coming from the steps below and pushed opened the doors into the dining room in panic. He hid behind the door praying that no-one entered and saw a uniformed officer pass by on the outside.

Carlos could hear his heart beating so loud he was convinced any one close could hear it but after a few minutes he forced himself to creep down the centre of the dining room and look through the doors at the end to the kitchens. He saw a large room with floor to ceiling freezers and stainless steel work surfaces and cookers but no staff at all. Quietly he opened the doors and looked in the nearest fridge and couldn't resist taking a few slices of cold meats from some of the anti-pasta trays that had been stored in there. Not exactly the Savoy but absolutely delicious after all the rubbish he'd been eating.

After grazing on items from various fridges he decided that he'd better leave before he took too much and silently left the kitchen and dining room. After seeing the laundry list in his cabin he had thought of one possible way of finding new clothes. As the Windjammer offered such a service, there must be a laundry somewhere in the ship where garments were cleaned and there was a chance, just a small chance, he could find something that might fit and which looked more respectable than his present clothes. His best guess was that such a facility would be forward near the crew quarters and he decided to find it.

It was 3.00 a.m. when he made his way to the next level down and started his search. By now he reckoned the only crew awake would be the officers in the wheelhouse sailing the ship but he searched quietly as he was very close to their sleeping quarters as he could hear by the occasional snore. It took 40 minutes to find the laundry and check that it was empty. He could smell detergent and see the line of washers and dryers in the dark but he needed more light. He pushed the doors closed behind him and found the light switch. There were lines of wooden racks with piles of clean and pressed clothes on many of them each with a room number label. After a search he found a dark blue Nike track suit from one rack, a pair of cream shorts and polo shirt from another and some underwear and socks.

The weather was still warm and Carlos was anxious to have clothing that matched what other passengers were likely to be wearing when they docked in Charleston. It was important that he didn't stand out and not wear anything that was so individual that the real owner could identify his own garment instantly. Hopefully these garments fitted that criteria and Carlos put them in a laundry bag to take them back to his cabin. There was always the chance that the owners would complain so loudly that it created a ship-wide search but he thought that it was unlikely judging by the huge number of garments in the laundry.

Fantoni reversed his journey without incident and locked himself in his cabin, drinking a bottle of water and lying down on his bunk and tried to plan his next moves. He dearly wanted to communicate with Dane and Joanne Li to discuss things but everyone had agreed before the trip that smartphones were dangerous and could be traced too easily, so should only be used when really important. That moment wasn't yet.

He drifted off to sleep and must have slept for hours because he woke with a shock, sunlight streaming through the porthole and somebody hammering on the door.

Chapter 21

Wolf Bayer was enjoying himself in the way only Bayer could. The two hookers had cost him a fortune but the pimp had assured him that they were disposable, being newly trafficked from Eastern Europe with no history. Bayer was in London for the next Salimond meeting and had rented a large apartment in Docklands with a fantastic view of the Thames and all the bank buildings. It had taken him an hour to line the room with heavy duty polythene but he knew that when he enjoyed himself, he tended to make a lot of mess.

The second hooker went by the name of Inga and thought she'd seen most things but when she met Bayer she instinctively felt that she was in trouble. When she saw the plastic sheeting, she knew her instincts were right and she tried to leave the room but was confronted by the tall German with a large handgun in one hand and stopped. Her need for drugs had made Inga do all kinds of disgusting things but she hadn't been in fear of her life very often. This was different and she felt astonishing pain as something lashed her and her flimsy top was flayed off her back. Through her tears she could see the old guy had some kind of special whip in his hand and seemed to be grunting with pleasure or effort as he snapped the leather thongs across her buttocks with a noise that sounded like someone whipping up a team of horses in an old movie. She tried to run away from the pain but slipped on her own blood and struggled to protect her legs as the sadist attempted to flay her alive as she lay curled up like a child on the plastic. Inga could hear the whip thongs hit her body and knew that unless she made an effort now, she would be dead. She gathered herself up off the floor and rushed at the man, surprising him with a strength that even surprised herself and pushed past him to the outer door. She tried in vain to open it and looked around for some other way out.

Bayer loved it when they fought back and this tall blonde was exceptional – so exceptional that he'd been shoved back on his arse by her headlong rush. The other hooker he'd used up earlier had been Chinese or Thai and was disappointing. He'd flayed her to death far too quickly and vowed not to employ any young Asiatics again. There was something far too submissive about these girls and they were nowhere near as much fun. With the spirited ones he played all kinds of games and sometimes allowed them to think they'd escaped before catching them later and killing them. With Inga she'd genuinely escaped the first room but he wasn't a merciful man so followed her out to the door and quietly shot her in the back of the head.

Dubai was the place that Salimond normally had their meetings as they had the use of a suite in the Burj Al Arab which had the highest levels of security. This time it suited the three main members of the board to meet in London because they all wanted to see the first Greenwatch units still on test in the centre of the city. Now the meeting was to be at Claridges and was due to take place tomorrow and Bayer had got some good news for his fellow board members. In the meantime London had plenty of other attractions for a man of his taste and he decided to relax in one of the other rooms and gather his strength.

Bayer had been the CEO of one of the leading German car groups for years as his family owned a large proportion of the shares. The group had been falsifying the emissions and fuel economy for decades and no-one had really noticed. Then the VAG group had been caught out and his company implicated as well as other manufacturers from Japan also had to clean up their acts rather quickly. Despite the huge scandal, lawyers managed to hide the facts and delay compensation claims for years. Even today many owners have still not been made aware of any pay-outs or remedial actions that the guilty car makers might have made. It has been an unparalleled exercise in obfuscation but the old fashioned makers knew that things couldn't be delayed forever.

Greenwatch was a delaying tactic that Bayer thought would give them another 5 years in Europe and indefinitely in other parts of the globe. When the scientist originally presented the technology to him as head of the automotive group, he saw just how much of a threat it was and wanted to own it rather than give a more scrupulous person the chance to change the world. So he and his partners had set up Salimond and his team worked out a technical add-on which could manipulate the figures when required.

As Wolf Bayer lay back on the huge bed in the apartment, he could hear the forensic crew cleaning up in the adjoining room and knew that they would leave virtually no evidence of his dirty games. The joy of being so incredibly rich and well-connected was that you could find someone to do almost any job and do it well. The hookers' bodies would be mincemeat by now and feeding the fishes somewhere out in the Thames estuary. The apartment had been rented for the next month by a Panama shell company and would be returned to its original pristine state well before the end. No one in the UK would be looking for the hookers anyway as in their countries of origin, disappearing women are as common as corrupt officials.

Bayer had an excellent night's sleep and made his way to Claridges early the next morning. It wasn't his favourite hotel but the driver dropped him immediately outside and he had to admit that the entrance with its flags and wide art deco canopy was impressive. He booked in for the first time and was taken up to the Kings Suite which was far too stark for his taste but at least comfortable. The porter left with a twenty pound tip which improved his attitude and he looked at himself critically in one of the floor to ceiling mirrors. Wolf Bayer wasn't bad for a man of 70 as his six foot two inch frame was still as straight as ever and his iron grey hair still immaculate but his eyes looked strange. Someone had told him once that eyes were the window to the soul, if so, then his soul was in a cold place.

He met the rest of the Salimond board an hour later in the St James Room which had been swept for devices by an ex CIA expert just minutes before. He'd had problems with the Japanese partner a couple of weeks previously when the boss had tried to resign because of the elimination of various people who threatened their project. Bayer had refused that attempt vigorously and there had been no trouble from that quarter since. Ms Tanaka, their representative, was sitting at the table in the board room exactly on time and looked as inscrutable as ever.

There had never been any doubt about the commitment of the other member of the board present. Sheikh Bin Hadad was in a beautiful handmade Saville Row suit and not in traditional dress but the views of his family were extremely old fashioned when it came to oil. His family had been raking in billions for years and throwing money at the local population and the army also for years to discourage anything radical like human rights or democracy. But the family was getting larger every week and they all wanted their cut. The sheikh and his immediate advisors had been investing abroad and trying to diversify but they needed at least ten more years before they could exit without problems.

Bayer called the meeting to order and prepared to deliver his report with his usual style which had once been described secretly by an underling as being like an aristocrat addressing a tribe of pygmies. The rest tolerated this approach and waited patiently for the tone to moderate, which it normally did after the first five minutes.

"You saw at the last meeting just how successful we have been selling Greenwatch into new markets and since then I have had positive response from five governments in Africa and four in Asia who are prepared to invest in Greenwatch <u>and</u> its additional programme. As you know this programme can reduce pollution readings by up to 50%. One of the African states," Bayer paused with a chuckle. "One of them wanted to increase the reduction to 100% but I had to say no... A pity really because he was offering a serious premium." The two others looked mildly amused but made no comment because they had bigger worries than just money or profit.

"The other benefit as you will remember is that wherever Greenwatch gives a city a clean bill of health, we can also sell our older more polluting vehicles and you can sell them oil at premium prices Sheikh.... as long as you pay the backhanders as well of course."

"But it's not all good news. I know you are all concerned about our one-time sales director Carlos Fantoni."

Ms Tanaka looked up and said. "The man seems to have more lives than a cat.. Have we found him and finished him off yet?

"No, but..." Bayer stopped whilst the curses in different languages reached their natural end.   "But we will have the problem solved in the next few days."

"We have heard that before." Sheikh Bin Hadad shouted with barely concealed anger. "You told us he was to be assassinated weeks ago in Panama."

"Yes I did and that assassination attempt failed but Fantoni now has more enemies than you can possibly imagine and I think we can forget about him – he's becoming irrelevant anyway."

"Listen, this sounds like bullshit to me..Tanaka interjected with real venom. "Hattori Kenshin will not like this when I tell him."

"I know that your owner is not a patient man but I would ask you to listen to the rest of my news before you report back." The Japanese woman looked angry but nodded her head and the Arab took another sip of his coffee and looked sceptical.

Over the next hour Bayer outlined the situation with Greenwatch starting with London. In this city the test had been an astounding success and the voters had loved it. The mayor had passed the budgets for its expansion throughout the city and central government were seeing it as a major policy advantage for the rest of the country. This was despite the fact MI5 had found out about the bribery involved and the way the Greenwatch system could be hacked into so it showed false readings. Someone in Westminster had apparently valued this so much they'd arranged for Diane Fallows expose to be discredited before publication and have her eliminated. The Prime Minister and the US President had talked briefly and both agreed anything that interfered with the introduction of Greenwatch was to be avoided 'at all costs.'

In the beginning it was planned that in western cities, Greenwatch would show true readings for the first few months whilst governments tried various methods of improvement. After a year or so Salimond would then have secretly reduced the figures allowing effectively everything to return to near normal with petrol vehicles no longer seen as the killers. But with London, the mayor had effectively become part of the conspiracy from the start. This was an unexpected bonus for Salimond and Bayer could see that the implications were not lost on the rest of the board.

The US was under even more pressure to make Greenwatch a success despite their knowledge of its capacity to deceive. Bayer confirmed that the test in Boston had been equally successful in terms of identifying real pollution problems and turning on voters. More importantly it was likely to win the President a second term in office because he had promised a nationwide introduction. For once not even the senate, which had the normal amount of opposing factions, could find much to object to.

The only thing that could ruin Greenwatch was lack of trust. There was a huge amount of cynicism about the automotive industry and government after the emission scandals of the early 21st century. Many people remembered that at one time they were told to buy diesel because it was better for the planet, only to be told a few years later that they were villains. They were told not to buy gas guzzlers and opted for supposedly economic cars only to find that the figures quoted in the ads for petrol consumption and emissions were lies. The public didn't trust anyone and though innovators like Tesla grew the electric market rapidly, they ended up mainly selling expensive cars and nobody seemed to agree on an electric charging system for volume cars. So the traditional car makers were able to avoid dramatic change by minor improvements to their performance that quite often were not real solutions.

Bayer reminded everyone that the only person left who was a threat to the trust in Greenwatch was Fantoni. Diane Fallow the journalist and her source Duckley were now history, Professor Coombes the inventor who'd threatened to go rogue had been eliminated and any social media critical of the system had been obliterated for ever.

Tanaka was becoming more than a little impatient with this monologue, most of which she knew from other sources and interjected

"All very impressive, Mr Bayer but can I remind you of my chief's concern mentioned last meeting. Yes, he wants to know that Fantoni is no longer a problem but he is also concerned about Joanne Li – who has proved herself to be a campaigner who is difficult to silence – what about her?"

Annoyed that his speech had been interrupted but conscious that he was only talking to two people and may have been pontificating, he sat down and lowered his voice. "Sorry if I was going into too much detail but there have been so many adjustments to our original plans over the last few weeks – most of which are positive – and I wanted to fill you in. Let me concentrate on the essentials."
"We don't have to worry about Mr Fantoni. We have information from Mr Kowolski of the CIA about his whereabouts. He has been smuggled on board a ship and is at sea at the moment but we know he is bound for Boston, USA."
"How do we know that?" Sheikh Hadad asked.
"Let us say that the US people applied strong pressure to the smuggler to reveal his destination."
"OK, but can't we intercept Fantoni before he arrives?" Tanaka asked.
"The US agencies have far more resources than we have and they think that intercepting a cruise ship at sea, would create far too much publicity. They seem certain that Boston is his destination and that's the place to intercept him."
"How can we trust the US people?" The sheikh asked.
"The last thing that the President wants is anything that affects his re-election campaign and Greenwatch is its cornerstone. I talked to the President's aide a couple of days ago and he has authorized the most extreme measures to stop Fantoni. Various government agencies and an independent contractor will be at Boston to ensure that Fantoni ceases to be a problem."
"When is he due to arrive in Boston?"
"In about a week's time."

The group considered the implications of Bayer's news but could not deny the logic of what was being planned. They had all seen the TV and seen the impact of the 'Vote for Me and Breathe Easy' commercials that had been running for months in the US. It may be an unholy alliance had been created between the Presidential team and Salimond but neither party wanted Fantoni to create problems now. After the election it might be different but there were signs from the aide that the administration might find it useful to be able to censor the Greenwatch read outs too.

Bayer knew that Washington had seen some recent pollution statistics and were desperate for no one else to see them. In 2019 the American Lung Association had said that dozens of cities in the US from California all the way to Alaska had unhealthy air. Back then they said that 133.9 million US citizens lived in unhealthy areas and had greatly increased chances of medical problems like lung cancer, asthma and many other life limiting conditions. Since then, the situation had got worse. The latest report on air quality was confidential but the Presidential team knew it was only a matter of time before it was leaked. The public health issues were bad enough but in the US especially, where lawyers had type actions off to a fine art, the legal implications were catastrophic.

The truth was that no one knew how to solve air quality it was too big a problem. Politicians were playing for time and had been for decades. Bayer hadn't predicted just how much the capacity of Greenwatch to hide the true situation would appeal to 'Respectable' politicians. The President and the Prime Minister may have found out about this by accident but they now saw its advantages 100%.

Strangely, the Boston Greenwatch test had shown that the public were shocked by the true figures. They trusted the politicians who'd installed it despite the fact the mayor of Boston had been in charge when pollution got bad, his approval ratings went up after he put in Greenwatch. The one thing everyone knew is that public trust is what made Greenwatch so powerful. Allow anyone to destroy that trust and the effects would be catastrophic.

Bayer had showed the board just how many new allies they now had and tried to finish the meeting on an optimistic note but was stopped by that persistent bitch Tanaka who reminded him that he hadn't answered the question of Joanne Li. Thinking quietly that he'd love to have this troublesome woman at the end of one of his favourite whips, he concentrated on his answer.
"The US have already hacked into her Corporate Li's blog and removed any past material. They have promised to add all kinds of information over the next few days that will make her look ridiculous. You know, conspiracy theories, alien landings and all kinds of material. The fact that a couple of years ago she was held by the New Zealand government because of her conspiracy theories will be released to the press. Her partner Dane Morgan will also be extradited over the next few weeks as an 'undesirable'. She has no evidence and will look ridiculous if she makes any claims."
"I will pass this on to my associates." Tanaka stood up, bowed

formally to Bayer, gathered up her briefcase and left the room. As soon as she was in Claridges' foyer she pulled out her mobile and phoned her boss on a secure line. Hattori Kenshin was not greatly reassured by what he heard but agreed to keep their involvement at a much lower level from this point on.

Sheikh Bin Hadad was much less concerned about the dangers of exposure and believed that the measures that Bayer had described would get rid of Fantoni. He was by nature an optimist and saw that Greenwatch would be sold into Africa as an open door to selling them his family oil. In fact Bayer had suggested a contra-deal where buyers of Greenwatch got his 'cleaner' oil at a special rate. He loved the idea.

Wolf Bayer had a direct number for the Presidential Aide and called him after the meeting asking if he had any further information about Fantoni and whether he was certain he would be entering the US in Boston. The aide disliked the German intensely and thought him an arrogant piece of shit but the President had said to cooperate with him until after the election because both wanted Fantoni out of the way.

The aide said he'd double check with the operatives on the ground and phoned Kowolski who patiently listened to the enquiry and then gave his reasons. First the smuggler under intense interrogation had said that Boston was his destination and Kowolski had done enough torturing in his life to know when a subject was telling the truth. Secondly, it is where Joanne Li and Dane Morgan had returned to and they are his only allies. Thirdly, it is the site of the first Greenwatch test so it makes sense. The ship is due to arrive on a Tuesday in October, just days before the elections and too late for him to cause serious problems. The aide was convinced and asked him what measures had been put in place to ensure that Fantoni didn't escape again. Kowolski outlined the measures that he'd put in place and reassured the aide that Fantoni would be eliminated in a way that was not going to embarrass anybody in Washington.

Though he believed his own logic completely, Kowolski was a careful man and detailed an agency guy to man the cameras at the next stop which was Charleston to check for his target too. The security cameras there had special face-recognition software which could pick up Fantoni from fifty yards should he be crazy enough to jump ship. But Kowolski was betting his pension on Boston which would be tied up so tight that even an ant couldn't get through. And with an English psychopath leading the welcoming committee,

Fantoni would enter the Promised Land in as vicious a manner as possible.

Alexander Brown had found over the last few years that he could focus his rage. As a surgeon in the army, he had to avoid any emotion and keep cool no matter how many broken bodies he was sent from the battlefield. Then one day he discovered the joy of taking the life of a particularly obnoxious master sergeant and realised that by focussing his rage and using cold steel he got an almost sexual thrill. It was also extremely profitable and Brown's image as the English Gentleman Assassin who never failed had got him numerous lucrative contracts over the last 10 years.

The consortium of oil producers who'd employed him to take out Fantoni in London all those months ago had paid their 30% deposit but not got any result. The fact that he'd failed in Panama had been bad for his image and he'd returned the deposit with the assurance that he'd complete the contract anyway but free of charge. The search for Fantoni had cost him a significant number of dollars but he'd found out that his quarry might be landing in Nassau sometime over the next few days but nothing else. He'd spent hours meeting passengers without success, then his schedule was changed by one of his new American friends.

After the call from the Washington spook, Kowolski had to change his plans. The intelligence was that Fantoni would be landing in Boston on a Tuesday on Windjammer which Brown saw was a four-masted tea clipper just like the one he'd seen in the Bahamas. This gave him a certain amount of concern and he double-checked the schedule but the spook was convinced that Boston was where he could be found. Knowing that US Intelligence is not always the most reliable source he questioned it again, but the CIA were certain. As the agency or one of its shadow organisations was paying twice his normal contract fee, he agreed, thinking that this might turn out to be a profitable trip after all.

Brown had been employed by Homeland Security, NSA or CIA or whatever set of initials they were using that month and had been well paid. But he was under no illusions and he had an extremely devious mind, so his reading of this particular contract was as follows. Firstly, the agency would not be choosing an English assassin just because they liked him. Secondly, they wouldn't just be relying on Brown, no matter how good he was because the target was too important, so they would have a back-up team.
Paranoia can be a useful quality in the assassination business and

Brown's paranoid mind told him that it was being used because if he succeeded or even if he failed then the CIA could say with truth that he'd been originally employed by a group of Arab oil tycoons to kill Fantoni. He also suspected that the US back up team were there to take him out whilst he was attempting the killing and would end up heroes trying valiantly to save Fantoni, but failing.

The more Alexander Brown considered his reading of the situation in Boston, the more it made sense. He checked his online bank account and found that someone had already credited a considerable amount of money to his account via an odd Dubai account. In the past payment had been much slower and for 'consultancy services' given to a US corporation based in Grand Cayman. Knowing that there were likely problems associated with this contract didn't alter the fact that he still needed to kill Fantoni to maintain his 100% record.

Brown got the keys to his modest apartment in the centre of Boston and got a cab across town. If the driver had an opinion about the tall gentleman in the ancient black suit he kept it to himself, there was something rather sinister about his passenger that he couldn't quite explain. Brown went up to the fifth floor and opened his door. Inside was a large living room with old fashioned windows looking across the business district. With a sigh Alexander Brown stripped down to his waistcoat, took the sword from its narrow tube and started to practise thrusts and parries in the way he had done virtually every day since he was an Olympic fencing champion. The movements got swifter and more fluid as he imagined Fantoni in front of him and just what damage he could do to the man who had become such a frustration in his ordered life.

.

Chapter 22

Carlos Fantoni was terrified that his trip out last night for food and clothes had been observed and that the assassin had found him. He hadn't seen anyone but perhaps there were security cameras or something else he hadn't considered. The knocking on his door hadn't stopped and he couldn't ignore it because now there was a soft voice calling outside for him to open up and do it quickly. He opened the door a crack and saw the steward who'd got him on board in the first place with a plate in his hand. Fantoni grabbed it with thanks in Spanish and locked the door again.

It took a good few minutes for his breathing to return to normal and then he tucked into a plate of pasta with a tomato sauce that was actually very good. He opened a fresh bottle of water and relaxed for the first time and considered his next move. His original strategy had been to keep on the boat until Boston and that is what they'd paid the smuggler for. But the timing was not good, it was only a week before the election and he and Joanne needed as much time as possible to find some way of getting their message on a major TV channel. He was under no illusions about the difficulty he faced convincing the media because he had little evidence and he bet that the material Diane Fallow had gathered for the FT had died with her.

But as the main person involved in selling Greenwatch for Salimond he had more credibility than anyone else left alive. He had hoped to get off in Nassau but it had proved impossible so his next opportunity was Charleston, South Carolina. He used his smartphone to do a little research and if he could get off there and his passport held up, then there were regular flights to Boston. Overall, he could save around three or four vital days getting to Dane and Jo, so he had to try.

Thinking his situation through, his other problem was that someone involved in his escape may have been persuaded to talk otherwise the assassin would not have been there to meet passengers at the last port. There was a chance he might also be in Charleston but Fantoni hoped there was just a chance he'd been discouraged by not finding him at Nassau. It was certain however, he would be in Boston because that was the destination Fantoni had paid the smuggler to get to. It was a risk at either port, but Carlos needed to get off and Charleston was his best bet. He just needed to be really clever how he did it.

That night Carlos crept out of the cabin again. It was about 3.00

a.m. and the air on the top deck was wonderfully cool. He sat at a table on the sundeck and watched the stars and planets in the night sky that was wonderfully clear and noticed somebody had left a hat and sunglasses on another table. Sunset was a big deal on this ship and the crew played beautiful music and raised the sails on nights when the weather was good. He suspected that someone had left both whilst watching the sun going down but it gave him just the hint of an idea. Later he went back to the laundry and looked through the racks for a highly specific set of clothing. It took a lot of time but eventually he found what he hoped would work and returned to his cabin for a rest.

Charles Towne, South Carolina was founded in 1670 by a group of English gentlemen who recognised the value of its sheltered anchorage. It became a highly successful port during the years when rice and cotton was exported all round the world. Sadly, slaves to work the plantation were also imported in great numbers and sold in the market square. The town became immensely prosperous and the merchant houses and trading buildings were as impressive as anywhere in the Deep South. Then in 1861 the Civil War started here and eventually the city was occupied by Union Forces and destroyed.

Though the town went into decline it became of strategic importance again in WW2 and gained prosperity. The historic value of this area was recognised some years ago and many of the oldest buildings have been restored. This area is on the end of the peninsular and is famous for its tall, narrow homes, wrought iron balconies, and leafy courtyards.

The unique qualities of this area were recognised by two extremely upmarket cruise companies as a different destination for their well travelled passengers. Windjammer had added this to their itinerary a couple of years ago along with Boston. It was ideal for those becoming more interested in US history and had been growing steadily in popularity.

The weather was always a concern at this time of year but forecasting was now so good that Windjammer hadn't been bothered by anything greater than a force 6 in the years it had been using the route. If it had to stay in a port because of a bad forecast then the passengers generally looked at the horizon, nodded sagely and felt like proper seafarers whilst ordering another Plymouth Gin.

Carlos didn't think that making calls was safe but felt secure enough to google stuff about his destination so had done a fair amount of research on the area. He also knew from the daily itinerary dropped into the other cabins that Windjammer was due to dock in Charleston in five hours' time which was mid morning local time. But he still didn't know whether it was to tie up to the quay or transport passengers by tender. He hoped with all his heart that it was the former or his plan would have less chance to work.

He looked in the mirror and shaved his face as closely as he could. He then did something he had never done before, which was to shave his legs and arms. The feeling was extremely odd but essential to his disguise. As a Peruvian man with a certain amount of Inca blood he had smooth features, olive skin and extremely unusual slanted eyes, which made him stand out from the crowd. His other unusual feature was his prematurely white hair but after a few weeks at sea it had grown enough to show but was still only a few inches in length. He was not tall but still had the slim body that had seen him through so many sets of tennis in his youth.

A few hours before the arrival he tried on the outfit he'd selected from the trips down to the laundry. The shorts and track suit he put in the backpack for later but the dark blue linen summer dress, size 16, fitted him rather well and was loose enough to disguise his lack of breasts and long sleeved so his muscles were hidden. He had no choice but to wear his old trainers but they didn't look as odd as he'd feared. He'd tried the outfit on several times before and walked up the corridor a few times until it felt more natural but now came the real test, leaving the ship in front of the other passengers. He planned to leave his exit until the very last minute so that nobody had the time to look at him too closely.

He took off his clothes and lay back on his bunk, which was starting to smell like an old friend and tried to catch some sleep. His mind was obviously working whilst he was unconscious and he woke up with the conviction that he needed to leave with a group of people and not wait to the end as he'd originally planned.

He also woke up with a start as he could hear feet running on the deck above and realised that he had slept for four hours. He looked out of the porthole and could see a coastline quite close with old fashioned houses and gardens that swept down to the sea. He opened the door very carefully and heard the announcement that they would be docking in twenty minutes and would all passengers be ready for disembarkation as there would be coaches ready to take them on the New England Tour or the walk round the historic centre of the town and Deep South lunch. Thankfully he realised that they would be mooring at a quay and he wouldn't have to brave half an hour of intense scrutiny in a small boat. He ate what was edible from the fridge, had a drink of water and decided to have a quick shower and shave before he left.

He emerged from the bathroom fragrant with the last of the shower gel and gradually dressed in each piece of clothing, trying to think like the sophisticated American or Italian woman he imagined owned the dress. He heard the ship gently slide down the quay and heard the shouts of the crew as they threw the ropes to the waiting men. Gradually the ship slid to a halt and he could hear the familiar noise of the gangplank being slid out and secured. He heard the engines stop and the silence from the adjoining area to his cabin as the diesels came to rest. Looking out of the window he could see bright sunshine on the marina and some super yachts parked on the adjoining walkway and realised that the weather was perfect for his outfit.

Carlos looked in the mirror as he tried the stolen Gucci sunglasses and broad-brimmed straw hat on his head and didn't see much other than a blur. Thinking it through he realised that these were obviously prescription glasses and he needed to be careful otherwise he'd fall into the water or bump into a Sunseeker or something. He drew a big breath and squeezed out of the cabin, walking down the corridor until he reached the gangway up to the next level. As he started up the steps, he heard very loud American voices and pushed past them. As a discouragement to others he clamped his mobile to his ear and argued in a soft Spanish voice to someone at the other end. If anyone had been able to understand his Spanish, they would have been convinced that he/she was devastated about the behaviour of her partner Miguel and was going to leave him the minute she returned home.

He realised what a deterrent the mobile conversation was to others and enjoyed acting this role and kept it running as he went up to the level where passengers were leaving on the gangplank. He sincerely hoped that no-one would recognise his hat or dress and waited until a group of large Americans gathered in a group ready to go in single file down the wooden walkway. Much to his amazement a huge guy in a bright Hawaiian shirt stepped to one side to let him go first and he stepped forward with a muttered "gracias" and went down to the bottom and on to the planking of the marina walkway.

A few hundred people were on the walkway and were forced to form a narrow, slow moving queue in order to make any progress. Carlos kept up his argument with his mystery partner and tried to gently push ahead so he could see what was ahead. Last time he'd tried to leave the clipper he was stopped by the assassin so he had to hope that his progress wasn't stopped by him or anybody he recognised. He was in the US now so he was closer to his destination but also in the home ground of those spooks who'd tried to stop him before.

Squinting from under his hat he could see that all passengers were exiting through a gate in a high security fence and showing their passports to the officers. This would be the first time he'd used the false passport so he pulled it out of his bag and opened it on the front page.
As he got closer to his turn, he looked carefully through the chain-link fence and couldn't see anyone that resembled the guy in Edwardian dress. The officer looked bored and barely checked the documents in front of him but as he stepped up to the gate, he had a horrible thought. The passport was for a man not a woman! God, he thought, no time to hesitate so he added a tirade of angry Spanish into the phone and passed his documents over. The man looked startled but other loud American voices were complaining about the ridiculous wait behind and he handed the passport back to Carlos who pushed ahead so he could catch up with those ahead.

As he walked down the final path to where he could see a number of coaches parked, he saw a guy who looked as though he worked for the military or one of the agencies who interrogated him. He was standing by a booth with a number of security cameras which pointed to all parts of the marina and which was occupied by someone in a naval uniform.
"Which trip are you going on? "The fellow passenger's question shocked him into attention.
Thinking back to the announcement and reverting to English, Carlos said "Old T..Town," with a nervous stutter.
"Me too." The guy said and walked alongside, blocking the view of the cameras as they walked together towards a bus with Heritage Tour written on the outside.

Hoping that his disguise wasn't so good that this Yank wanted to flirt with him he shuffled along and saw the marina shower/toilet block ahead. Making his excuses in English he rushed over to the building and pushed his way into the main doors and was faced with guy in a smart blazer behind a desk. Reverting to Spanish Carlos asked for the loos and was guided through a side door and down a corridor where he could see both male and female signs. Having a crisis of gender Carlos thought quickly and decided that a 'woman' in a gents would create far less fuss than the reverse and pushed into the gents. Luckily the room wasn't crowded and he could just see and hear a couple of men at the far end having a shower who hadn't seen him. He pushed into a cubical and locked the door, considering his dress options. Though the female outfit had worked so far, he really didn't think it would work much longer. He had been in crowds, and where he was going he would be under far more scrutiny, so unless he was trying to pretend to be transgender then he needed to change. Also thinking about it clearly, he had a male passport and needed to look like a plausible male traveller.

Carlos looked at the stuff left in the backpack. First there were lots of hundred dollar notes – which would be essential later because he didn't have any cards. It was still around 20 degrees out there and sunny and sailors tend to be incredibly casual, even scruffy round their boats. The track suit was possibility but really didn't feel right. The simple cream shorts fitted him well and one of the original white T-Shirts still looked serviceable so he put them on. He felt a lot more confident but realised he had to get rid of his other outfit. He tried to rip the hat but it was too strong so he folded it up as tightly as possible and did the same with the dress, putting them both out of sight in the top of the pack.

Feeling more human, he went for a wee, washed his hands and face and walked back down the corridor to reception. The guy in the blazer wasn't there so Carlos pressed the exit button and was about to walk out when a thought occurred to him. His white hair was still short but it was a feature that stood out, he thought for a moment and turned back into the building and headed for the chandlers he'd seen. It was more like an upmarket sailing clothes store really and Carlos looked around for any hat that covered his hair and looked appropriate. The Sunseeker baseball hat covered his head and looked fine.

Carlos left the building and headed away from the boats, over on the far side of the car park he could see his fellow passengers boarding the coach. He looked back and could see the agency guy looking over to the boats and then started down the quay to check out the rest of the area. He realised he needed to get out and began walking along the road as fast as possible, his heart hammering. After five minutes he passed through the barrier guarding the marina and kept walking, realising he needed to find somewhere to stop and plan his next move.

The first bar he came across looked a little downmarket for the marina's normal clientele and was called Firenze. Knowing that this was Italian and hoping for the first decent cup of coffee he'd had for months, he opened the door. Inside was a reassuringly large Gaggia coffee machine resplendent in chrome and brass and a swarthy guy leaning on the bar. Carlos had only managed basic Italian but attempted to order in Italian. The guy looked shocked but impressed that anyone could order a double expresso and glass of water so well despite not being Italian.

He took his time and produced a tiny cup of liquid stimulant and Carlos sat down and sipped it with obvious pleasure. The bartender was second generation Italian but shared all his ancestors' veneration for good food, good wine and good coffee. The problem was in South Carolina you didn't get that many people who appreciated it as much. Seeing the man's quite unusual looks, the bartender asked in Italian where his customer was from and seeing the concentration on his face repeated it in English.
"Lima." Carlos said in English.
"Jeez you're a long way from home – have you just come in by boat or something."
"Yes"

The guy had been in the US Navy and visited Peru and they chatted for a while about the beauty of the country and other places including Panama where Carlos had said that he'd embarked originally. They talked about the supertanker entrance that had been opened since the guy had been through and the crazy size of the vessels going through. After a while the guy asked what he was doing next and Carlos decided he needed a little local knowledge and admitted that he didn't know this area and needed to get to Boston urgently.

The barman told him where some local stores were for supplies and offered him the name of a cousin who ran a cheap taxi service. Sensing a good deal, Carlos said to ring the cousin to see what he would charge for a morning's hire. The barkeep went to the back of the cafe and whispered in Italian on the mobile and came back with a figure. Carlos knew about bartering and offered 50% in the traditional manner and after a few more stages they settled on 75% with honour on both sides.
Carlos had a pastry and another coffee and asked for the taxi in half an hour. He took his drink over to the window and enjoyed the flaky delicious sweetness of the cake. A police car slowly cruised by

outside and Carlos pulled involuntarily away from the glass. The bartender had seen all kinds of people in his life and suspected that he was on the run.
"Somebody after you?
He nodded and gave him the excuse that he'd jumped ship and just needed to get to Boston in a hurry or things would get a lot worse.
"Have you got plenty of money?"
"Enough" Carlos said guardedly.
"Well Roberto, my cousin has lots of contacts who might be able to help."
"Thanks, but we'll see how it goes."

The guy nodded and Carlos went back to his plans in silence. The barman went back to washing glasses and plates and stacking them on the shelves behind. When the taxi arrived outside, it was an old Lancia with nothing usual like a taxi sign or licence and the driver, who was holding open the rear door for him, looked like an older version of the bartender. Carlos did not trust him.

A few miles away Pete Davis was in a bind. He'd been told by Kowolski to man the cameras and check whether a fugitive called Fantoni came off a ship called Windjammer, but everything about this mission had been a farce. Firstly, when he arrived at the marina and shown his ID nobody had known he was coming and refused to let him into the customs/security office. It had taken ages for them to agree anyone to check passengers but then a navy officer was given a poor quality photograph of a white haired guy to put in the system and too little time. Bromby had to stand outside and check the departing passengers visually which had been difficult because the queue was crowded and he didn't have a clear field of vision.

After fifteen minutes observation of all passengers who had now left the marina, neither watcher had a positive ID. Davis and the navy guy checked over the footage and the system had pulled up no-one certain. Three people were seen as being men of approximately the right size but when analysed, each image was discounted in turn as the target. There was one image that conformed to roughly the right build but that was female, obscured by other people and wearing a hat.
The big hat had been a little suspicious at this time of year but nothing positive. Now the agent couldn't work out whether to phone Kowolski or not. His boss was a vicious bastard who treated his staff almost as bad as he treated his prisoners and was distracted by an operation in Boston they were planning. In the end Davis compromised and pulled in few favours with the local police chief

and got him to circulate Fantoni's mug shot, saying that he was an important fugitive.

The two Ford Interceptors were squad cars that had been fitted with the latest tech a few years ago and the alert flashed on their screens a few seconds later. The Harley Davidsons had similar alerts but police motorcyclists were supposed to stop before they looked at them on their tablets. No one did but the shot of the white haired guy with the slightly unusual face was difficult to see because the quality was bad. What was totally clear was that he was a dangerous fugitive, wanted by Washington and all the officers could see promotion in the wind if they found him. The shot had obviously been taken in some kind of prison like Guantanamo because he was wearing an orange jumpsuit and he had a rough black beard that contrasted strangely with his shock of white hair.

Within five minutes the two Ford squad cars and one Harley – all in their distinctive Charleston black and white livery – were joined by the unmarked Dodge Charger used for pursuit work. All were circling the marina area in a show of force not seen since the police chief had been up for election.

As the final squad car was entering the area, Carlos decided that he had no choice but to trust the driver for the moment and settled back into the lovely leather of the old Lancia Fulvia and asked the guy where was the best place to buy some clothes and a new mobile. Carlos explained that he had been in an accident a few days previously and had lost most of his gear. He could see the Italian nodding sympathetically in the mirror whilst driving at speed down the highway and suspected that his genetics would mean he drove like a madman most of the time, trying to be a Fangio or some other Italian racing legend of the last century.
"Fiorelli is a great place to buy clothes and he's a relation - so you'll get a great deal." The guy said in a deep south drawl totally at odds with his looks.
"OK, let's have a look." Carlos answered wondering just how many other relations there were in this man's family.

The shop was a double fronted architectural gem with wrought iron balconies and climbing vines. Inside was clothing he hadn't seen since Salimond had bought him work outfits in London. Some of the Italian designer suits were thousands of dollars and Carlos said in reasonable Italian that they were out of his league. The manager nodded and sized him up and saw him as 40 inch chest, 32 inch waist, 5 feet 10 inch guy which was pretty close to an average

Italian man. He thought for a while and took him to a rack of suits on a sale rack that he said were the previous year's styles but perfectly acceptable to most men.

Carlos chose a dark blue single breasted suit in a light wool and looked around until he saw some racks of shirts. He chose a narrow blue stripe, button down style in cotton and a similar style in white. At this point he asked the manager what the cost was and he played with his calculator for a few seconds before coming up with a figure that anyone could tell was wildly optimistic. Fantoni said nothing but went over and tried on a pair of English brogues and looked at an Italian leather overnight bag and various socks and underwear. He bundled them all up and walked back to the till and said that he would pay the original figure quoted if all the items were included. The manager laughed as if this was the silliest idea he'd ever heard and they started on a series of offers and counter offers which kept them both entertained for two minutes. After agreement, Carlos went to the fitting room and changed. Whilst he was out of sight, he checked his money and did a mental calculation as to what he would need for taxi, plane tickets etc. and realised he still had enough of the original Black Card money to cover everything likely.

On the way out he picked up a light coat which cost him a hundred dollar note and Carlos went out to the Lancia wishing the manager happiness as he left. The Manager of Fiorelli was happy at the way he had managed to get rid of some old stock but worried that he'd lost the art of barter and been beaten by an unusual foreign guy. He also had to admit that the guy looked a million dollars in the outfit and knew how to choose clothes like an Italian.

Back in the Lancia, Fantoni asked the guy where to buy a phone and was surprised that he didn't have a relative selling them. In the end his driver took him to a strange shop in a back street and Carlos bought three inexpensive smartphones that could be disposed of after use. He asked the drive to stop at a coffee shop or bar where he could eat and he was dropped at a small bistro in the business centre. Carlos agreed that the driver would return in an hour and went in for a plate of Creole Fish stew and a glass of beer.

Using one of the phones, Carlos rang up Delta Airlines, who he knew flew direct to Boston and said he needed to get there quickly and when was the next possible flight. The office mentioned a flight in four hours and Carlos explained he wanted to pay cash as he'd had a credit card cloned so it was arranged that he would pay at the Delta desk. He then did a little more research ate his food and waited for his driver to arrive.

Charleston police officer O'Mally had been cruising the marina area for an hour or two looking for the fugitive. Some of the bars near the docks had an early trade and always had their share of drug dealers, drunks and derelicts. So, when a wild haired guy shot out of one of them and looked terrified when he saw the squad car, O'Mally gave him special attention. He had white hair, a black beard and had started to run clumsily down the road. The cop floored the accelerator and caught up with him in seconds, then his partner leapt out of the car and grabbed the guy whilst reading out the standard warning.

The criminal turned and tried to throw a punch which missed the cop by inches, he tried to reach for his pocket but the cop hit him with a right cross which was one to be proud of. The guy went down like a sack of potatoes and was cuffed. O'Mally looked closely at him, thought that it looked like the fugitive and called it in. Within five minutes he was in an ambulance and the squad car was following them to the hospital. Feeling proud of his cops and anxious to take credit, the Chief called off the search and eventually remembered to call the CIA watcher he'd talked to earlier. They agreed that the Chief would meet him at the hospital when the guy recovered consciousness.

Carlos Fantoni now had to assume the identity of Juan Lopez who was of Spanish nationality according to the passport he'd been given in Panama. His Spanish was pretty perfect but with a Peruvian accent which would confuse anyone from Spain. But he thought the chances of that happening was low compared to the risk of using a false passport anyway. As this was a US internal flight, he hoped that security would be less than international flights and although the documents looked good, he really didn't know about their quality. His original passport had been left in the hotel safe in Boston along with his clothes and personal affects. As to what happened to them after he was abducted, he had no idea, but he hoped at least his passport had been stored because he needed to get his original name and identity back before too long.

Fantoni at least looked like the respectable and stylish businessman he'd been a few months ago. The new suit and shirt fitted him beautifully and the driver looked with approval after he emerged from Fiorelli gentlemen's outfitters.
"I told you this was a good place."
"Yeh, thanks." Carlos responded.

"Where next?"
"The Charles Towne Hotel please." Carlos requested, thinking yet again that he really didn't trust this man.

After 20 minutes of crazy driving the Lancia pulled into the forecourt of the old fashioned hotel and a doorman came out to open the rear door. Fantoni handed him a small wad of dollar bills and said that he might be staying at the hotel overnight and would call the driver in the morning. The driver looked astonished but had no chance to stop Fantoni as he was already out of the car and rushing into the hotel. Carlos was in the foyer before the guy had time to think and saw the Lancia wait for a few minutes and then pull out into the traffic with a squeal of its tyres.

Fantoni went to the lavatory and then walked back to the foyer and asked the receptionist to arrange a taxi to the airport. Carlos hadn't wanted the driver to know where he was going and didn't want to give him any opportunity to steal his remaining dollars. He might be getting paranoid but as he was being sought by the CIA, gangsters and just about everyone else, paranoia might be a little justified.

The only people he trusted, the only people who shared his need to expose the Greenwatch scandal were Joanne Li and Dane Morgan and he hadn't been able to contact them for weeks. They had arranged a simple code that he would use when he was close to arriving in Boston so he pulled out his mobile and sent the text message. Carlos knew that they were expecting him to arrive by boat so he had to find some way to change that expectation.

This taxi was an official cab and it made the short journey to the airport without incident. The cab dropped him at the terminal and Carlos pushed his way through the crowd of business people at arrivals and looked for the Delta Airlines desk. On the way he remembered to dump the mobile he'd used in a rubbish bin and pulled out the second phone. At the desk he initially spoke in Spanish and seeing the confusion on the girl's face, reverted to accented English and requested the ticket he'd reserved by phone. To avoid suspicion Carlos used the card cloning story again and got sympathetic noises from the little blonde who said the exact same thing happened to her on a trip to Europe last year and Amex took forever to send her a new one. Then the little Mexican looking guy next to her said he'd had the same with Visa on a trip back to Mexico. It seemed a common problem and the two assistants eventually issued his one-way ticket and boarding pass with a cheery "Adios."

Carlos had got quite good, he thought, over the last few weeks at becoming different people. His command of languages helped but he couldn't do much about his appearance which was too Inca to fit in over here or in Europe. Some people found it attractive and Carlos felt a pang of sadness as he thought of Diane Fallow the reporter who'd discovered the Greenwatch conspiracy and become his lover. She had been murdered before she could publish and her story killed off. Carlos was determined to prove her right and expose her murderer but first he had to get to Boston. The Delta flight was due to leave in just over an hour and judging by the number of people in the lounge, it was going to be a busy flight.

Carlos pulled out his passport, memorised his new name and joined the queue for security hoping that the passport was good enough to get past the big black guy checking documents. He could hear his own heart beating and tried to look calm.

Chapter 23

Joanne and Dane had been quietly going crazy. It had been ages since they'd seen Carlos Fantoni, not since they had handed him over to the smuggler who got him on board the clipper in Panama. They'd had a pre-arranged text from the guy to say it had gone well but no direct contact with Carlos. Everyone was too paranoid to use mobiles as they knew due to the resources GCHQ and the US agencies had, they would probably be traced. So they'd arranged a simple text code to be sent when he was getting near and hoped that it wouldn't trigger any interest.

They had to organise Fantoni's journey in a hurry without really having time to work out the implications of sending him by sailing ship. When they saw how many days the voyage would take, they realised just how late he would arrive. The original plan was for him to be there in the last few weeks of the Presidential campaign so he could cause maximum embarrassment at one of the conventions. But the way it was working he would arrive in the last few days with no power to influence anything. They sat round the table in Boston with Professor Li and brainstormed how to compensate for the lack of Fantoni's presence and really not got any real answers.

There was a serious lack of evidence. Jo's blog had been wiped with all the important stuff like Dane's shots of the original abduction and the Carlos interview where he exposed Wolf Bayer and all the Greenwatch crew. Everything had been wiped off Dane's camera and laptop too so they were without anything. One hope had been the Cloud and as this type of back up was used by Dane Morgan they'd quietly hoped that this had not been tampered with. To all of them the Cloud was a mysterious concept but it was impossible to interfere with, according to one of Dane's old contacts in IT. In desperation Jo called a contact in one of the social media companies who was more tech-savvy than anyone else they knew and he agreed to come over. Emile Sanders had been in love with Joanne Li since they'd been at college but had always looked about twelve years old. Years later he still looked like a boy but had retired after a sparkling career with Facebook, Instagram and various other platforms. He listened to the explanation about the lost material from Dane's camera and nodded sadly when Jo said that she thought Washington had been behind it. He still thought the backup would be safe and spent an hour and a full bottle of Barolo trying to find it. At the end slightly bleary eyed he had to admit defeat.

This was a real blow to Jo and Dane as they had absolutely nothing else. It wasn't only their recent history that had gone, the SCC environmental disaster he had discovered 18 months ago had been exposed on the Corporate Li's blog and now that had gone too. Some of the traditional media might have that story on their files, but the blog was personal. Dane had rescued her in New Zealand because of that story and they wouldn't have met without it. They had used the Corporate Li's blog after that as a way of getting the story out without apparently breaking the non disclosure agreements they had been forced to sign. And it had worked, a First Minister had resigned and an evil CEO had been killed because they had been exposed. More importantly the pollution of a beautiful lake had been revealed and the company responsible had been forced to clean it up. This was their history and someone had wiped it out.

Professor Li asked his friend from Shelford, James Spencer to join their brainstorming session. He and the Professor had been highly critical of their University at the beginning when they'd not questioned the claim that Greenwatch had been invented at Shelford, which was tenuous to say the least. Yet the institution had accepted an extremely valuable donation from Salimond which the two professors thought was extremely damaging to its reputation and was effectively bribery. The Chancellor had not admitted any fault and the only result of the confrontation so far was that the Business Manager had been asked to resign.

Dane and Joanne suggested that the meeting place be changed because of security. They had decided to inform Spencer about the full story of Greenwatch, Fantoni, the abduction and everything since. He had a good brain and had been there when Dane returned to the Grosvenor Club trying to find his shoes all those months ago, so he had witnessed the beginning of this extraordinary story. They met at the university common room and spent ten minutes bringing him up to date. Initially he found it difficult to believe and thought that it might be one of Dane's strange jokes. The look on everyone's face showed that they were deadly serious.

The thing that made the whole thing so unreal was just how well the Greenwatch test was going in Boston. Mayor Bonelli was now just off life support but already taking credit for the test which was doing so well. Republican ratings had improved exponentially since the test started and the President had been filmed at the mayor's bedside, more than once, talking about the success of the 'Vote for Me and Breathe Easy' campaign. Spencer couldn't believe that any politician could be so heartless as to use Greenwatch to spread lies. Dane and Jo needed Fantoni to prove that it was true.

Spencer suspected that US politicians were faced with an impossible task in cleaning up the cities and might be tempted to hide the true situation. But it was the highest possible risk if they did and they were literally playing with people's lives.

James Spencer lectured in economics and often had heated discussions with Professor Li about the benefits of science in the real world. But they were both incensed by the way money had compromised their hallowed institution and had started to achieve some changes to college policy. Their politics were very different normally and Li's republican zeal was countered by Spencer's democrat conscience. This was offended mightily by the dirty tricks and violent actions that the incumbent President had apparently sanctioned in order to stop Carlos Fantoni.

After an hour of intense brainstorming Jo, Dane and the two professors had achieved very little. Spencer knew an influential Democratic senator and offered to bring him into the conversation but there was a worry that his party was so far behind at present that he would be seen as a sore loser and not believed. Jo had good contacts with the environmental media and some of the local TV stations but without Fantoni they had no evidence and even the bravest of programmes would need something tangible before they ran anything as controversial as this. In short, they needed Fantoni.

The group tried to work out any way that they could get Fantoni off the ship early but didn't have the resources to intercept Windjammer. Then a text message had come from an unknown number. CB21:30Air and Jo had screamed so loud that Dane jumped up out of the easy chair.

Fantoni remembered the simple text – C for Carlos. B for Boston and originally it was just to say Today. That code would have been understood as Windjammer docking in Boston today, get down to the harbour and meet me! He tried to think of something that Jo would still understand that would alert her of his arrival on the Delta flight without being obvious to anyone monitoring incoming calls to her phone. He had deliberated for a long time in Charleston and then sent the text knowing that in a few minutes the mobile would be at the bottom of a bin.

He was in the queue for the Delta Airlines flight and in front was a family of people of colour who looked extremely prosperous and when Carlos considered the history of the area and the way that much of its prosperity was based on the exploitation of slaves, it was a little reassuring that at least some of their descendants had made good. Now he had his own injustices to fight and was determined not to be stopped at this point.

The customs check official looked at the well dressed guy and tried to figure out his origins. It was a game he played with himself on busy days to keep himself sane. The passenger was medium height, a very fit looking 30 something and had short white hair which made him stand out. He thought he was some form of Asian maybe or he might be American Indian as the slant of the eyes was quite unusual. He stopped and looked at the passport – Juan Lopez – Spanish. Well, he never would have guessed Spanish thought the guard, but then he didn't see that many Spaniards and waved him through with a pleasant smile.

Carlos drew breath and tried to calm himself as he walked down the corridor towards the departure gate. His heart was still hammering in his chest and he kept the deep breathing going until it started to slow. After a while he settled down and hid behind a newspaper he'd picked up in the terminal, the front page was all about the election and had a photograph of the President and Mayor Bonelli of Boston with a write up of the campaign so far.

Bonelli had been the politician he'd first sold Greenwatch to in the US and he remembered the big mayor who'd seen the potential and signed up for the first test. Fantoni was surprised to read that he'd had a major heart attack a few weeks ago and was still in hospital. Looking at the photograph it was clear that he was well enough to be part of the campaign even from his sick bed.
Fantoni was weeks out of date as he hadn't got much news on the ship, so the article was really interesting. He suspected the paper had Republican sympathies but the President had obviously done hugely well with his Breathe Easy approach and seemed to be committed to environmental improvements in a way that no previous administration had. Greenwatch was central to that campaign and the party had committed to install units in the top 10 cities with bad air quality before the end of next year.

Carlos looked at the editorial with astonishment. He knew better than most people just how bad the air was in those cities, which stretched from California to Alaska.
He knew that the Greenwatch units used properly, would not tell any

lies and the amount of dangerous particulates shown on the monitors would really frighten the local populations. So the extent of the promise was astonishing and Fantoni could only see three possible reasons why:
1. The President was making promises that he would never keep, just to get elected.
2. He was genuinely planning to clean up the cities.
3. He was planning to use the special software at some point and falsify the readings.

Analysing the likely options was difficult because he hadn't been brought up in the warped, cynical families who had dominated the US political scene before and after Obama. He had learned a lot during his sales' trips to the US and realised that most of the politicians were obsessed with apparent success more than principals. But scared of failure, media criticism and litigations more than anything. This applied to both parties but as the Republicans were in power then the principal was doubly true.

Of the possible reasons, Carlos thought that Option 1 was unlikely because although he might slow down the installation a little, the cities that had been highlighted as bad air places would demand Greenwatch on their streets and not allow it to be halted.
Option 2 was what he hoped the President wanted to do but the measures required would be dramatic including a ban on all traditional vehicles and changing public transport to electric. After all this time and all the evidence presented, surely one President would have the courage to bite the bullet and do it? But it would be difficult to sell the sacrifices required by the general public if they were really going to make the big changes. They might have to change their cars, their heating systems and all kinds of other things and that would be difficult for many to accept.

Option 3 was what Fantoni really feared. If the President was re-elected then he might be tempted to install Greenwatch, make some comparatively minor changes and then falsify the readings so that the improvements were overstated. Politicians are such short term thinkers and are only concerned about their next term in office. It might take years before the true situation was seen and then it would be someone else's problem. Republicans might justify things in their own minds by thinking that it gave them more time to solve the problem properly or they might just hope that the whole situation became much less of a public concern and they could ignore it.

As a scientist, Fantoni knew that radical change was needed and the reason that Salimond had originally backed Greenwatch was that it was seriously good technology but if corrupted it could give them an extra five or even ten years before they had to change their dirty habits.

As he walked up to the embarkation area Carlos knew there was only one way to ensure that the President made the right choice which was to make everything public knowledge as soon as possible and take Greenwatch out of political control.

After twenty minutes hiding behind the paper and memorising in his mind his new name and nationality, the girl on the gate desk picked up the microphone and announced that the Delta flight would be delayed because of a technical difficulty. There were collective groans from the other passengers and Carlos started to panic. Had someone double checked his ID, had someone from the CIA recognised him? He looked around for anyone new coming into the lounge and tried to control his breathing.

"Every time I try to get to Boston in a hurry, Delta screw it up."

Fantoni looked across at the short, fat guy in the sweaty white shirt and tartan trousers, who was complaining loudly to anyone who cared to listen and thought that if anyone looked less like a government agent, then he had not seen one. Fantoni tried to ignore him and nod sympathetically but it was hard to avoid the eye contact.

"Si eez veery bad." Fantoni said in a reasonably good Spanish accent.

"You Mexican?"

"No Espanol."

That seemed to shut the guy up and Fantoni decided to go to the lavatory to avoid further contact and be out of sight. He spent twenty minutes hiding in a cubicle before he heard the Delta girl saying that the technical problem had been solved and that embarkation would take place in ten minutes. He waited 10 and then went to the basins to check his appearance. Actually, the good shirt and suit fitted him extremely well and made him look like a prosperous businessman. He needed a shave but so many men sported stubble these days, it didn't matter and his white hair had grown but was nothing like his original style. He couldn't do much about his face but gave it a good wash and tried to dry it, thinking that perhaps he would have been better with a hat but it was too late now and he just needed to trust fate and hope that Jo and Dane had got the message and were at O'Hare airport to meet him when he arrived.

It had taken a few minutes for Jo to decipher the text message. CB she knew meant Carlos and Boston which was simple. But they hadn't expected the text for a few days yet as the ship wasn't due in Boston until then. So something had changed and they knew that Carlos would have been worrying about the delays as much as they had. She realised that Windjammer has stopped earlier that day in Charleston and started to work out what he'd done. Looking online she checked incoming flights to Boston Logan and found what she needed.

"Listen everyone" she said quietly to the rest of the team. "I've worked out the text and Carlos will be coming in to Boston at 21:30 tonight by Delta Airlines."

They were still gathered round a low coffee table in one of the meeting areas and there was a silence as everyone considered how this affected the campaign they'd been planning over the last few hours.

"Brilliant, absolutely brilliant, but we better drive to the airport and get him to safety as soon as possible." Dane's English accent was more pronounced when he was excited which Jo loved and he jumped up and started to leave before Jo grabbed his arm and persuaded him to sit back down until they had time to consider the implications. Dane had been sitting for hours which was more than enough for any man and was desperate for action, but could see that Jo was right and slumped back down with a sigh.

Jo looked around the room and saw odd groups of families, students and staff and no one who looked suspicious or who could overhear them.

"We all met here because I thought there was every chance my parents' home had been bugged."

Professor Li looked shocked but agreed that it was the safest assumption and Jo continued.

"We can obviously meet here again but I suggest that all of us are careful of what we say at home. There are two things that we need to agree urgently, firstly who meets him at the airport and then where he can stay to be safe."

The group discussed the best options for both and eventually came to the conclusion that as Dane wasn't a US citizen and his visa could be revoked instantly, he should stay home at the moment. Of the rest of the group, Carlos would only recognise Jo, so she had to be there. Dane didn't like the idea of not being there with her but couldn't deny the logic, he remembered the threats of the US agent at the Grosvenor Club all those weeks ago and knew Jo was right. It was logical therefore, that she went with Professor Li who was a respected local academic who the authorities would find difficult to snatch or extradite without serious implications.

When it came to where Carlos Fantoni would be hidden, they had some real difficulty. The Li's home would be an obvious target for anyone looking for him and putting him in a hotel seemed far too risky. After a while James Spencer volunteered his place as a refuge and the group realised it was a decent option. His wife was away visiting relations in Ireland and wouldn't be back for weeks. He hadn't really been involved with Dane and Jo's campaign and wouldn't be on any agencies databases as a potential contact. He was a US citizen with impeccable lineage and as fellow academics Spencer and Li had every excuse to speak on a regular basis so planning meetings were easy to facilitate. Everyone agreed on the immediate plan and realised they had a couple of hours to put things in place before Fantoni arrived.

A few miles away in the office Kowolski occupied occasionally when he was in the US, he was going over his plans to plausibly eliminate Carlos Fantoni when he arrived in a couple of days. This was totally undercover even to the FBI and other local agencies because the Presidential aide wanted it that way. Which meant that he was using a lot fewer people and knew that increased the chances of a cock-up. He had an almost superstitious belief that every plan had a hidden mistake, something that took endless reviews to find and only when he found it did he relax and feel happy. In this case, he hadn't prepared for the eventuality if there was bad weather and the ship had to go to the outer marina. Having now covered that base Kowolski lit another illegal cigarette and leant back.

Kowolski knew that what he was doing was illegal but his agency had no real legal structure anyway and often had a brief that would have given those old ladies in the senate apoplexy. In this case he was confident that dealing with the White House was as safe as anything else he'd been asked to do over the last few years. The President was going to be re-elected and would end up on the side of the angels but he had a fall back plan just in case.

Alexander Brown was an English assassin and part of Kowolski's plan. He'd asked to be the first in the reception committee when Fantoni arrived and they'd agreed Brown was perfect - he looked like an old time villain with his odd dress and sword and he was desperate to deal with Fantoni. If anyone afterwards researched his funding, they'd find the contract on Fantoni had been paid for by someone in Iran and people would draw their own conclusions. Kowolski had agreed to let Brown have first stab at Fantoni but planned to kill him immediately after. As far as the agency was concerned having an agent killing a known assassin was good TV. If that was after the assassin had killed a chap who'd been trying to clean up the world, then that was very, very sad.

Kowolski had an email from the colleague who'd been monitoring all incoming communications to the Li household and been checking videos. There had been dozens of calls and emails over the last few days but nothing suspicious but there were some texts from unknown numbers to Jo's phone a couple of hours ago. Kowolski scanned them briefly and decided to wander out of the office for a little fresh air and come back when he could concentrate.

He lit up a Marlborough before he got out of the lift which got shocked gasps from the women in the same car and exhaled smoke with an audible sigh exiting with a traditional middle fingered salute to the rest of the occupants. Outside it was late evening and Kowolski strolled down the street trying to work out why it was so quiet. He saw the green box on the pole and remembered that when the Greenwatch units on test flashed red, the mayor banned cars for 24 hours and everyone obeyed. He blew cigarette smoke at the unit and laughed nastily at his own thoughts. Generally, he didn't believe much in air pollution or any of that crap, his father had been in a coal town and breathed in smoke for ever and he'd lasted 80 years. Personally, the only pollution he believed in was people pollution from terrorists and misfits - he enjoyed cleaning them out more than anything.

After twenty minutes hard walking and two more cigarettes, Kowolski felt refreshed enough to go back to the office and read through his emails again. He put his eye against the retinal scanner and the outer office door opened and he followed a similar process with eye and voice checks on the inner door and entered the office he'd occupied for the last few days. The last texts had come into Joanne Li's mobile about 18:00 hours Eastern Seaboard Time and his associate had tried to chase the identity of the mobile user and found nothing. The fact it was a 'burner' might be significant but the fact it was from South Carolina was a bit of a mystery. Recent satellite images had shown the Windjammer to be at sea and to the best of their knowledge Fantoni was still there. Something bothered him so he looked again at the text CB21:30Air. The second part of the text could obviously be a time and Air could be a flight but who was CB?

Kowolski switched to the live feed from the Li house and saw Dane

Morgan sitting at the kitchen table with Mrs Li. Turning up the sound he heard that they were talking about New Zealand and how Mrs Li wanted to visit there but was worried about the length of the flight. Dane was encouraging her to go... Kowolski pulled out the earphone and wondered where Joanne Li was. He checked cameras in the other rooms and she wasn't there. It was unusual for her and Dane not to be together but not unique because he went to the Grosvenor Club sometimes without her. Kowolski looked at his watch and realised that it was nearly 9.00 o'clock – 21:00 and that if 21:30 was a flight then he had no time at all to get to Boston Logan. C might be Carlos, B might be Boston – shit if he was right, he was almost too late. He grabbed his gun and jacket and ran to the door.

Carlos Fantoni got through the check-in at the gate with no problem and tried to avoid the big sweaty guy who had button-holed him earlier and was still loudly complaining about the flight. He had tried to talk again but Fantoni hit him with a blast of fluent Spanish that seemed to deter him. In the end Fantoni was sat next to a business woman who nodded in a friendly manner and after take off she fired up her iPad, put in some earphones and seemed to be drafting a report.
After half an hour Fantoni got out of the seat and went up the aisle to the lavatories at the back. He couldn't see anyone that looked suspicious and thought that he'd become quite clever at recognising men who might be from a government agency. They all looked like versions of the men who'd abducted him at the Grosvenor Club all those weeks ago – broad, black suited, 30 something in age and mainly white. He couldn't see anyone who resembled that description but wasn't going to bet his life on his quality of agent recognition, so he kept himself out of sight for as long as possible. The flight was just over two hours and the original delay on departure seemed to be have been made up in transit because the Captain came on the tannoy and said proudly that they would be arriving at Logan at 21:30 as scheduled.

The crew went to their stations for landing and Fantoni could see the lights of the city and its hi-rise business district as the plane banked and turned for its final approach. Fantoni could feel the knot in his stomach getting tighter as the aircraft descended and smoothly touched down. There were the normal announcements and the plane taxied slowly to its bay and passengers started to unbuckle and stand up, opening the overhead lockers and taking out their cases. Fantoni just had the leather shoulder bag and pulled it out of the locker, thinking that it had very little in it except for a new shirt, underwear, his Nike trainers and the track suit he'd stolen off the ship a few days ago. The only other thing which might have caused comment was the remaining cash. He hadn't counted it but there was still a significant wad of $100 bills left after he'd paid for all the clothes, tickets and taxis he'd had to buy earlier in the day.

Memorising his Juan Lopez ID and trying to look as unconcerned as other passengers on the flight, Fantoni followed everyone off the aircraft and kept walking.

Kowolski might have made it, the big V8 in the Dodge Charger started with a satisfying roar in the underground car park and he hammered it round each corner with the tyres squealing. He nearly rammed the barrier and got his card in so fast that the system rejected his attempt. Breathing deeply and concentrating he put the card in correctly and saw the barrier lift slowly up. It had already been ten minutes since he'd seen the email and he had to get to the airport on time or he might miss Fantoni. That is if his theory about the text made any sense.

He accelerated out of the car park and swung the Dodge left so he could take the interstate to the airport, he was doing about 70 when he saw the illuminated cones across the road and tried to weave round them but found himself facing a Boston City squad car and a large police officer pointing a radar gun.

Kowolski was in a serious quandary. Nobody, especially the cops, knew what he was doing and the last thing he wanted to do was leave an official trail. So he braked heavily and stopped the Dodge within a few feet of the officer, buzzing the driver's window down so he could speak to the cop.
"What's the problem, officer?" Kowolski asked with barely concealed contempt.
"You." Said the cop, looking at the read-out on the back of the radar gun. "You were doing over 70 when I clocked you."
Kowolski was tempted to blow the cop away but knew that he was wearing a body camera and film would be relayed to headquarters as he spoke. "Really sorry officer, I've been working late and I really needed to get to the airport."
"That's not all sir, you were driving in the centre of Boston on one of the Mayor's Red Days when all traffic is banned and cars disobeying this regulation are impounded and drivers fined one thousand dollars. Please step out of the car sir." The cop didn't like the look of this driver and drew his gun.
"Officer, I'm on official business and I must get to the airport – it's a matter of national security."

"Sir, just get out of your vehicle." The cop raised his gun and levelled it at Kowolski.

"OK, OK." Kowolski knew that he had no option and got out of the vehicle with his hands up.

"Officer, I'd like to show you my ID, so I'm putting my hand inside my jacket, OK?"

The cop nodded and Kowolski pulled out his wallet and in the process, it was impossible not to show the shoulder holster he wore, which made the cop even more nervous. He carefully looked at the CIA card which was one of a number of alternative ID's that Kowolski could have shown and called in to HQ on his throat mic to check it out. The cop was an old hand and had encountered the odd spook before but kept his gun levelled on Kowolski for what felt like hours before he was allowed on his way.

Kowolski was furious. He looked down at his watch and realised that the plane would have landed ages ago. Still he gunned the Dodge now he was out of the Mayor's Red Zone and was outside the Arrivals terminal just twenty minutes later. It was difficult to see anything in the lights of the terminal building as there were dozens of people dropping off and collecting friends and family. He decided to park the Dodge illegally and walk back to see if he could see anything.

Professor Li drove a Toyota plug-in hybrid that was about five years old because he wasn't quite brave enough to go fully electric. His daughter scoffed at his attitude and scolded him every time he got it out of the garage, saying that he didn't need a car at all and should help save the planet and use public transport. He loved her too much to point out the fact that she was normally complaining about his profligacy when being given a lift in the very same car. But no one could doubt her sincerity when it came to the big issues like global warming and pollution and she had nearly lost her life trying to expose an environmental disaster a few months back. So he kept his mouth shut and listened more to her causes these days and tried to help. Which is why he was outside Boston Logan airport at the moment trying to rescue a fugitive he'd never met.

One of the great advantages of having a hybrid car at this airport was that there were hundreds of parking spaces dedicated to low emission vehicles and lots of charging points. The Professor and Joanne had arrived an hour before the flight was due and found a dedicated space very close to the pickup point at Arrivals. Jo looked at her flight app and waited till she knew the Delta plane had landed and passengers were off loaded. She then left the car and entered the terminal so she could check the gate hadn't changed on the screens inside and said that she would phone her father when she had Carlos so he could drive to the pickup area near the building.

It felt like Joanne hadn't seen Fantoni for months and so much had happened. She knew that his false passport was in the name of Lopez and he was supposed to be Spanish but when they last saw him, he'd had his head shaved and been dressed to look like a port worker. If the text meant what they thought it meant, then he'd managed to get off the ship and get through security, so he had been extremely clever or incredibly lucky. They knew he was well educated - getting a double first from a top US college whilst holding down a national tennis scholarship needed intelligence and determination, but this sort of challenge was something different.

Joanne couldn't imagine how people managed to assume another identity. Some actors like Marlon Brando and Richard Burton had got into "Method Acting" so much that in their minds, they actually became the people they were portraying. Dane said his mum had given up trying to argue with his father Eugene because when he was on a major con and was playing aristocracy or a major land owner, that is what he truly believed and nothing would persuade him differently.
To have got so far Carlos – or Juan – as it said on his passport must have had some similar qualities. They knew about his ability with languages, but impersonating a character was a different thing altogether. He was not an average looking sort of guy and he didn't look exactly European, so he'd obviously found some way of coping.

Joanne stood by the barrier and a trickle of people started to come through. There were only two other domestic flights on the board and those seemed to have cleared ten minutes ago. The one that she thought he must be on was the Charleston flight which was the only one due to arrive at 21:30 as mentioned on the text. It was also the only other town which Carlos could have got off the Windjammer since Nassau, so everyone was hoping their logic was correct.

She concentrated carefully, the first couple of passengers were white males being met by families who looked as though they did this meeting weekly, the second was a black female who ran out with her mobile clamped to her ear. The third group was a mixed bag of a teenager with a backpack the size of a small car, a fat guy with a loud shirt and behind him a slim man in a business suit who was almost hidden in the crowd.

"Federer," Jo shouted because she knew that Fantoni had always idolised him during his tennis career and because in the heat of the moment she couldn't remember the false name he'd been given on the passport. The guy hesitated and looked over with a flash of recognition and walked quickly over to her keeping his head well down from any cameras. She grabbed him by the arm and hustled him across the concourse and out through the doors whilst texting her father.

The Toyota was outside at the curb when Jo got there and they pushed through the crowd of other meeters and greeters and luggage. Carlos didn't recognise the tall man holding open the rear door but presumed that this was Jo's father. He looked around 55 years and was smiling at him in a slightly bemused way but looked friendly enough so Carlos threw himself and his bag inside the car and Jo followed. After the last few weeks of imprisonment, hiding and subterfuge, Fantoni was just grateful to have someone he knew to talk to and smiled over to Jo.

"Thank God you understood my message, the thought of doing what I have to do over the next few days without your help, was not good. But... oh jesu.."

Jo could see that Carlos was looking out of the car window at a man running past, a man who he seemed to recognise.

The Professor seemed to understand and pulled smoothly out of the bay and accelerated away from the airport. They didn't talk for the next few minutes until they were a few miles away from the terminal and on the road to the city centre. Then Jo asked what had scared Carlos so much and he tried to explain that he didn't remember the guy's name but he'd been the vicious bastard who'd abducted him from the Grosvenor Club and who'd been his chief jailer in Panama. They considered the implications of that and Jo reassured him that the car had darkened windows so the agent couldn't have seen him and that they were taking him to a place of safety right away. Then they would discuss their plan of attack. Carlos slumped back in the seat and looked exhausted.

Professor James Spencer lived in an early 1900's house well outside the city centre so they were not affected by the mayor's daily ban on traffic. They were able to pull up his drive which was protected by mature trees on each side and drive straight into the vast garage which only had one other car – a vintage Corvette – which was up on a ramp to one side. The little Toyota was able to fit in with plenty of space and they got out of the car looking around for the exit. A large figure came out of a single door ahead of them and used a remote to shut the doors behind them.

"Welcome to Spencer mansions," the voice boomed out and the two older men embraced in a familiar fashion before he kissed Jo on both cheeks and went round to Carlos giving him a firm handshake and a welcoming smile. Carlos instantly liked Spencer, he had that affability that big, round men sometimes have but eyes that shone with humour and intelligence. James Spencer had been at the Grosvenor when Dane returned with the wrong shoes but had never met Fantoni himself. Jo had told him a fair amount about his background, so he knew that tennis had been his passion and that he'd given up everything to get degrees to help him in his environmental work. So he was no college jock with all muscle and no brain.

They shared a pot of coffee in a kitchen that showed the absence of Spencer's wife but the brew was Peruvian and excellent. The Professor explained that Dane and Mrs Li were at home, hopefully putting on a show and looking as though nothing untoward was happening for any watchers or listeners who might be observing. Spencer laughed derisively because he thought the Li's had become totally paranoid but Carlos quietly reassured him that with the government anything was possible - even murder.

It was late and Fantoni was obviously absolutely wiped out but before he went to bed Jo told him the bad news that everything they'd done on camera, the video and all the blogs had been destroyed. He was absolutely devastated and put his head on his hands and slumped. The team could see that this could easily be the end of the line for Fantoni and Jo knew that she had to bring something positive to the conversation. She went over to him and touched him gently on the shoulder.
"Listen we're going to re-do the video of you tomorrow and we've got some TV contacts who are interested. Don't give up, Greenwatch is too important."
"I think you need some sleep, or you'll be fit for nothing, come on I'll show you to your room." Spencer picked up Fantoni's shoulder bag and led the way out of the kitchen and Fantoni followed looking like he had all the troubles in the world on his shoulders. Spencer showed him into a quiet side room with an en-suite shower room and left him in peace.

Carlos stripped off and put his suit on a wooden hanger in an old pitch pine wardrobe that smelt of mothballs. His shirt, socks and underwear felt as though they'd been worn for months so he bundled them up and put them in a wicker laundry basket in the bathroom. He had very little to wear but he couldn't care about that now, so he mastered the controls and stepped into the steaming shower for about five minutes and started to scrub the dirt of weeks off his body. He really couldn't remember when he'd last had a good long soak, the boat facilities had been small and the prison showers had been primitive, so it had probably been on the last night in the Boston hotel. He found an old towelling robe on the back of the door and went back to the bedroom. He lay down on the deep patterned quilt and tried to think through his next actions and remember what he'd planned to do and gradually realised that his head was heavy, too heavy and that he couldn't think straight any more.

Spencer went into the room at 7.00 a.m. and saw that Fantoni was still unconscious. It was a weekend so there was no pressure on him to go to college but they wanted to get Fantoni videoed as soon as possible so they could approach some of the TV journalists that Joanne knew. There were so few truly independent reporters and most of the media was influenced by one party or another, but Jo knew a few who were as committed to the environment as much as she was.

They decided that the study in this house was suitable as it had all the trappings of an academic's study like panelled walls, bookshelves, ancient desk and would be difficult for anyone to identify where it was. Dane was going to do the video using his equipment as he had everything he needed at Jo's house. They were being careful about communications at present but they'd agreed last night that he would come over about 10.30 a.m. and set everything up. Professor Spencer left it for an hour or so and went in to rouse Fantoni. He saw terror on his face as Carlos struggled to remember where he was but he pulled himself together and promised to be down at 9.30 for breakfast.

Spencer went down and started to prepare his favourite breakfast, thinking rather morbidly that it might be the breakfast of a condemned man, if they didn't have success over the next 24 hours. He didn't know it but the smoked haddock omelette was perfect for Fantoni and reminded him of breakfast in the Savoy with Diane Fallow eons ago. Fantoni finished every crumb and had two cups of expresso and felt as ready for action as he'd felt for months. He was wearing a brand new shirt and the suit had been brushed down and he was newly shaved. All he needed now was Dane Morgan and his camera.

The mayor had decreed that today was a green day which meant traffic was allowed in the centre, so Dane was able to use the

Toyota and at 10.00 a.m. Jo and himself went out and pretended to shop for a while. They couldn't spot anyone following but these days it could be a drone or even a satellite and they would never see them. They didn't want anyone to know they were going to Spencer's place so they parked in an underground car park and then split up with Joanne going in and out of supermarkets using different doors and Dane running by a circuitous route. They aimed to make it difficult for watchers without making it too obvious.

Dane worried that everyone was getting a little paranoid. He agreed that the Li home was probably bugged but thought Carlos was being a little too suspicious when it came to the airport. As far as the government was concerned Fantoni was arriving by sea in a couple of days so why would anyone be at the airport. Dane remembered the guy, he was the thug with the card that said he was from the US Environmental Agency and his name was Kowolski. If they had decoded the text and worked out when he was arriving, why hadn't they got him?

All the general precautions he understood, the Li's house must be bugged, that was logical. People would be watching for Joanne, he understood that. He also knew that if he himself transgressed in any way – even a parking ticket – the US would have him extradited in a moment. They all agreed that getting Fantoni on camera was the most urgent thing and he had everything he needed in his pack.

He arrived at the Spencer house and kept to the edge of the drive under the shadow of the trees and slipped down the side of the house. Feeling like a criminal, he knocked on the kitchen window and James quickly opened the door and pulled him inside..
"Oh God it's the Irish Limey, creeping in like a criminal just like his ancestors." Spencer greeted him with a laugh.
"And it's the failed colonial economist who's eaten all the donuts." Answered Dane with a smile.
They met originally at one of Professor Li's parties when Dane had first come over to be with Jo and got on well. Dane Morgan had an unusual sense of humour and enjoyed pricking the egos of pretentious people. In England it was known colloquially as 'Taking the piss out of people' and it had already got him into a few misunderstandings in the US. Luckily he was tall and hard enough looking for people not to be too aggressive so they normally just put it down to eccentricity. In Spencer he found a fellow practitioner and they always spent the first few minutes sparring verbally.

Carlos came in and they shook hands. Over a coffee he brought

Dane up to date with what had happened since Panama. When he heard how he'd managed on the Windjammer and got off by dressing as a woman it was impossible not to admire his resourcefulness. The guy had fortitude too, after the privations of prison and the death of his girlfriend, to be that determined to carry on was extraordinary. The fact that many people involved in Greenwatch like the journalist Fallow and the inventor Coombes had been killed in strange circumstances, tended to back up Fantoni's belief that there was a team out to get him. His description of the English assassin who'd tried to get him in London was like something out of a cheap horror comic but Fantoni obviously found him terrifying.

Dane had his own mystery. At Jo's insistence he had tried to get his father Eugene on his mobile three or four times without result. Eugene was a devious bastard but they hadn't seen him since they'd split from him at the Panama prison. The contact he'd given them to get Fantoni out had been invaluable but had cost a lot of money. Looking back on things, Dane thought that Eugene's decision to return by boat had been strange but Eugene had mysteriously disappeared on a number of occasions before and had always turned up again like a bad penny.

Dane went through to the study and set up his camera and lights. Carlos was already sitting behind the desk and was running through the script he had written on a few sheets of paper. When he'd done this before in the motel room in Panama, he'd been extremely convincing and done it in one take. This time he had to be even more believable because none of the other shots of his arrest or imprisonment were now available. Dane looked at the screen and asked whether Fantoni was ready, when he nodded, Dane started the camera running.

"My name is Carlos Fantoni, I was Chief Development Officer of the company who introduced Greenwatch to the USA. Now I am on the run and other whistleblowers have been killed because we were trying to tell the truth about the Greenwatch system and its capacity to falsify results. Someone working for your President had me abducted in Boston, illegally imprisoned in Panama and attempted to kill me. Now I am demanding that your President allows independent oversight of the Greenwatch test in Boston and everywhere it is used on a permanent basis." Fantoni paused, looked at his notes and continued. "Millions of lives are at stake - in the US alone there are 133 million men, women and children who are breathing air that can kill them. Greenwatch can help you solve this but if it is left to politicians or industrialists then they will find a way to alter the readings.

Listen, my own parents died of bad air in Lima so I couldn't be more serious about this. Greenwatch can save lives but behind it is a company called Salimond and they bought it because they are frightened of it. Salimond is run by a man called Wolf Bayer who works for a major automotive group. The other directors are from oil companies and industrialists and they have a strong vested interest in keeping the gas guzzlers on the road. They will do anything to keep their profits rolling in, a dedicated journalist from the Financial Times was killed and the inventor of Greenwatch, Doctor Coombes was murdered before he could expose the truth. Now they are after me. Your President has promised to clean up the cities with Greenwatch if he's re-elected. Don't trust him. Let me show the American public how to protect themselves against these environmental killers."

Carlos ended his presentation and Dane turned the tripod light off. Fantoni wanted to see the film so Dane switched it through to the laptop and played it two or three times to see whether he had covered everything. Most people don't really like themselves on film and Carlos Fantoni was no exception but Dane reassured him that he'd covered everything important and his presentation was excellent. It was the truth, he'd seen a number of professionals with experience and rehearsals that had done a worse job. His sincerity shone through and he was sure that Jo would find it convincing. The problem was that they couldn't transmit the film electronically to her because they were concerned it might be interfered with, putting it on a memory stick was a little archaic but in the end Dane just stuck the laptop back in his pack and jogged back to the shopping centre where Jo had been on the longest shopping spree in her history and visible to most of the cameras in the area. She walked back with loads of bags to the car park and when Dane showed her the film, she seemed satisfied. They hid the Mac and exited to the cameras out on the main street chatting together like a couple who's had a great days shopping and headed back to the Li house.

Kowolski had been five minutes late getting to the airport the previous night and then thirty minutes trying to persuade the security guy to show him the CCTV footage. In the end the guy was even more afraid of breaking the data protection rules written on his heart than threats of violent retribution from Kowolski. What made it more difficult was that the security guy wanted to call the cops first and Kowolski knew that would create problems as he was doing all this undercover. In the end the agent pulled out his phone and showed him a shot of Fantoni he'd taken in the Panama prison which showed a bearded, white haired guy in a Guantanamo style orange boiler suit and asked him to check the last hours footage to see if there was anyone like him coming through. The security guy was more convinced by the outfit than Kowolski's story as he'd seen all those nasty terrorists in the high security prisons wearing them after 9/11 and eventually agreed to look.

The CIA guy was frustrated like hell but couldn't see any other way of checking the footage without blowing his cover so sat down outside the security office and had an illegal cigarette. The smoke alarms went off and Kowolski had to explain yet again why he was breaking the rules and apologise.

The truth was the security guy was a little OCD and the quality of the footage he was looking at was a little inferior. He took things literally and was looking for a white haired, bearded guy and he found him eventually. So after an hour he called Kowolski into his office and showed him the results of his search. The guy had come in on a flight at 20:00 hours according to the counter beneath the screen and Kowolski looked at him with utter amazement. The subject had white hair and was bearded but around 20 stone in weight and about 60 years old. The agent asked to look at anything around 21:30 and the security guy looked hurt.
"Listen sir, I do this every day – it's my job, I haven't missed anything."
Kowolski bit his lip and tried to be polite, which was difficult because all he really wanted was another Marlborough and then he could think. "What's your name, son?"
"Arnold, sir – Steve Arnold."
"Well Steve, these terrorists are expert at disguise – so expert that even you wouldn't pick them up. I'm just going to phone Washington, please get me the coverage from 21.00 to 22.00 on screen and I'll be back in five minutes."

Kowolski hoped that the threat of Washington would make the difference and found the nearest outside door and went through it lighting up as he went and with his phone clamped to his ear. He called his office and asked what was going on in the Li household. The surveillance team were listening 24 hours a day and had nothing to report other than Dane and Mrs Li had been discussing New Zealand and holiday plans. Absolutely nothing had been said about Carlos Fantoni, Greenwatch or anything else suspicious.

Kowolski returned to the security office ten minutes later and the guard was almost overcome by the smell of cigarettes which he hated with a passion. He started to run the footage at high speed so that the agent would be gone as soon as possible and stopped a couple of times when the agent requested clarification of the image. There had been three flights within the hour specified and groups of people had come out together which sometimes made it difficult. The guard had been apologetic about the quality and asked the agent to complain officially because he had been trying to get funding for an upgrade for years.

Kowolski had taken another phone call from the team watching the Li house which affected the urgency of his search tremendously. The watchers said Joanne Li had returned and had been discussing plans with Dane Morgan to meet Fantoni down at the marina in two days' time so the general view of the observers was that the airport trip was a waste of time. Quietly Kowolski agreed with them and scanned the remaining footage quickly noticing just one guy who might have been Fantoni but he didn't have the shock of white hair and looked more like a prosperous businessman than the fugitive. The agent cursed silently to himself and departed the office quickly but something, just something was bothering him about the security footage he'd seen but he couldn't work out why.

Chapter 24

Senator David Eveson was a religious man. He was also a rich man because his parents had run an advertising agency from the 1970's and done successful campaigns for the new airlines who were just starting to offer cheaper flights to Europe and Asia. Several of their campaigns had won worldwide acclaim for their creativity and then they branched out into automotive, handling some of the new European and Japanese cars that were trying to break into the US market. By emphasising the quality and design superiority they managed to make inroads into the US market which had been almost entirely US brands. They'd kept the agency creative, resisted takeover bids from the Madison Avenue conglomerates and made lots of money.

When they handed the business over to David in the 2000's he'd seen no problem with a religious man being in the selling business. His parents had been staunch Baptists and had a strict moral code which was only to advertise things they believed in and be honest in their advertising and be highly creative. David had the same code and some of his parents' flair but saw a different future for the business. He came up with a social media platform before virtually anyone else because he loved the idea of good people talking to each other on a worldwide basis without it costing them anything. The fact that his clients could also use it to get through to a market with a conscience was a bonus.

After several years developing his online business he realised that he could use his skills and help people more by going into politics. During his youth the Bush years had sickened him and it was only when Obama got in that he saw a ray of hope. It was inevitable that he would choose the Democrat side and he started the long term planning needed to become a senator. By current standards he had poor funding and had put only a few million of his own money into campaigns but had much of his agency creativity and a lot of his social media strategy to make his campaign really fly. The Trump era only made him angry and the fact that people like him were now able to harness many of the same promotional skills as he had but with hugely larger budgets made him fear for the future. But Eveson had been a campaigning senator for years now and hadn't lost his zeal for the righteous fight.

The present incumbent of the White House had a campaign that the Democrats would have died for. He'd got into office for the first term on a peace-loving, America first ticket and Senator Eveson had hoped for someone who might genuinely care about the people – even if he was a Republican. But as his term went on, he realised that he hadn't done anything that was in his original manifesto to help the poor and unemployed. Then around a year ago when campaigning for his re-election had really started, he came up with Greenwatch, which was a real game changer.

Eveson's fellow democrats couldn't figure it out, there had been all kinds of scary statistics coming out of the World Health Organisation and US groups about air pollution but no-one had the courage to face it. The fact that oil and automotive money had funded so much in US politics didn't encourage anyone to stand on principle. Electric cars had helped a little, improved engine efficiency helped but most politicians knew that dramatic measures were necessary and they wouldn't be popular with the public. So leaders tended to avoid the data and kick the problem down the road for the next administration to deal with.

David Eveson had two kids and a wife who he'd loved for twenty years. They lived in Washington and you could see the dirty air every time he drove to work in his Tesla. He had seen in the press the way that London had started the change things a year or so back and admired their courage. When you saw how many schools they'd found that were surrounded by air that could slow down child development, cause allergies and even kill, you knew why it was necessary. He hadn't known it then but they were using Greenwatch in its first world test.

The Republican President had obviously seen the same test and recognised its potential. The Boston test of Greenwatch had all the opposition on the back foot and wishing they'd thought of it. The way this had been extended into the national 'Vote for Me and Breathe Easy' campaign by the White House team was an approach Eveson would have been proud of in his agency days. It had given the President unusual levels of backing from his own party and given him a seemingly unassailable lead in the polls over the Democrats.

The eldest child in the Eveson family was Emily and ever since she'd been 8 years old she'd had to use an inhaler. The doctors said it was asthma but her Grandma said it was because of bad air created by the increasing levels of traffic in the city and pointed out that her generation hadn't suffered the amount of respiratory problems or allergies that were affecting people now. David understood her concerns and had considered moving out of the city

– he certainly had the money – but his conscience told him to stay and solve the problem, not run away.

Every Sunday David and his family knelt down to pray and the children asked for God to help all those less fortunate than themselves. To his shame, in his heart, David asked Him to find some way to stop the Republicans winning in the election on the second Thursday in November because he knew they were far from godly.

The Li household was like some sort of strange reality TV show where everyone was acting oddly because they knew, or were fairly certain they knew that they were being watched and listened to by some government agency. Not everyone had the acting ability to carry it off – Mrs Li in particular thought that they were all mad and kept her comments banal in the extreme and kept to her office doing bank work. But the rest were convinced and had already carried out a scripted conversation in the kitchen that appeared to confirm they were planning to get Fantoni from the marina as had been the original idea. Real conversations had to take place at the college or at James Spencer's house where there was little chance of being overheard. Joanne saw the new video that Dane had done of Carlos Fantoni and approved – his sincerity had shone through and now she just had to work out how to use it.

Dane and Joanne went to an underground car park and tried to work out a plan of attack. Whilst they were occupied with that Professor Spencer was on another mission and one that he hoped wouldn't blow security. At the moment Fantoni was on a false passport and had one set of clothes and all his original wardrobe and documents were in the Boston hotel he'd been staying in the night before he was abducted from the Grosvenor Club. Academics still write to each other occasionally using old fashioned pen and paper so he had some impressive college letterheads in his desk drawer. He told Carlos what he intended and after a few moments consideration he nodded and pulled a blank letterhead and pen towards him.

After scribbling a few notes on the pad Fantoni dated the top and hand wrote a letter to the manager explaining that he'd been in an accident and unavoidably detained for many weeks and wanted to settle his outstanding bill. He had authorised Professor James Spencer to pay this and to pick up his effects from the wardrobe and his personal documents which had been in the safe.

Many hotels have a real problem with the personal effects of guests who either disappear or abscond whilst staying there. Personal things like clothes and toiletries can be put in storage for a few months in case the guest has a valid reason for his disappearance but eventually they will be sent to a charity or dumped. Documents and money, especially in a hotel safe need more careful handling in case estate lawyers or police eventually track the guest down.

James Spencer was a well known local academic who was quoted regularly on economic matters whenever anything dramatic happened in the local financial world. He knew the hotel manager from one of the college/business networking clubs that met quarterly to encourage links between the two sectors. When he called the hotel, he eventually got through and asked to meet the manager on a matter of some importance. The manager thought the academic a little eccentric but was delighted to meet him later that morning. Before he hung up, Spencer mentioned that he would be discussing a Doctor Fantoni who'd stayed at the hotel back around August and would appreciate total confidentiality on the matter until they'd had time to discuss it. After the call, the Manager put the name on his database and found that he'd had one of the suites and stayed a couple of times but the last visit had not been paid for and his financial guy had found difficulty tracing the company he worked for.

He met James Spencer in the breakfast room because it was light and sun-filled but empty at this time of day. Spencer was a large man who looked more like a successful farmer than an academic which the tweed suit he was wearing seemed to emphasise. But he was sharp of mind and vicious in his humorous criticism of some of the great and good who attended their meetings.

The Professor demanded tea and cakes and a waiter hurried off to comply whilst the manager patiently waited for Spencer to get to the point. Eventually he said that Dr Fantoni had been caught in the bed of one of the married academics and had to leave in a hurry. His problems were compounded by an auto accident which had him hospitalised and unconscious in another state. He was recovered now but didn't want to break cover yet. Spencer handed over the letter and got his wallet out saying that he would pay the outstanding bill and could he have Fantoni's effects if they were still available.

There is a set of guidelines that most hotel groups follow called the Hotelkeepers' Guide which sets standards in all kinds of areas including lost property and guest security. One of the sections deals with unpaid bills and property left in rooms and safes. The convention is that clothing can be held on to for at least three

months by housekeeping, then sorted and sent to charities or dumped.
Documents such as passports and wallets left in safes should be kept for a lot longer, up to a year in many cases. Then managers would normally dispose of them in a manner considered most appropriate.

Some hotels have a surprisingly high level of left property. The manager remembered a previous establishment where five guests seemed to have disappeared leaving their possessions behind. On three of these it was simply people leaving without payment and hoping to delay pursuit by leaving a few meaningless clothes in a wardrobe. But the remaining cases were more complicated, on one it was an elderly man who was developing dementia and who genuinely couldn't remember where he was staying. The other was a businessman who'd been in town for a meeting and been knocked down and killed by a taxi. With him it had taken months for people to trace where he'd been staying and collect his possessions.

The manager brought the credit card machine over and Spencer paid the $530 debt that had been left when Fantoni had gone and arranged for someone to open the hotel safe and bring down anything left in his name. Saying that, getting housekeeping to check the store would take around 30 minutes and the manager asked whether Spencer would wait. He confirmed that he would be happy to stay as long as there were more beautiful cakes. The manager forced a smile but thought having an aged debt cleared off his books was worth the investment and asked the waiter to bring another afternoon tea for the academic.

It took only a few minutes for Spencer to demolish the tray of cakes by which time the manager had returned with a large envelope with a room number, date and the name Fantoni written on the outside. Spencer considered taking it unopened but in the end, curiosity got the better of him and he ripped open the package and spread the contents on the table in front of him. There was a Peruvian passport, a wallet with lots of cards and cash and an iPad. He put everything back in the envelope and nodded at the hotel guy whilst having a final sip of tea.
"James have you come here by car?"
"No"
"Well you will need some kind of transport to carry all Mr Fantoni's clothing and cases. They are all up in reception as we speak."

James Spencer should have realised that someone as elegant as

Carlos Fantoni would not have travelled light. Luckily there was a Samsonite case and he was able to put everything inside before asking reception to arrange a taxi. Spencer thanked everyone and wheeled the luggage out of the hotel and looked round for the cab. He may have been catching the collective paranoia being felt in the Li household but he was slightly suspicious of the large SUV with the blacked out windows that was parked across the road and wondered whether he should have taken the risk of coming.

He shrugged to himself, it was too late now and got into the cab thinking that if someone from the FBI had realised he'd picked up Fantoni's stuff then perhaps they'd think he was arriving at the marina in a couple of days as originally scheduled. The taxi took around twenty minutes and Spencer couldn't see anyone following like the big black SUV, but he supposed that surveillance was a little more sophisticated than that now. He dragged the case in through his front door and slammed it behind him. Fantoni was waiting in the hall and thanked him profusely. It was obvious that after months of effectively being someone else, having his passport and wallet back helped him feel a little bit like his old self.

Before he took everything up to his bedroom Carlos checked what the hotel bill had been and handed over the cash from the half empty bag of hundred dollar notes, joking with Spencer that he hoped he didn't mind payment in dirty money. Spencer had no idea what he meant and had to get Fantoni to tell him what happened when Dane and Jo used the black card to draw a hundred thousand dollars from the Panama Gulf Bank ATM. Spencer was mightily amused by the thought of Dane Morgan trying to stuff endless notes from the machine down his trousers as they poured out of the machine but said that dollars were dollars any way you got them.

Carlos dragged the case up the stairs to his room and took the clothes out. There wasn't much that hadn't been tainted by contact with Salimond and Wolf Bayer. The suits were tailor made from Hunters of Saville Row, the shirts from Turnbull & Asser and the shoes Grensons. All of these were arranged by Bayer when he was making Fantoni presentable before the London test and he loved them. There was more in the apartment in Panama City but he never wanted to go there again. He also wondered what had happened to his lab and research facility there that had been so much a part of Greenwatch at the start.

Carlos looked at the wallet, which was personal because his lover Diane Fallow had bought it for him. It wasn't particularly expensive but she had put her photograph in the clear plastic window inside, which made it priceless. He looked at the picture now and felt a deep, empty, sadness that she'd been killed because she knew too much about Greenwatch. He put on a clean pair of trousers and a shirt from the case, which smelt a little musty but nothing to worry about and wandered back downstairs to the office. Spencer was sitting behind the desk on his laptop and Carlos asked what was going to happen next.

"It's a bit difficult to know yet, I think Joanne has contacted some TV people she knows but everyone is obsessed with the election on Thursday and I'm not sure she can get their interest."

Carlos had had months to think of possible stratagems and asked who was the Democrat contender in the Presidential race and could we contact them?

"The main contender is Wilt Henning but we can't get close to him this late in the process as he's up to his neck in party meetings trying to cover up why he's so far behind. Sadly, and I'm a Democrat, it's because he had a lousy campaign and has the personality of a concrete block."

"Have you any other ideas? If not, I'll just walk into the CNN office and tell them all." Carlos said with more determination than conviction.

"Listen I have one other man who might help, but I have to talk to the others first." Spencer picked up the phone and asked Fantoni to stay indoors whilst he went out to visit these people.

The meeting was in the underground car park near the shopping mall and it was just Jo in the other car. She was exhausted having tried to interest many of her media contacts in a story which sounded crazy. She didn't want to show the video and give the game away until someone showed definite interest. Inevitably they couldn't see the potential without it and though they respected Jo they had plenty of news to cover without it. So Professor Spencer reminded her he had a contact in the Democrats who he trusted him implicitly. Jo was hesitant but desperate enough to say yes to a first contact.

James Spencer had met David Eveson a couple of years ago when he'd heard there was a politician prepared to back certain charities and lobby for them in Washington. Spencer had a mother who lasted until the age of 92 but whose last few years had been ruined by dementia. After her death he vowed to start a charity that would be dedicated to research into the best treatment and care for this disease. A young senator had also been trying to start a similar charity and they met at the university. He had backed the project wholeheartedly and there was now a care home in Washington that had made huge strides in the care of patients with Alzheimers and dementia. Senator Eveson had used his lobbying and marketing skills to raise funding and get cross-party support.

Spencer had the senator's direct number and called him. "Senator it's James Spencer, I suppose you are just a little busy at the moment."
"Good day Professor, yes we're busy losing the election at the moment. But it's always good to talk to someone normal, how can I help?"
"If I told you that Greenwatch is a fraud, would this be of interest to you?" Spencer couldn't resist a touch of the dramatic and was rewarded by an audible gasp at the other end.
"Knowing your strange sense of humour James, I would ask you to repeat that slowly."
"Greenwatch …. the system that the President says will clean up our cities... has been designed so it can be used to falsify the readings when politicians need it to."
"Can you prove that," the Senator asked.
"No, but I have someone here who can."
"Who is that?"
"The man who sold the idea to the mayor of Boston and who lead the team who installed it in London."
"Bloody hell, why didn't you tell me this a few weeks or even days ago, I could have really used it then."
"Because the CIA or another set of spooks had him incarcerated in some hell hole in Panama so he couldn't talk. Listen I'll send you an interview we did with him yesterday."

Eveson gave the Professor a private email address and the academic found the interview and sent it through immediately, saying that he would wait by the phone until he'd seen it. Carlos had listened to most of the conversation between the two and hoped the senator was a better politician than all the rest he'd met so far. From the mayor and council staff in London, to the mayor of Boston right up to the Presidential team in Washington, it seemed to him that they were all self-serving bastards who would kill rather than lose power. When he was an ambitious kid in Lima he'd seen the corruption there amongst local politicians but thought that when he'd got to the civilised West it would be different – it wasn't, it was just that the pay-offs were bigger.

The phone rang after half an hour and Spencer put in on speaker, telling Carlos that it was the senator.

"Unbelievable, absolutely unbelievable. I can't believe that even our president would get involved with such a bunch of crooks. To be honest James, it's all a bit too much like some sort of mystery story for me to use."

Carlos Fantoni couldn't resist an interjection. "Senator, if you don't believe me talk to Joanne Li and her partner, they saw my abduction and rescued me from the prison in Panama."

"Joanne Li, the journalist – the one who exposed that environmental disaster a year back?" The Senator asked impatiently.

"Yes, I believe so. Her father is Professor Li."

"Oh.... well that might make a difference... Listen, get Joanne to call me on this number and I'll consider whether I can use this.. but honestly, have you any idea how late all this is?"

They ended the call and Spencer had to throw caution to the wind and send a text to Jo asking her to call Senator Eveson right away, without really explaining why. Hoping that she would find somewhere secure to make the call, they sat down and waited.

It seemed hours but was actually fifty minutes and Eveson called back and asked Fantoni whether he was willing for his film to be shown on a channel Eveson was involved with. Fantoni confirmed that as long as it was used to get to the truth then he was happy. Obviously, however, he wanted to know what the plan was and what further part he could play. Eveson said he would be talking to a number of people but hoped to get the film broadcasted sometime over the next 24 hours.

It was a pity that Joanne was in Boston because a story like this needed a journalist or presenter to introduce the film of Carlos otherwise it was just a statement from a foreign guy and why should anyone believe him. Joanne was a US citizen, she was a journalist and though no-one would remember it, she uncovered a major environmental disaster only a few months ago. David thought about it quickly and asked her to come to Washington as soon as humanly possible.

Joanne booked a direct flight for later in the day using American Airlines. The flight only took an hour and a half and the senator promised to meet her, which surprised her because she thought he would have been involved in the pre-election campaign in some way. The fact he was getting involved personally either meant he thought Fantoni was vital to his campaign or that he had done everything possible on other matters and had some time on his hands. Time would tell.

Joanne had to take the call from Senator Eveson but it was difficult from a security point of view. She hadn't really known what it was about because Professor Spencer hadn't wanted to give anything away on a text which might be monitored. The whole Li family were being incredibly careful not to mention Fantoni anywhere round the house but Spencer had been relentless in his questioning and all Jo could do was to move into the garage to avoid the obvious hotspots of kitchen or living room. None the less, she was able to confirm many things the senator wanted to know and mentioned that her blog and original film had been wiped off the net like it had never existed. Eveson was astonished when she said it had even gone from the Cloud back-up as he only knew of one government department who could do that which was normally only used for anti terrorist work. He said he would use his old marketing agency specialists and see whether the Corporate Li's material could be recovered and was interested in taking the Fantoni story further. For the moment he just needed Jo and the Fantoni interview but if the film got traction, then Carlos Fantoni himself would be vital for congressional hearings or interviews by the police.

Whilst Jo was on the way to the airport there was a major alert in another part of Boston. The crew in Kowolski's office who were monitoring the Li household had got terminally bored listening to the family talking about holidays, relations and Dane Morgan's opinion of US photographers and almost missed the fact Jo had received a call a few hours previously and obviously tried to find somewhere quiet to take it. Luckily the whole house was covered by devices and even the garage had a microphone so they heard her mention Fantoni and an interview with him yesterday. They almost discounted it because the boss had mentioned a previous film that had been eliminated but then she discussed how they might use it now and called the person at the other end senator. It took a while longer to establish that the person calling Jo was Senator Eveson and everyone agreed that Kowolski needed to be informed immediately.

Eveson was not seen as a friend by many of the more clandestine agencies in the US. After one killing scandal involving an innocent man of Pakistani origin, Eveson had conducted a campaign to get transparency from some of the less known enforcement agencies. He demanded their objectives and funding sources were made public and that whoever had been behind the killing was brought to justice. He failed but his ability to motivate large numbers of mainly young people by using his social media networks frightened the establishment, who tried to ruin his reputation by creating a misinformation campaign to blacken his name. It died because no-one could find anything other than good things in Eveson's background and he was seen to be one of the most dedicated senators in the business.

Kowolski didn't like the call at all. To his mind Eveson was a do-gooding pansy who should really give up politics and spend more time with his family. But he needed to be watched and any connection with Joanne Li and Fantoni was dangerous, very dangerous. Kowolski left his apartment and drove to the office demanding a report from all the watchers as to the whereabouts of everyone in the Li household and warned the rest of the team to be on standby for Fantoni's arrival on Windjammer in a few hours. As he lit his first Marlborough and the car filled with wonderful, illegal smoke he remembered what had bothered his sub-conscious after he'd been at the airport. That stupid little Toyota he'd run past had a licence plate that was on his list and he just remembered that it belonged to Professor Li.

Kowolski hadn't seen any sign of Fantoni when he'd been through the CCTV but the quality had been so bad that he couldn't be certain. Everything was starting to support his theory that the original text meant Fantoni was already here and was going to threaten the President. In some way or other. Kowolski pulled in to the side of the road and phoned the President's special aide he'd dealt with in Panama. To say that he was annoyed despite all Kowolski's reassurances, Fantoni was probably at large and planning mayhem would be an understatement and the agent sensed that he too was going to have an unpleasant time telling the President. After all, they were on the eve of the election and things had been going brilliantly well for the Republicans but a big media problem now could be a catastrophe.

Kowolski knew that both parties to this conversation could have a bleak future if they allowed anything bad to happen. Presidents don't get into office without having a ruthless streak and he needed to think quickly. After agreeing some actions with the stunned official at the other end of the call, he also called the assassin Brown and put him on immediate stand-by.

Alexander Brown had been in Boston for a day checking out the marina and working out his plan of attack for when the Windjammer came in. The only disadvantage he had with the vintage look he preferred whilst working was that people in hotels tended to remember him. So he quite often booked private houses or Airbnb so he had the privacy. He'd booked an apartment overlooking the harbour and enjoyed the views but it was planning and executing the kills that gave him most pleasure. He was getting slightly concerned about his need for bloody drama as his last kill - the Bishop in Lima - had not made him any profit. It had been good though, he hated Priests from his days at public school in England and the gothic charm of disembowelling a man of the cloth in his own cathedral had been irresistible.

He put it down to Fantoni. That man had escaped him once in London and again in Panama which for an assassin who was known as one who always got his quarry was extremely damaging. And because of the idiots who work for the CIA, he could have missed him again.

When he was an army surgeon, they called it the 'yipps' after eight hours of straight surgery on some of the most damaged bodies ever encountered, a surgeon would make a mistake so catastrophic that it might have killed the patient. They knew the mistake they'd made and spent time trying to make it right but then on the next body they'd do something stupid again. Doctors who'd done a few tours reckoned that it was a psychological thing. Any surgeon can only handle so much pressure and in the end the mind and body are forced to make mistakes so they had to stop otherwise they themselves would become casualties with no chance of survival. Brown had found his own way of coping which was to kill people, but outside the operating theatre, starting with an obnoxious US Master Sergeant and then for money.

Alexander Brown hadn't trusted the CIA agent in the first place and was convinced he'd been set up to take the rap for Fantoni's killing anyway. With the change of plan, he had to think independently and work out where Fantoni was likely to be and eliminate him before Washington had time to fuck the whole thing up again. He had some contacts who might help and was looking forward to the lovely sound of his rapier cutting into Peruvian flesh. This time it was personal.

Chapter 25

Carlos Fantoni was feeling incredibly frustrated with his inability to achieve anything quickly and was tempted to break out of Spencer's house and call the cops or something. Every time he switched on the TV it was about the election and when he saw that smooth talking President it hurt. The message about the Greenwatch fraud still hadn't got through and though Jo and Dane were in Washington trying to change that now, he felt powerless.

He looked down at the Rolex GMT-Master on his wrist and thought back to when Wolf Bayer had bought it for him at the Harrods store in London. It had a world time function and Bayer had said that with all the world travel he'd be doing with Greenwatch a gentleman needed a good watch. The watch had been with his passport and other gear that Spencer brought from the hotel. Despite its connection with his naïve past, he enjoyed wearing it. The Rolex was tough, functional and not flashy like the bejewelled monstrosity Bayer wore to show how rich he was.

Carlos looked at the watch, checked the time, and decided he must do something for himself. He did a time zone calculation and called London, knowing that it was 8.30 a.m. and that any top class editor would have been in for an hour or so checking the overnight stories on his computer and planning the next edition. The last time he'd spoken to the editor was when he'd learned about Diane Fallow's murder and the memory of her still haunted him. As a friendly gesture, the editor had given Carlos his direct number and he got through after a couple of the long rings.
"Financial Times." A gruff voice with a cockney accent said suspiciously, not knowing the incoming number on his screen.
"Carlos Fantoni," identified the caller whose vaguely foreign voice the newsman knew from the past.
"Yes, Mr Fantoni." He said guardedly thinking that he didn't have time to be some type of bereavement councillor even though Fallow had been his favourite junior reporter before her career had been cut tragically short.
"Diane Fallow was killed because of Greenwatch, not drugs, she was getting close to some very important people – you must listen."
"Yeh, yeh, that's not what the police found and they investigated it thoroughly, that bastard Duckley's house was full of money and drugs," said the editor wanting to hang-up.
"It's just not true, let me send you an interview I did on film, I'm in Boston at the moment where Greenwatch is also on test – please, you must see the interview" rushed Fantoni sensing that the editor

was losing patience.

"What interview?"

"It's me exposing everything bad about Salimond, Greenwatch and the President."

"This sounds like paranoia not news." The newsman said sadly.

"Well Senator Eveson believes me even if you don't and he's using it in a broadcast that he's doing tonight in Washington." Fantoni said angrily.

"David Eveson, the black senator who was in the news a few months ago with his campaign for transparency in the secret services?"

"I think so."

The senator had been newsworthy even in Britain and apparently as straight as a die, so the editor started to be a little more interested.

"Well OK, send me the film and I'll call you back on this number – but don't hold out too much hope. Diane's death was properly investigated."

"Don't forget that Diane was the one who found out about the Greenwatch scandal first – she deserves a medal or something." Fantoni said quietly.

"Just send me the film."

"I'll send you what I've done so far but the senator is doing the rest tonight."

"Send it now, please." The senator had his own broadcast channel so the newsman knew that anything he used was likely to be seen by quite a few people. He didn't want the FT to be upstaged by any damn Yank social media, so he looked eagerly on his screen for anything incoming.

GCHQ in Cheltenham monitored telephone traffic just like its US equivalent and had software that was triggered by certain key words and phrases. Greenwatch was such a word and Diane Fallow a name of interest so the combination was significant enough to alert a human being in MI6. The duty officer looked down his list and called his senior officer who was on holiday at his place in Southwold, Suffolk. At that point the man was sitting in the Sole Bay pub having consumed two pints of Adnams bitter and was not best pleased. He pulled his labrador out from under the table and went outside to get a better signal. What he heard didn't give him any joy at all and would please the PM even less.

Joanne Li sat at a desk in Eveson's studio and consulted her notes. The senator thought she looked brilliant on camera. Tall, slim, with an unusual beauty that she seemed totally unconscious of and green eyes that shone with intelligence in close ups. She might look rather exotic but her voice was pure Boston. She sounded like the well educated all-American girl that she was. When it came to communicating facts, she was a natural and Eveson had no problem trusting her ability. She was sitting in front of a green screen his technicians would eventually overlay with shots of Greenwatch on test and the President, but first the plan was for her to introduce herself. He knew that she intended to be honest despite the gagging agreements they'd signed.

"My name is Joanne Li and I am an environmental journalist with 5 years experience working in different parts of the world. Last year my partner Dane Morgan and myself discovered a major chemical spill in New Zealand and managed to expose the people behind it. But a few weeks ago we discovered a cover up right here in the United States which is even more important and which could kill millions of people across the world if not stopped. First of all I'd like to show an interview with a man called Carlos Fantoni whose parents died of air pollution and who has tried to dedicate his life to exposing the bad air in our cities. But he was abducted, imprisoned and almost killed to prevent him talking. We believe that US special forces and maybe even the President's staff were involved. Let me show you the film."

The film was only five minutes long but its content was so damning that Fantoni's statement could have looked like an unbelievable fantasy if Joanne hadn't given it such a good introduction. Even so, the senator thought that some of his audience were likely to find it difficult to believe anyone involved with the President of the United States could be so devious and violent, so he decided on the spur of the moment to add his own weight to the argument at the end.

Dane felt as though he was contributing nothing to the process. He had been the first to spot the abduction and started the whole investigation but he felt powerless to help now. He wasn't a US citizen and he wasn't patient with politicians, who he had found to be two-faced bastards. He had to do something so he took shots during the interview and as he looked through the lens, he remembered just how much he loved this woman. It wasn't just her beauty, ever since he had rescued her from that squalid shed half way up the Remarkable Mountains he'd been amazed by her capacity to deal with tough situations. She'd been fragile at first but within a few weeks she had been out again looking for corporate malfeasance again. God he needed this woman and looking at her behind the desk, he remembered the intensity of their first lovemaking in Thailand and felt an embarrassing tension in his groin which didn't respect the seriousness of the situation at all. She was looking directly at him from across the room and could see a bulge in his chinos which almost made her lose her cool.

Senator Eveson stepped up to the desk and gently moved her out of shot. She was surprised as David wasn't originally going to take part in the interview and there was no part in the script for him. But she sensed that Eveson was starting to banish his own doubts and fully believe their story. A few words from him might help the credibility of the story tremendously. It was his channel after all.

"Brothers and sisters. You know that I try to follow the Lord and take the righteous path when it comes to politics. But there are temptations, Lord there are temptations. Some of you may be voting for our President and I would ask you to think about your conscience and vote for our brother in the Democrats instead.

I agreed to show this interview with Mr Fantoni because pollution is killing our children and Greenwatch seemed to be a way we could measure it. My own son suffers with bad asthma and my wife and I both think that the air in the city has caused it. The President promised he would stop bad air but I think that he was a false prophet or at least misguided. Our sister Joanne and brother Carlos have put themselves in danger so we can see the truth and we all need to pull together to make sure that whoever wins really does clean up our cities. My son Joseph will be grateful when they do." Eveson paused for dramatic effect and then went on. "At the end of this message friends, we will tell you how to use Facebook, Twitter, Instagram and all the other channels to ensure the righteous message gets to our new President. Brothers and Sisters, it's not too late to make a difference."

Joanne found Eveson's style on the broadcast rather too evangelical for her taste and totally different from the urbane style he adopted normally. But this was a religious channel with many thousands of followers and it was a powerful force for good. The main thing was Jo knew just how effective a lobby group could be with the right tools and Eveson was passing those on to them. The ripple effect could be dramatic on the edge of an election.

The FT editor thought about calling Fantoni back but decided to not go ahead and time was short. The original film from him looked unbelievable but he was a scientist, an intelligent guy and Fallow had obviously cared deeply for him but this was a hard business and he had a deadline to meet. But he took the trouble to look at Senator Eveson's broadcast later and it changed his mind completely. The journalist Joanne Li had a good reputation, she came across well and he believed her. The senator was a little too bible-belt for him but there was no doubt he had credibility and if he backed this then it would get traction. So he remembered what Fantoni had said on the phone – this exposé started with his reporter and there was the sniff of an exclusive if he acted now.

The next day's Financial Times front page was all about the US elections and the almost certain return of the incumbent with in depth analysis of the financial prospects for the US, China and the rest of the world. It had taken a few years for the markets to recover after the corona virus that had shut everything down in 2020 and there was a vulnerability to the world economy that had never been there before. So confidence was everything.

On page five there was a half column article written by the editor himself which showed that the paper was backing the Fantoni story in its own way. **Suspicions about Financial Times reporter's murder.** In the text it said that a US investigation into Greenwatch, the environmental monitor being tested in London and Boston had started and there were suspicions that whistleblowers had been abducted and killed to prevent them exposing problems with the Greenwatch system. Diane Fallow, a journalist from this paper was murdered a few months ago whilst following up a story involving Greenwatch. Whilst her murder was considered to be drug related at the time this puts great doubt on that explanation. According to one reliable source Fallow was the first person to have uncovered this scandal. We have asked the London police for a comment which has not yet been forthcoming.

Certain people in high places wondered whether getting rid of Carlos Fantoni was a physical impossibility. He'd been targeted by an oil cartel in London, the CIA in Panama and even his old employers Salimond wanted him dead. But every time they tried to get him he'd been rescued or disappeared. The London station boss called him Macaverty with obvious admiration which confused his underlings until someone quietly googled it and found a poem by T. S. Eliot about a nefarious criminal cat who did dastardly deeds but when the police came 'Macavity wasn't there.' But the grim faces around the office were anything but poetic now that the watchers and listeners knew that Fantoni was in Boston and making problems. Plans of an extreme nature were being discussed since they knew where he was staying and included taking him and if necessary, everyone else in that neighbourhood out in some kind of accident.

The President had been incandescent with rage after the British PM called him whilst he was preparing his victory speech with members of his staff. The fact that Fantoni wasn't dead and was in Boston two days early making mischief was cataclysmic. The fact that he'd been told this by the Brits and not his own staff made it worse. Luckily he was able to keep his cool on the phone and pretend that he knew already. He realised that PM had his own reasons to keep the Greenwatch story clean. But when the upper class bastard offered to have Fantoni taken out by the SAS in Boston it was too much to bear and the President threw his mobile across the room.

The special aide and Kowolski had known about Fantoni's early arrival but hoped to take him out before the President knew. They hadn't known exactly where he was and surveillance had told them nothing until yesterday but by then Fantoni had broken cover. Then GCHQ told Washington first and the local Boston team were in the shit.

A little later the shit got a lot deeper when a member of the team had sent him a link to Senator Eveson's broadcast which included Joanne Li, Fantoni and the good Senator himself. Senator Eveson was a man to be watched, the campaigning bastard had almost got Kowolski's department funding taken away and its objectives revealed. Transparency is not welcome when one of your aims is to eliminate enemies of the state without benefit of trial. But his bosses managed to avoid that crisis by sending a few damaging photographs to the right people and suddenly funding was back. Eveson himself appeared to be squeaky clean unfortunately and deeply religious. His blogs and website had thousands of followers many of whom had been tweeting and emailing the President about Greenwatch, Fantoni and US dirty tricks. The mainstream media hadn't taken it up yet but it was just a matter of time.

An hour's travel away in a side office of the White House and away from the noisy celebrations, the President, his special aide and a wizened old lawyer called Edgar Bleach met in private. It was said that Bleach knew more about the way that Washington worked than anyone and had been trusted in times of difficulty by two previous Presidents who'd been close to scandal. He was totally loyal to any President as long as they were Republican and he hated Democrats with a maniacal fever. Over the last few hours they had shown him the Eveson broadcast and given him an edited version of what had happened to Fantoni, Greenwatch and the election campaign. Bleach looked worried which was unusual and asked a number of extremely searching questions.

After ten minutes consideration Bleach said that he would come up with a detailed further plan but any plan to eliminate Fantoni needed to be carried out immediately. In his opinion there could be ways of the President salvaging the Greenwatch idea and still coming out of this intact. But if Fantoni was put in front of congress or allowed on mainstream TV then the shit storm could be so great it could discredit the leader completely. Furthermore, it could lead to impeachment and his need to resign from office.

The President was stunned and looked over to his aide whispering that he should contact Kowolski immediately. Bleach was over the far corner of the room on his iPad looking at emails and the aide ran passed him with his phone clamped to his ear and a grim expression on his face, which confused the White House staff outside who were still celebrating.

The lawyer came back to the desk and said he would leave now but have something for the President by 9.00 a.m. the following morning. The leader nodded in thanks and stretched out his legs, it had been a long day and a long campaign and he desperately needed to rest. As he shut his eyes for a few minutes he remembered that he had promised the English PM the US would remove Fantoni – that was doubly urgent now.

The President left the crowded offices and went up to his bedroom. His wife was elsewhere with the party faithful and he needed some rest. He lay back on the big bed and closed his eyes; amazingly he slept. After the short rest he felt refreshed. It was an ability he'd had since he was a young man in private practice. 15 - 20 hour days were the norm and you didn't get to the top by sleeping all night. He'd found that 10 minutes shuteye gave him at least a couple of hours of work time concentration. After the nap he woke with a totally positive attitude knowing that things would be alright. He had an almost uncanny ability to reinvent the truth in his own mind and the President could now see himself denying that he'd ever heard of the Peruvian scientist – it had been Bonelli who'd met him after all. But he could dedicate himself truly to solving city pollution before his final term of office finished. It would be a heroic ending to a great career.

The President felt hugely better. He drew himself up to his full height, checked his carefully coiffured hair in the gilded mirror and knew that destiny had brought him to this place.

Kowolski was considering defecting to Russia. The situation had gone from bad to worse when the Presidential Aide who'd spent so much time conspiring with him to silence Fantoni now demanded an explanation as to why he wasn't dead already. Having not liked the answer the aide fired Kowolski and told him to go on leave. The whole thing was fucking crazy, no other team knew the target as well as Kowolski. Fantoni was only going to make trouble, especially for Kowolski because he was the one who had abducted and imprisoned him. He needed to be got rid of but in a way that didn't rebound back in his face.

Kowolski knew that his own career was probably dead but that if he could find a way of dealing with Fantoni that was untraceable then he might just survive. He already had someone who was deadly efficient, highly motivated and employed by someone else. He had already planned to use him at Boston marina but now he needed to bring everything forward to urgent. Brown was already in Boston and they knew where Fantoni was. All Kowolski had to do was bring the two of them together.

Joanne and Dane knew that they had failed. The Fantoni broadcast got thousands of hits but was too late to do anything other than create a last minute slump in the President's approval ratings. Eveson summed it up.
"The data on voter opinion was significant but time was against us, so it is almost inevitable that the Republican President will be back in the White House in the next few hours."
"That's bad news but exposing the Greenwatch fraud and the killings is still the major objective. We might not be able to change the election but there is still a huge amount we've got to do." Joanne knew that in the confusion of post election, it would be easy to lose sight of their major objective.
"Yeh, I've been thinking about that and I agree, we've got to keep this thing alive because in the media, memories are short."
"Agreed" said Jo and Dane simultaneously.
"So I think I need to come to Boston and do some more interviews, after all it's where the Greenwatch units are on test and where Fantoni is." The senator stood up and said, "I've got some political work to do now – tell you what, I'll be there in 48 hours – is that OK?"
"Yes and I'm sure that we could find some space at my parents' place." Jo said.
"Brilliant, I've always wanted to meet Professor Li after I heard his lecture on 18th Century anti-slavery law all those years ago."
"Great, see you then." Jo said with the amazement that many children have when somebody praises a parent.

"The only issue might be your mayor. Bonelli and I are not exactly close."

Dane and Jo just wanted to get back to Boston and Carlos Fantoni but there were no flights until early morning. They were terrified of contacting him directly because the minute anyone from the dark side knew where he was, they knew he would still be in incredible danger. All they dared do was to contact Professor Li and say they couldn't get back until the morning and that there would be another guest staying for a few days. They knew Carlos would by now, have seen the broadcast on the Eveson channel but also be aware from TV that the President was almost certainly to be re-elected. They knew this would be incredibly upsetting for him and hoped that James Spencer could reassure him.

The fact that Eveson was coming to Boston might help keep the story alive but it needed something bigger than a religious channel to take it up. The Boston pair went down to the ground floor where a beautiful man on reception called a cab. As they sat they looked round the walls at some of the work the Eveson agency had done over the last 50 years. The early work was for causes and charities that the agency had supported from the beginning but also work for other clients in automotive and air travel. Dane could see why they won awards on a regular basis as the ads were beautifully designed and the commercials highly creative. They needed something equally creative to counter the 'Breathe Easy' campaign but they were too late.

They sat together in the taxi with their hips touching and Dane could feel every bit of her side and its warmth through the silk as she pressed closer. It was totally inappropriate in the circumstances but Dane was incredibly turned on. Gently she stroked his right thigh until she got closer to the hard lump in his groin. Quietly she found the zip and pulled it down slipping her slender fingers into the gap. Looking at her, he could tell that she was as turned on as he was, her lips were moist and parted, her skin glowed and those wonderful green eyes were unfocussed. It took a while to realise that the taxi had stopped and the guy was shouting in some strange accent over his shoulder.
Dane wondered whether he could get out of the taxi without embarrassing himself but slid out of the car and into a cold wind that nearly cooled his arousal. Jo grabbed his arm and they registered quickly finding that The Eveson Agency were picking up the tab. They looked at each other and knew just what they would be doing in their room for the next hour or so.

Chapter 26

The Boston mayor was delighted by two things. Firstly, his health was almost back to normal, he had lost loads of weight in hospital and felt better. The doctors had put a really clever device in his heart and it was beating more strongly than ever. The health of his city had also improved since the Greenwatch units had been installed as he had banned petrol vehicles in the centre on some days, installed some electric buses and announced a future ban on taxis that were not electric. This meant that the Greenwatch units flashed red less often, meaning fewer pollutants in the air.

His staff told him that the sparrows had stopped dying in such numbers and the undercover clean-up squads who had been cleaning up the corpses overnight for months had found very few over recent days. He'd spent more than a few days looking at the birds in the trees outside the hospital and had a member of staff bring in a bird book and he was becoming quite an expert.

The call from Fantoni a couple of months ago had been the thing that had nearly killed him. He was the first to be told that Greenwatch had been designed so that its results could be falsified. At the time he'd thought that could be an advantage and passed on the news to the President's office. Bonelli had heard nothing from Fantoni after that and presumed that Washington had dealt with the problem permanently. But the near death experience had changed him. Bonelli had been given a copy of 'Silent Spring' whilst he was in hospital and for the first time he'd started to think about the environment. The world had suffered many things over the last decades including AIDs, Corona Virus and SARS and Bonelli suspected that many of them were caused by the greed of men like himself. He was determined to clean up his city for real now and the last thing he needed was anyone causing problems and interfering.

The real cause of his heart attack had been the journalist Joanne Li and her constant harassment. His brain had obliterated that last call but his memory was returning and he remembered the call accusing the US of abducting Fantoni. The thought of that interfering bitch gave him palpitations even now and he tried the deep breathing the doctor had taught him and the warning buzz on his monitor gradually faded.

The other thing that had pleased Bonelli earlier was the news that his friend the President had been re-elected and it had been the mayor's Greenwatch project that had inspired the Presidential campaign and undoubtedly help him win it, against the odds. Bonelli's own campaign was next year and the mayor was hoping for all kinds of help from Washington in return. Though mayoral elections are not as party political everyone knew about Bonelli's politics and that he was unlikely to get support from any Democrats.

The Eveson broadcast had almost put him back in hospital. He picked it up many hours late and it had almost everything in it that he hated and feared. Joanne Li introducing a believable Fantoni and the whole thing being hosted by the hated Senator Eveson. The accusations about Greenwatch obviously hadn't changed the election result as they'd only been seen by a few thousand god-botherers. But if this ever went mainstream then it might cause chaos. As Boston was the place where Greenwatch started and he was the man who agreed to it, Bonelli needed to come up with an aggressive plan of defence otherwise he might never get the chance to show what a changed man he was.

Dane and Jo caught the first Delta flight to Boston and slept most of the way. The lovemaking the previous night had been monumental and lasted far longer than any session they'd experienced so far. After the foreplay in the taxi Dane had been more than ready but Jo insisted that he had a cool shower in the hotel ensuite. When he emerged, Jo was going through a series of yoga stretches whilst he towelled off. The sight of her moving through the plank and bridge positions was lovely and an incredible turn-on. She had a beautiful body which apart from those wonderful breasts and gently rounded tummy, had not a trace of excess flesh. He put cream on her body whilst she exercised and saw her skin change to goosebumps. Eventually her orgasm forced her to collapse and she told him to wait and sit cross legged on the floor.

After a few seconds Jo lifted herself onto him and he was trapped in the most erotic way in some kind of sexual lotus position. She squeezed him and nibbled his ears in the most arousing way and it took supreme control to last around ten minutes before they came together. That was just the start of a few hours of lovemaking at an intensity Dane had never known. When the alarm went off at 6.00 a.m. the next morning, he felt like he'd been through a triathlon and was starving and went down to breakfast whilst she gradually got herself ready. He had never got into the American habit of pancakes and was ravenous, so he looked round the coffee shop for something else. Coffee in the morning was also a little too American and he found some English Breakfast tea and put two bags in the largest mug he could find. Then he had a large plate of scrambled eggs and bacon and sat down with a satisfied sigh. Joanne was amazing and he had never met a woman who was so intelligent but also so sensual. She had been brilliant at the studio and the film had gone well but as he could see from the TV screen on the wall of the coffee shop, the President had won the election and was smiling broadly as he passed through the crowd in Washington. He knew that Jo wouldn't let it rest there and that Fantoni was crucial for the next stage because only he and Wolf Bayer knew the truth.

Dane woke up when the aircraft was making its final decent and the stewardess was making the normal announcements. His long legs barely fitted in the space between his seat and the one in front but he'd been able to stretch a bit as the seat next to him was unoccupied. He sat upright, fastened his seat belt whilst looking across at Jo and smiling. As always, she looked immaculate and rested and gave a wonderfully knowing smile back.

The Professor met them at the terminal and knew they would want to see Fantoni as soon as possible, but they were hampered by security. As he suspected, the car was bugged so he concentrated on general stuff about the college such as the argument between the two Professors and Chancellor about the Salimond Research grant. The grant was worth millions and had led to some people at the top turning a blind eye to the rather tenuous claims that Greenwatch had been developed at the institution. The inventor, Coombes had been there briefly and left under a cloud so the Professors' said that the grant should be returned. The Chancellor disagreed as the research would benefit mankind and the only concession was that the Business Manager who had brokered the deal had been asked to resign.

The Professor told them that Spencer had tried to contact Dr Coombes at Salimond in Panama City by email and telephone and failed on both counts. Eventually someone from the lab had responded by email and attached a press clipping from the local paper showing that Coombes had been killed in the most sadistic way possible. Thinking carefully about what she could say in the car, Joanne said little but remembered vividly what had happened to the inventor whilst he was on the way to give evidence. Dane squeezed her arm as the memory haunted them both – the stakes had been high and Coombes had lost in a horrible way. They had to talk more openly so the Professor pulled into the underground car park again and they all got out and walked far away from the Toyota.
"We need to get to Carlos now, I am really worried about him." Jo

said with passion.
"Don't you think they'll stop trying to get him now?" Dane enquired. "He's been on film and told everything and yet the old President is back again."
"No I don't." Jo said.
"I think Jo's right, when you analyse things, he's the only evidence we've got that Salimond intended Greenwatch to deceive people. Everyone else who might have helped is dead except Wolf Bayer and he was the evil bastard behind all this." The Professor added sadly.

They were eager to get back to Fantoni but first they had to play their normal game of hide and seek in case the authorities didn't know where he was. Jo went to the shops and the Professor and Dane went back to the car and drove in the direction of the Li house, hoping that any watchers would assume that to be their destination. After a few minutes Dane slipped out of the Toyota whilst it was under some trees and jogged in the opposite direction pulling a baseball cap down over his eyes. Under another tree he took off his outer layer, tied it round his waist and ran faster towards Spencer's house. When he arrived, he followed the same procedure and slid into the drive under cover of the evergreens and down the side, knocking on the study window as he went. It was a couple of days since they'd seen Carlos and too dangerous to contact him, so Dane was anxious to see what shape he was in.

Fantoni was feeling shamefaced having finally admitted to Spencer that he'd broken the rules and contacted London the previous day. As Dane entered the study, he could see the two men were facing each other and the Professor was purple with rage.
"Do you realise what you've done? You've probably told everyone where we are!"
Fantoni just shook his head and looked down. It took a few minutes for Spencer to calm down enough to tell Dane about the call to the Financial Times and the film sent by email. Dane was equally horrified when he realised that all the subterfuge and all the games to keep his position secret might have been wasted. The chances were that any such calls were being monitored and that anyone who mentioned Fantoni or Greenwatch would trigger an alarm in the US or UK. Dane had to move fast and find somewhere else for Fantoni before it was too late.

Alexander Brown was living in a private house in Boston that he had rented online. He didn't trust the yanks or anyone else anymore and had used his own resources including new backup identity and credit cards. He had his needs and had wandered out the previous night trying to find a victim worthy of him. The cop hadn't been particularly challenging but at least he'd been given time to draw his gun. The assassin had walked over to a part of the city that seemed to appear in the crime pages more than most and looked for an area where dealers might be operating. The fact he was wearing his Edwardian frock coat and wing collar might have drawn some attention but it was dark and it was ages before the big black guy tried to turn him over. He pulled out some kind of machete but really had no idea how to use it. He obviously wanted Brown to step off the street so he could rob him and Brown complied, trying to look worried. He stepped into a room occupied by two other guys who looked like they'd appeared in early episodes of 'The Wire' with all the tattoos, gold jewellery and guns.

Alexander liked room to move so he made some by withdrawing the blade from its holder and piercing the machete guy between the eyes with a straight thrust that went straight through the brain and felled him like a humane killer takes down a bull. Brown was fast, too fast for the others as their feeble minds couldn't work out what was happening. The man moved like a dancer pulling the long blade out of the head with a sound like a knife scraping on stone. The boss had time to see a wafer thin stream of blood pump out of Waldo and tried to reach for the gun which was only inches from his right hand. Curiously his hand wouldn't move and he felt a warm, wet feeling on his front and looked down where he could see a mass of entrails. After a few seconds he realised they were his.

Brown abhorred drugs as he'd seen what they'd done to good men in Afghanistan and Iran. But drug dealers have loads of money and as he found a few thousand dollars in the house, he was quite happy to use this to finance the next stage of the operation. He had millions in his accounts in Panama but accessing it here was more difficult. He normally operated in Europe and had only been lured over here because of Fantoni so it wasn't home ground.

The money for the assassination had been paid into his account months ago and he would have fulfilled the contract if Fantoni hadn't been snatched at the Savoy. The CIA had also paid him but he seriously suspected them of double dealing. It was hard to tell who was friend and who was foe at the moment but one thing was certain, his reputation. He had never failed on a contract and this was not going to be the first.

The cop had been a happy accident when Brown left the drug den.

He was exiting down the alley with a bag of money over his shoulder when he was confronted by a policeman. The officer was surprised to see a white man in fancy dress coming out of a known dealer's address. He was even more amazed when the man asked him to draw his gun and drew out a long blade. The assassin slashed the cop across the neck and noticed with distain that his custom made swordstick was covered with blood. He wiped it across the cop's greatcoat and walked away looking for cameras then realised the local residents would have taken those out years go.

Brown had his best contacts in Europe and one woman in an office in GCHQ had been useful in the past finding telephone conversations and emails. She was employed by the South American section and could speak Spanish and Portuguese and lived alone in a flat in the centre of Cheltenham. Agatha had met Brown at a regimental dinner 10 years ago when he had still been a surgeon and her brother had been a Captain in the Irish Guards. She was immediately attracted to the tall doctor in the vintage uniform and Brown realised that this woman might be useful. He spent a night with her at his club in London and occasionally renewed the relationship when he was in England.

Over those first few weeks Brown had carefully built up his pedigree, which was that he worked for one of the more secret departments associated with MI6. She had gradually told him more about what she did in Cheltenham and the exchange of secrets made her more trusting. She was deeply patriotic and Brown had always been careful to say he was after terrorists or anti-British agents when he asked her for information. On this occasion he asked her for any information on the location of a foreign agent called Carlos Fantoni.

Agatha Howley was in love with the ex-soldier who called himself Alexander Brown but even more, she was in love with the idea of a patriotic spy frustrated by the endless bureaucracy that stopped him acting when action was really needed. She could see those frustrations around her with data protection, health and safety and all the other rules that got in the way of action. She was happy to help him but knew that secrecy was essential otherwise his mission might be compromised. The name Carlos Fantoni sounded foreign and Agatha imagined some kind of Latin drug runner or Spanish terrorist and put the name into a search engine on her computer. What she found was that a lot of important people were after Fantoni and that he was obviously a serious threat. Luckily she was able to pass on information that included Carlos Fantoni's current location.

Brown actually quite enjoyed the Bond and Moneypenny type relationship they'd built up and never had it been more productive. He now knew for sure that Fantoni was in Boston, his address and contact details – he even had a grid reference. He made a note to himself to send Agatha some flowers and went on Google Earth. Within seconds the app had shown an aerial shot of a prosperous suburb around two miles from the centre and a line of detached red brick houses that looked as though they were early 20th century. He could see that the house had a large wooded garden and that there were at least two ways an enterprising assassin might get in with relatively low chance of discovery.

As the computer worked, he absent-mindedly honed the edge of his second sword which he hadn't used since the priest in Lima. The blade was an original having been made in 1820 by Josiah Wilkinson for an ancestor of Browns whose crest was engraved on the ebony sleeve. It had a wider blade than the foil he'd used the previous night and he felt that it did a more satisfactory disembowelment. He knew that if anybody deserved the full treatment it was Mr Carlos Fantoni and time was of the essence.

Dane was in a quandary. He couldn't think of anywhere that was safe to move Fantoni and couldn't really contact anyone who knew Boston better. Fantoni was pale and to give him something to do Dane told him to pack some essentials in a backpack and wear suitable gear because they might have to run somewhere quickly. Carlos disappeared up to his room and Dane whispered in Spencer's ear whilst he planned his next move. First, he went up to the second floor and into the rooms which offered the best views of the road at the front and the rear garden. He'd done the same thing every day and nothing at the back looked different. But to be sure, he put the big telephoto lens on the Nikon and covered every blade of grass until he could be sure. The front was more difficult as it was obscured by trees and bushes but he repeated the process from two rooms and could see nothing suspicious. Then on the second pass a truck or van pulled up on the opposite side of the lane and Dane couldn't see inside because of some kind of smoked glass. Dane waited five minutes and no-one got out. Dane didn't know whether he was suffering from general paranoia but he couldn't help thinking about the number of hours the dark forces had since Fantoni had called London. He shouted for Carlos.

Carlos was ready when Dane went downstairs. His hair still wasn't the recognisable mop of white but his face would be recognised by face recognition systems, so Spencer found a pair of spectacles and a Giants baseball cap to help confuse the watchers. The Professor quietly confirmed that he'd managed the booking and Dane nodded to Carlos as they quietly slipped out of the house the back way and onto a service road that fed the main road.

Carlos had the natural fitness of a born sportsman and Dane enjoyed a fast run every few days, so it only took a few minutes for them to find a pace that suited them both. The tall man and smaller companion didn't stand out as they looked like dozens of other runners who ran in the city every day. It was getting colder but the air was now cleaner and many had joined their ranks over the last few weeks. The mayor was even talking about sponsoring a series of new runs for older people as part of his fitness campaign.

Dane was enjoying the exercise and for Carlos it was the first time he'd run for months but you could tell he was enjoying every step. He stopped as if hit when he saw the first Greenwatch unit on a pole and then recovered his composure. Both knew that the city was full of cameras and tried to avoid delays or obvious places. For Dane, the route now had a special significance as it was repeating the run back to the place where all this mystery had started.

The Grosvenor Club was an old-fashioned club in many ways. In the 19th Century its members had been drawn from a large area and comprised merchants, farmers and bankers. Many came by train or ship for business meeting and stayed overnight. Following the lead of many London clubs like the Reform or Guards, it had around a dozen rooms that members could use if stuck in the city. The rooms were basic and without amenities such as en-suite bathrooms but they were comfortable. Dane had asked the Professor to book two rooms in his name for the next week.

It took 30 minutes to reach the club and Dane was grateful for the break. Carlos was pushing himself and fitter so the effort of keeping up was starting to hurt. Dane pressed the buzzer on the outside door and hoped the club wasn't too busy.
"Mr Morgan, are you back already?"
Marvelling at Gerald and his amazing memory Dane nodded and mentioned their booking. The Secretary took them to an old registration book and started to sign them in when Dane put his hand gently on the page. "Could you put the rooms in Spencer's name and not ours please Gerald?"
Gerald looked worried but also looked the kind of man who didn't

mind bending a few rules.

"Do you remember those thugs who abducted my friend here?" Dane whispered.

"Yes of course, I've never had such rude people in this club and they threatened me. Mr Morgan I don't like people who threaten me."

"Well they're after Mr Fantoni here and I'm trying to keep him safe."

"I thought I recognised you sir. You were one of the best young tennis players in the All-American Cup. You were an absolute natural."

Fantoni smiled and his face lit up. "Thank you Gerald - sometimes I wish that I'd never stopped."

Gerald nodded sagely and said he'd sort out the registration and watch out for any strangers. He put the book down and led them through the club to the back and up some carpeted stairs to a corridor of rooms. "There are no other quests this week so you'll have it to yourself – let me know if anything is needed."

Dane opened the second door on the left and threw his pack on the single bed then moved on to the adjoining room where Fantoni did the same. There was an old fashioned bathroom and separate lavatory opposite so they had everything they needed accept food. Carlos sat in the chair by the window and nodded at Dane who went to the bathroom and washed off the sweat of the run. There was no shower but the old iron bath looked large enough to hold a party in. He sat on the end of the bed and tried to plan what to do next.

Joanne wondered what had happened to Dane and phoned Professor Spencer. He just said that Dane had gone out with a friend for a run. Knowing their concerns about Fantoni, it didn't take any imagination to work out who the friend was but it was worrying that Carlos felt the need to leave the safe haven of the Spencer place.

Her parents were fine about Senator Eveson's arrival tomorrow as the house had six bedrooms and enough bathrooms to satisfy an incontinent drunk. Having thought it through Joanne agreed that the best way to progress things would be for Eveson to do some interviews with Fantoni in the centre of Boston and explain just how the politicians and Wolf Bayer intended to manipulate the Greenwatch system. The other angle Jo was considering was Shelford University and for the senator to confront the Chancellor about the money Salimond had poured in. This might be productive but it certainly would be counterproductive when it came to her father's career prospects.

Mayor Bonelli was obviously a major target. He had been the first to hear about the problems with Greenwatch and must have been the cause of Fantoni's abduction. There were rumours that Mayor Bonelli had gone all green since his heart attack and was a changed man. But his principles might be tested if he knew David Eveson was in his city. There was evidence of their changed mayor when she switched on the TV in the kitchen and saw Bonelli in a bright green track suit surrounded by people in matching gear. Turning up the sound, she saw him being interviewed by someone running alongside. "Congratulations to my friend the President on his election. You will remember his promise, 'Vote for Me and Breathe Easy' – well we in Boston made that happen. My investment in Greenwatch made that promise possible....." Bonelli stopped dramatically and looked directly at the camera. "It's working really well but as with everything good, there are trendy lefties out there trying to cause trouble - trying to kill things and I just wish they'd...." Bonelli decided he'd said enough and ran off followed by his pack of acolytes.

Jo knew that Mayor Bonelli had been the first man in the US to learn about Greenwatch's guilty secret. Carlos had told them about the call he'd got from the journalist Fallow and his demand to Bonelli that he stop the test here in Boston. What happened after that happened incredibly quickly and they could only guess that the mayor had been terrified of exposure and contacted the FBI, CIA or some other set of dangerous initials. They had acted very quickly and Jo knew from Carlos that he had been abducted from the Grosvenor Club only an hour or so later.

It was slightly scary that Dane had taken Carlos back to the place where all this started but he had to make a decision quickly and didn't really know anywhere else. In normal times they might have gone to the police but with senior politicians involved you really couldn't rely on them. Anyway the Grosvenor Club was not the first place anyone would look, Jo hadn't known they had rooms and she doubted that many others did either.

Dane had an ability to befriend people and find out things which she admired. Gerald, the secretary of the club was a prime example and Dane got him to give some Real Tennis lessons when he first arrived and he now loved playing this ancient game. He would have checked out the rest of the place and known its history within hours of joining.

As long as Carlos stayed out of the rest of the club, then he was probably quite safe as the US Environmental Agents and that thug Kowolski wouldn't look there. But it was likely that the Li household had more microphones than the Symphony Hall and maybe some cameras too, so they needed to keep up their game of charades when they were all together.

Carlos Fantoni was exhausted. It was a big day tomorrow and he knew that Jo was bringing over a Senator Eveson who he had seen on TV backing up his film. He sounded like one of those TV preachers Carlos used to see on the television in Peru all those years ago but Joanne said he was a good man. Dane had dropped in a pizza, a bottle of Argentinian Malbec and water half an hour ago, apologising that he hadn't been able to find any Peruvian wine. Carlos agreed to stay on the top floor and not go down to the club under any circumstances. Dane had given him another burner telephone but told him not to use it unless it was an emergency. He left for the Li household from the back of the club where hopefully no-one could see him.
"Where do you think Mr Fantoni got to?" Professor Li said mustering his considerable acting skills.
"I think he must be in Washington." Mrs Li said.
"Why Washington?"
"Well we saw that interview with him on the Eveson show with Joanne and so I think he would have stayed there, do you understand my logic?"
"I suppose so, but Jo's back here now so why not Fantoni."
"Washington is where all the action is, I'm sure that's where the young man is."
"You are probably right dear."

After a performance they could be proud of, the two split and went back to their offices to real work on their computers. Joanne and Dane met for a coffee later and continued the play acting pretending that Fantoni was in Washington. They really weren't sure whether anyone was really observing them and whether the performances were believable but it was worth trying to cause confusion. After the Senator arrived tomorrow to stay, it was going to be very difficult to keep any pretence up any longer. If Fantoni and the team wanted to change things and expose the scandal then tomorrow was when they had to do it.

David Eveson had spent a few hours just thinking about his trip to Boston and what his real objectives were. Now that it was too late to influence the choice of President perhaps his first aim might be to find some way to influence that man's behaviour for the better. With him basking in the glow of a successful re-election campaign and surrounded by fawning staff that was going to take some doing. But what was at stake was the health of the nation and every time he looked at his son's inhaler, he realised that it had a very personal importance.

He hadn't met Fantoni yet but Eveson believed he was a hugely principled man who had been exploited by a company with the worst of intentions. His researchers had found out a little about Salimond and its board members. The fact there were directors with a background in the German automotive industry, Japanese manufacturing and Oil was significant. And something did not feel right, the funding was huge and in the Panama Gulf Bank, not the most respectable of institutions. Also none of the companies that the directors had originally worked for mentioned Salimond in their reports or admitted to any connection. Wolf Bayer the boss of Salimond had also had a split with other members of the family owning one of prestige German car brands according to the recent financial press.

So Salimond was looking increasingly dubious and Eveson thought that it might be used to embarrass the President into good behaviour. Because Greenwatch was worth saving, if Fantoni was right the units on test in London were incredibly accurate and very popular. But they had to be operated by trustworthy people – certainly not Republicans financed by the oil and auto magnates.
Eveson was under no illusions about his own channel and that his own level of faith was not shared by many people in the government. He needed someone who was hardnosed, independent and who could get this exposed on mainstream TV.

Wyatt Boyle had a weekly interview programme that boasted viewing figures about half the level of the old classics like the Ed Sullivan show which meant that in today's multi-channel world, he was doing incredibly well. He interviewed interesting people, not just stars, he dealt with real issues and he couldn't be bought. He enjoyed getting out of the studio and on to the streets as much as he could because that kept him honest.

Boyle didn't share Eveson's faith but he trusted his integrity so when the senator sent him a ten bullet point idea for an interview in Boston he looked at it carefully. Eveson wasn't a bullshitter and the only other time he'd contacted him was a couple of years ago when he was trying to get some transparency from the government on the financing of undercover agencies. On that occasion Boyle hadn't helped but a few weeks later he wished he had because all kinds of bad stuff was being covered up. He'd seen Greenwatch on the news and it looked a good idea so if someone was trying to misuse it then it needed to be exposed. He told his staff to arrange a team to go to Boston and fired off an email to Eveson.

David Eveson was just reading a story to his kids when the email came through and he was amazed. He sent a text to Joanne right away to say that Wayne Boyle was coming over with a team tomorrow and had agreed to interview Fantoni and herself. He was pretty sure that Jo would have heard of him – everyone had – and would be able to work out the best place to do the interview and think things through. As before the key person was Carlos Fantoni and he needed to be ready to answer questions from one of the toughest interviewers in the business.

Dane was trying to read Jo's expression after she'd had a bleep that indicated an incoming text. It seemed like a cross between excitement and terror and as they were in the Li home any words had to be chosen carefully. She passed over the phone and Dane could see what the excitement was about – even he had heard of Boyle and if he didn't get their story exposure then no-one could.

He couldn't stop worrying about Fantoni alone in the club and wondered whether he should have stayed with him. But they'd agreed originally to keep things as normal as possible so the watchers didn't smell a rat.

Dane hadn't used his original phone for months having used burners for security reasons. But he'd kept his old mobile charged in the kitchen ever since Jo had stuck it together again. It really shocked him when the iPhone rang with that familiar tone. Picking it up, he could see that the call was from his mother in England. His first feeling was guilt because other than one call from the hotel in Panama he hadn't been in touch. They were close in many ways but she was not a regular caller and many weeks often went by without calls being exchanged.
"I hope you are OK son?"
"Sure Mum."
"Listen I had a call from the police this morning and I'm afraid that they've found your father's body."
"God Mum, what did they tell you?" Dane asked thinking back to when they'd last seen Eugene heading to the water.
"Apparently he'd been stabbed quite a few times and dumped in the river – they only recognised him by his dental work apparently. They

eventually traced me because he was on some criminal database and I was listed as his next of kin."
"Mum that's awful – did they have any idea who did it?"
"No, but your father moved in some pretty dangerous circles – he wasn't the nicest man as you know."
"What about funerals and stuff?"
"They asked me if I wanted his ashes and I said no, just bury them there where he spent most of his life – the thought of having him back in this house made me feel sick."
"I understand Mum. I can tell you that we saw him in Panama a month back and he helped us a lot – perhaps he wasn't all bad – I'll call you in a couple of days Mum, OK?"
"I'd like to believe that he did some good in his life, but I didn't see it." She said sadly.
"I'll talk to you soon – honestly." Dane could see that everyone else in the room had stopped talking and sensed that something was wrong.
"OK, but don't leave it so long – I worry about you."

Thinking that his mum was sounding older, Dane promised to call soon and thought back to that mad chase through the jungle when they had rescued Fantoni. Eugene's help had been invaluable, his contact had smuggled him out and it looked as though Eugene himself had paid the price for being involved. Dane had grown up hating his father and what his cons and frauds had done to his mother. But at least there was now something a little more positive to look back on.
Sensing that everyone round the table was waiting expectantly for an explanation, Dane just said that he'd been told his father had been killed. But that they'd not been close. Strangely Joanne was more affected than he expected and burst into tears. She had tried to reconcile father and son in Panama and rather liked the old rogue but realised that she really couldn't explain to her parents until they were on safer ground.

Anyway, they all left the kitchen and went to their respective rooms and Jo put her arm round Dane but realised he really wasn't upset.
"He was a terrible fraud, you know – he even embezzled his wife's – my mum's inheritance."
Joanne nodded sympathetically and waited for him to continue "But everyone loved him, even in prison he got half the warders investing in one of his crazy schemes – anyway we've got something more important than him to work out." Dane suggested a walk and they put on coats and went out of the house and down the street looking for cars or people who might be observing them. Dane said that in

view of all the changes to the interview, he needed to go to the Grosvenor Club early in the morning and tell Fantoni that Wayne Boyle was arriving to interview him. Jo agreed and wondered where the best place was to carry out the filming.

Alexander Brown walked the short distance to the address he'd been given for the call from Fantoni which his informant had said was owned by a Professor Spencer only to see Fantoni run out with a taller man in the direction of the city centre. Kowolski had given him a file of key people a few weeks ago and he identified the taller man as Dane Morgan, photographer and partner to Joanne Li, journalist. Kowolski had labelled them both as dangerous to the mission, whatever that meant. That was a few hours ago and he had taken residence in a white panel van opposite waiting for them to return. In the end Morgan returned by himself, picked up a bag and then travelled by taxi to what was identified as the Li household.

Brown settled down for what could be a long night waiting for Fantoni to emerge but called Kowolski and asked whether Carlos Fantoni was hiding in the Li house because he was there ready to carry out his contract. The agent seemed surprised that he'd made it that far and said they had twenty devices in the house and Fantoni was not there. The assassin didn't have much respect for their agents but they certainly knew how to do surveillance, so Brown knew that Fantoni was elsewhere. All he had to do was to follow Morgan when he came out and he was certain he would find his quarry.

Alexander might favour ancient ways of killing but he was not a technophobe. He had a portable laser sensor which he placed across the front door of the old house knowing that if the door opened and someone crossed the threshold then he would have plenty of warning. It woke him up at 6.30 a.m. as Dane Morgan exited the home wearing his track suit. Brown was not a fan of what the Americans called jogging but he was able to follow Morgan in the big Ford at a reasonable distance feeling fairly certain he would make contact with Fantoni as soon as he could.

Even after a night's sleep in the vehicle, Brown looked immaculate having shaved with a 1990's Ronson portable electric and cleaned his teeth. He was not dressed for the kill but his frock coat and wing collared shirt hung in a suit bag in the back. The Hacket tweed jacket worn over a woollen Smedley shirt looked expensive and classic. The moleskin trousers fitted perfectly, he felt ready for anything and touched the top of his Wilkinson rapier in anticipation.

Brown had no problem following Dane as he kept up a steady speed and the streets were quite empty and the tall chap in the red baseball cap could be seen easily. Only when he got closer to the centre did one-way systems make life a little more difficult. But the grid system of most US cities made it easier and Brown managed by accelerating to the next block and catching up with his target as he crossed the intersection. Only after twenty minutes did Brown find it impossible and that was when Morgan ran into a pedestrian-only zone and he was forced to park. He caught up with Dane Morgan as he was delayed when talking into the phone entry system of an old building. After Morgan had entered, Brown walked up to the door and noticed the brass plate to the side which stated that this was the Grosvenor Sports and Athletic Club.

Wyatt Boyle hadn't become a success by just listening to senators – even if they were unusually honest and he'd decided that this story needed a little more spice. He'd read about the Greenwatch test in Boston and knew that Eveson and the journalist Joanne Li wanted to reveal some dirty tricks associated with it. But you needed to hear both sides of the story so Boyle invited Mayor Bonelli to attend an interview at a studio he'd rented at midday in Boston. Bonelli sounded incredibly happy to make himself available and said he'd clear his diary. If the mayor had known what Boyle had in store for him, he would have avoided it like the plague.

Boyle would be in Boston early and planned to meet his team at the Grosvenor Club where this whole story started. Carlos Fantoni was central to this whole thing because without him there was no proof of anything. He had seen the statement Fantoni made on film a few days ago and apart from the fact he looked like somebody out of an Inca painting, he came across as intelligent, sincere but not exactly dynamic. Mayor Bonelli was ebullient and media trained so had a natural advantage in any confrontation between the two men and Boyle needed to deal with that to get at the truth. The only missing element was Salimond, which as the developer of Greenwatch and the company behind the conspiracy, he would really have liked them to be represented. Senator Eveson had passed on what research his people had done but they appeared to be in Panama. This might turn out to be a major flaw in his plan but hopefully they or their lawyers, would have chance for redress after the programme went out.

Dane pressed the Grosvenor entry system and Gerald answered and opened the doors. Some members exercised and showered before work as the club opening time was 6.00 a.m. on weekdays so the Grosvenor already had a few people in. But he managed to avoid them and went up the stairs at the back of the club as fast as he could.

He was extremely uneasy because he'd had to leave Carlos there on his own and his instincts told him he had been followed from Jo's house. He'd tried to catch people out by changing route and stopping suddenly but hadn't seen anything unusual. In the end, he just put it down to natural paranoia.

Dane knocked on the second door on the landing and whispered his name. Fantoni opened the door a few inches and looked through the gap. It was hard to work out who was more relieved and Dane sensed just how much pressure Carlos had been under for the last few months. Imprisonment, attempts on his life, the death of his girlfriend and his desperate need to get the truth out. A weaker man would have broken under the strain. Dane embraced him which surprised them both as it was a little too Latin for Dane's normal attitude to meeting and greeting.

Fantoni was anxious to know what the plans were for the day and Dane gave him a quick rundown of what he knew so far but added that with Wyatt Boyle involved some of it might change. One thing for sure was that the team would be at the Grosvenor at 10.00 a.m. and everything else would follow after that. Fantoni looked at his watch and realised it was only 7.30 and really wasn't looking forward to waiting around in his bedroom for hours.

Sympathising with him, Dane suggested that he book a Real Tennis court and they have a few games whilst they were waiting. Fantoni couldn't have been more grateful and Dane went down to see Gerald and arrange things. Real Tennis dates back to the 15th Century in England and was even mentioned in Shakespeare. Henry VIII had a court in Hampton Court and there are still just a few courts in England, Australia and the US. The one at the Grosvenor was there when the club was founded and was protected against redevelopment by all sorts of ancient covenants.

Whilst it is the origin of the present lawn tennis game, the court looks radically different with walls and shelves you can play off. Gerald was a first class coach and loved people playing whenever he could persuade them – which wasn't very often. Dane showed promise but Fantoni was a tennis prodigy and it would be fascinating to watch him adjust to the game. He found rackets and a bag of balls and passed them over to Dane saying that he could have the court for as long as he liked. Morgan thanked him and went back to Fantoni's room.

The coach wouldn't have approved completely of their kit but Carlos and Dane managed to strip down to shorts, T-shirts and trainers. Looking down at his feet Dane could see the same Nikes that he'd had all those months ago at this very club and which had started this adventure. Carlos now had some cheap South American brand on his feet that they'd bought in Panama but they were perfectly serviceable. They joked about the mix-up in shoes and talked about the hidden black card that Dane had found as they walked down to the court.

Fantoni had forgotten how heavy the rackets were and that the balls were like miniature leather cannonballs but he felt at home for the first time in months. There were three windows and targets that proficient players could hit for points and numerous lines called chasers that created change of serve but Dane could only remember part of the rules and realised he needed another lesson. The big difference for Carlos was that you could play off the walls and he had fun experimenting with deflections and rebounds for around ten minutes. The net was about the only thing that this game had in common with its successor and whenever the ball came his side Dane hit it back often deflecting it off the slanting ledge that ran around three sides of the court. After a while he noticed that the ball from Fantoni was getting faster and he was getting in a real sweat getting to the ball. In terms of therapy for Carlos, this was working but Dane needed more coaching if he was ever going to give him any kind of game.

At that moment Gerald was occupied signing in a gentleman from London who was taking advantage of the twinning arrangement they had with the Guards and RAC. Alexander Brown asked to be given a tour and Gerald had obliged happily showing him the members lounge, gym, squash courts and pool.

Gerald obviously mentioned the Real Tennis courts and the man showed great interest stating that he'd played at the Queens Club as a youth and found the game fascinating. Finally, he asked about accommodation and Gerald confirmed that they had a few rooms for members but they were fairly basic. Brown signed in as a visiting member and asked whether he could use the facilities right away because he was only in town for a few hours. Gerald was happy to comply and Brown left for a few moments returning with a large suit bag. As before he was carrying an elegant stick which Brown said he'd needed since Afghanistan. Gerald nodded sympathetically and buzzed him through to the changing rooms.

Carlos was feeling hugely better, he didn't understand the rules of this arcane game but he felt at home for the first time in months. Tennis had been his exit from the slums and temptations of Lima and his skills had gained him a great education in Peru and US. The gangster who'd sponsored his education had loved the game and loved even more the money he'd made betting on the boy's precocious talent.

When Carlos was on court his body came alive and his senses became heightened, even as a kid he could serve at around 90 mph and the number of aces was astonishing. In Peru he'd run out of opponents who he couldn't beat and it was only when he went to the West Coast College that he found some competition. Over the years there his interest in languages and academic subjects overtook that of his sport but he still found great physical satisfaction in playing.

Carlos realised the last time he played any kind of sport was here at the Grosvenor and that was months ago. His fitness wasn't perfect but as he tried forehand and backhand strokes he found himself loosening up and he felt the tension that had filled his body overnight was starting to flow away. He hit one of the net targets which rang the bells to show he had scored a point and then laughed – this was such a strange game. The balls were a cross between a tennis and a cricket ball and hurt when they hit you. Dane had surprised him early on with a serve that bounced off the wall and hit his forearm and the bruise was already turning blue.

Whilst he was playing his brain was running through the points he needed to make in the interview at an almost subconscious level. So far, his efforts had been frustrated by the lateness of his arrival in the US but he really needed to make today count. He hoped that his conversation with the editor of the Financial Times might have convinced him to investigate in London but he hadn't called back. That paper had the muscle to check out Salimond and do a forensic job on Wolf Bayer but he could only hope they believed him enough to start. But if they agreed with the story put out by the police that this was all about drugs and that Greenwatch wasn't involved, then Diane Fallow's death would have been wasted and the thought horrified Fantoni. It was her dedication to the truth that had inspired him and forced him to dedicate his life to exposing Salimond and all their trickery.

Today was all about Boston and the US. Although Joanne Li was an excellent ally and Senator Eveson seemed to be a believer, he knew that Wyatt Boyle would be forensic in his questioning and Fantoni was the only one who could give most of the answers.

Carlos was aware of a total silence on court and wondered what was happening. He realised that Dane hadn't returned any balls for what seemed like minutes and wondered if he was injured or resting. He looked down court for Dane and realised that he had dropped his racket with a loud clatter and was running towards the exit at the side of the net.

There was tall figure standing there in the shadows watching. As the man stepped on to the court he could see the black frock coat and spotless white wing collared shirt of the figure and Fantoni recognised him with an involuntarily shudder. With practised grace Alexander Brown withdrew the long blade from its holder and walked towards Fantoni who backed further into the corner until he could back no more..

Chapter 27

London had always been a favourite city of Wolf Bayer which was one of the reasons he had chosen it all those months ago for the first test for Greenwatch. Now it was becoming too dangerous for him to stay more than a few days. The first reason was his last sadistic episode had been a little too extreme and the pimp had recorded it all on camera. The East European women had given excellent sport and he had paid their procurer thousands but now the bastard was demanding more.

Bayer was worried that he was getting addicted to giving pain and taking too many risks. The last game had been exciting but it had cost the lives of two women. He reconciled himself by remembering that they were worthless stock and would have ended up in the gutter anyway. At least they had given him good enjoyment on the way but now their deaths might cause more unpleasantness than he'd expected.

The other reason that London was less attractive was that it had been chosen as the venue for what turned out to be a difficult Salimond board meeting. This had taken place at Claridges a couple of days ago and Ms Tanaka was the main problem once again. Despite Bayer's threats at the last meeting her boss, Hattori Kenshin had decided the project had no honour anymore and they were pulling out. They said they might leave their funding in the Panama Gulf Bank but Kenshin had made it clear that any mention of their group in connection with Salimond would have severe repercussions. As the Japanese involvement had recently created nothing but arguments, Bayer had agreed with some relief.

He had no complaint from the other board member at Claridges, Sheikh Bin Hadad. Oil prices were rising again and the sheikh was always happy when that happened and the deals that Wolf Bayer had negotiated in some African states had opened up new markets. Here the Greenwatch extra programme was used to provide false figures and consumption of old fashioned gas guzzlers and oil was going up. The only issue with this director was politics as Bayer knew there was always someone trying to backstab their way to the top of the family. So far, the sheikh had stayed on top.

Bayer's own family had been causing some problems over recent months and he really needed to be back in Stuttgart to solve them. An auntie had died who'd been part of his power base when he'd come up with the idea of using Greenwatch. Between them they controlled the majority of shares and held the same belief that the world needed the petrol engine. She ran a 5 litre Mercedes herself and a number of their own vehicles, all of which consumed lots of fuel and was shameless. Similar to himself, she thought that mankind had always used the earth's resources for its advancement or pleasure and that's the way it should continue. She hadn't believed in the nanny state and to her the most beautiful sound was not the sound of birds – it was the sound of a TVR V8 engine she had in her collection. Recently she died and her shares had passed to her son who was an accountant.

Rudi Bayer ran an electric car but tried not to use it. Most of the time he cycled or ran to the office which was only 5 miles away from his house. He was married to a lovely Finnish woman who was vegan and a charity worker. They had two children who were into wildlife and camping in the woods not far from their house. The fact that their father owned part of the company that made some of the most unashamedly powerful cars in the world had not yet become an embarrassment for the kids but his wife, when asked by her friends what he did, just said Rudi was an accountant. But the money was obscenely good and she salved her conscience by not taking a salary herself and giving huge donations to charity.

Rudi was embarrassed by the vehicles his company produced and also embarrassed by Wolf Bayer who he was convinced had been using the group as his own personal fiefdom for ages and his mother had been complicit. As a financial man he was also convinced that company money had been diverted into some dubious schemes for years and was determined to find what they were. He had approached the Chairman who had fobbed him off with the explanation that this was an international investment with a number of other large groups and that it had been cleared by the board years ago and was nothing to worry about.
In his own way, Rudi was just as driven as Wolf had been at the same age and recognised the need to have something on Wolf Bayer that he could use against him. Using his own money, he employed an investigation company that had been used by Deutsche Bank when he'd worked there and asked them to find out about his uncle. They could see a lucrative contract from someone who had been tipped by FAZ to be a future German business man of the year and who would almost certainly become a major corporate client in the future.

The Financial Times was another reason why Wolf Bayer was uncertain about staying in London as they seemed to be after him. The newspaper had survived when many others had failed because it still had journalists who investigated and writers who knew their subjects. Many other august titles had fired their staff and just ended up recycling press releases which in the end were rejected by readers. It helped that the FT had always specialised in financial matters and money had always been at the core of what business people and governments were interested in.

The editor J. R. Page was an old fashioned journalist who had a fascination with mathematics. Unlike just about every other human being, he loved looking at the detail of an annual report and dissecting the figures until he could see the hidden gems that Financial Directors had tried to hide. To him a set of company accounts were as interesting as Dickens and as exciting as Jack Reacher and he was forensic in his analysis. But he was also a great reporter of facts and believed that words needed to be used accurately.

Diane Fallow had also got it – she could capture the essence of a story in a few sentences. Even the crap work J. R. had given her as an apprentice like attending London Council meetings had been reported crisply. She hadn't shared his fascination with numbers but she was clearly an investigator with talent when it came to companies and institutions as she had shown at the beginning of the Greenwatch story. Page had originally thought that she'd been right about the bribes being paid to officials to get Greenwatch on test but wrong about the rest of the conspiracy. But her persistence had got her killed and now Carlos Fantoni was saying she'd been right about everything and that the editor needed to investigate Salimond and Wolf Bayer forensically out of respect for her. The US interview he'd seen the previous night had been convincing and J. R. suspected that it was just the start of a major exposure over there. But London was where everything had started and he'd decided to put some serious resources behind the investigation.

The FT had put in the story, questioning Diane Fallow's death, a couple of days ago and there had been no real reaction. Memories are short and most papers worldwide were obsessed with post US election analysis at the moment and the UK was no different.

The Carlos Fantoni interview had bothered him, the chap was so sincere and if there was truth in it there was the story of a lifetime. J. R. had tried to check out Salimond and knew the company had been registered in Panama a few years ago with substantial funds in the Panama Gulf Bank. Having a five star credit rating was one thing but having an impressive trading record was often more important when it came to assessing companies. Salimond had the feel of a shell company with a fine looking website and not much else.

The Salimond head office in Panama City never answered his calls or emails and its list of directors could easily be fictitious. Dr Coombes was on the website as the Scientific Director and inventor of Greenwatch. Research showed he had an excellent academic background and an impressive list of scientific papers to his name but when the editor googled his name all he got was an account of his horrific murder in Panama City a few weeks back.

J. R. Page looked back at the interview with Fantoni and remembered another key name in the story - Wolf Bayer. The name hadn't been mentioned in the Diane Fallows' file but she'd been investigating things locally and Fantoni himself had been the main Greenwatch representative in London. According to her investigation a Ric Duckley had definitely taken money and there were suspicions that his boss had taken even more. All this came to a premature end when they were both found dead in Duckley's flat which was full of drugs and money. At the time the editor hadn't questioned the police account but now he was determined to take this story as far as it could go.

Wolf Bayer was at least real and obviously had spent a certain amount of time in London. He had found photographs in the files of Bayer with his rare Porsche 550A Spyder at Goodwood Revival and opening the Anglo/German trade club meeting in Frankfurt last year. But it was a few pints in the Lamb and Flag with one of his fellow newsmen a few days later that had been more enlightening.

Damon Green was more tabloid than broadsheet and spent his life finding or inventing scurrilous gossip about stars and politicians. He couldn't have been more different from J. R. which is why they got on so well. He mentioned Bayer after a second pint of Fullers and got Damon's total attention.

"You mean this century's representative of the Master Race, by any chance?"

"What the hell do you mean, Damon?" The editor demanded thinking that the comment was poor taste even for him.

"Listen, his family go back years and they've always been in charge in that part of Germany. There are stories that his grandfather was in the SS and that his father was extremely right wing with some really dubious contacts in South America. Bayer is a bit of a genetic purity freak and insisted that his sisters only married pure stock from Bavaria. He himself married into the Hapsburg family but there were no kids and I think she died. There were rumours that charges of the violent rape of a Polish girl were quashed years ago but..."

"How do you know so much about Bayer?" J. R. interrupted suspiciously.

"I've been working on a feature for the Daily Mail about the new Nazis and his name kept on coming up."

"Typical Damon – have another pint."

"Since you're on expenses, I'll have a large McCallan instead please – what's your interest?"

J. R. went to the bar and ordered another round. He needed to be careful, Damon could be more than a little sensational in his stories sometimes but it was worth comparing notes, they were never going to be after the same stories.

They enjoyed a couple more hours in the pub but there wasn't much more that Damon could add that helped, other than the fact there were claims that Wolf Bayer frequented some pretty sick clubs and enjoyed giving pain. The tabloid hack had to admit he hadn't been able to substantiate any of this and Bayer had a fairly impressive legal team.

In the morning J. R. Page was back in the office trying to work out what to do next and decided the direct approach was best. As editor of the FT, he had a certain amount of power in the financial world so he emailed Wolf Bayer at the automotive group headquarters asking for an interview. As additional information, he sent a link to the broadcast on social media where Carlos Fantoni accused him of being behind a Greenwatch fraud. The editor copied the Managing Director of the company as well and hoped for swift response as TV in the US was already covering this story.

The Financial Times name worked its charm and Page had a promise from the MD within the hour to investigate and get back to him. The respondent explained that they had only been in the office for a couple of days but would respond quickly. This was a private company so not as open to outside pressures as PLC's but no one wanted anything nasty to appear in the FT.

Wolf Bayer had the call at 6.00 a.m. in the morning at his English home in Ascot. Bayer had four homes across the world which ranged in size from a two bedroomed apartment in Washington, a villa in Panama through to his vast Schloss in Germany. His home in the UK was one of his favourites and was a 1920's Arts & Crafts Mansion in 2 acres of parkland. He lived here most of the time and kept his collection of classic cars in almost as much luxury as he kept himself. He had a gardener, a driver and cook who lived above the outbuildings and catered for all his needs.

He took calls directly so the ringing of his mobile shocked him awake from his bedside table. He groggily answered in English and found that it was that boring young man, Rudi Bayer demanding to know why the Financial Times wanted to interview him.

He'd seen the email yesterday and decided to ignore it and would have left the country until all this died down but there was a Sotheby's auction in a week where an original 1930's Mercedes was up for sale that was reputed to have been the personal staff car of Himmler. He had to have it.

J. R. Page had eventually traced some of the other people who might have been involved with Salimond through a press contact in Dubai. She said that Bayer had regular meetings in the Burj with Ms Tanaka from Kenshin Global and Sheikh Bin Hadad but that local financial correspondents couldn't work out why such senior people from such different businesses should meet. Also, the cover at all the meetings had been at government levels of security which had intrigued everyone.

Knowing that both businesses had significant London investments, Page repeated the process he'd used on Bayer, sending interview requests to Tanaka and Bin Hadad along with the people listed as CEO of their respective groups. He was careful to attach the same link to the Fantoni interview so everyone could see the accusations he was making.

If Page could have seen the shit-storm he started, he would have been surprised and maybe a bit frightened. He was a numbers' man and used to the desperate way that people can react when the money starts to run out. But this was at a different level and if Fantoni was right then people had been killed to stop them telling the truth and Wolf Bayer had been responsible.

Bayer had four more calls in next hour and was starting to get concerned about his future. The call from Hattori Kenshin had been the most concerning. Hattori had raged about honour, the Samurai code and vowed that Bayer would regret every moment of his betrayal. Also his funds associated with Salimond had now all been withdrawn from the Panama Gulf Bank.

The call a few hours later was from Sheikh Bin Hadad's brother who said that there had been a family meeting because the Sheikh had suffered a massive heart attack and could no longer be in control of the business. He was on life support at a private clinic and was not expected to survive. Regrettably any business relationships between the Hadad family and Bayer would now end immediately.

Bayer realised that his situation was now perilous but at least he still had his Salimond black card and access to billions of dollars.

Elsewhere in London an office familiar with the Greenwatch/Fantoni/Bayer case received an urgent transcript of all the emails and calls and saw a political opportunity. During the Covid 19 pandemic the UK electorate became used to a more authoritative leadership and the nation still looked for a powerful Prime Minister. He knew that air pollution was an even greater danger and some people might judge any action that saved so many lives as worthwhile. Only history would judge thought the MI6 officer co-ordinating the exercise. But no historian was ever going to get this story through freedom of information he realised with a grim smile.

It was raining steadily in Ascot and Wolf Bayer had dined alone in the lovely book-lined study thinking about destiny. He had grown up in the family Schloss convinced he would be king, only to find that there weren't any kings anymore in Germany – not even any Kaisers. But he'd tried to run his company like a kingdom and it had worked for years with sales of their performance cars growing every year and profits growing even faster. He was the oldest working member of the family working so it was right he took all the important decisions. As to the non executive shareholders, as long as they got their substantial dividends every year, they hadn't cared what he did. Then he had been involved in a number of scandals with women so the rest of the family decided to promote him away from the trouble. They made him honorary President and gave him carte blanche on the Salimond project which he said would benefit the group immensely but which was secret even to other members of the family. He had revelled in this new role and reported to no-one but now his lifetime mission was looking challenging.

Bayer noticed that it was getting dark. He wasn't normally in Europe in the winter and the daylight stopped so early especially on stormy days like today. For the first time he was starting to feel threatened so he set the security system early and told his staff to go to their quarters.

He looked out of the study window and could see the trees blowing in the wind and the last of the leaves scattering across the lawn. The ten garages with his car collection were lit brightly over to the left and he thought about the Mercedes staff car that would occupy the remaining garage. There were rumours that his grandfather had travelled with Himmler on many occasions and maybe it was in that very car. He would bid whatever it took to get it but auctions didn't like cars with any kind of Nazi provenance so the price could easily be cheap for such an iconic vehicle.

Sometimes Bayer felt like a prisoner in his own house but in situations like this, security was reassuring. The security system had been designed by an Argentinian company who didn't care about the health and safety of intruders. But he had a remote control which kept him safe, so he summoned up his courage and walked out of the front door and towards his precious cars. He opened up the second garage and looked at the 1958 Porsche 356A Speedster that was one of his favourites. It had been owned by a minor German film star who had true Aryan beauty and who he'd been in love with as a boy. Its cream bodywork and tan hood had been lovingly restored but it was the engine that gave him most pleasure. He slid into the short bucket seat and started the engine, it started second time and the flat, rattly roar was muted. He revved it hard and the wonderful Boxer 4 engine burst into song so he revved it again even louder. Then every light in the building went out.

Chapter 28

In the Grosvenor Club, Dane Morgan was running as hard as he could towards the tall man in the entrance to the court. He had never seen the assassin before but Fantoni's description had been unmistakable as you don't see a man dressed in full Edwardian clothing very often. As Dane got close, he could see the dark eyes turning to him and realised he was in trouble.

Dane had been in hand to hand battles before but this man was a pro and looked unhurried as he took a step back then turned the rapier towards him. Dane saw the blade blur in front of him and then cross his body again. He felt nothing but after the momentum of his body stopped, he was unable to move or cry out. All he could see was the blood pumping out of his chest.

Carlos Fantoni was backing away in terror but when he saw Dane slashed, something clicked in his brain and he knew that he wasn't going to go down without a fight. He was desperate to get to the man who'd become his friend, the man who'd helped rescue him but the assassin was in the way and there was no way out.

He took a deep breath and realised he felt on familiar ground for the first time in months. He had a racket in his hand, a ball in the other and he was on a tennis court. The racket may have been wood, the ball may have been solid leather and the court may have had strange angles but he felt at home. He knew that psycho Brown was after him but here he felt he could defend himself for a while. Fantoni looked down at the canvas bag of 6 balls at his feet and hoped that it would be enough.

Kowolski had tracked Brown ever since he'd given him Fantoni's location and the drones had done a good job though they were not as useful in inner city areas. But there was more CCTV and a smart system that links the two. Although he was supposedly off the case, he still had access to all the technology so his plan remained the same. To ensure that Brown killed Fantoni then he would heroically kill Brown - sadly too late to stop the assassination.

With his pedigree, Alexander Brown could certainly be stitched up as an enemy of the people and a legitimate target for himself. Kowolski was just a few minutes behind him and surprised to be back at the Grosvenor. As before the smart-ass door man made a fuss and he had to dig out his ID and remember that last time he showed the US Environmental Protection card. The delay was frustrating as was the few more minutes it had taken for Gerald to tell him where Carlos Fantoni was and direct him to the tennis court. Part of the problem was another group hammering on the door and demanding attention. Kowolski drew his gun and moved swiftly down the corridor to where Alexander Brown was hopefully killing Fantoni.

In the old days Carlos could deliver balls at over 100 mph with millimetre precision which is why he got an uncanny number of winning aces. But this time the target was human and moving. None the less the first ball hit Brown on the shoulder and it obviously hurt because he stopped and rubbed it with his hand. The second was aimed at his head but his target ducked away. The third hit home and glanced off the man's ear and drew blood which enraged him and he roared with anger. The fourth was his best to date and the ball hit Brown somewhere around the eyes. Fantoni only had two balls left and Brown wasn't stopping, in fact he picked up his blade and was moving towards him with a new determination. Then the assassin's head seemed to explode in a red mist and the sound of a gunshot followed a nano-second later.

Bradley Kowolski now knew that Fantoni was a kind of immortal or something. He'd given the assassin more than enough time to complete the contract but when he arrived, there was a body on the floor but Fantoni was still alive. To add complication, he found himself on camera because a TV team had arrived and were recording everything. A woman was screaming and Brown was moving towards his prey so he had to kill Brown otherwise it would have been obvious who the target was. Now I'm a fucking hero and I'm going to be appearing live on the Wyatt Boyle show he thought a few minutes later after he recognised the team. And Fantoni is still alive which probably means that the President's office will be fucking incandescent with rage.

Carlos Fantoni got over the shock and ran over to Dane, whose body was lying slumped on the far side of the court. He was surprised to see Joanne there before him, screaming into her phone and demanding an ambulance. Dane looked a bloody mess and he appeared to be just about breathing but the gashes across his arm and chest looked awful. The strangest thing was the thug who had abducted him in the first place, appeared to be the man who'd just saved his life?

A TV crew seemed to be filming everything and the familiar figure of Wyatt Boyle was there. He vaguely remembered that he was due to be interviewed this morning but for the moment just felt a deep sadness about Dane. After about 10 minutes the paramedics arrived and spent a long time trying to get a battlefield dressing on Dane's front before putting him safely on a stretcher. Joanne was inconsolable and racked with sobs but went with the ambulance when it finally left for the Boston General, blue lights flashing.

Carlos Fantoni was stunned and realised that everyone he knew had gone. But through the shock he realised he still had to continue or all this tragedy would be wasted. He chatted to Boyle who was pleased that Fantoni wanted to carry on and they discussed how to script this now that Joanne Li had gone. Fantoni suggested that the team buttonholed Kowolski and explained that his saviour had also been his abductor and jailor. The interviewer thought that this was a great idea but when they tried to find him, he'd disappeared from the club.

Kowolski may have been a thug but he was a government trained one, so he knew that he had to write a report of what happened. He went back to the office and worked on his computer for an hour writing the truth about everything that had happened. He then made some suggestions as to how the occurrences could be explained and sent the email to the Presidential Aide and his ultimate boss. He then wrote his resignation letter and left it on his boss's desk. His final job was to wipe his gun clean, gather all his ID's and leave them in his desk drawer. Kowolski then used his personal mobile and booked a last minute fishing trip to Canada which started the following day. He didn't hold up much hope that they'd let him enjoy it but he'd given his marriage, his health and everything else to the agency, so he reckoned he deserved one chance at the holiday of a lifetime.

The President and his aide were more than a little distracted. Boyle had got his early footage on the morning TV news. The stop press text running across the bottom of the screen was **Government agent stops assassination.** The sequence of the assassin advancing menacingly towards a helpless Fantoni was repeated endlessly during the morning with Kowolski clearly identified as his saviour. The fact that Boyle was to interview Fantoni in a couple of hours concerned them both and the fact they were now powerless to do anything, depressed even the constantly optimistic President. The President called his old advisor who listened patiently for a while and then hung up the phone.

Joanne Li had been outside the Emergency Room for an hour and the team hadn't stopped working on Dane. After a while an exhausted nurse came out and asked what relationship she had with the patent. She burst into tears and the nurse waited patiently whilst she composed herself enough to say "partner." Which seemed so inadequate, so trivial that she added fiancée but the nurse seemed to understand and said that she must be prepared for bad news as his condition was critical. She also said that staying was pointless as Dane would not be able to see or hear her but to leave her number at the reception desk and the doctor would call the minute there was anything to report.

Jo looked at her blood stained front and realised that Dane was only in ER because of the Greenwatch investigation. If he could, he would be saying get out of here and help Fantoni bring those bastards to justice. She looked at her watch and called Fantoni's number hoping that she could get through before he went into the studio.

At that point Mayor Bonelli was in blissful ignorance and having a sparkling water in the Green Room alongside the studio. He'd been locked away preparing for his big interview and hadn't seen any news. Even if he had seen the footage, it would have been hard to identify the man on court as the cool businessman who'd sold him the idea of Greenwatch all those months ago.

Wyatt Boyle had the broadcaster's skill of assimilating facts and getting to the essence very quickly. He'd spent the night before looking at the previous video done by Fantoni and talked with Joanne and Carlos himself. He had more than enough to use before he'd witnessed the attempt on Fantoni's life by someone who looked like something out of a Victorian nightmare. Now he had the making of a ratings busting programme.

He'd planned to start with just Bonelli and then bring in Senator Eveson, leaving Fantoni until the end. That was when he thought Joanne Li wouldn't be with them because she was outside the Emergency Room praying for her partner. Now he was going to use her close to the start but would use his instinct as to when was the right time. The fact that her partner Dane Morgan had been with her from the beginning of this investigation and was dying because of it added as much drama as anyone needed.

Boyle went into the green room five minutes before the interview as he normally did with guests. Bonelli looked a much fitter version of the man Boyle had seen from the files and he remembered that the man had a pretty massive heart attack a few months ago. For a moment he wondered whether he might be too fragile for the grilling

Boyle planned and asked him about his health. Bonelli had proudly mentioned the device monitoring his heart and confirmed that the specialists had declared that he was fit enough for anything. Boyle considered that good enough for him and left the room, saying that an assistant would collect him in a few minutes.

"Mayor Bonelli, you were the man who first agreed to have Greenwatch on test in the US."
"That is correct."
"Why did you think it was a good idea for Boston?"
"I had been really concerned about the air quality in Boston and I knew that it was killing people, especially our children - so I had to act. I had also seen the results from a test in London and the data was impressive."
"Any problems with the test so far?" Boyle asked, aware that this was the baited hook an honourable man would take.
"No, it's a great success and that's why I suggested it to the President and he used it as part of his re-election campaign – which as you know, he won convincingly." Bonelli said with a self-satisfied smile.
"So no problems – what about those comments on Senator Eveson's broadcast a couple of nights ago?"
"Just more lies from someone whose party just lost – it's sad how low politics are these days." Said Bonelli in an affronted tone.
Hearing on his earpiece that his other guest had arrived, Boyle held up his hand and waited for the tension to build.
"I'm sorry mayor, but I have just heard that Joanne Li is available after all..." and turned to the camera. "Joanne is an experienced Boston reporter who has been at the bedside of her partner in hospital. He was attacked earlier today in an incident that we think could be related to this investigation." Bonelli looked tight lipped and shocked as an ashen faced Joanne Li sat in the chair alongside him and couldn't help noticing the blood on her front and the fact that Boyle had used the word Investigation, which was news to him. Boyle asked her how Morgan was, but she just shook her head sadly and requested if she could ask Bonelli some questions herself. Boyle nodded and Jo turned to the mayor.
"Who gave you all the facts on the Greenwatch system originally?"
Bonelli seemed to think the question banal but answered eventually.
"It was a Mr Fantoni from a company called Salimond. My department and Washington checked them out and they had an excellent track record. As I said they had tested Greenwatch in London and the results were impressive."
"Mr Fantoni, Mr Carlos Fantoni?" Jo repeated.
"Yes..." said Bonelli guardedly.

"And did you hear anything else from him during the test?"
"No absolutely nothing."
"And you didn't have him abducted from the Grosvenor Club here in Boston. Then illegally imprisoned and nearly killed in Panama?" Jo asked with quiet intensity.
"No.. of course not." Bonelli answered with a noticeable tremor and was obviously about to leave.
Boyle held up his hand. "Don't go Mayor Bonelli – we have someone else for you to meet."

Carlos Fantoni had showered and changed into a suit and looked exactly like the respectable man who'd sold Greenwatch into Europe and the US. He came and sat in the other spare seat and on Boyle's request gave an excellent summary of why he had believed in the Greenwatch system in the beginning and the shock when his journalist contact in London found out that the readouts could be falsified. At this point Joanne interrupted with a question for Fantoni.
"Mr Fantoni this must have been quite a shock - did you tell anyone about this problem?"
"Of course, I telephoned Mayor Bonelli immediately and told him to stop the Boston test right away."
"No you didn't" Bonelli spluttered.
"Of course I did and I sent an email too – both of which will be recorded somewhere I suppose." Fantoni said. As the mayor rose to leave, Boyle gave him an ironic farewell wave and went back to Fantoni. "What happened then Mr Fantoni?"
"I was arrested by someone who claimed to be from the US Environmental Protection team, I was drugged and imprisoned somewhere outside the States. Eventually I found out it was Panama."
"What happened there?" Boyle asked.
"I was interrogated and beaten up. They wanted to know whether I was going to expose the problems with Greenwatch."
"So they knew that you'd tried to warn someone in the US about the Greenwatch fraud." Boyle asked pointedly.
"They knew within a couple of hours of my warning to Mayor Bonelli, so either he told them or someone bugged his phone."
"Which backs up your statement that you told Bonelli as fast as you could."
Joanne nodded to Wyatt Boyle. "Yes Ms Li, you want to make a point."
"Yes, if my partner Dane Morgan hadn't seen Carlos being abducted then none of this interview could have happened. Because of him we started this investigation and had to rescue Carlos from Panama. Someone is prepared to go to any lengths to keep this

scandal quiet which is why Dane is at death's door right now."
"Greenwatch has been a threat to a lot of powerful people and I have been attacked in London and here. If it hadn't been for Dane and Jo, I would be dead." Fantoni said emotionally.
Joanne heard a buzzing from her phone and excused herself saying that it was the hospital about Dane.

Dane Morgan knew instinctively that he had a choice as he floated above the team working on his body. He thought back to the landscapes he had captured for a moment, a second of his life. The snow covered peaks of the Remarkable Mountains as he floated above them, the steamy forests of Costa Rica as he drifted through them, the dawn mists of England as he looked down at them.
His love for Joanne Li had been elemental but it was of a transient world. His choice was to continue as half a man or become a greater part of the earth. He could become the gentle rain as it pattered on the leaves in a wood, he could blow like the warm wind as it blew from the south or be the raging sea as it carved away at the cliffs of some far cape. He knew that Joanne Li had her own path in this world and was tempted to let his body give up and go back to its maker.

Wyatt heard on his earpiece that Joanne had heard bad news on her phone and was too distraught to return to the studio. He tried to explain to the audience that Ms Li had to return to the hospital and had just one final question for Carlos Fantoni.
"Mr Fantoni, do you regret having persuaded the city of Boston to invest in Greenwatch?"
"No the system itself is extremely reliable, I spent months checking it out in the first place. But someone is able to hack into the system or alter its readouts, I don't know how precisely."
"Who do you blame for this problem." Boyle asked.
"I had the impression there were some shadowy figures at a very high level – maybe even government level behind my imprisonment. But the real blame lies with Wolf Bayer, he's the boss of Salimond.
"Wolf Bayer is a name we've not heard before."
"He persuaded me that he and a number of like-minded industrialists had financed the whole operation because they had a conscience about all the pollution they had created but that they needed to stay in the background because their shareholders would reject anything that reduced their income. It seemed believable then.." Fantoni added in an embarrassed tone.
"Thank you Mr Fantoni. I think this has been one of the most extraordinary interviews I've done in ten years but before I finish, I'd like to ask Senator Eveson to join us who told me about this story a

couple of days ago."

The senator walked in looking incredibly concerned and sat in the seat Joanne had vacated.

"Briefly, Senator you've heard the statements from Ms Li and Mr Fantoni, can I have any concluding observations you might want to make as the only politician left in the room?"

"I am not going to say too much for two reasons. Firstly, I think that Joanne Li and Carlos Fantoni have said it all. Secondly, I think that this will be the subject of some kind of congressional enquiry and I wouldn't want to compromise anything. But if there is one lesson I think we should all learn, when it comes to something as vital as air quality, we cannot put it in the hands of our politicians. And I say that as a politician myself."

"Thank you Senator, thank you Mr Fantoni."

The filming finished and Boyle joined his crew at the back of the studio shaking their heads at the piece of broadcasting history they'd taken part in. Fantoni stood forlornly to one side and the senator tried to console him. Dane's injuries had been horrifying and the fact that he had only been saved from the assassin by the man he recognised as Kowolski was totally confusing.

Carlos needed somewhere to rest and collect his thoughts. Eventually Joanne called his mobile and said that Dane's condition was critical but he should stay at her parents' house for a while and plan their next moves. He agreed gratefully.

The broadcasts would be seen by millions of people – probably billions of people worldwide over the following days. The early assassination attempt and the interviews later had shocked everyone. The social media storm afterwards had been at hurricane level and fed into an underlying disgust about what big business and elected governments would do to cover up scandal or protect profit. The fact that the whole thing looked like one of the later episodes of House of Cards or Mission Impossible should have made the whole thing unbelievable but it didn't.

The President denied any connection with the scandal immediately and severely criticised Mayor Bonelli for his apparent duplicity. He'd worked out there was little evidence directly linking him personally with any of the dirty tricks. The fact that Fantoni had recognised a picture of his special aide from an election publicity shot gave him some problems, but the aide could be sacrificed if really necessary. Kowolski and his team had received no direct orders from the President and confusingly, now seemed to be the man who saved

Fantoni. The main thing for the moment was to remember that he, the President, had no direct links with this problem that couldn't be severed like a gangrenous limb if necessary. This might become important because he knew Senator Eveson was trying to whip up enough support for a congressional enquiry and he was getting quite a lot of support. Ever since the Covid 19 outbreak and the tens of thousands of people who were thought to have died needlessly in the US because of Trump's chaotic approach, the Republican Party had been trying to build up trust. The fact that he had been re-elected was testament to the fact his approach was working but he knew that trust was fragile and events like this scandal could bring it into question once again.

Thinking positively, however, the President realised that Covid had shown many voters that their politicians were important to their survival in times of emergency. He remembered TV coverage of places like London, Paris and Sydney where the streets were empty because their leaders told them to stay home. In more recent times he knew that people had accepted traffic bans in London and Boston on certain days because they trusted the Greenwatch readouts. But these measures were just like a sticking plaster on a gaping wound.

The President now knew that he was destined to help his people and bring them clean air but they had to be guided carefully. The true figures were just too horrendous - 133 million people in the US suffered from bad air and everything from arrested child development through to the growth of dementia were part of its effects. No voter would accept the measures really needed like a total ban of petrol and diesel engines. It wasn't just cars, it was public transport, home heating, power stations – everything. Most voters in the US and UK would feel that it was like a return to the dark ages and throw their leaders out.

Wolf Bayer had requested a secret meeting with the President before the Boston test and one of his major financial backers from the oil lobby had been present. It had been the first time he'd heard about Salimond and learned about the extra programme which could be added to Greenwatch to alter its accuracy. At the time he'd been shocked but when Bayer said that all Salimond was trying to do was buy an extra ten years of normality, he sat back down. Bayer said that most car manufacturers were developing zero emission engines and that the oil producers were developing much cleaner fuels but they both needed more time. Greenwatch without modification was a huge threat to this development because it was too accurate which was why Salimond had taken it over and created modifications.

Wolf Bayer had said with apparent honesty that it was a war and this time the enemy was bad air. Just like in previous wars, intelligent leaders used newspapers to spread an edited version of news that was good for morale and he said that Greenwatch could be used to give the public tailored data and not frighten them needlessly.

The President was now back in the White House and remembered all those early conversations with Bayer. His campaign forced him to use Greenwatch in his final term and he hadn't worked out whether to use its modifications or not. He'd just seen the Wyatt Boyle show and do-gooders like Fantoni and Joanne Li were a serious threat to his plans but he needed to find a way to eliminate them or avoid them. First, he had to stay in office because he was genuinely convinced there was no better man to bring clean air to the people than himself. People had died and would continue to die during this campaign but as far as the President was concerned, they were casualties of war.

Joanne Li was desperately worried about Dane. The call that made her leave the TV interview had been from the hospital. She was told that the surgeons had amputated Danes left arm and that he was still close to death. They said he would be in an induced coma for days until they worked out what blood loss and the wounds had done to his system. Joanne tried visiting each day for the next week but saw no change so concentrated on essentials. The first call to his mother had been devastating for her and Joanne remembered that she had only just got news of her husband's death. Eugene may have been a bastard but his loss must have meant something. His Mum's first instinct was to come over to Boston but Jo tried to discourage her, saying that she would call daily or when she had any definite news about Dane. The hospital warned them both that it would probably be two or three weeks before they could judge his chances of survival.

Joanne needed to work to keep herself sane during those first weeks. The Professor had found someone from the college to do a sweep of the Li home and found numerous devices, which were now in a pile in the garden. So those involved were now able to have an initial meeting in the kitchen and talk with reasonable confidence. Round the table were Mr and Mrs Li, Joanne, Carlos Fantoni and James Spencer and they all agreed that getting

Greenwatch re-engineered so it couldn't be hacked into was the first priority. Spencer had an excellent suggestion.
"The research grant that Shelford was given by Salimond for environmental studies is worth millions. Very little of it has been utilised because Professor Li and myself have been complaining loudly about the lack of diligence used before it was accepted. After all the TV, I don't think the Chancellor will refuse if we say that it should be used to make Greenwatch hackproof – we could end up with something Shelford could be proud of." It was agreed that this was an excellent idea and Professor Li contacted the Chancellor's office later in the day to say that in view of the media coverage on Greenwatch, they thought a meeting was extremely urgent.

The meeting was the following day and Professor Li and Carlos Fantoni attended. The upshot after a hard fought battle was that Shelford agreed to finance the reworking of the technology and Fantoni was put on contract as their consultant on the project. The fact that Joanne was due to be interviewed on the next Wyatt Boyle show may have had some influence on their decision. Emphasising the fact that there were Greenwatch units on their doorstep, they both insisted that the first report on feasibility needed to be delivered at speed.

The Chancellor only made one relevant remark which was the question of intellectual property rights and wouldn't somebody have a legal case against them if they started altering the technology. Carlos thought about it for a few minutes and agreed that it was a possibility but as Salimond had always pretended that the technology partly came Shelford it was unlikely. Also, as Coombes the inventor had been murdered and Wolf Bayer the boss was on the run, it was really low risk. Finally, the administrator agreed it would far worse to be associated with an invention that had the capacity to deceive and do nothing about it.

The most invisible man in Boston was Bonelli who had complained of chest pains immediately after the interview and checked himself into a private clinic. Joanne thought his most likely course of action would be resignation but she was wrong. His first defence by press release was that he hadn't directly had any conversation with Fantoni and any message left by him might have been missed. Dealing with the convenient abduction of Fantoni immediately after the call, he stated that this must have been authorised by Washington as the US Environmental Agency was based there and not Boston. He then reassured his electorate that using Greenwatch was his idea and it had already made Boston a cleaner city. He was totally committed to that aim and refuted in the strongest terms that he would falsify the air pollution figures.

Jo admired what was a masterpiece of misinformation but realised Bonelli wasn't going to go without a fight. As she had never thought he was the major motivator behind the deaths and dirty tricks of the last few months, she thought she could live with him remaining in office, as long as he didn't object to the re-engineering of Greenwatch or someone else having an oversight on the project.

Within two weeks the university had found an initial fix for the Salimond extra programme and had incorporated it in some of the units on test in Boston. They hadn't even told Bonelli about the change but local media covered the demonstration where Fantoni tried to hack into the system using the method originally offered by Wolf Bayer. What happened then is the Greenwatch unit flashed the word **HACKED** in red, demonstrating very visibly that the unit had been compromised. As a good bit of local theatre Fantoni stated that any geeks who could alter the read-out would get 1000 dollars. The media loved the challenge.

Joanne appeared on the regular Wyatt Boyle show two weeks after the attack and stole the show. Her intelligence and sincerity shown through and her description of Dane Morgan's condition brought tears to the eyes. When the programme had shown some of his work and they could see the stunning landscapes he had captured on film they realised what a talent was at death's door. Someone started a crowdfunding appeal to cover his medical costs immediately after the show and within hours it amounted to thousands of dollars.

Boyle had invited Senator Eveson on the show too. Both of them demanded the President answer the charges that Carlos Fantoni raised and that his special aide be made available for interview. The aide was a new line of attack that Carlos recognised from some of the shots of the winning team in Washington. It was the same guy who'd come to his cell in Panama and tried to persuade him to drop the Greenwatch exposé, now he was pictured next to the President.
After the show and before Jo returned to Boston, Wyatt Boyle offered her a job. He suggested a year's contract as their Environmental Investigator. Basically, a monthly slot on his TV programme to investigate Greenwatch, false claims and environmental disasters worldwide. Use of Greenwatch was obviously first on the agenda. She hesitated but Boyle said that he understood she wouldn't be going anywhere until Dane's condition

was known. She had gratefully agreed to consider the opportunity over the next few days and rushed off to the airport.

When she arrived at Boston she went straight to the hospital. This time they had moved him to a different ward and she could see him through the glass and to her amazement he appeared to be moving. His long frame appeared to have lost substance and weight and he was still hooked up to all kind of electronics. But there were signs of movement.

Of his attacker there was little to report. The police had established that he had a British Passport and were fairly certain it was not in his real name. They had apparently sent his fingerprints and photograph to the UK and Interpol and were awaiting a response. Joanne was sceptical about their reliability as they had been fighting against government opposition for months and at least one of the potential employers of the assassin was the government itself. The Wyatt Boyle show was a brilliant medium for airing such worries and there were signs that someone in authority was at least listening.

When the Li team analysed just how many people might have wanted to keep the Greenwatch secret hidden, they came up with a long list. Firstly, someone at Salimond itself was an obvious contender, but anyone who wanted to keep petrol consumption high would be a candidate and that was everybody from car makers to oil producers. As they'd also found, governments also had plenty of reasons why they didn't want to deal with the problem of pollution. So the assassin could have had plenty of masters willing to pay his contract.

Carlos Fantoni knew that if he wanted to achieve his main objectives – which was to ensure that Greenwatch was used properly and find the criminals behind the fraud – then he needed to go to London. He now had a new official role as a Consultant for Shelford Environmental and generous funding (originally given by Salimond) but he felt nervous about the trip. The truth was he felt exhausted after all the pressure of the last few months and very much alone. When he'd last been in London, he'd stayed at the Savoy, had a driver and a small team with him. He'd also had Diane Fallow to talk to and share things he'd never shared with anyone. Now with Joanne and the Li team doing a good job of keeping pressure on Bonelli and the Presidential team, he was becoming superfluous in the US. His account of what had happened had been shown dozens of times and he really couldn't add any more weight to their campaign. So he needed to grow some 'cajonas' and book his flight to London.

He needed to meet the editor of the Financial Times and see how his side of the investigation was progressing. Wolf Bayer was not a major focus in the US and yet he was the mastermind behind the whole thing and needed to be brought to justice. Also, he needed to see the head of London local authority again and ensure that all the Greenwatch units already there were altered to incorporate the updated protection. The embarrassment Fantoni had with this meeting was the bribe Wolf Bayer had forced him to hand over to some of the senior people to get the system adopted by London. He remembered even now the shame he'd felt when he'd used the special black card at the Panama Gulf Bank and left with bags full of money. He knew the junior guy, Duckley had been killed but presumably his boss was still there and he wasn't sure whether he should be looking for some kind of justice.

Fantoni called J. R. Page at the Financial Times and updated him, requesting a meeting as soon as possible. He also emailed the Greater London Council with a warning that the Greenwatch system had been compromised and suggested some dates. He booked the Savoy again as he remembered the good times he'd had there and didn't really know any other hotels. He felt safer knowing that the terrible nightmare of an assassin couldn't get him anymore but what he didn't know was that a number of very powerful people were hoping to ensure that any meetings he had were as unproductive as possible. Also that the danger had not gone away.

Chapter 29

Wolf Bayer was scared witless. Whoever had killed all the lights at his home had managed to disable a security system that was supposed to take out any intruder permanently. The Argentinian who'd sold it to him had done a wonderful demonstration where they all watched on infra-red and thermal video as a criminal crossed an open space in total darkness and triggered some kind of beam. A high intensity light picked him up and a silenced, rapid fire system cut him to pieces. It was impressive.

He could still hear the wonderful Boxer flat 4 engine in the Porsche rumbling behind him in the garage and realised that the solution was literally in his own hands. He reached across and switched on the headlights, shoved the stick into first gear and shot out of the garage yanking the wheel to the right so that he could get to the gates but scraping the rear end as did so. His clutch control was not as good as it used to be but he slammed it into second and slid onto the drive.
The engine behind was screaming at him and he could see two figures in the headlights crouched down ahead of him but he didn't dare try to find third. He could just see where his gates were and if he could get onto the main London road, he had a chance. The Porsche only had a top speed of around 90 but its handling was wonderful if you didn't lose concentration. He floored the accelerator and felt the rear wheels spin on the gravel.

J. R. Page was surprised in two ways since he'd emailed Wolf Bayer and the other supposed directors of the Salimond Group. He'd traced the automotive group Bayer was also President of and the main companies who the other directors were involved with and copied their MD's with the same Greenwatch email. The first surprise was how quickly someone from the parent companies responded – it was minutes. The answers may have been uninformative but someone out there was definitely on guard. Even the power of the Financial Times name didn't work that fast. The second surprise, however, was that none of those listed as the Salimond directors responded at all.
The editor had also contacted the Panama Gulf Bank and requested some financial information. When he'd done that a few months ago he'd been given a basic set of figures that hadn't raised any suspicions and he'd been given a triple A credit rating. This time there was no response at all for several days and then a denial that the bank knew of any such business. J. R. had the impression that someone was metaphorically pulling up their drawbridge and

preparing for a long siege. Unfortunately, Panama was not as transparent as a banking area as many others and Page didn't really have any contacts there. So he was going to have to concentrate on the people involved in the deal in the UK and US.

The call from Mr Fantoni opened up a number of new possibilities. Inevitably Page had seen the Wyatt Boyle interviews – half the world seemed to have seen the attempt on Fantoni's life and the absolute verbal destruction of the mayor of Boston afterwards. But the big target was the President himself and it did look as though he was just ignoring all the pressure and just sitting tight. In an impatient media world that might be all he had to do knowing some other crisis would hit the headlines soon and everyone would forget.

Joanne Li, however, looked to be a tenacious woman and if anybody could keep the fires of accusation bright then it might be her. J. R. vaguely recognised her and when he googled the name, he remembered that she'd exposed malpractice in a global Thai based company that would have destroyed them if the Chinese hadn't stepped in. He always suspected there had been a lot more scandal behind that but it had been covered up at a very high level and he couldn't make any kind of story out of it – regrettably.

Her partner Dane Morgan was mentioned in much of the research and J. R. had seen his work in London years ago. The small gallery in Knightsbridge had done a retrospective of his work and even now the editor could picture the stunning panoramas of mountains, deserts and jungles in some incredibly remote parts of the world. He regretted not having bought one then as there are so few British photographers still in existence with that kind of talent. And judging by the reports he was hearing, he was unlikely to survive the assassination attempt.

The Financial Times is a respected financial institution and not a tabloid. Much of the information that came out of the US interviews was like something out of a Lee Child's or a John Grisham novel – killings and kidnaps were not FT territory. Business and Government policy were its mainstay and Page was going to put a full team on this and re-open the Diane Fallow file. Corruption was definitely what Fallow had suspected and that was right up J. R.'s street. Having Carlos Fantoni in town would be a great help in the investigation.

South of the River and well away from HQ, two people from two organisations with letters and numbers in their name were meeting to discuss something that would never be recorded and never be admitted. According to popular legend the two outfits were always at each other's throats and never co-operated but in this case it wasn't true. The subject of their conversation was a foreign national who'd been a 'person of interest' for over a year. The fact that he would be entering the country soon had caused some consternation in Downing Street and County Hall. Two organisations who also didn't often agree but in these exceptional circumstances they were absolutely of the same mind. It had been hoped that the person concerned would have been eliminated months ago but the cousins who took on that responsibility had made a complete Horlicks of the job.

Perceived wisdom from the Lords and Masters was that elimination was not now an option as the exposè of all dirty tricks on a popular TV show was best left for the US authorities to explain. The fact that the assassin was British was a potential problem and he had a history of working for anyone including the CIA but that could be dealt with. It was known that the assassin's original client had been a cartel of Middle Eastern oil families, so that could be leaked if necessary.

The Gods were worried, however and the officers had a suspicion that they knew what it was. Corruption in the Council had become a problem and at least one council official had been removed in a plausible but permanent way by one of their associates. But this went higher and someone had obviously signed up for that secret extra programme that falsified Greenwatch results and which was the basis of the scandal in the US coverage. As Greenwatch was due to roll out to other large UK cities over the next year, this was unlikely to be someone with just local jurisdiction. So it came from the top.

The political pressures in the UK were quite different to those applying in the US. The London mayor was popular and wasn't in any kind of pre-election fervour. The Prime Minister in England is not actually directly appointed by the public and he or she is appointed or dismissed by their party. The Tory's had come into power a couple of years ago with a good majority and there wasn't the same pressure for a general election or a change of leader. Unless there was a national scandal or a death in office.

The Covid 19 tragedy and its handling had been not just a national disaster it had been a global catastrophe. The UK government hadn't done everything right and the economy never quite recovered to its previous good health but neither had anybody else's. The opposition parties had been in disarray during the crisis and ripped apart by infighting for some years after so they hadn't been much challenge to anyone. Now for most people, the virus was a distant bad memory and the political situation was very different.

The green benches of the House of Commons were full for the first time in years. Angela Law was making her first speech as leader of Her Majesty's Opposition. She had an impeccable pedigree being the great granddaughter of a Scottish mining union leader and an English women's rights campaigner. Her own job had been as international human rights lawyer for Amnesty and she was a mesmerizing speaker who'd been seen on TV programmes defending the rights of the unseen and forgotten for years. Her rise through her own party had been meteoric, missing out the normal local government stages and going straight to party headquarters. She succeeded in the end because she ignored party politics and for once was liked by members and voters. Previous leaders had succeeded in getting one or the other on side but not both.

The leader of the house stood up from the woolsack and formally welcomed the leader of the opposition to speak and members from both sides hushed in expectation. She looked impressive, tall, slim, pale faced and with slightly hawk nose. Nobody would call her beautiful but she was what the Victorian novelists would have called handsome. The head of dark curls was unruly but tucked inside the trademark red silk bandana which was the only colour she wore.
"I put it to the Right Honourable Leader opposite that he in conjunction with the Mayor of London has been part of a conspiracy that has already killed three people and is likely to kill thousands in this city alone..."
The house erupted in absolute uproar. Opposite were standing on their feet waving their order papers and shouting and screaming at the top of their voices. The Speaker was shouting "Order.. Order!" Behind her Angela could see her own party – first in shocked silence because they had no idea what she had been talking about - they had thought it was going to be about education cuts - not killings. After a few seconds when they realised just how much she had rattled the PM they stood and shouted in the sheer joy of the House at its chaotic best.

It took fully ten minutes for the Speaker to get control and by that time the press box had already sent their photos and headline stories and it was already appearing on social media. Angela Law stood up throughout in dignified silence, waiting for her chance to continue. But first the PM against all protocol stood up and interrupted. He was a dignified man able to hold his own in most arguments but he was clearly very angry.

"That was the most outrageous accusation I have ever heard in the House. Ms Law is a lawyer and knows all about the privileges of speaking in this House so I cannot take her to court for libel. But if she thinks that I am going to continue on this subject – whatever her fevered imagination supposes - then she is sadly mistaken... Education is the subject we all were expecting but if Ms Law thinks the subject of our children's future isn't worth talking about then I find that very sad." The PM shuffled his papers and sat down to enthusiastic cheers from his own back benchers.

"This government has been in power during the worst period for child education and you have cut budgets in real terms every year.." Angela looked at her back benchers and realised they were sinking back into the standard opposition routine of listening enthusiastically to their leader and heckling the PM or front bench in power, so she needed to shake everyone up. "Those children will not benefit if their brains are damaged by pollution or they die prematurely. Over 2000 schools in England are in areas where air quality is well below World Health standards. The Prime Minister is part of a conspiracy and they will continue to die for years to come. Greenwatch is not part of the solution – it's the problem...."

If anything, the House was in even more uproar than before and the Speaker failed to get control. The noise was more like a hundred rioting baboons and the PM picked up his papers and left followed by his front bench. The Speaker asked an official to silence all the microphones and closed the House for the ancient charge of Riot and Disorder – a statute that had never been used before.

BBC 6.00 o'clock news showed Angela Law's maiden speech as leader and her first personal charge on the Prime Minister and later footage of him storming out. Scenes of absolute pandemonium were shown in the chamber and old leaders dragged in to accuse present leaders of bringing the House into disrepute. A Channel 4 documentary was even cobbled together quickly with snippets of the worst behaviour in the Commons since TV became more common in the 1960's. It wasn't an edifying sight. Despite it all, Angela Law came across as dignified and principled although no-one in the media had the slightest idea what the charges were. Curiosity was rampant, however, and with her background the presenters speculated whether it was some kind of human rights breach she was accusing the Prime Minister of.

Angela Law had been given the information about Greenwatch by Senator Eveson a man with similar politics who she had met at an

Amnesty Conference some time ago. Eveson had read about her appointment as leader of the socialists in England and sent a copy of the Wyatt Boyle interview with a few explanatory notes. As the senator knew that Greenwatch had been on test first in London he thought that she might find it useful. As an additional piece of information, he'd added that Carlos Fantoni, the man first promoting the Greenwatch system would be coming to London over the next few days and he had given him her number. She responded gratefully and had an assistant do some research. What she found astonished her and the name Wolf Bayer mentioned by Fantoni was one she'd encountered before.

Carlos Fantoni had chosen to fly directly from Boston on the early British Airways flight leaving at 7.30 a.m. The last time he'd come through Boston had been on a false passport and he'd been trying to remember enough Spanish to justify the nationality on his documents. It felt like a lifetime ago but it was only a few weeks and Carlos was relieved to be using his genuine passport again and felt almost relaxed. He had told his story and knew that Joanne would make sure it didn't get forgotten by the politicians in the United States. She had a regular slot on the Wyatt Boyle show now and looked as though she had found her forte – she could write and she could deliver those environmental messages that had only been seen by a small audience before – now they were reaching millions.

The only heartache was Dane Morgan and the panic she showed every time her mobile rang and it was the hospital. There were signs of movement but surgeons were non committal about his chances still as they worried about brain damage. Even if his brain functions were OK, the thought of how a great photographer could work with one arm worried them all.

Fantoni had his own mission now and just a seven hour flight to clarify his objectives. He had a brief conversation with the senator which helped a lot to improve his confidence. Eveson's evangelical zeal had rubbed off on him and he knew he was on a righteous mission which could help save mankind. Sometimes Carlos had to remind himself of his own roots and the poverty of Lima. His Mother had died coughing up blood in a poor tenement because of polluted air, his father shortly after. This mission really mattered.

The Senator had also helped in a really practical way by giving him the number of Angela Law and saying that she could be a real ally in the city. Because other than the editor of the Financial Times, who he'd only talked to a couple of times, he knew no-one. With his new position with Shelford Environmental he had emailed J. R. Page and arranged to meet him tomorrow at 6.30 a.m. He'd also arranged an appointment with the head of the London Council the day afterwards to discuss the Greenwatch updates and this had been confirmed. The main objective, however, was to bring to justice Wolf Bayer, Salimond and all those who were part of the conspiracy.

Fantoni was travelling Business Class which made him feel guilty but it was Shelford policy. In the Salimond days it would have been first class and a private car at each end so he didn't quite feel such a capitalist lackey. The extra space was welcome and the good food went down well but most of the time he spent sleeping. After around 6 hours the Captain announced they would be arriving twenty minutes early and the weather in London was cloudy with a ground temperature of eight degrees centigrade. As they started their descent Carlos could see the river Thames through a gap in the clouds and the high buildings of the financial sector. Ten minutes later they were on the ground and taxiing to the BA stand. He took his leather weekend bag out of the overhead locker and while waiting, he switched on his new mobile phone and checked messages. He'd never got into the habit of leaving the phone on flight mode because he actually enjoyed the peace during a flight. Now however, there were about twenty messages – most of which were people trying to sell him something. It was astonishing, he thought how quickly the marketing men catch up with you even when your phone is only a couple of days old.

Two messages were more important. J. R. Page double-checking the arrangements. Also Angela Law requesting a meeting s.a.p. and confirming her mobile number. He answered them both saying that he'd arrived at Heathrow whilst waiting in the Other Nationality queue at passport control and wondered whether to take the train into the centre or taxi it. He'd never had to worry before as the Salimond Bentley and driver had always met him. The queue seemed to stretch forever and looking around he saw just about every race, colour and dress but no-one who looked quite like himself. Eventually he was told not to use the automated passport scanners and directed to one of the normal booths. Behind the counter was a tired looking Sikh in a turban who looked at his documents for a long time and was obviously checking something on his computer. Thinking that it would be ironic if he had problems coming through here with his real passport after getting through in the US with false papers, he waited with a polite smile on his face. Eventually the officer said there was a problem with his documents and that somebody senior would come down to see him.

After a few minutes a Sergeant in the uniform of the Metropolitan Police and a bulky man in plain clothes came to the far side of passport control and checked that he was Carlos Fantoni. When he confirmed his identity, he was asked to accompany them to the security office. When he tried to protest, he was grabbed by the arm and pulled forcefully out of the control area, down some steps and into a closed office. Behind the desk was a man with pebble thick horn rimmed glasses who was already checking his passport.

"Mr Fantoni, my name is Bryce and I have a warrant for your arrest."

"That's ridiculous – what on earth is the charge?" Carlos asked feeling as though he was in some melodrama.

"You are charged with serious fraud. That on the 16th day of March you did sell a system known as Greenwatch to the London Council knowing that it was not fit for purpose. You do not have to say anything now, but anything you do say may be taken down in evidence and used against you." The man waited for a response and having received none, nodded to the officers who took him away.

"What about my luggage? There is some vital equipment in there."

"We already have it." The man said as he rose from the desk and as he left Carlos couldn't help noticing the black shoulder holster he wore under his jacket.

Fantoni found himself in handcuffs and being hustled out of the airport building to the curb side where there was a black van with metal grating on the outside of the windows. He was pushed into the back of the vehicle which only had a bench seat, and tried to hang on as the police van rushed away with its siren blaring.

It was still daylight when the vehicle pulled into the rear of a modern building on Victoria Embankment and went through an impressive number of security checks. Terrorism was still a threat worldwide and London was an obvious target for fundamentalists of all kinds. Fantoni was pulled out of the van and put through the process he'd seen on the TV dramas – photographs, fingerprints and personal effects were logged with impersonal efficiency. Only then did he remember his part in the drama.

"Have I been charged?" He said angrily.

The uniformed cop nodded.

"Don't I get a lawyer?"

There was a silence and he was ushered down a long corridor with metal doors until he reached his cell. The door was opened and he was gently pushed in.

For an innocent man, Fantoni was getting rather too familiar with prison cells. This one was relatively clean and a lot cooler than the last one but shared the same basic equipment. The small window at the top was glazed so no spiders would come through this one. But Fantoni sensed that there were other threats he needed to be aware of here. Thinking back to the charge, Carlos realised just how beautifully he had been stitched up. Somebody powerful didn't want him causing problems in London and meeting J. R. Page or the council. What better way to stop him than to charge him with being behind the whole Greenwatch scam. He had been guilty of bribery of an official – that was true – so why not charge him with everything else too? The fact is the police could keep him for days, weeks if they hinted at some sort of terrorist connection, so by the time he ever got to court then the FT might have lost interest and those really responsible could have disappeared. The British didn't need to have him killed to silence him, they just needed to keep him incarcerated and get his story discredited - it was incredibly frustrating.

The next day J. R. Page was at his desk at 6.30 as agreed. He logged on to his computer, checked the overnight stories and went through the normal meeting with his team. Another retail group was on the edge of extinction in the UK, a disruption to oil flow in the Middle East was causing dramatic increases in prices. And in the US there had been unusual activity on the Nasdaq which was supposed to indicate a likely takeover by the Chinese of one of the big names. The news distracted J. R. for several hours before he realised that Fantoni hadn't turned up for the meeting. Annoyed that after all that fuss the man hadn't arrived, J. R. called his mobile and got an unobtainable answer. He knew that he'd arrived at Heathrow because he'd emailed, he also knew that Fantoni was desperate to meet and wouldn't have cancelled. The editor was under no illusions as to the level of opposition Fantoni might face when trying to expose this potential disaster. So he called over one of his web specialists and asked whether he knew any way of tracking someone else's mobile phone.

The young man had never been addressed by the god that was J. R. and wondered whether this was some kind of morality or ethics check. His brain slipped back to cases in his prehistory when journalists had been jailed for hacking into film star telephones and didn't know quite what to answer. When his god told him to "fucking wake up, you silly bastard – I'm being serious!" He nodded and took down the number. Most phones have a tracking facility and the journalist was lucky first time by trying the iPhone locator. When he found where it was, he was shocked enough to triple check it, but

when he was sure he tentatively knocked on the boss's door.
"The telephone is in London and on the Embankment sir."
"Do you think he's lost his phone?" the editor asked.
"No boss, I've checked three times and it's inside New Scotland Yard."
"Fuck" he said and dismissed the guy from his office. After a couple of minutes, he had a strategy in mind and thought that it was time he used a few tricks of his own.
The FT website posted it first and many people saw the hard copy later. The front page carried a story that the editor inserted at the last moment before press.
Greenwatch Expert Goes Missing.
The rest of the story named Carlos Fantoni mentioned his appearance on US TV and confirmed that he had arrived early at Heathrow on the British Airways flight at 10.10 a.m. There were unconfirmed rumours that he had been arrested before he could be interviewed by this paper about problems with the Greenwatch system being tested in London. The Financial Times asked for urgent confirmation of his arrest by New Scotland Yard.

The story was also seen by Angela Law in her run through of all the early editions. Her office contacted the FT and within a couple of minutes the two of them were speaking directly. It took about ten minutes for both parties to compare notes about how they knew Carlos Fantoni as Angela knew Senator Eveson quite well and J. R. had heard of him by reputation. Page was able to add background information about his reporter Diane Fallow and the corruption investigation which got her killed. J. R. told Angela that with recent events it had become obvious that the reporter had been right and the whole Greenwatch thing had been covered up in the most violent way possible. It had taken a while for both of them to grasp the scale of it – kidnappings in Boston, killings in Panama and assassination attempts in the US. Yet the whole thing had started in London and the first death was probably Diane Fallow – his reporter. The person who was the cause of all this mayhem according to Fantoni and his own research was a powerful man called Wolf Bayer. Law had heard of him because of a human rights case she'd been involved in some years ago and he was an evil man. The only other person who had been part of the action since the start and who'd been targeted too was Carlos Fantoni himself. He had disappeared and J. R. told Angela Law where his likely location was and left it for her to consider.

Fantoni was actually in an interview room with a glass screen covering the top half of the facing wall. Everyone knew from the movies that behind the screen was where the real people stood whilst a succession of hard-bitten thugs sat across the desk trying to break the poor prisoner down. It was a surprise when a slender young man with rather effeminate mannerisms sat down and asked him if he would like a cup of tea or a cafe latte.

Playing along with the act, Carlos requested a pot of Earl Grey and the man left and returned five minutes later with a dirty plastic mug full of a dark brown liquid that could have been almost anything. Carlos ignored it and demanded a lawyer.

"We don't have lawyers here, we have solicitors." The man said with a noticeable lisp.

"In that case I want a solicitor."

"Good luck with that request.... You will be lucky to get away with just fraud, my boss wants to charge you with manslaughter."

"Don't be ridiculous – I want a solicitor."

"People have died.. Children would have died in the Greenwatch test area because it gave out false readings and everyone thought they were safe."

"That is outrageous – I am in London to make sure Greenwatch is safe..."

"Were you not the person – the expert who persuaded London Council to buy Greenwatch?"

"Yes but." Carlos realised that he needed to stop because the supposedly gentle nature of the man had changed completely and he knew that if he mentioned bribes then he would have to be truthful. Silence was his best protection, he needed to be quiet. "I demand a solicitor and a telephone."

The interrogator had an excellent track record. Despite his rather gender-ambiguous look he was as tough as they come and competed in iron-man events on a regular basis. On the first, he had turned up in a pink Lycra outfit which had caused a fellow competitor to ask whether he should really be in iron-woman. The same man couldn't get close to the pink outfit in any of the tasks and decided to shut up next time they met and work on his own training. So the officer had great stamina and could have kept up the questioning for hours but he was dealing with a highly intelligent subject who had obviously decided that he wouldn't be provoked and wouldn't co-operate any more. After an hour he nodded at the screen behind him and a uniformed sergeant came in and stood impassively at the back and he left the room.

Behind the one-way mirror was the Police Commissioner and a suited man who might have been MI6 or one of the less official units involved with State Security. The interrogator shook his head in disappointment and apologised for the lack of progress. The Commissioner had a call on her phone and swore like a docker which shocked the interrogator and worried the other man.

"Our own security is obviously full of holes. Carlos Fucking Fantoni is on the front page of the Financial Times and they know we've got him."

The Commissioner dismissed the interrogator who was glad to get out of the room and back to the less scary people he normally dealt with, like criminals. The suited man was tasked with discrediting or eliminating Fantoni and anyone else who might cause problems for Number 10. He thought they had been doing quite well on security but New Scotland Yard was evidently full of leaks.

The main reception at New Scotland Yard was used to all kinds of visitors. By 11.00 a.m. they had seen a group of police cadets on training, a school trip and lawyers doing client visits. But they didn't normally see the Leader of Her Majesty's Opposition and a camera crew. The people on reception had all seen Angela Law on TV News confronting the PM and had chatted for half their shift as to what the fuss was all about. She was even more impressive as she stood in front of them, dressed in black and with a scarlet bandana. She handed over what appeared to be a legal document bound in ribbon and demanded to see a Mr Carlos Fantoni. The fact that everything was being filmed was intimidating but after looking at her computer, the receptionist couldn't find anyone of that name who was either staff or visitor. She was sure that filming was against the rules but arguing with this woman was above her pay grade and looked at the roster for the most senior officer on duty.

When she had talked to J. R. earlier, Angela Law formulated a plan which wasn't strictly legal but thought would be effective. It was based on the essential weaknesses of most institutions that serve the public. They are terrified about negative publicity and only the most senior officers have the balls to stand up to intense media pressure. Secondly, they lack confidence in their own security and efficiency so they are never sure they know what their organisation is doing. It was also the weekend so all the people with the balls were probably in the pub or sitting in front of a log fire at their weekend cottage.

First, she had to have a meeting with the inner circle which was the Shadow Cabinet and explain what she planned to do next. The confrontation with the PM had raised her to hero status amongst Labour members but only the people round the table here knew what it was all about. She called Senator Eveson the minute she'd heard about Fantoni's disappearance and told the group that Eveson was going to try to apply pressure on the UK Government from Washington but he wasn't expecting too much cooperation. There had been concern from the oldest member of her team that she was in danger of bringing the reputation of politics into disrepute but he was shouted down by the others. Law said in total seriousness, "that if the senator was right, then the people behind Greenwatch had killed and kidnapped to keep their secrets and the Tories were in league with them. Fantoni was trying to expose them and surprise, surprise, the man had been taken. Unless we want this place to turn into a police state then it is our mission to find him."

The shadow cabinet were inspired, this woman knew how to excite everyone and was the best chance they'd had of winning the next election since Blair. She'd phoned a camera crew she knew in Covent Garden and they arranged to meet at New Scotland Yard. Listening to Eveson it was obvious that the man Fantoni had suffered all kinds of challenges and dangers. It was about time he was set free and she wasn't going to leave there until he was found.

Carlos was back in his cell and starting to lose hope. Another stained plastic tray of food and cold tea had been there when he returned and apart from the sliced carrot it was hard to identify what was in the meal. He hadn't had a proper meal since the aircraft and he was ravenous enough to eat almost anything. He forced a forkful into his mouth and forced it down – at least it had some taste. The desert was sickly sweet red goo and he shovelled that down too. The food had some effect and he hoped that his friends in the US and maybe J. R. Page would be wondering where he was. With a pang he remembered that Dane Morgan was still fighting for his life after trying to save him and wouldn't be aware of anything.

The Commissioner of Police had been half way home when a deputy called in absolute panic. When the Chief Superintendent on call had said that Angela Law was in New Scotland Yard with a camera crew her first thought was that this was a wind-up. When he went on to say that Law was there for Fantoni and wouldn't leave without him she went cold. The head of London Police hadn't risen to the dizzy heights of running the Met without recognising a winner and in her opinion, Law was a definite next leader of the country. The present PM and his party were in decline and so she had a choice. Either keep Fantoni illegally detained for a few more days as the PM had demanded or let him go now and back a winner. She told the Chief Super to tell Angela Law that she would be there in 10 minutes, switched on the blue light and made the Jaguar really move through London.

Carlos couldn't believe what was happening, he'd just sat down on his bunk in despair when a large police sergeant slammed open the cell door and threw in his clothes, passport and told him to be ready in five minutes or he'd be there "for the rest of his fuckin natural."
As he left Carlos shouted back that if he didn't have the rest of his luggage too, he wasn't going anywhere. There was a very British curse from the corridor and the cop stamped off leaving the door open. He wondered what was going on and dared to hope that someone might have been working for his release.

He got ready quickly, looked in the steel mirror and waited. It seemed hours before the sergeant returned who then escorted him along the corridor and through numerous security checks to a point where the cop had to scan his pass and do a retinal check. Eventually Carlos Fantoni found himself in what appeared to be an underground garage where another cop was standing with his luggage. He checked his personal effects and had his wallet, passport and luggage but no mobile. He requested his phone but was pushed with great force out through the barrier and into the road without it.

It was raining and he could see what he thought must be the Thames across the road and started pulling his case away from the building as fast as he could. The rain was cold and Carlos realised he wasn't dressed for London in January and looked around for a black cab. Eventually one stopped and Carlos pulled everything inside and asked for the Savoy Hotel in Central London. Only a few yards away in the reception of New Scotland Yard, two very different women faced each other. The Commissioner was skinny, sinewy, lined but with an inner power that wasn't often refused. The first thing she did was to get her sergeants to forcibly confiscate the camera and sound equipment. When the crew tried to object, she told them that filming in any police station was highly illegal and they could be imprisoned for months under anti-terrorist legislation. They handed it over without further comment.

Angela Law was about six inches taller and about a stone heavier and was battle-hardened against powerful people. But there were battles worth fighting and those that were not. She demanded to know whether a Carlos Fantoni was in custody and if so what he was charged with. The Commissioner pretended to call on her mobile and walked to the far end of the room speaking animatedly. When she returned, she confirmed that Mr Fantoni had been in custody briefly after an anonymous tip off but had been released without charge earlier in the day.

London was still looking very Christmassy and Fantoni realised that he'd missed the festive season completely. As the black cab pulled into the Savoy, he hoped they still had his booking despite his late arrival. He looked up at the elegant name plate above the doors and remembered those happy weeks a million years ago. The doormen were still the same, elegant in tails and top hats and he wondered if the Italian head waiter would still recognise him. But it was breakfast in the suite with Diane Fallow that he'd really miss. There was a polite cough from outside the cab and he realised that the doorman was waiting. He paid the driver and hoisted his gear out of the cab. He walked over to the reception and apologised for not being able to call and said that he'd been involved in an accident and been delayed. He looked unshaven and slightly disreputable but the Savoy had an excellent database and knew how many times he had been before.
"Will it be your normal suite, Mr Fantoni?"
"Sadly no, I've changed job and my new employers have a different policy."
"So this will not be chargeable to Salimond as it was before?"
"No I am now with Shelford Environmental." Said Carlos handing over a card.
"That's fine sir and we will upgrade you to a junior suite on the south side at no extra cost. After all, you did become quite a regular, didn't you sir."
Carlos realised he didn't have a mobile and needed to make some calls from the room. So he thanked the receptionist and went towards the lift followed by an extremely attentive member of staff with his bags. He stopped and realised that all the numbers he wanted were on the missing mobile and asked them to get J. R. Page at the Financial Times and put him through to the room.
He made it to the room on the fifth floor in double-quick time and heard the phone ringing as he entered. He slipped twenty dollars to the boy nodding apologetically and ran to the phone.
"You certainly know how to live you people don't you." J. R.'s east end edge was much more apparent and Carlos tried to explain. "Don't worry I'm only joking and after where you've been you probably deserve it."
Fantoni gave him a quick summary of what had happened at the airport and his incarceration at New Scotland Yard. He said he'd got everything back apart from his mobile but someone had obviously been through his luggage. Everything still seemed to be there but he needed to get in touch with everyone he was due to meet again.

J.R said he had lots to tell him and that they needed to meet up as soon as possible. That evening in the Savoy Cocktail Bar was where they agreed to meet.

First, he went out and bought a new phone. He passed the door of Simpsons where he had met Diane and really wondered whether he should be staying somewhere else – everywhere was a reminder of the first and last woman he'd ever loved. But he walked on until he found a small alley off the Strand on the way to the Covent Garden shop that reception had recommended. He ended up with an iPhone 9 and realised that it was the first one in months that wasn't a throwaway burner. He paid on his new company credit card and walked back to the hotel.

It was 4.00 p.m. and he hadn't eaten proper food for days. He felt ridiculous but he ordered afternoon tea for two in his room. Whilst he was waiting, he got the phone out of its box and ensured it was charging. He looked at the Omega and realised that it was 11.00 a.m. in Boston and used the hotel phone to ring Joanne Li. What he really needed to do was check how Dane was as they would be worried – he'd been out of contact for 24 hours and they'd be thinking the worst. Whilst he was waiting to be connected there was a knock on the door and he reached over to open it. A waiter in full livery was wheeling a three-tier trolley that was packed with cakes and sandwiches. On the top was a china teapot with matching cups and he poured himself a delicate cup of Darjeeling whilst reaching for a crustless cucumber sandwich. He managed about six tiny morsels before he had a cream cake and another cup of tea. After prison food, it was about as different as you could imagine but he redialled Joanne and tried to resist another cake. The call to Joanne was difficult because she was at Dane's bedside and he'd had a relapse. Carlos could hear the alarms going as she struggled to concentrate on what he was saying. The urgent buzzing of the life support systems sounded terrifying and she was obviously forced out of his room whilst the doctors tried to deal with it.

Dane Morgan had saved him more than once and had become a friend whilst they were hiding out in Panama and Carlos felt absolutely powerless. He just said that everything was OK in London but for her to call him the minute she knew anything about Dane. Before he hung up, he said that he had a new phone and would text the number through. Immediately after the call he did that and lay down on the bed hoping the phone would be charged quick enough for him to receive calls from Boston. The alarm on his watch woke him half an hour before his meeting and he was amazed that he had slept at all. He checked for any incoming messages on the iPhone and there was nothing so he went to the wardrobe and checked what he'd brought with him. In the old Salimond days he had enjoyed wearing good clothes and Bayer had made sure he had outfits from the best of the London tailors. He hadn't really had the chance to dress up since and knew that clothes were only a veneer but it made him feel better. He had a tweed jacket from Huntsman and a pair of Levis he was going to wear but worried that the Savoy might refuse the jeans, so changed to a pair of dark wool trousers that fitted him perfectly. The Grenson brogues reminded him of Dane as he wore them whenever he wasn't in Nikes.

He'd spoken to J. R. Page on many occasions but never met him. One of the advantages of looking like an Inca was that people tended to recognise him rather quickly in Europe. So he went down to the bar at 6.00 o'clock and looked round the room. He hesitated for a few seconds and an older shaven headed guy stood up and mentioned his name. They ordered drinks and J.R asked a striking woman by his side what she wanted and she requested a Guinness. Carlos asked for a Plymouth Gin and tonic. J. R. said he would have a Brandy Alexander. The barman was slightly nonplussed by the beer request but went off to sort the order. They went to a corner away from the bar and J. R. gestured to the woman to his left.
"I know you haven't met, but I thought that you'd like to meet the woman who got you out of jail."
Fantoni leant over and shook the long elegant hand of a woman he vaguely recognised from somewhere and looked suitably confused.
"This is Angela Law, leader of the opposition and friend of Senator Eveson. She's a brilliant lawyer and though I don't share her politics I think she will be running the country before long."
"Well thank you Ms Law, I'm glad to be out of there for sure."
The drinks arrived and Carlos spent a few minutes giving her a brief summary of his history with Greenwatch and what he intended to do to ensure that it was used properly in London and the UK.
She listened attentively and asked questions about the Shelford update and the political situation in the US before nodding at J. R. in approval. Carlos didn't want anyone to be in doubt about the other main aim of his trip which was justice.
"One man was prepared for millions to die just so his company didn't lose profit. This evil man took a good idea – Greenwatch – and turned it into a lie. He manipulated people like me and we worked for him. He is evil."
"Wolf Bayer?" J. R. questioned.
"Of course."
Angela Law asked a few questions about him and made a few

notes. She had heard of the German automotive family he was from but her main knowledge was of a human rights case some years ago where he had been accused of a kind of human slavery and her practice had got involved.

Page updated Carlos with the demands the FT made for interviews with Bayer and the other Salimond directors and the fact the whole board seemed to be disintegrating with a Sheikh been deposed and the Henshin Empire pulling out all funding. Of Bayer there was no sign at all and his family company had issued a statement that Wolf Bayer had no executive involvement in the automotive group and had left five years ago to 'enjoy a well-earned retirement.' Page added that his enquiries at the Panama Gulf Bank had been equally fruitless and according to them Salimond didn't exist. Fantoni pulled out his wallet and showed them both the special black card he'd been given which had almost unlimited drawing rights. J. R. was fascinated and they agreed to visit the local branch of Panama Gulf Bank the following day.

Fantoni had learnt not to trust politicians but there were notable exceptions such as the Senator and hopefully, Angela Law. He still felt very much on his own over here and had a meeting scheduled with the head of Greater London Council which could get difficult. J.R. thought about it for a while and suggested that he attended with Carlos. It would be rather irregular but the FT was seen by most as a respectable, factual newspaper and as it was one of his reporters who had uncovered anomalies with Greenwatch originally, he thought that his own board would understand. The editor had considerable autonomy but he was not without other responsibilities. Carlos hadn't mentioned the bribe involved in the original process but wasn't going to bring it up now if he succeeded in getting the Shelford anti-hacking device installed in the London test units immediately.

Angela Law had re-run the original Wyatt Boyle interview several times and realised that the Senator had made an excellent point at the end. Both the US and UK had badly polluted cities and getting Greenwatch in all of them was literally a matter of life and death. It was far too important to be in the hands of any politician. She would give the matter considerable thought as it could be the most important issue she could ever deal with. The group finished their drinks, exchanged numbers and J.R said that he would be back at the Savoy at 9.30 a.m. tomorrow morning to collect Fantoni.

Wolf Bayer gunned the Porsche engine and slid onto the main road, changing into third and reaching 50 in seconds. It was dark, wet and he seemed to have escaped his attackers for now. There appeared to be gaps in the traffic and he overtook three or four commuters who were all happy to dawdle around and knew there was a junction coming up. He double de-clutch down to second gear and went round the roundabout in a controlled drift which frightened the shit of a woman in a Range Rover already going round.. He needed time to think and this car stood out far too much and anybody with access to CCTV would pick it up too quickly.

He couldn't go home, that was for sure and whoever had killed his security system was a pro and wanted his blood. He had plenty of enemies at the moment – the gangsters who'd sourced that white trash he'd had fun with had threatened him and Hattori Kenshin who'd been part of the consortium had promised all kinds of revenge. On a less violent note, the Financial Times were doing a forensic job on his background as well. There was no point in going to Coworth Park or any of the upmarket hotels around Ascot because that would be the first place they would look so he headed for Slough.

He managed to keep on small roads and go round Windsor so he only had a few yards of road where he thought there might have been cameras. Luckily he'd had his short leather jacket and wallet when he'd crossed to the garage otherwise he would have been in trouble. He couldn't trust his staff because they'd either been bribed or neutralised by his assailants or they would have come to his rescue. For the moment he had to look after himself.

He found a small B&B on the outskirts of Slough which had a large covered carport. In January it was unlikely to be fully booked and there was a vacancy sign hanging in the front window. He parked the car at the back and walked round to the front door. He rang the bell and eventually a large white-haired woman with what he thought was a Polish accent opened the door suspiciously. Thinking it was his destiny to be surrounded by Eastern European trash he explained that he had car trouble and needed a room for the night. They came to terms and was shown to a room with more different patterns than he'd ever seen before in one place and given the key. A few minutes later with a mug of instant coffee in his hand he tried to plan his escape. After his MD had seen the Fantoni interview he had an email officially ending his relationship with Salimond and all his company credit cards were cancelled. His assets were worth millions but what he needed was swift cash as his standard account had been dented badly by his last car purchase. What he needed was plenty of cash so he could get to Panama where a few of his like-minded friends could help him disappear whilst he sold some of his precious cars and homes. Luckily there was an account that had a very healthy balance he could access and very few people knew about it.

J. R. Page had a few doubts overnight as to whether he was doing the right thing by accompanying Fantoni to the bank. He had plenty of other things to do and his deputy wasn't quite ready – mind you he'd been saying that to himself for years and knew in his heart he was good. So he handed things over and went to the Savoy. Fantoni was waiting for him in reception chatting to the girl in German and Page marvelled at his ability with languages. The man obviously spoke Peruvian but apparently had fluency in many other languages as well. Compared to J.R.'s halting French and native English he was an absolute genius and knew that even if he hadn't been a tennis star, Fantoni would have found another way out of the slums of Lima.

Fantoni's first question surprised Page.
"What is NSPCC?"
"It's a kids' charity and does a lot of good – its been around for years - why?"
"I'll tell you later.."
They travelled across town to Canary Wharf which took a long time and Fantoni noticed just how many diesels and petrol vehicles were still spewing out fumes. Page had an electric Nissan which was small but saved him loads of tax and congestion charges. It took a while to find the bank even though Fantoni had been there before but eventually he could see the high-rise Panama Gulf Bank and they parked by an ATM with the hazard warning lights on.

Suggesting Page stayed in the car, Carlos got out and walked quickly over to the cash machine and appeared to be reading the screen. It took about three or four minutes and Page could see the black hat of a traffic warden in his rear view mirror coming menacingly down the street when Fantoni wrenched open the car door laughing hysterically. Page floored the accelerator leaving a frustrated warden desperately trying to catch up but the Nissan showed surprising pickup speed and they headed out of the area.

Half an hour later the treasurer of a well known charity sat back in his knackered old chair and thanked the Lord for providence. The NSPCC was a large charity but they had lost lots of income during the Covid 19 outbreak because of all the events that had been cancelled. There was also less money everywhere after that and fundraising was nowhere near its previous levels. Yet children needed help more than ever as sadly people still take it out on kids especially when things are difficult. The anonymous donation of £5,455,000 pounds had been a strange amount but he'd checked it plenty of times and it seemed legit and had cleared into the NSPCC account.

Carlos Fantoni felt better than he'd felt for weeks having used his black card for something that would do good. But he was still worried about Dane Morgan and the crisis after talking to Jo. There had been no messages and the time in Boston meant he couldn't call for a couple of hours yet. He had to concentrate on the here and now, the next meeting was crucial.

The meeting at the London Council was less difficult than he'd feared. He'd decided to ignore the bribe, which he hadn't mentioned to J. R. Page anyway. Having the editor with him had helped, Fantoni explained that the Financial Times was doing a major feature on the London test and that the editor had kindly agreed to be there. Fantoni opened the meeting by referring to the difficulties the system had in Boston and that there might well be a congressional enquiry on who had tried to interfere with the efficiency of Greenwatch. But he was sure they'd seen much of this on US TV already. Looking around he could see from the nods that everyone was aware.

He went on to explain the changes Shelford University had made and that these updates would be installed free of charge unless there were any objections. One suited man at the back who looked as though he'd come out of the parliamentary official handbook asked about compensation for any of the false readings the Greenwatch units might have shown during the test.
"There was nothing wrong with the test units at all. Someone would have had to hack into them to change them. In the states there are suspicions that politicians were trying to falsify readings but I'm sure that no-one here would do that – would they?" Fantoni looked round and no-one answered
"It's worth reminding you that these changes are to make them hack-proof and Greenwatch will insist on some kind of independent oversight in future. Remember you got these units virtually free and judging by the figures you need them in just about every city in the UK too. Any more questions?"
The Council official who'd taken the biggest bribe thanked his lucky stars and was determined not to rock any kind of boat. Fantoni hadn't mentioned him or that idiot Duckley who'd also been on the

take. He'd died because he'd been stupid enough to throw his money around and blabbed to a reporter whilst the others had kept the money safe and quiet. Greenwatch was essential after all and the updates made perfect sense. The roll out to the rest of the capital was now inevitable but what Downing Street would do with the entire country was a different question. The costs and behaviour change required to stop pollution would be enormous.

J. R. Page was fascinated by the politics and could see why Fantoni was so good at getting the message across. He was lucid, intelligent and committed to the cleaning up of the world and he intended to give him a full page interview in the paper this week. The more positive coverage he got the more protected he was from the dirty tricks that had bedevilled them. Angela Law was also a potential asset but he wasn't quite sure how that would work to Fantoni's advantage. She had challenged the PM in a big way and the impact of that would be seen in the next House of Commons Prime Ministers question time soon.

On the way back to his office he couldn't resist asking what Fantoni had been doing at the bank earlier. He was strangely enigmatic but put a black card with strange markings on it in the central well and said "That was making sure that the last of the dirty money is being used for a good cause." Fantoni started chuckling to himself and Page couldn't get anything more from him.

Wolf Bayer had endured Mrs Polanski's 'full English' and gone into a Tesco Express for the first time so he could get some toiletries. He smiled politely and booked an extra night at the B&B saying that he had to go to town for a few hours and would leave the car parked undercover. He then had the indignity of having to share the train with blacks, Asians and all kinds of trash just to get his mission accomplished. There was absolutely no point in going by car as it was daylight and he could be identified too easily. In desperation he tried his home number on his mobile but just got a number unobtainable message.

When he got off at Canary Wharf, he felt a little more at ease. People were dressed in suits and looked respectable unlike those peasants on the train. When he saw the tall towers and saw the bank names he almost felt at home. This was his territory and he strode down the side streets until he saw the gold windows of the bank - his bank, which had backed his enterprises and held his money for years.

He had chosen the Panama Gulf Bank all those years ago because his father had said that his associates banked there after the war and it was reliable and discrete. He didn't want to be seen inside as there were always cameras and this was London not Panama so he drew out the master black card and put it in the slot as he had done on many previous occasions. The card asked for what currency he required so he stated dollars and then what amount. He requested enough to cover his expenses for the next few weeks but the system refused his demand. He went through the system five more times and then asked for a balance. The figure on screen was 3 dollars and 50 cents. Bayer felt sick, there had been millions in there even after the Japanese pulled out their funding so where was it? He staggered away from the machine knowing that he was doomed unless he could find some cash.

He had to repeat the indignity of trains and underground back to Slough and decide what to do. At the B&B he had to face the Polish cow demanding money for the next night up front and pay out of the diminishing wad of cash in his wallet. He had twenty thousand dollars and ten thousand Euros in the safe in his house and some gold. Visiting his house could be suicidal but he had to try so he called his house number again and this time his man answered.
"The Bayer Residence"
"Smithers, I was attacked two days ago and just about escaped, what happened to you?"
"We were all kept locked up sir, it was dreadful."
"What happened?"
"The police came and we were let out and they have been trying to reach you since."
"Smithers, if they call, tell them I am away for a few weeks and will be in touch."
"Fine sir. Will you be back here at all?"
"Not sure. Now back to your duties and remember, when I have staff I expect them to look after me not leave me at the mercy of criminals. You will be lucky to keep your job after what I have been through."
Bayer hung up and decided that he needed to take a risk. At three in the morning, he started the Porsche and backed out onto the road. It was dark, cold and raining but there wasn't much traffic just the odd minicab and truck delivering to the shops. He made good progress past Eaton and across country towards his house in Ascot. There was a lot of open countryside and he kept looking in his rear mirror and couldn't see any other headlights so he hoped that no-one was following. The big danger however, could well be ahead.

There was a very positive double page spread in the FT the day after the Council Meeting extolling the benefits of Greenwatch and pointing out the business benefits of cleaning up the UK's cities. It reminded everyone of the frightening consequences of bad air quality – 7 million people dying prematurely every year worldwide according to the World Health Organisation. 40 cities in the UK with pollution well above WHO levels which shortened children's lives and reduced their mental and physical development. London alone was estimated to kill around 9,000 people prematurely every year because of air pollution. In financial terms air pollution in Europe was estimated to cost around €1.5trn – roughly a quarter of the continent's GDP according to a study. So the financial and business reasons for an efficient air quality monitoring system were extremely convincing.

There was a lengthy interview with Carlos Fantoni of Shelford Environmental titled **The FTSE 100 need to clean up their act.** Alongside was a photograph of him with his trademark shock of white hair standing next to one of the Greenwatch units situated in the high-rise banking district.
This deliberately provocative statement used data from the US to show that many of the politician were partly financed by the oil and automotive industries which had, according to Fantoni caused all kinds of problems in the development of Greenwatch including an attempt to subvert its purpose and falsify its results. This meant a new system had to be developed that was tamper-proof. Fantoni then stated that the UK top companies and politicians needed to learn from this experience, clean up their environmental policies and commit to independent monitoring.
'**Whereabouts of Wolf Bayer unknown.**' This final subhead allowed Fantoni to lead into a warning to any nation or city who had bought a system from him that its results could not be trusted. Also that the man seemed to have disappeared and was not available for comment.
Reaction to the FT feature was immediate. Hits on the website were in the thousands, evening television had interviews by Greenwatch units with shocked commentators requoting the death figures. Predictably one tabloid had the headline **Don't Cry Wolf** and a photograph of him with fangs photoshopped in, talking about the search for the villain mentioned in the FT piece.

The politicians in power knew that they had been out manoeuvred for the moment and needed to sanitise anything in their past connected to Wolf Bayer or Greenwatch. They postponed any sort of action against Carlos Fantoni and asked the specialists to stand down. For the moment they had to consider more immediate things like how to deal with Angela Law's next attack in the House of Commons.

A few hours before dawn the Porsche moved with its lights off down the road at the edge of his grounds and Wolf Bayer hoped that the idiots who worked for him had turned the alarm off. He parked 20 yards away from the gates and walked in the darkness feeling along the wall to the entrance. The wind was blowing through the trees and it was cold as he edged along trying to listen for any noise. He looked round and the gates were open so he summoned up his courage and moved down the drive towards the house, looking on both sides for anyone who might be crouched there. He knew there was a sensor beam across the drive when the system was switched on, which triggered the lights. So he found a piece of wood and threw in front of him and waited for the lights to blaze on. After a few seconds he breathed in relief as he realised it was probably still switched off. Just as well, he thought, as the system triggered a far more deadly response a little nearer the house.

His house was in total darkness and the wind was blowing the dead leaves across the garden in front of him. All the windows looked out like blind eyes and there was absolutely no sign of life at all from the main building or the staff quarters. He cautiously moved forward getting the keys out of his jacket and heading for the back door which he thought would be safer. There were no lights from anywhere and Bayer wondered whether the electricity was still cut off. He found the keyhole and quietly inserted and turned the key. Inside he dare not try the lights so stopped for what seemed like hours and just listened. He could hear the ticking of his father's big clock from the hall and moved through the kitchen, feeling his way to the table where he always kept a torch and quickly testing it inside his jacket. It worked and he moved, still in darkness to the study where the safe was. Every sound seemed magnified and he could hear the mechanism of the clock his father had sworn belonged to the Fuhrer. He felt a little more confident now and moved to the second door off the hall, turning the metal handle and pushing the big door inwards. Inside he could hear the creepers rattling on the outside of the study window and moved to the far wall where the safe was hidden behind some beautiful panelling. He needed the torch now and shielded it in his hand as he found the release catch. Pressing the button, a panel slid out of sight revealing a very modern Swiss safe.

Soon he thought, I can be out of here, just a few thousand dollars, some Euros and maybe the diamonds, sadly the gold will be too heavy, then I can be back in Panama and enjoying life properly. His hand brushed across a few DVD's and he remembered the films he'd taken in happier times and those women who'd given him such sport. He was tempted, really tempted to take them in but decided against. He found a briefcase by the side of the desk and started to stuff in the dollars, euros and diamonds and was wondering whether he should go upstairs for a suitcase when he was aware of a change in the darkness; something made the short hairs on his body rise in fear. He stood stock still, transfixed and could still not see anything, then something sharp pricked his neck.

The House of Commons was full of anticipation. After the chaos a couple of days ago the green benches on both sides were crammed. The Prime Minister was scheduled to revisit the education debate which had been foreshortened by Angela Law and her outrageous accusations. The speaker looked down from the woolsack with a mixture of fear and anticipation as he didn't want to have to close the Commons again and be infamous for years after.

The Prime Minister delivered a standard statement about their increases in budget and improvement in child literacy and numeracy over their years in office. Much to the Tories surprise nobody opposite heckled and they started to fear another parliamentary ambush.
"Does the Prime Minister know just how many schools in Great Britain are surrounded by areas that the WHO consider to have dangerous air? Also, does the Prime Minister know that this pollution inhibits their ability to learn and physical development?" The labour MPs were somewhat disappointed with the lack of drama in their leader's question this time. But judging by the frantic shuffling of papers and urgent conversations close to the PM they could see the questions had caused consternation.
"I'm afraid that I don't have that data to hand at present but my honourable friend opposite will be aware that it is our intention to make the roll out of Greenwatch to the rest of the UK as part of our election manifesto." The PM sat down to resounding cheers from his back benchers.
"Since you don't seem to care about the numbers of schools where the air is killing pupils, let me enlighten you. According to reliable data there are 6,500 schools in the UK where the air is deadly dangerous."
"As I said, we are planning to introduce Greenwatch...." The Prime Minister interjected but Law had not yet finished.
"Are yes. Greenwatch is where even the Financial Times – not

normally a fan of this party – warned that certain politicians - maybe those with strong connections to the oil and automotive industries - had conspired to falsify its results and discredit its supporters. Does the Prime Minister know any such people?" The uproar was not quite as great as previous but it was close, everyone had seen the FT and knew its implications. The Speaker allowed the uproar to die down and noticed that Law was standing and still had the floor.
"The final part of my question is simple. We all know there could be an election next year and that Greenwatch will be a major issue. Shelford Environmental and Greenwatch expert Carlos Fantoni suggest that air quality is too important to be left in the hands of one political party. My question to the Honourable Leader is that if my party committed now to Greenwatch being a matter for cross party agreement only, would the Conservatives agree?" Law allowed the question to gather impact and went on. "Furthermore, we in the Labour party would commit to independent scrutiny from the World Health Organisation. Would he?"
The Prime Minister prevaricated about not having produced its manifesto yet and the disgusting way that yet again the Honourable Member had broken parliamentary rules but most members knew that this was possibly the most important interchange they'd seen in the house since the Covid-19 days. Most knew in their heart of hearts that Angela Law was likely to win the next election and that the offer to effectively take Greenwatch away from party politics was a serious consideration. When the PM got back to his office there was an email from Angela Law offering to discuss the matter in private. This was real politics and he needed to consider his position with his most trusted advisors..

Carlos Fantoni had watched the speech from J.R.'s office and been stunned by Law's offer. He had mentioned the hope a cross party agreement might work in the States but thought that technically it would be difficult to achieve. He'd also hoped that some kind of oversight whether it be academic or health would be possible but the World Health Organisation would be ideal if it got its act together. In the last great emergency, many accused it of being slow and bureaucratic in the extreme but gradually it started to get organised. Global Warming, Habitat Loss, Water and Air Pollution were all related and all global concerns where a non political viewpoint is useful. Greenwatch or something like it was needed in cities everywhere yet opposition from entrenched interests like oil and power is also everywhere. This needs to be overcome by honesty, trust and science if we are to survive as a species. Fantoni realised that it was early but couldn't wait to phone Senator Eveson and Jo with the news.

A meeting took place in a small mews house on the edge of Chelsea Barracks. It had the advantage of having a rear entrance close to parking which was not overlooked by anyone. The Prime Minister owned it personally and always thought that the market value of five million would be a useful reserve if things went tits up politically. And that was a distinct possibility judging by recent events. If he lost the election and resigned then his pension would be inadequate for a couple with their tastes, though he could make a few hundred thousand by joining the speaker circuit and becoming a non-exec like all his predecessors. There could be a problem however as many of the companies who might have offered the usual non executive positions were the ones who felt threatened by Greenwatch and the environmentalists.

Angela Law arrived wearing Levis and a leather jacket and was not surprised to see the PM wearing his trademark pinstriped suit. She always imagined he'd been born in a miniature version of that suit – a thought that amused her when he was pontificating at the despatch box. He may have been a stuck up tailors dummy but he had a good brain and the native cunning of a third-generation Tory politician. So she had to play this carefully as too much was at stake for her to fail.

After the usual pleasantries and a pot of extremely good tea, complete with Spode cups and an antique silver strainer that she was tempted to pocket, she got down to business.

"There is evidence that you personally negotiated with a company called Salimond to invest in the Greenwatch extra package which would falsify the results when you rolled it out nationwide."

"That is outrageous and certainly not true – I honestly think you are deranged, I thought you'd asked for this meeting to apologise." The PM spluttered.

"I also have heard from an extremely reliable source in MI6 that you ordered them to remove Carlos Fantoni and sanctioned another clean up operation involving a London journalist."

"Leaks, bloody false news – this is total rubbish."

"I am aware that this may never get to court but I think that you are a despicable man. I am told that you conspired with others like Wolf Bayer to prevent anyone seeing the true picture of pollution in our cities. I suspect you were motivated by greed and that your friends in the oil business were concerned that someone might damage their profits. Unless you agree to my cross party idea then the election campaign is going to get really dirty and you will be the one who will be damaged. Or you could choose to be the one who history remembers as the Prime Minister who helped save thousands of lives. Your choice?"

Angela Law picked up her case and left the house hoping that the recording she'd made was adequate. She breathed the winter air outside and felt a profound relief she was out of there. It had been a risky thing to do but they would see in the House of Commons over the next few months whether she had achieved anything worthwhile.

Carlos Fantoni reckoned he had done as much as he could for the moment and was anxious to get back to the States. Shelford had already produced enough updates for the Greenwatch units on test in London and their installation didn't need him there. The experts would be able to tell remotely from Boston when they had been fixed. Greater London Council would send an official order for the roll-out to the city inside the M25 but they had a lot of planning to do first. The first stage would be to change all council operated vehicles to electric and restrict other heavy vehicles coming in to electric or zero emission during the day.

The council was also working on a pollution forecast in the same way they already provided weather and pollen. The air quality forecast would be based on Greenwatch data and if too bad then vehicles would be banned for the day. The city was targeting a 50% reduction in a whole list of dangerous chemicals within five years and Carlos could not fault their ambition. The rest of the UK would have to wait until after the general election but if Angela Law got her cross party agreement then it should be considerably easier than he had ever anticipated.

Carlos looked around his hotel room and knew he loved it here in London as he had some good friends here now. He planned to meet them for another drink in the Savoy Cocktail bar and then be on his way. The only thing he had failed on was finding Wolf Bayer and whilst he was unpunished nothing would be satisfactory, nothing would be finished. He didn't know who had killed Diane Fallow or been behind some of the other killings but in his heart, he knew that Bayer had some part of it. Anybody who could allow the death of so many innocent people just to protect their profits was capable of all kinds of inhumanity.

Wolf Bayer was paralysed. He could see something familiar and with a supreme effort of concentration he recognised it. It was the dashboard of his 1938 Mercedes Saloon and he was sitting in the driver's seat. He could see the large Bosch dial with the chrome edging and the figures from 0 to 120 kph going round the edge. He could see the huge steering wheel ahead of him with his hands in the classic 'ten to two' position but he couldn't move them no matter how hard he tried. He could feel the big engine vibrating through the wheel and wondered vaguely why he'd chosen this car and not the Porsche. It took a while, but he discovered he was in one of his own garages and there was someone in a black outfit with goggles looking in through the car window. The man smiled and then forced something down Bayer's throat which he felt, but he realised in horror that he could do absolutely nothing about it.

Chapter 30

In Boston General, Dane Morgan wondered whether a one-armed photographer was going to impress anyone. His rather warped British sense of humour wondered whether they would want anyone so 'short handed' or work with someone who was 'armless' and who'd 'chucked his hand in'. Puns were giving him some entertainment but Joanne had no idea what he was gibbering about and thought it was the pain-killers. But the doctors were pleased with him.

Crowdfunding raised more than enough for his treatment and Dane had some medical insurance but it was very basic and only covered a fraction of the cost of this operation. His non-existent arm had stopped giving him so much pain and now they had worked out the cause of the relapse a few days ago and changed his medication, they thought he could be released within days. Joanne had actually touched the stump of his left arm and not found it disgusting. It was just above the wrist and the surgeons had done a good job. It was the vast amount of blood he had lost during the attack that had worried the team. But now they were convinced that he was in reasonable shape physically and mentally and were talking about releasing him. Dane had a lot of catching up to do. His conversations with Carlos and Joanne had brought him reasonably up to date with the Greenwatch campaign but he was naturally curious about the man who'd nearly killed him.

The assassin who'd attacked him had been a mystery as he'd obviously done a lot to cover up his past and Dane suspected that at least one of his possible employers was the government itself who wouldn't really want to investigate. Eventually they found out he was listed in British military records as Alexander Brown, army surgeon. According to Interpol he had worked as an assassin for around 10 years and had a unique modus operandi which was to always use a rapier or swordstick just like the one left at the Grosvenor Club. This had allowed police to link it to a string of murders in Panama and Boston. Investigating this further, Dane was able to find out that one of them was Dr Coombes who'd been on his way to confess to them on camera, another had been a priest in the cathedral where he'd met Eugene Morgan all those weeks ago. The other person who'd disappeared and turned up dead in Panama at about the same time was Eugene himself. There hadn't been enough of his body left to know how he was killed, but the assassin had to be the most likely suspect.

It was a dead cop and some dealers in Boston that had been the most recent murders and which had given the investigation extra impetus and led to the other murders being linked. The house Brown rented had also been found which had given them other weapons and evidence. Within the narrow field of assassination Brown was known as a high price, top quality professional who had never failed to get his target. With this record Fantoni and Dane himself had to consider themselves incredibly fortunate to be still alive. The mystery remained as to who had employed the assassin and why the thug who'd abducted Carlos in the first place had saved him.

Dane returned to the Li home to recover and spent hours discussing their aims with the rest of the team. He had missed so much in the beginning – the Wyatt Boyle regular weekly slot Jo now had and the way the Senator had been pushing for a congressional enquiry. But not enough progress had been made in the US and the people that mattered – the President, his aide and that thug Kowolski – were still carrying on regardless. The conversation he'd had a few hours ago with Fantoni in London seemed more hopeful but the criminal mastermind behind the whole thing was still missing. There were too many loose ends for Dane and he needed to get out of bed and help.

Kowolski had been in Canada hiding at a fishing lodge after he'd escaped from the Grosvenor Club. The most unusual thing about him was that he was a hero. The assassination attempt had been shown again on TV and when a big guy in a tartan lumber jacket looked at the coverage, he recognised him. He couldn't deny it, the camera was just a couple of feet away from his face when he blew that psycho Brown away. The fisherman bought him a Bud then everyone else bought him one which made for an extremely convivial night.

Kowolski had done some extremely bad things in his life. He'd killed women and children – anyone that Uncle Sam wanted taken out. And he had never been too worried about collateral damage as long as the target was eliminated. The one thing he'd never done is become a hero, so the novelty and free beer was quite enjoyable. But he didn't want his masters to know where he was now because he suspected that a heroic death was the last thing they were thinking about for him. The fishing was good and he'd told his friends in the lodge he would be there another week and not to blow his cover. They slapped him on the back with comradely bonhomie and thought it was great to have someone like Kowolski protecting their continent. The great thing he enjoyed in addition to the free drinks was smoking.

The lodge prided itself on being free of all restrictions so he didn't have to sneak out for a smoke anymore, he was free to have a brandy at 6.00 a. m., a pack of Marlbrough in the morning and whatever he wanted was fine. People smoked pipes, cigars and cigarettes and Kowolski loved coming down in the early evening to see a pall of tobacco smoke hanging from the bar ceiling. It was just like the old days. Also just like the old days, Kowolski woke up in his bunk tight chested from the cigarettes, hung over from the beer and yet after a few coughs and a shower he was fit for fishing again.

He reckoned that it would take his Lords and Masters weeks, if not months, to find him. He'd resigned and technically he was entitled to so many months of back leave so they might not care. But he'd embarrassed them and though they would be distracted with all the post election furore for a while they'd remember eventually. Then someone would want to take him out in a clean up exercise. His partner in the original snatch of Fantoni to Panama had already been sent to Vietnam on another mission and Kowolski had been unable to reach him since. Funnily enough, he thought, his appearance on TV might just delay their action a little longer.

Kowolski had managed another week of great fishing before anyone found him and then the peace was shattered by a familiar sound. He was sitting on the verandah one evening having another Marlbrough and enjoying the lovely winter scenery when he heard it. The Sikorsky UH-60 had an individual sound that he remembered from many missions. The fact that the helicopter had come over the hill without any attempt at stealth gave him some hope but he really thought they could have used something smaller and less obvious. The Black Hawk settled down by the lake by which time all the other guests were out of the lodge with their jaws on their chests. Kowolski tried to look confident as he pulled on his big boots and set off down the hill to where someone was getting out of the helicopter's side door.

The Presidential special aide was not the leader's favourite person anymore but he had one great advantage. As they say in the movies, he knew where all the bodies were buried and as such he was the only person the President was able to talk to. With senators, journalists and TV people all trying to depose him, he needed all the help he could get.

Operations like this were also going to be his main mission for a while as no one else could be trusted. He hated helicopters, he hated the cold outdoors and he hated Kowolski for failing to arrange Fantoni's death - so this combined everything he hated in one place. He struggled out of his straps and jumped clumsily out of the Black Hawk trying not to be decapitated by the rotors. He crouched down and ran away from the gunship to where he could see Kowolski crouching at a safe distance. Only then did the idiot pilot decide to shut down the engine and make it easier. Kowolski just about recognised the aide in his huge flight suit and realised that he was too much of a pansy to be a physical threat. The other guys in the Black Hawk were a different matter and now they'd shut the engine down he was doubly wary.

"What the fuck do you want?" Kowolski asked with his mouth close to the aide's ear.

"If the President wanted you dead, you'd be dead by now – I thought you guys were good at undercover – you left a trail that a boy scout could follow."

"I wasn't trying to hide – I just wanted out of this business."

"Were you planning a TV career perhaps?" The aide said nastily. "The President wants you well away from Washington for a year and out of sight. He's given you a new job and a new identity and if you do it properly maybe you'll stay alive." The aide handed him a large brown envelope and struggled back through the wind which was starting to get up ominously. The Black Hawk took off a few seconds later and Kowolski held the package close to his chest and struggled back up the hill to where an adoring group of fellow fishermen waited. Thinking that his heroic status must have been hugely enhanced by a US helicopter coming to hand him his mission papers he went to his room quickly and opened the package. The contents were 1. A new US Passport and set of credit cards. 2. An ID in his new name stating that he was a CIA officer stationed in Anchorage, Alaska. 3. Instructions to set up a new office for the agency. The rest were just background details for his new identity along with standard Health & Safety and HR type information sent to all new officers. Kowolski was shocked that they'd found him so quickly and astonished that he still appeared to be on the payroll. He'd never heard of fucking Anchorage and Alaska was the end of the world, but he was still alive.

Joanne felt they had the full team together for the first time in weeks. Carlos was back in Boston staying at the Li home. Dane was out of hospital looking pale but gorgeous as always, even with the end of his left sleeve of his shirt hanging empty. Professor Li and Professor Spencer were also there trying not to worry at how gaunt

Dane Morgan was looking. None of them had seen him in hospital because Jo had been the only one allowed and the tall muscular young Englishman was now a shadow of himself. Thinking that this was getting a little too depressing, somebody had to break the spell. "What's the matter, haven't you ever seen a one-armed man before?" Dane asked with a grim smile.
"Not since the Fugitive film." Said James Spencer.
"Don't forget Nelson – he was English." Said Jo, picking up the tone.
"Another great Englishman here to save the world." Said Dane.
After breaking the ice and forcing everyone back into character, Dane asked for an update from Carlos as most of the local news he knew from Jo's bedside chats in hospital. London sounded as though a lot had been achieved and the Greenwatch project might be safe – especially if both main parties agreed to independent scrutiny of the units before the election. The newspaperman Page also seemed like a useful ally, Dane had worked with them before supplying jungle shots for a feature on deforestation and they had a brilliant reputation.

The only strange thing about the meeting later was the camera. Dane picked up a Nikon and practised one handed shooting members of the team which he found tiring. Everyone knew that he'd made his living from photography before he'd lost his arm but with all the concentration on Greenwatch it was hard to remember that of all the people round the table he must feel the most insecure. Carlos Fantoni was employed by Shelford, Joanne had a regular slot on the Wyatt Boyle show and a burgeoning career in media. The two Professors were still in place at the university and an even greater part of its future development plans. Dane was in his 30's and not poor but had to rebuild his career completely with one less hand than when he'd started. So he was experimenting with the smaller Nikon he had first photographed Carlos with all those months ago. Looking across the table he realised that the shock of premature white hair which had stood out so well on those shots, was back to its full glory.
"It's months since the President got re-elected and Dane was attacked – I think we really need to concentrate on what we want to achieve over the next couple of months." Joanne asked everyone. Dane put his camera down with a sigh and absent-mindedly looked at the shots he'd taken on the back on his camera. The others had each been concentrating on their own areas of interest and it was a good discipline to think of real aims and objectives. So they were all silent for a while and Dane who had become impatient, couldn't help adding. "Who are the guilty ones and how do we get them." Joanne thought that Carlos might have answered but he looked pointedly at

her so she put her views first.

"Mayor Bonelli, he started the dirty tricks first, the thug Kowolski and whoever was with him, who took Carlos in the first place. And the President."

"What about that Presidential aide I recognised from the election shots – he interrogated me and looked like Kowolski's boss." Fantoni added.

"Yeh, so him too. "Joanne added. "Anybody else to add?

"Just Salimond and Wolf Bayer who started the whole con. But I really don't think we can do much from here." Carlos added. "And J.R. is going to ring me with an update on that investigation later."

Since he was quite enjoying himself in the chairman's role, he asked a final and fundamental question before they broke up the meeting to compile their plans. Dane stood up and asked.

"But apart from getting bad people to justice what is our main long term objective? – Carlos, you should answer first."

"Getting Greenwatch installed safely worldwide has got to be the main thing – it can save millions of lives as you know."

The nods around the table were enough to convince them that nothing was more important than that. The group split up and agreed to meet when they had some new ideas about how they might achieve some of these aims and get justice.

One of their targets, Mayor Bonelli, surprised them all just days later. Bonelli had hidden in a private nursing home after being very publicly accused of fraud and criminal deception on the Wyatt Boyle show. He hadn't expected anything but complements for his vision in testing Greenwatch but had been ambushed by Fantoni who accused him of covering up the warnings on the system and arranging for him to be snatched. Despite the fact he'd had a genuine heart attack earlier in the year he knew he couldn't pretend he was at deaths door for much longer.

The irony was that Bonelli was a true believer in the system now and loved the way that he'd helped clean up the city. He loved that the sparrows and thrushes were chirping in the trees and not falling dead to the floor as they used to. He'd even heard that a rare finch had been seen in the city for the first time in a century. He was fitter himself and normally ran a couple of miles across the city and enjoyed the winter air. He'd done good things like banning traffic from the centre on bad air days. Now he needed to come clean with everyone else.

He surprised everyone, including himself, by ringing Joanne Li arguably the woman who caused his real heart attack with her constant harassment about the environment. It was a call made on impulse but at least she listened and after considerable discussion agreed to his proposal. A week later Jo was in the studio for her normal environmental slot on the Wyatt Boyle show only this time she had Mayor Bonelli alongside.

Boyle had ten minutes' notice of this but went with it. The original confrontation with Bonelli and his storming out had done wonders for his ratings so he was hoping for some more fireworks. Just to add more spice, he replayed the first interview with Fantoni accusing Bonelli and his swift exit. Then he introduced Joanne who was now almost as good as Boyle at live studio work.
"A month back we accused Mayor Bonelli of all kinds of dirty tricks connected with Greenwatch and he felt the need to leave. But a couple of days ago he rang and asked me for a chance to put his side of the story and Wyatt agreed. Over to you Mayor Bonelli."
"Thank you Ms Li. This is in the nature of a confession, Carlos Fantoni did leave a message for me, demanding that I stopped the Greenwatch test because he was concerned that its readings could be tampered with. Knowing that Greenwatch was a key part of the Presidential campaign I panicked and passed on the information to a senior member of his staff. What happened to Carlos Fantoni or anyone else in this terrible story had nothing to do with me."
"Who did you tell in Washington?" Jo could not resist interrupting.
"I'm sorry, I can't tell you that – that is up to them. But before I finish, I would like to say that I am now totally committed to Greenwatch and the cleaning up of my city. I have already changed so many things; I've banned traffic on certain days and have a city wide fitness campaign. Since the heart attack I'm a changed man. Do you know that the birds are back in the city, even a rare finch that hasn't been seen for a hundred years....."
"Thank you Mayor Bonelli, thank you Joanne." Boyle smoothly finished up with a request direct to camera that someone in the President's office would come clean and then as the President's ad used to say, 'we could all breathe easy.'

Senator Eveson watched the broadcast with astonishment. He had disliked the man intensely because he thought he had been a self-serving, profiteering Republican. But he believed Bonelli's confession and lots of other senators and state governors might have been convinced too. His attempt to get the two thirds required to insist on an impeachment had been stalling but this might just give his campaign a boost. He had also been watching with interest the progress in London and J. R. Page had sent a video of the extraordinary offer made by Angela Law in the House of Commons.

As it was his own idea to bring some independence to Greenwatch monitoring he felt some satisfaction.

Having also seen the interview, the President felt as though his balls were being squeezed and not in a good way. Bonelli seemed to have fed him to the dogs and the demands coming from Wyatt Boyle and co to subject his aide and himself to an official investigation were becoming incessant. His aide may have been his right hand during the last few months but as that interfering bastard Dane Morgan had found out – sometimes you have to cut off a hand in order to survive.

Back in Boston, the Greenwatch Six as those who were now working together round the Li kitchen table jokingly called themselves, were in a quandary. Predictably it was Dane who had named them after groups of dissidents or wrongly accused like the Birmingham Six or Hampstead Four. Dane was really back on form and his humour had improved day by day as he adjusted physically to the demands of Photography with one hand. The fact that he'd still got the left forearm helped as he had found he could rest the Nikon on it and still produce great shots. Those he'd taken of the group the previous week were good and Joanne couldn't work out how he managed to capture personalities on film. His landscapes had been the thing that had captured her heart originally but he used a camera the way a great artist uses paint. He always added something – an essence or an insight, Jo couldn't work it out. But it was obvious he had got his mojo back. Another thing had helped. The Eveson Agency had asked whether they could buy the copyright on two of his old shots of the Remarkable Range in New Zealand as they wanted to use them in a campaign for an ethical Canadian Sparkling Water brand. The fee they were offering for worldwide usage was generous and Dane liked the product. The other thing was an email from J. R. Page asking him to come to London to discuss a new assignment for the Weekend FT which might involve the sort of work he and Joanne Li had been doing on damaged landscapes. He didn't know the editor personally but Carlos spoke of him highly and he was definitely an influential friend as far as the Greenwatch Six were concerned.

Dane also felt that after all the trauma of the last months he needed to visit his mother in England. He emailed J. R. and confirmed that he could be there in two weeks and FaceTimed his mother who asked pointedly whether she was going to meet Ms Li this time or whether she was his secret.
The quandary faced by the Greenwatch Six was who they were

after now Mayor Bonelli had confessed to at least part of his sins. Carlos and Dane reckoned that the aide was the only practical target because his testimony was the only way they might get evidence that the President had been behind all the dirty tricks. Now they even knew his name.

Months later and Special Aide, Steve Bannerman still hadn't given in to the pressure from Joanne Li, the Wyatt Boyle show or anyone else to talk about Greenwatch. As the most senior aide he was used to pressure but the last year had been challenging. He knew that the pressure was starting to tell on the President and thought that Kowolski was also a potential security threat even in Alaska. So the instruction to visit him in Fairbanks and assess the level of risk was not a total surprise. What would have surprised him was the message Kowolski had received directly from the President.

Fairbanks, Alaska in early spring could still boast minus 30 degrees. Kowolski had arrived when it had been even colder and had set up a CIA office in one of the few office rental areas with a decent view and Arctic quality insulation. One didn't put CIA on the nameplate so he'd used his old US Environmental Agency identity. The irony was that even by industrial standards the air quality round here was abysmal and a pall of smoke normally hung over the town from every building burning logs on his journey in from the hotel. The smoke in his office was even worse but that was from the 40 or more Marlborough he enjoyed in solitary glory every day. He still didn't know why he had been sent here but the direct call from the President gave him one very good reason. His mission was to ensure that the Presidential Aide suffered an extremely plausible and totally terminal accident.

Steve Bannerman had checked on the local website as to the likely climate and had dressed in his Aspen Ski gear but the reality was nothing like Aspen. The cold when he left the station was bad enough to have formed icicles on Kowolski's recently acquired beard and made his own head hurt even under his ski hat. He looked around at his fellow passengers and realised that he needed a parka or something else as an extra layer and a pair of snow boots. Everyone else looked as though they'd stepped out of an Arctic expedition movie.
"You certainly know how to blend in with the crowds don't you?" Kowolski sneered whilst trying to light a cigarette under the cover of the station entrance. "And you've chosen the busiest day of the year to come – it's the Fairbank's dog sled competition."
The aide tried to look as though he knew all about it and failed. But

as they drove into town for him to buy some extra clothes, he could see the posters everywhere. Fairbanks is only famous for a few things – the Northern Lights, The Ice Sculptures and the Annual Dog Sled Race. "Mush, Mush" was all he could think of saying.

He found an outdoor clothing store and invested in a pair of Caribou boots and a fur lined Parka with a hood and put one layer of ski clothing back in his case. This he dumped in Kowolski's jeep and they walked to where a team of four pairs of dogs and a sled were ready to set off. He didn't find it thrilling, the fact that anyone would voluntarily set off for a 1000 mile race through the toughest country and climate he could imagine was incomprehensible to him.
"Can you drive a snowmobile?" Kowolski asked and when he nodded said. "I've arranged a quick guided tour of the area with a local guy who showed me round when I first came. I've got a doctor's appointment later, so I've arranged it for then, OK?"
They went for coffee in a cafe full of Nanook of the North lookalikes and Bannerman tried to remember that he was there to check out Kowolski and not to enjoy himself. They had not exactly bonded in the brief time they'd been together and the new facial hair just made him look like a thug with a beard. The fact Kowolski had shot the assassin and not Fantoni had not been forgotten by anyone in Washington but luckily the media hadn't found him in this godforsaken hole.

Four thousand miles away and forty degrees warmer, Dane and Jo were in London having a drink with J. R. Page in The Lamb & Flag, Covent Garden. The bar was a real surprise for Jo as she'd never experienced that wonderful British institution, the city pub. The atmosphere was unlike any of the bars in Boston or anywhere else she'd travelled. There were local tradesmen in their overalls, bankers in their suits and even a female barrister with her wig hung on a hook behind her. Everyone seemed to have pints of beer and Dane had ordered a Black Sheep and J.R. a Fullers. She looked down the array of pumps behind the small bar and asked for a pint of Guinness. The noise and laughter was infectious but J. R. looked extremely grim.

They arrived at Heathrow a week ago and spent it with Dane's Mother in Oxfordshire. She lived in an old cottage on the edge of a lovely stone town that nestled under the Bledlow Ridge. Rosemary Morgan had been unmoved by the death of Eugene and Joanne realised what a bastard he must have been for a lovely woman like her to be indifferent. Dane's amputation and the story behind it had her in floods of tears however, then incredibly angry that anyone should try and cover up such pollution. She'd seen the search for Wolf Bayer in the papers but hadn't realised that he was the mastermind behind the whole thing.

Dane had travelled in to London from Oxfordshire on the coach for a meeting with J. R. on the second day. They sorted the business out in an hour and Dane was now employed by the Financial Times doing a series of photographs of 'Threatened Landscapes' worldwide. These included the Amazon Rainforest, Borneo Jungle and Costa Rican Cloud Forests and were an attempt to show the real danger of these disappearing because of over exploitation. It was a fantastic opportunity but Dane couldn't help asking about Bayer and Salimond as soon as he could. Page said that it was frustrating because the police didn't seem interested despite the coverage but he had an ex SIS operative who might just help. No matter how much he tried to stoke it up, the media interest in Bayer was starting to wane but Angela Law had helped by mentioning him in Prime Minister's Question Time. The PM had denied any connection with him.

After arranging to meet again at the end of the week Dane returned on the luxury coach to the Watlington turn and then ran the three miles from the M40 junction. It was March and he could see just the start of new green in the hedgerows but it didn't feel much warmer. A cruel wind was blowing up the lane and it was starting to get dark as he sprinted the last few yards to the cottage. Joanne was on her laptop as he opened the door and she smiled that lovely smile. She'd been talking to Carlos and he said that there was good news from Washington. Apparently, the President had agreed to his aide attending a special enquiry convened by Eveson and a select committee of other politicians. This was to take place in three weeks' time when Bannerman had returned from an official visit to Alaska.

The person most shocked by this arrangement would have been Steve Bannerman. He was dressed in a set of grimy overalls and crash helmet and could barely see anything through the cracked visor. The guy Kowolski had introduced him to, was a local judging by his eyes, and that was all he could see through the gap in his helmet. He'd tried to talk health and safety but the guy grunted, fired up both snowmobiles, said a few words which could have been Inuit and roared off at great speed waving for him to follow.

The aide was not going to be embarrassed in front of Kowolski, so wound up the throttle and shot after the guide, who was already out of the yard and speeding up towards a track into the woods he could see a few hundred yards away. The snow was starting to fall heavier now and the big flakes made it even harder to see so Bannerman wiped his visor with his gloved hand and tried to follow. The guide was going faster and pulling further ahead so Bannerman had to increase speed and the trees were crowding in on both sides and amplifying the big engine noise but he kept his nerve. He got closer and followed the guide through two narrow bends that almost had him off the machine but he steadied the snowmobile and they burst out of the trees into a clearing. The guide stopped for a few seconds 50 yards ahead to check he was still behind and then accelerated out of the clearing and up a steep track on the far side. Bannerman powered after him with a roar and entered the forest again at speed and realised that he couldn't see the guide's machine anymore. He twisted the throttle and tried to catch up but the track got rougher and narrower, forcing him to slow down and stop. He was frozen, lost and relieved to be alive then saw the guide appear about 100 yards up the track waving frantically through the blizzard for him to come. The guy disappeared in a flurry of snow and Bannerman roared after him not wanting to lose him again. He saw the hairpin bend at the top almost too late and powered through it at speed feeling the machine slide. The fallen log a few yards round was impossible to avoid and the aide knew he was in big trouble. The last thing he remembered was flying through the air in slow motion and hitting a pine trunk with a sickening crunch which was beyond pain.

The death of the President's chief aide was announced on CBS News with great solemnity. His wife and children had only heard an hour previously when a tearful President had called them himself from the White House. It was hard for Mrs Bannerman to believe that her husband had been so foolhardy. He hated the cold, didn't like exercise and planned everything meticulously. The TV had said that he'd been killed trying to race his snowmobile in thick snow and hit a tree – that was not the Steve Bannerman they knew.

She remembered he had been worried for some reason about the trip to Alaska and that he had been upset by all the media pressure the President and himself were under, but he had reassured them it was all hot air and would die down soon. Now he was dead. With a sense of disbelief, she unlocked his study and went through to his desk. There on his computer was a handwritten envelope with the words "*Please open in the event of my death.*"

The news broadcast was seen by Carlos who immediately

suspected foul play. People who tried to expose this President ended up dead and the aide was the only direct link between him and all the bad things that had happened since he'd tried to expose the Greenwatch fraud. The official enquiry that Senator Eveson had forced out of the President was now dead in the water as its star witness was in the morgue. He picked up his phone and called Dane telling him that the official enquiry they'd been promised was now unlikely to happen.

Dane picked up the news in the Lamb and Flag in London and passed it on to Jo and J. R. Page. He had been looking depressed anyway and the implications of the aide's death were not lost on him. They moved away from the bar and found a free alcove at the back of the pub where the noise was a little less and tried to talk. It was obvious that something had upset J. R. before they'd had the news from the US and he was trying to decide what to tell them.

The editor had been pursuing Wolf Bayer in his newspaper and online for months despite opposition from some members of his board who were starting to think that the story had died weeks ago and the editor was showing signs of obsession. Politics had also reared its ugly head when Angela Law mentioned it in Parliament – a woman who some directors thought was the devil as far as the FT was concerned.

He'd paid for the investigator himself. This was a woman who'd worked for the UK intelligence agencies for twenty years before being retired ten years early because she had been whistleblower on a particularly nasty operation which had an unacceptable collateral damage level. In some ways she reminded J. R. of the sort of woman Diane Fallow might have become – principled, persistent and well connected. He'd given her the task of finding out about Wolf Bayer and she'd come up with nothing until last night and what he'd seen had turned him stomach. Now he couldn't decide whether to show Dane and Joanne or not. The investigator also had an idea as to where Bayer was hiding and if she was right then they really should tell the police.
"Look J.R., there is something bothering you, what is it?"
"Something I really wish I hadn't seen." Admitted J. R. with his East End accent more pronounced than they'd ever heard it. "But I can't unsee it and it's a bloodbath.."
"Listen, I was in the army, I've seen all kinds of things – you'd better show me." Dane said.
J. R. pulled out his iPad and pointed the screen towards Dane who put his body between it and Jo. The film lasted about three minutes

and involved a tall, older man torturing a couple of women – one a tall blonde and the other Thai or Chinese. The detail was horrific; one was virtually flayed alive and the other whipped and shot. Blood and guts were everywhere and the sadism involved was more sickening than anything Dane had ever seen. The detail on film was horrible and the man involved was very clearly Wolf Bayer. Joanne could see the horror reflected on Dane's face and just asked for an explanation.

"It's that sadistic bastard Wolf Bayer and I'd love to kill him myself after seeing that."

"So you can see why I was upset." J. R. said. "I wasn't sure whether to show it at all."

Dane pushed out of his seat and went to the bar for another round. He needed just a moment to collect his thoughts and cool down. It was strange, he knew Bayer was capable of putting thousands of people at risk by falsifying the Greenwatch data but how anyone could be cruel to defenceless women was incomprehensible. He took the pints back to the alcove and they sat in silence for a few minutes.

"Carlos will want to know how do we find Wolf Bayer." Joanne asked, shaking them out of their torpor.

"Can you be back at the office tomorrow morning?" J. R. asked.

The editor said he thought they might find him but it was about an hour's car journey. He had also considered telling the police but judging by the way they'd tried to stitch up Carlos there was a risk that someone might try to cover up anything they found.

Someone at Government level didn't want the world to know about the scandal, someone influential enough to get Fantoni arrested on false charges a couple of weeks back. So he thought they'd better get the proof themselves and tell the Police later.

The next morning the weather had reverted to winter and storm force winds battered the coach as it went up the hill on the M40 and threatened to blow it into the next lane. It took an hour to get to London central because the rain was sheeting down and the temperature had dropped enough for snow. J. R. picked them up in his small electric Nissan and they headed out of the city with his sat nav giving directions. Joanne couldn't believe just how many old diesels and gas guzzling 4x4's there were still on the road and could see why the politicians were always going to have difficulty getting people here to change their habits and why manipulation of the pollution figures might be tempting. Bad air is a silent killer and it takes years to feel the effect and by then, sadistic bastards like Wolf Bayer would have made another few billion.

The sat nav was saying they had arrived at their destination but all they could see in the wind and rain was a long high wall that seemed to go on for miles. J. R. slowed the car down to a crawl, there were very few other vehicles and apart from one white van that roared past with its lights on full beam, the lane seemed deserted. Page seemed to be looking for something and eventually he pulled into a drive. Through the struggling wipers they could see a pair of tall iron gates set between large stone gateposts with some kind of legendary animal on the top. Dane pulled up the hood on his Rohan waterproof and began to wrench open the door, Jo started to join him.

"Just wait for a minute whilst I check things out – it's evil weather out there." Dane pushed the door open against the wind. He couldn't believe the rain or sleet driving against his face and had to tighten the hood on his waterproof as he staggered to the gates which he could just see in the headlights. Looking up, there was a security camera which seemed to be smashed and further ahead he saw a gap in the gates which he was able to squeeze through. There in front of him was a long drive, a large house and outbuildings to the left and right. It looked totally deserted and there was not a light to be seen anywhere. He checked the name and description of the home against the information the editor had been given and tried to open the main gate fully. He then walked back to the car and shouted into the driver's window.

"It's the right name and the house fits the description, but it doesn't look occupied – I'm just going further down the drive in case there is anything more to see." Joanne shouted something from the back but he couldn't hear, so struggling against the wind, he returned to the relative shelter of the gate post. He tried to open the gate again but having one hand wasn't helping and the cold and effort required made it ache like hell. Dane squeezed back through the gap and started down the drive and thought he could see something white across the lawn but couldn't work out what it was.

Dane wasn't a superstitious man but this house felt wrong. The darkness of the storm didn't help but he felt his skin crawling like a kid reading a bloody ghost story. He nearly jumped in fright as an arm grabbed him from behind and he realised that Jo had followed him despite his warnings. She gripped his arm tightly and he realised that she was spooked too. J. R. had stayed with the car and Dane didn't blame him – having the editor of the FT caught breaking and entering really would be news for the tabloids.

The rain was turning to sleet as they got closer to the house. J. R.'s informant had said to check the garages so they turned right at the top of the drive and Dane could then see what the white shape was.

It looked like an old Porsche and he reckoned about a hundred grand's worth of motor had been abandoned with the hood and driver's door open to the elements. He crept past the Porsche and tried the garage door behind but inside it was empty. Over the next few minutes they tried four more garages and found Porsches, Mercedes and all kinds of classics but nothing else. The last outbuilding was a double garage and the wind tried to rip it out of Dane's hand as he wrenched it open. Inside there was a car that looked like it had come from a Nazi newsreel and Joanne gasped and recoiled at the smell that came from within.

Chapter 31

The 'suicide' of Wolf Bayer had an ironic justice to it. Having him asphyxiated by a rubber tube connecting the exhaust pipe to the interior of the old Mercedes would have taken someone with a black sense of humour to devise. As Bayer was happy for thousands of people to believe in Greenwatch and die of bad air, it couldn't have been more appropriate. The police said they had found no note but the death certificate still stated 'suicide by suffocation' as the cause. Everyone, especially Carlos Fantoni was delighted about his demise and just wanted to ensure that the rest of the installation in the UK went without a hitch. The Financial Times had a damning obituary for Bayer and named the other members of the Salimond board who they suspected had been part of the Greenwatch conspiracy.

Angela Law had repeated her forensic questioning of the PM in the House of Commons but he had repeated his well-rehearsed denials. She reiterated her support for the Mk 2 Greenwatch unit being installed in the rest of the UK and repeated the assurance that this would be a matter of cross party agreement if she won the election or not. But she added the proviso that independent monitoring by someone like the World Health Organisation was an essential part of the deal.

Dane and Joanne returned to Boston where things looked less optimistic when it came to bringing the President to account. The death of the aide, Steve Bannerman seemed to have eliminated the last link between the President and what happened to Fantoni. It was unlikely that a brute like Kowolski would have had direct contact with the oval office and he was a complication anyway. The fact that he killed the assassin they now knew to be Alexander Brown before he attacked Fantoni was inexplicable and he had disappeared immediately after. It was a fact the Greenwatch Six discussed that night – everyone who might interfere with the President's plans seemed to disappear. Bannerman was the latest.

If the President of the United States had his way, Kowolski would be the next, though it might take a few months. He'd seen Kowolski's medical records and knew about the shadow on his lungs, so it appealed to send him to Fairbanks, Alaska for two reasons. Firstly, it was about as remote as you can get from Washington. Secondly it has some of the worst air quality of any city in the USA and he knew that pollution and 40 cigarettes a day would get rid of him rapidly enough. Other people might have considered that cruel but Kowolski had failed to kill Fantoni more than once and you didn't get to the top in this business by rewarding failure.

Mayor Bonelli was no longer an ally but the President knew he wasn't a threat as his own part in the conspiracy was almost as dirty as his and he intended to keep that quiet. Bonelli had actually turned into a genuine believer. He had installed the new Shelford modified Greenwatch units in record time and enlarged the test area. The idea of automated and autonomous e-driving had been pioneered in Somerville, a suburb of Boston back in the 2020's but had died out after the Covid-19 pandemic and a huge reduction in investment had followed. He had given the area special funding and a boost by saying that all local public transport needed to be pollution free and automated within two years.

Bonelli could see that Boston was improving every day and now it was spring you could hear the birdsong in the trees every morning. The birds that had suffocated to death only a few months ago were back in greater numbers than had been seen since the 1800's. It was too early to measure changes in human health but the Greenwatch units hadn't flashed red for weeks and that was a great reflection on the measures Bonelli had introduced. It was very early but Bonelli had already let a few friends in the media know that he would be interested in running for President next time around. Carlos Fantoni had suggested that first he should show real commitment to the cause by testifying against the existing President. Bonelli shook his head at the naivety of the suggestion and what with the death of the aide there was even less chance that anyone would bring him to impeachment or any kind of justice.

The small church in Washington was packed with people and a small number of them were genuine mourners. Amongst them was Mrs Julie Bannerman and her two children, Donald and Frances, who were uncomfortably shuffling into the front pew trying to avoid the cameras. The family had wanted a small service but the President insisted on this media circus because it gave him the chance to deliver the eulogy personally. Again, he had been in tears on the telephone when he called Julie a few weeks back and said they would like to arrange the memorial service. The President had said that the State would take care of all the costs and her pension would be supplemented by a special 'death on active service' award he had arranged. Julie was in despair at the time and it had been easier to say yes.

Now she saw the tall grey haired figure with the stoop walk to the pulpit and knew that it had been a mistake. The spray-on tan and the weather beaten good looks were just too practised and too media savvy to be believable to her. She barely registered the words or the crocodile tears but as the coffin made its progress through the open doors of the furnace, covered in the stars and stripes, she heard the last post and realised her husband had gone. She burst into tears and was comforted by her two children – an event that the five cameras hidden around the church loved. She tried to leave the church, obviously in great distress, and with a wonderfully spontaneous gesture, the President rushed from his seat to comfort her as she walked down the aisle and they went out into the spring sunshine together. In the safety of the funeral limousine and away from all the Presidential circus she and the kids held each other tight and after a few minutes she asked the driver to take them home as soon as possible. The President had arranged for mourners to be given drinks and canapés in the White House but Julie couldn't face any more posturing and falseness so she asked the driver to pass on her apologies.

Back in the Washington house, where they had shared so many plans, she felt better. Steve had so many ideals at the beginning and had a brilliant mind but they gradually became less important. He was surrounded by accomplished people and eventually realised that he was never going to be a leader but could achieve some of his ambitions if he joined the right team. Winning was all his boss wanted to do and Steve had helped him with meticulous planning of his campaigns. He became indispensable but as things got tougher in the re-election campaign, Julie could see her husband becoming more disillusioned and a little frightened about some of the things he was being asked to do.

Steve hadn't said anything but she knew his trip to Panama had been particularly stressful. Julie opened up his office once again and went back to the note he had left on his computer. She had read the long personal note from him which was full of emotion but not looked at the file he had left on his computer or carried out the rest of his instructions. Her instincts told her it would be a gruelling experience and she still couldn't handle it as her emotions were so raw after the funeral. But she promised her dead husband and herself that she would open the file on his birthday in a few weeks' time and follow the instructions exactly.

Joanne and Dane saw the President's eulogy on the news and were amazed at his capacity to fake things. After a few weeks back in Boston and the months spent with Jo during her recovery from the kidnap, Dane was anxious to return to Europe but when the

Financial Times contract started, his first assignment was in New Zealand and the next was in Costa Rica, so he realised he could be based anywhere. Joanne understood his attitude and knew he had effectively put his career on hold for a year whilst he looked after her in the difficult times after the kidnap. But she had a burgeoning career on the Wyatt Boyle show now and her Corporate Li's blog had grown hugely. So they had come to a parting. They loved each other passionately but agreed to separate for a few months and then review their situation. They both felt they had spent months of their lives trying to bring people involved in the Greenwatch fraud to justice and that frustratingly, the man in Washington was still beyond their reach.

Carlos Fantoni returned to Panama to see who from the Salimond lab was worth offering a job and to salvage any equipment. From what he had learned, Salimond had disappeared so successfully that even the Panama Gulf Bank claimed never to have heard of it. So the risk of anyone objecting to him stealing scientists or equipment was zero. He still kept the black card in his wallet as a memento of those days when he could draw unlimited money and now his expenses from Shelford Environmental were more restricted, but enough for any reasonable job.

His next stop was going to be Lima, his home town and the start of a sale's drive to get Greenwatch installed in major cities in South America. He had no family left in Peru as his parents had died years ago and the Mafia don who had paid for his education had been shot in a gangland feud. But he intended to enjoy a few games at the Lima Lawn Tennis Club that he'd helped start as people still remembered him as a rising junior star. Fantoni was as happy as any dedicated man can be with a whole world to help clean up. But there were so many loose ends – he didn't know who had killed Diane Fallow – a death that still gave him pain. He didn't know who killed Wolf Bayer but whoever it was had his total gratitude. According to J. R. Page the likelihood was that it was either a Japanese industrialist called Hattori Kenshin or MI6. The politicians seemed to be the ones who always managed to slip through the net and to see the President on the TV every night on CNN spouting plausible platitudes about the environment, really rankled.

Bradley Kowolski slipped back into Boston with a lot more stealth than he'd left. The trapper's beard and fishing hat had confused everyone as did the fact he'd used his original passport. He knew that as far as his original team was concerned, he was on sabbatical and bet on the fact that no-one would have dared clear his office or change his security clearance. He was right and by the time he'd got to the office he was clean shaven and looked his ugly, old self. It was Sunday, the place was deserted and he didn't give a damn about the security camera footage because by the time it was checked, he really wouldn't care. He was driven by an anger that had consumed him ever since the aide Bannerman had said over coffee in Fairbanks that the President had chosen this part of Alaska for him because the air quality was so bad and they knew he had a bad chest condition.

The aide had just been trying to trade insults and he had certainly paid for the comment a few hours later but Kowolski was angry that his President was trying to kill him in such a cowardly way.
The clinic in Fairbanks had been very good. It was used to dealing with respiratory problems and when Kowolski found out what his prognosis was, something snapped in his brain. Three months was all the specialist said, the last of which would be best spent in a hospice. It was too late for chemo or any other of the aggressive treatments but with the right drugs now he might have a month to sort his affairs out in relative comfort. He had paid privately so was certain his employers would hear nothing and set about closing the Fairbanks office immediately.

After Boston he booked flights to Washington and spent a night in a small hotel. In the morning he caught the early shuttle carrying just a small bag which he stowed in the locker above and then checked a few things on his iPad. The bag contained his medication and toiletries, underwear and a clean shirt and tie. The only other item was a tubular object about the size of a shaving foam canister that he thought was made of graphite and wouldn't show up on the scanners. The device had been created through 3D printing in China and had fascinated his colleagues when it had been confiscated on a drugs raid. It had attracted no attention from the checks at both ends of the journey and was now in his inside pocket along with a tube of antacid tablets.

Julie Bannerman tried to watch the video her husband had made at his death bed confession but couldn't bear it. He was more worried than she had ever seen him and it was obvious he had a real belief that he wasn't going to survive the trip to Alaska. According to him, the man he was going to see, Kowolski, was a trained killer and there was a fair chance that he wouldn't return. In Steve's meticulous way, he then outlined how the President had used him and Kowolski to stop Carlos Fantoni from exposing the problems on Greenwatch and if necessary, arrange for his termination. She was shocked to the core but followed his instructions implicitly as to the various people the confession should be forwarded to.

The President had a new aide who had the great advantage of being black, female, intelligent and with no knowledge of recent events, she ticked all the boxes as far as he was concerned. She had seen the pressure for an official investigation of his behaviour from Senator Eveson and dozens of other people, but had been abroad during the time in question, so knew nothing until a few minutes ago.

The email had come in to Steve Bannerman's old White House address and the first thing she noticed was that it had been sent by Julie, his wife. The second was a copy of a group email sent to Senator Eveson, Joanne Li and Wyatt Boyle earlier.

The video took fifteen minutes for her to see and it was a detailed and emotional account of what her predecessor had been asked to do to silence Carlos Fantoni and cover up problems with Greenwatch that would have de-railed the President's re-election campaign. The aide felt that she knew far too much about the past for comfort now and really wondered if she wanted this job. Its last incumbent was dead and if Bannerman was right then her new boss deserved impeachment.

As per Steve's detailed instructions, his video had been sent to Joanne Li, Eveson and Wyatt Boyle an hour before it was sent to his old desk.

Joanne Li had nearly missed it in the mass of other emails but luckily had recognised the aide's surname and opened it. It was still quite early and she'd just shown it to Dane when a FaceTime call came in from Wyatt Boyle and the Senator. Looking at the other two, she could tell that they couldn't believe their luck. The death of the aide Bannerman had effectively killed off their chances of getting an official enquiry. This changed absolutely everything.

Wyatt Boyle looked at his watch and realised it was only an hour to the weekly Presidential Press Briefing.

"Listen, you guys, I've got a colleague who's at the White House right now. She's waiting for the weekly briefing. Can I get her to ask a question on this? For once we might catch the slippery bastard out." Boyle asked excitedly.

She would have liked more notice but Joanne called Carlos and he thought it was too good an opportunity to miss. Press Briefings are live and seen by millions and the next one was in an hour. They signed off and Boyle sent detailed instructions to his journalist.

Joanne and Dane went back to the kitchen and poured themselves a mug of Costa Rican coffee. The rest of the Greenwatch Six deserved to see this – especially Carlos – so she quickly emailed them to watch the daily briefing. He was in Lima now but hopefully CNN or one of the other channels would carry it. The Professors were working but she had an acknowledgement from Spencer and knew there would be places they could see the broadcast at the college.

After one term of office already, the President was well practised at the press briefings and he'd learned to send a deputy when something bad was happening and be there himself when it was good news. This time the economic growth figures were looking optimistic and he wanted to talk about his plans to clean up more cities that had bad air. His campaign 'Vote for Me and Breathe Easy' had been a winner and now that those Democrat shits in the media couldn't get any evidence that he'd conspired to falsify the Greenwatch figures, he was a lot more confident.

The oil and automotive lobby had been a constant problem as over the years they had contributed millions to his campaign fund. Greenwatch had always been something they had tried to prevent but now that was unstoppable. What the President had agreed with them – in return for a large boost in funding and a lucrative consultancy on retirement – was to delay each city's introduction by as long as possible. With plausible reasons like research, testing and consumer attitude surveys in each area he reckoned that Greenwatch installation could be put back for three or four years. The cost in bad health might be significant but at least no one could accuse them of totally ignoring the problem. The President with unintended black humour, told the oil people that the delay would give everyone 'breathing space.'

The only other problem was the resignation of his new aide. She had departed with immediate effect for 'personal reasons' and already left the White House. It was an annoyance but a lesson to him never to employ female, young and black staff again as they obviously couldn't handle the pressure. He didn't think he was a white supremacist or anything like that, but history showed that white males of the right class had always been best at running countries. He went down the long corridor, lined with pictures of previous leaders, to the press conference with four trusted advisors. It always reminded him of a Greek or Roman general surrounded by his phalanx of guards on the way to send his troops into battle. He rather enjoyed the parallel and sped up so his underlings had to scurry after him.

Dane and Jo were able to see the news briefing live as was Carlos in Lima who'd found it on some channel or other. The scene was familiar with the raised lectern centre stage with the blue graphic of the White House building behind and the words spelling it out underneath in case anyone didn't know where they were. To the left was the Stars and Stripes and the flagpole with the bright gold eagle on the top. Already assembled were notables including one general, two government officials and one female advisor. As always, Joanne marvelled at the fact they always seemed to find a representative selection of races and gender on the dais to show how much they were into equality. As yet there was no President and the assembly tried to look intelligent and expectant and, in many cases, just looked like stuffed dummies. The camera was positioned over lines of black seats occupied by the press and Joanne tried to guess where Wyatt Boyle's associate might be. There was the sound of frantic motor drives from off-stage and it was obvious that the star had arrived.

It took a few minutes for the President to take his place and then the press briefing took its normal course with the leader calling out named correspondents who then asked questions that to Dane and Jo seemed fairly innocuous. It took ten minutes before he called the TV journalist and a small Hispanic looking girl stood up and everyone in Boston held their breath.
"Mr President, an hour ago we received a video from your aide – your late aide – Steve Bannerman in which he accused you of a number of crimes concerning Greenwatch and the abduction of a Carlos Fantoni. He also suggested that we investigate the circumstances of his own death because he strongly suspected that he was going to be assassinated. Do you have any comments Mr President?"
The uproar in the chamber was extraordinary with everyone standing and shouting and the President raised his hand to try and restore order. He was shaken and had difficulty remembering exactly what she'd said so bullshit seemed the only answer. He raised his voice and glared at the woman. "Ms Luiz, can I say that this is the most outrageous....... this is the most scurrilous..."
The President stopped and seemed transfixed by another figure who had risen from the side of the auditorium and was slowly moving towards the assembly of leaders. The man looked familiar, he was wearing a crumpled suit, a White House security pass and appeared to be carrying a grey tube in his hand. One person tried to stop him and was dropped by a straight jab to the throat and others scrambled away from the threat until only an aged General in full

dress uniform stood between him and the President. That only delayed the agent for a few seconds before he stood in front of the leader he had hated for years. There was a sound like a pop of compressed air and a bullet hit the President in the forehead and he went down in a spray of blood. Before anyone else could react, Kowolski put the weapon in his own mouth and blew himself away.

Epilogue

Exactly a 1000 days on from that fateful first day at the Grosvenor Club in Boston, Dane Morgan was still running. So much was the same but so much had changed. Dane still wore the Nike Air shoes he'd always run in and carried the small Nikon in his backpack in case he saw a shot that needed taking. But he had one less hand and a lot less happiness than he'd had then.

The series on 'Threatened Landscapes' for the Financial Times had turned him into a minor celebrity and taken him to some beautiful but endangered places. He'd seen again the hard, white beauty of the Chilean glaciers and saw huge pieces sheering off the ice cliffs due to global warming. He'd hacked his way through hot steaming jungles surrounded by the sound of howler monkeys and saw the wonderful iridescence of the hummingbirds only to find virgin forest being illegally felled for profit a few yards ahead. He'd taken some of the best photographs of his life so far but the experience had turned him into a climate and environment evangelist as committed as Joanne Li.

His anger with Wolf Bayer and what Salimond had tried to do with Greenwatch had barely abated and he knew there were other companies and governments out there who were prepared to kill people and destroy the planet just so they could increase profits or maintain power. Bayer had died a horrible death and been disowned by the German automotive family which had spawned him but it wasn't enough. The only positive outcome of the Bayer scandal was that the boss of the same company had committed to a 90% reduction in the pollution created by its vehicles in the next 10 years. Dane didn't know whether he could believe them but it was a good sign and as always, independent monitoring was the key to trust.

In Washington immediately after the assassination of the President, his deputy Joe Baker took over and had stayed in office despite numerous attempts to impeach the dead leader. Republicans had tried to blame Bannerman and Kowolski and claim that the President had known nothing but no one really believed them. Lawyers on both sides as always, seemed able to keep the fight bubbling for years without resolution and still showed no sign of solving anything.

Mayor Bonelli was a revelation, he had genuinely cleaned up his city over the last few years and would definitely be a contender for the next Presidential election where he might be facing Senator Eveson as the most likely Democrat candidate. Interestingly, they both agreed that Greenwatch should be rolled out throughout the country and subject to independent verification.

They had learned something from the experience in London. Angela Law had helped the Labour Party win the last General Election and kept her promise with Greenwatch which was planned to roll out to other UK cities with Carlos Fantoni supervising the installation. The World Health Organisation had agreed to independently monitor the readouts and publicise the figures so that there was no chance of political interference.

Joanne Li had every media success she had ever wished for. Ratings for her slot on the Wyatt Boyle show peaked over the first year but settled down to a level that the producers were extremely happy about. She was dealing with environmental matters which had hardly been box office before and she was reaching new younger audiences. Her Corporate Li's blog now had millions of followers worldwide and she was seen as a major influencer. But on her weekly trip to Washington one night, she realised that she wasn't happy anymore. It took time to admit to herself that she missed the simple joy of working with and loving Dane Morgan. Together they were far stronger and there was so much to do as companies were still trying to rape the world and getting cleverer at covering it up. She picked up her phone and called a number she had learned by heart years ago.

Carlos Fantoni had seemed to do so well in Peru and Brazil with Greenwatch on those first visits and created a lot of media interest. Dealing with the politicians there was more complicated but he had made some progress despite the lack of bribes paid. London had been excellent for him since the change of government and plenty of other European cities had followed its lead and were testing the new system. In the US, Boston was a casebook example of how to use the units and clean up a city. So most people had heard about Greenwatch and seemed to want him to succeed, which made his present predicament even stranger.

Carlos had woken up in a stinking cellar running with water, which he thought must be somewhere in London. The guns he was facing were real and his three captors looked deadly in their combat gear. After they slapped him awake, they switched on a spotlight which illuminated him brightly and he was told that he was going to record a message on camera for Joanne Li. Any deviation from the script they were holding and he would have an eye gouged out. The huge knife on the table in front of him looked like it had been in a Rambo movie and he felt his bowels loosen.

Printed in Great Britain
by Amazon